The Princess Shoppe

by

Kerry Blaisdell

This is a work of fiction. Names, characters, places, and incidents are either the product of the author's imagination or are used fictitiously, and any resemblance to actual persons living or dead, business establishments, events, or locales, is entirely coincidental.

The Princess Shoppe

Lello Ball Enterprises
P.O. Box 331
Beaverton, OR 97075

Publishing History: First Edition, 2024
Print ISBN 978-1-951141-10-3
Digital ISBN 978-1-951141-11-0

Published in the United States of America

The shorter man stepped forward.

He had a hawkish nose and aristocratic features. "Ms. Kincade? I am Tarek Cassar. I wish to say that the episode upstairs was most regrettable."

Allie felt herself flush. "Sorry about that. Again."

"Do not concern yourself. We understand."

"You do?"

Bathroom Guy's expression hadn't changed. For some reason, she couldn't get a bead on him. In their grand total of two encounters, he'd been mad, amused, encouraging, and mad again. Yet he also seemed at home in his own skin, like no matter where he found himself, he *belonged.*

Or maybe he was just too good-looking. Like Bobby, but with more "there" there.

She glanced away. "Mr. Cassar—"

"Please, call me Tarek."

Bathroom Guy shot Cassar a surprised look, then grimaced and checked his watch. Tarek stared pointedly, and Bathroom Guy said, "Sorry. Hoping to hurry this up."

You and me both, Allie thought. To Tarek she said, "Is there something I can do for you? I have an appointment."

He bowed. "I will be brief. I am most sorry for any distress Mr. Peerless caused you, but I believe I may be able to help."

"What? You help me?"

Bathroom Guy frowned some more, and Allie gave up. Tarek was easier. He beamed now, pleased with himself, or with her, she wasn't sure which.

"Yes. It is clear that you are in need of employment."

"I can't argue with that. But, er, what do *you* need?"

"A princess. The job is yours, if you will take it."

Romantic Suspense: PUBLISH OR PERISH

"…a gripping suspense which I couldn't put down… Having diverse characters rounded out the story nicely. Fans of Harlan Coben and J. D. Robb will be as captivated as I was. Highly recommend!"

~ N.N. Light's Book Heaven

"I loved this book…especially Vin's uncle Azi who suffers from Down Syndrome but doesn't let it stand in his way. All in all a wonderful story that also touches on the problem of autism, vaccinations and Down Syndrome."

~ The Paranormal Romance Guild

"…I wouldn't hesitate to recommend this book! It will keep you guessing. If you love romance and suspense go out and get Publish or Perish. You won't regret it!"

~ Romance Book Addicts

Contemporary Fantasy: THE DEAD SERIES

"The supernatural mystery and suspense elements drive the fast-paced plot forward... Balanced with a sense of fun and quirky situations, Debriefing the Dead is excellently imaginative and hard to put down."

~ Reader's Favorite

"Fans of television shows like 'Constantine' or 'Supernatural' will absolutely love [WAKING THE DEAD]…The main character, Hyacinth, is phenomenal and develops so much in this book."

~ InD'tale Magazine

"Ms. Blaisdell is a master storyteller...So many twists and turns will have you sitting on the edge of your seat!"

~Still Moments Magazine

Dedication

My deepest gratitude to Teri Brown, critique partner and goal-setter extraordinaire. Your faith in me and my writing has kept me going through the hard times. And your faith in this story in particular gave me the push I needed to finally get it out there. Gracias!

ONCE UPON A TIME…

*In olden times, when wishing still
helped, there lived a king whose
daughters were all beautiful.*

~The Frog King, or Iron Heinrich

Chapter One

She'd lost the house. She didn't even own it, but she'd lost it all the same.

Sitting on the can in the men's room at Peerless PI's was the last place anyone should hear such devastating news, especially a woman. Allie Kincade tried not to squirm, to keep her blue unisex running shoes planted below her jeans and act-slash-think like a guy, though how she should do that, she had no idea. Most men didn't seem to think about *anything* beyond their own desires, getting that next brass ring—or keeping their dicks happy.

For instance, at least one of the two men standing at the urinals had wanted nothing more than to get into Allie's pants from the moment they'd met. Even after ending it three years ago, Bobby Peerless still managed to unzip her every few months. They'd go a few weeks, and then Allie'd remember why they broke up, which usually happened when another of Bobby's girlfriends called to remind her.

But that wasn't what made her nails dig into her palms now. They would never last; she knew that. He was a fun roll in the hay, a warm body when the loneliness was too much. But what she *hadn't* known when she quit the police academy and sacrificed her personal savings—and her personal life—helping him start the agency, was that his dick wasn't the only carrot he'd be dangling in front of her.

"Let me break the news to Allie," he said now, finishing up the destruction of her life as he zipped, flushed, and moved to the sink. "Then we'll announce your partnership."

"Sure thing." Another zip and flush.

Frank Timarco.

Allie clenched her jaw. Bad enough the women's room door was stuck again. Worse that Bobby and Frank unknowingly followed her in here and had emptied their bladders while Bobby dropped his bombshell. Worst of all that *Frank* had gotten *her* promotion. Four years of her life, literally pissed away. But if Bobby knew she'd overheard, *while* tending to her own business, it would be too much.

Please let them leave, she thought, feeling sick as they ripped paper towels from the dispenser, still chatting.

She *would* lose the house. Allie'd only found the tiny split-level in South San Francisco by accident and could barely afford the earnest money—twenty thousand dollars—let alone the down payment. The mortgage approval depended on the letter Bobby'd written, swearing her income would increase when she became partner.

But the wording he'd used—

Son-of-a-bitch!

He hadn't even lied; he'd never intended to make her partner and kept the letter vague on purpose: *At such time as Ms. Kincade is promoted to full partner*—no date mentioned—*her income will most certainly increase...*

Hot tears threatened. *Dad, I know you said to think before mouthing off. But even you'd agree that now is yelling time, not thinking time.*

Of course, Patrick Kincade also would've been oblivious to his only child's plight, even if he weren't dead. How many times had Allie's mom tried to make a life for them, only to be ripped away by his quest for the ever-elusive university tenure? Even after Sara Jane died when Allie was eight, he'd buried her quickly and moved on again. The only reason he'd stayed more than a year in San

Francisco was because he'd died here.

Bobby and Frank finally exited the bathroom, and Allie performed her own wipe-zip-flush, then gave the stall door vicious kick to open it. "Bastard! Goddamn son-of-a—"

"Is there a problem?" asked the man using the urinal.

Allie froze. "What the hell are you doing here?"

"Isn't it obvious?"

His blond brows snapped together over a nose that slanted, just a bit, downstage left, and Allie's face heated. In his thirties, he wore expensive jeans and a tan blazer that hugged his broad shoulders. His stance was aggressively wide, and she had to look up to meet his fierce gold-brown gaze. Apparently, even at five-ten, she could still feel petite.

He gave himself a shake and tucked the important parts out of sight—not that she was looking—then turned to the sink, jaw set in an uncompromising line.

"Oh. Sorry," she managed, suddenly deflated. "Women's room door is stuck again. I couldn't hold it, and…" She stopped. "They left. I waited until they left."

He tore a towel off with a fast tug. "If you mean the two men here before, they went out as I came in."

The heat came back and Allie moved to the other sink. "Right. Well, it's been nice."

His penetrating gaze tracked her in the mirror. "You always beat up the hardware, or is this your first?"

"Why do you care?"

"Just making conversation."

"In the john? Who knew Club Urinal was such a hotspot."

He actually laughed at that, his stony expression melting in a way that sent the heat from her face tingling all over her body. Just like her dad used to do with her mom, turning on the charm when she needed to stay mad.

She said, "It's none of your business why I'm here."

"Have it your way." His gaze lingered appreciatively on her own important parts, and he seemed suddenly at ease.

Which was just plain annoying. "If you're done browsing, you can leave and let me finish in peace."

"Squatter's rights?" His eyes twinkled, until he saw her expression and reached for the door. "Never mind. Nice meeting you. Let's do it again sometime. How about the women's room in an hour?"

Allie started to tell him off, but he laughed again and escaped. Instead, she splashed water on her neck. It didn't help. Her brain whirled, replaying Bobby's words over and over. She faced her pale, taut reflection in the mirror.

"You're going to chew Bobby out, aren't you? Even though you'll lose your job *and* the house. Damn it!"

She'd make him give her the partnership, the raise, the works. She was a good PI, not to mention the money she'd given him to start this place. What a dumb mistake that was. Just like her mom. Bobby couldn't back out *again*. She'd get the house—her own little piece of the Bay Area pie. Suburban enough that she could almost afford it, urban enough to make bussing easy. And she'd finally have roots.

Mom, I wish you were here. You'd be so proud. I'm finally going to have the home you tried to give me.

If Bobby-the-Prick Peerless thought he could take this from her and give it to Frank, he had another think coming.

~:~:~

Matt Wilcox made his way through the austere grey halls of the private investigation firm his boss, Tarek Cassar, had insisted they hire, and thought about the woman in the men's room. She was mad as hell, ready to murder the first hapless jerk who crossed her path, which happened to be him. Luckily, she'd been too surprised to find him there taking a leak to do any actual damage.

And she looked like she could do damage.

Though it'd been nearly three years, Matt's military training kicked in, and he catalogued everything about her, filing it away for later. Tall with strong arms below the sleeves of her yellow tee. A tee that did nice things to her breasts, like cling to them and show off their bounce. A hint of bare stomach had led his gaze to the waist of her jeans, and from there over her smooth hips to her long, long legs.

He shook his head. She was right. Her situation was none of his concern. His job was placating Tarek and finding the princesses, so he could get on with his life.

At least the encounter had added interest to an otherwise wasted day. He entered the waiting area just as Tarek disappeared into one of the offices. Crap. By the time Matt followed him in, Tarek sat in a leather chair across from an ostentatious mahogany desk. He threw Matt a disapproving look; he knew Matt didn't want to hire a PI, and probably thought he was late from the bathroom on purpose.

Just to tweak him, Matt leaned against a bookcase on the back wall instead of taking a seat. Besides, standing was easier on his injured leg, though Tarek didn't know that.

Peerless—now *there* was a name to live up to—was one of the men from the john. He smiled at Matt and came from behind the desk to offer his hand. "I'm Bobby. You must be Wilcox. GrimmLand Theme Park police, right?"

His grip was firm, but his obsequious tone set Matt's teeth on edge, and his light hair and gray eyes were as bland as his office. Matt extricated his hand and fought the urge to wipe it on his pants. "Security Engineer."

"What's the difference?"

"Architectural engineering. I designed the park's security systems, the entrances and exits, underground maintenance tunnels, stuff like that. I'm not a watch dog."

"Interesting." Peerless flashed a grin obviously meant as buddy-buddy and returned to his seat. "Your friend Tarek here was just filling me in on the disappearances."

Tarek's jaw tightened, and Matt guessed Peerless hadn't been given "first name" permission. Good. Maybe the lack of respect would piss Tarek off so they could leave.

"Oh? Did he mention the police found no evidence of foul play? What makes you think you will?"

Peerless said, "Just because they didn't find anything doesn't mean there's nothing to find. Three actresses in a month, gone with no leads? Sounds to me like GrimmLand's got a problem. A real *security* problem."

"Are you implying this is an inside job?"

Tarek raised his perfectly manicured hand in a placating gesture. "Forgive my colleague, Mr. Peerless. Mr. Wilcox believes he must solve these heinous crimes himself."

Peerless lifted an eyebrow. "I thought he wasn't a cop?"

"He is not. Mr. Wilcox's contract ends this month, but he feels a certain…obligation to stay. However, I believe hiring a private investigator of your caliber is best."

Matt drawled, "Or the cops could be right. Maybe the actresses got bored with their crappy jobs or finally got their big breaks. Happens all the time in LA."

Tarek shot Matt a look. "How can you say that? Three cast members vanish in a matter of weeks?" He pulled a handkerchief out and wiped his brow, then folded it meticulously and replaced it. "Two have removed from their apartments, leaving all their possessions behind, and we have been unable to settle their paychecks. Absurd."

Peerless cut in, "I'm with you on that one, buddy."

Tarek's mouth pulled down, but his tone was neutral. "Please, Mr. Peerless. Continue."

"Call me Bobby." When, after a beat, Tarek didn't reciprocate, Peerless cleared his throat and faced Matt. "I was explaining to Mr. Cassar that I have just the agent for you. I'm announcing a new partner soon or I'd go myself."

"Mr. Peerless," Tarek said. "Perhaps I was unclear. This matter is of the utmost urgency and is also very…delicate. I was told by an agency in San Diego that you specialize in cases requiring discretion. A subordinate will not do; we must have only the highest trained individual. If word of this leaks out, my cousin's reputation will be ruined."

"He's GrimmLand's owner, right?" Peerless slid a stack of manila folders closer, opening the top one. "Roland, King of Luradel. Wow. You really related to a king?"

Tarek answered stiffly, "Our fathers were twins, yes."

"Does that make you a prince?"

"No."

"But you're a member of the, what's it called, the Royal Court or something, right?"

"I have only visited Luradel, never lived there."

Peerless's face fell, probably seeing his billables drop without the royal connection. "Right. You were born in—" He rifled through the folder. "Here it is. Zulfiqar. The internet didn't have much on it. Where is it, again?"

Tarek's scowl deepened. "Near Syria, but that is of no consequence. It is Luradel we must consider."

"And where's that?"

"North of Austria. Perhaps you know where *that* is."

"Sure. I watched *The Sound of Music* as a kid."

For once Matt didn't blame Tarek for getting offended. Peerless's attitude was pretty cavalier for someone who wanted their business, and his knowledge of geography—and-or search engines—was appalling.

Besides, Tarek's late father's whole family was pushing

Tarek to find the missing women before Luradel's parliament convened in the fall. Matt had only one person on his case: King Roland himself, to whom he owed his life.

Still, he'd given too much of that life to Luradel's infighting. Time to be done with spies, assassins, and kidnappers. He'd put the remodel business on hold twice already; one client had bailed and more would follow. He needed to finish Darlene's house and start the next one, or the business would be DOA before it was established.

And the fastest way to achieve that was to placate Tarek and get back to GrimmLand, so he could uncover the truth.

Eyes on the prize, Wilcox, eyes on the prize.

He leaned forward. "Look, whoever does it, we need to find those women. If word gets out that GrimmLand harbors a kidnapper or, God forbid, a serial killer, Roland will be deposed and Luradel will end up in a civil war."

Peerless frowned. "I don't get that. Why?"

Matt willed himself to be patient. Just because he had been steeped in Luradel's conflicts so long, they seeped out his pores, didn't mean anyone else understood them. But if the region wasn't stabilized, the repercussions for the border where East met West were unthinkable.

He said, "Roland built the park for his adult daughter after someone tried to kill him. He wanted to hide her from the factions trying to steal the throne, but he bankrupted the royal coffers funding the park, and if his political enemies learn it's not secure—that he *endangered* the princess by sending her to America—they'll try to depose him."

"He spent their money and what's to show for it?" Peerless asked, showing a glimmer of his reputed smarts, and Matt wondered if some of the smarm was an act.

"There's also the problem of the princess herself."

Peerless glanced at his notes. "Laurette, right? Age

twenty-four, lives at the park?"

"For now. In a few months, she'll assume her place as heiress to Luradel's throne."

Tarek shifted, but Matt ignored him. Laurette couldn't succeed Roland *yet,* not until he overturned the law forbidding female successorship. And if he were deposed before the parliament voted, the fight for the throne would be bitter and long. With royal inter-marriages, other countries would be dragged into the conflict, including Zulfiqar, as Tarek's mother's family might make a claim.

Matt continued, "In any case, since we're here, and Tarek believes you can help, I expect you to assign your top investigator to handle this, fast, and with *zero* publicity."

Peerless nodded. "Of course. The man I have in mind has been with the agency for years."

"He must be discreet," Tarek said.

"Absolutely."

"And level-headed."

"Of course. *Every* agent at Peerless PI's is intelligent, professional, and would *never* crack under pressure."

A *thump!* came from the hall, then a *crash!,* and for the second time that day, Matt had a door kicked open at him. It bounced off the wall as the woman from the john burst in and shoved everything off Peerless's desk. His expression went from shocked to shuttered, and Matt would've bet the smarm knew *exactly* what had pissed her off.

"Allie—babe—this isn't a good time. I'm with clients."

"You bastard!"

She hadn't noticed Matt yet, and he sidled along the bookcase for a better view. She was more interesting to look at than he'd originally thought, with short brown hair and elfin features. Her large, dark eyes flashed beneath delicate brows, her cheekbones were high, and her full lips might have been soft and inviting if not pulled back in a snarl.

She bent to pick up a stack of fallen papers and Matt took the opportunity to admire her rear. Man, jeans looked good on women. Especially her. Then he spied the handgun tucked into her waistband and revised his estimation of her damage-capacity upwards.

Straightening, she hurled the papers at Peerless, who flung an arm up. "Hey! Knock it off!"

She grabbed more papers, and he rose, putting both the chair and desk between them. Tarek scowled and Matt grinned. In Tarek's opinion, a man who ran from conflict was weak; running *from a woman* was inexcusable.

Matt checked his watch: one-thirty. Excellent. They'd be home by dinner.

Oblivious to Matt's schedule, Allie chased Peerless side-to-side across the desk. "How *dare* you give my partnership to Frank! After all the money and work I put into this agency! You owe me that partnership, Bobby!"

"Calm down, Allie," Peerless said, which in Matt's opinion was the dumbest thing anyone could say to a woman, especially an angry one.

"I will *not* calm down! You led me on about the promotion, when you *knew* I'd lose my house and the earnest money. I'm out twenty grand, *all I had left of my dad's estate,* after investing the rest in this agency!"

"Now listen here—"

"No, you listen. Give me that partnership or—or—" She paused, vibrating with suppressed rage. "Or *I quit.*"

From the rigid set of Tarek's shoulders, he was not pleased. He might have his issues with equality of the sexes—he wasn't a fan of female successorship—but he believed women should be treated with respect and courtesy, neither of which Peerless exuded at the moment.

The jerk put his hands on the back of his chair, damn pleased with himself. "Okay, Allie." He waited until her shoulders sagged with relief before adding, "But as the saying goes, you can't quit, 'cause *you're fired.*"

Allie gasped, going stiff again. Her hand twitched toward her gun and Matt contemplated tackling her before she did anything illegal, when abruptly the fight left her. She turned and met Tarek's flat gaze. Then she saw Matt and froze again. A myriad of emotions crossed her face: recognition, embarrassment, and finally, resignation.

She said, "Sorry to barge in on you, er, again. You did say the women's room, right? My bad. And it hasn't been an hour yet."

He couldn't help it. His lips twitched up and her eyes sparked, from humor or rage, he couldn't tell. But at least she didn't look so beaten down.

Don't get sucked into the vortex. Besides, what could he do? Unemployment would cover her. She might lose her house and the earnest money—now *that* was a bitch—but it was hardly the end of the world.

She walked to the door and left, and Peerless heaved a sigh. "Sorry about Ms. Kincade's performance there. I assure you my other agents—"

"It is not a problem," Tarek said and rose.

Peerless's relief was palpable. "I'm glad to hear you say that. The agent I have in mind—"

"It is not a problem," Tarek interrupted, "because we are leaving."

Yes. Matt pushed off the bookcase.

Peerless paled, watching their commission vanish in a puff of his own oily smoke. "I swear my other agents—"

Tarek gave a short bow. "Good day, Mr. Peerless."

The asshole hurried around the desk. "Wait. I'll go

myself. Let me announce the partnership—"

"That will not be necessary," Tarek said

Perfect. They'd hop on that company jet—flying was *much* nicer than driving—and be home in no time. It would be a late dinner, but at least he'd get a minute to relax and have a beer on his deck, before facing it all again tomorrow.

Which made Tarek's next words hurt all the more.

"Mr. Peerless, I appreciate your efforts. However, I do not want anyone at Peerless PI's for this case. I have decided to hire Ms. Kincade instead."

Peerless looked as stunned as Matt. "You're joking."

Tarek didn't blink. "She is spirited and resourceful. Why should I not hire her?"

"Because—she—she's—"

"A loose cannon," Matt put in, earning a grateful look from the jerk, which he ignored. "If you're going to do this, at least hire someone who is technically employed as a PI."

Tarek remained unfazed. "She will start her own firm."

Peerless's mouth worked like a fish, and Matt thought hiring Allie might be worth it just to screw with him. But sanity prevailed and he tried again. "What about discretion? She just erupted all over her boss. How level-headed is that? Plus, we know zilch about her qualifications."

Peerless grasped at this like a lifeline. "She has none. She flunked the SFPD psych test. *Twice.*"

Tarek's lips curved in an unpleasant smile. "And yet you employed her for how long?"

Peerless's Adam's apple jumped as he tried—and failed—to find a good spin. "Five years," he said at last.

"Ah," Tarek said, and walked out the door and straight to the receptionist's desk, Matt on his heels. "Excuse me, can you please tell me where I may find Ms. Kincade?"

News traveled fast. The brunette's pleasant expression

soured and she said, "I believe Ms. Kincade no longer works here. If you like, I can ask Mr. Peerless to—"

"That is not necessary. Where may I find her desk?"

Faced with Tarek's unbending expression, the woman caved. "First aisle. Last desk on the end, by the windows."

"Thank you. Good day."

Matt hurried after him to Allie's empty desk. She'd either had little to retrieve or hadn't wasted time. Or both.

"Come. We may still catch her," Tarek said and took off again up the aisle, making Matt feel like he was on one of GrimmLand's more dizzying roller coasters.

"Wait—let's decide if she's right for the job first."

"She is perfect, because she is a woman."

Tarek reached the elevators and pressed the button, and Matt stopped in his tracks. "You *prefer* to hire a woman?"

"Of course. It is the best solution. She will go undercover as a princess and find the truth."

Tarek appeared sane, and yet…his eyes had an odd glint. He'd never chosen a woman over a man for any job. And Matt had *never* seen him so determined to hire anyone so clearly unstable, regardless of sex. Either way, *Matt* would be working with her. It would've been bad enough familiarizing a PI with the park's layout and security. But for Allie to go undercover, she'd need hours of training, on everything from park history to timekeeping.

If she took the job. But why wouldn't she, when Tarek, through Roland, had such deep pockets?

"Hell," he muttered as the elevator opened.

"Come again?"

"Nothing."

Matt stabbed the button for the lobby. As they began their descent, he felt the vortex sucking him in after all.

So much for my deck and my beer.

Chapter Two

Allie made it out to the parking lot, clutching one small cardboard box of her work stuff, before the fury quit sustaining her and stark terror took its place. She stopped next to her dad's ancient hatchback—the only thing of his she had left besides his books—and dropped the box, then sagged against the car.

What the hell have I done?

At least with a job, she might get the house. But with no income *and* no savings, she was screwed with a capital S. Maybe Bobby'd never make her partner, but he paid well, and she liked her job—liked the people she worked with.

Well, she liked the *other* people she worked with.

Still, Bobby wasn't all bad, and technically, he'd never *said* the partnership was hers. He'd hinted, and she'd assumed. The strong, kick-ass part of her suggested that the promotion was hers, regardless. But the emotional, terrified-of-financial-ruin part was stuck on, *Why the hell didn't you suck it up until you got the house and found a new job,* before *telling the old boss to shove it?*

She bumped the back of the car with her hip, then waited while the hatch decided if it would open or not. It released and rose an inch. With another nudge and the groan of dry hinges, it opened enough for her to drop the box on top of the preexisting junk before she slammed it shut again.

What now? She'd violated Patrick Kincade's Number One Rule of Economics: Never count your chicks before they hatch. She'd known she might not get the promotion, but she'd banked on the raise that went with it anyway.

Her cell rang, the screen showing her realtor's number. *Perfect timing.* "Hello?"

"Allie." Rianna sounded way too cheerful. "You busy?"

"Um. Not exactly."

"Great. Meet me at the house in half an hour? I found an inspector who can come today. If it passes and everything's a go with the owner's contingency, you could move in by Labor Day."

Allie straightened, heart pounding. "That soon?"

She felt Rianna's smile through the phone. "Yes. Your very own home, yard, the works. Speaking of which, my landscape guy called. He's giving you a *very* good rate on breaking up the side patio so you can have your garden."

Allie couldn't breathe. *Her garden.* She'd had one once, back before her mother died—before her dad's job as an Econ professor forced Allie to move with him every year or two, dragging her poor potted plants with her. So optimistic; they clung to life in their tight confines, and she'd yearned to set them free, to give them room to grow.

She'd almost given up on that dream. Now, here she was, a mere seven weeks—and one job—away from having not just a garden, but a whole yard.

Rianna said, "So you'll be there? I don't want you to worry, but the seller had another offer. You're still in first place. Don't panic. But it would be good to play nice, show him your offer's strong, and that we can close quickly."

Allie swallowed. *It will all work out.* She'd get another job, or two, or three. Whatever it took to *not* lose this house.

"Yes," she said firmly. "I'll be there."

"Wonderful! There's one more thing. The owner wants to add a clause to your contract about the earnest money…"

Allie listened with half an ear as the door to the building

opened, and the men from Bobby's office strode out. The shorter one made a beeline for her, while Bathroom Guy followed reluctantly. His jaw was even tighter than before, and she wondered if she'd imagined his encouragement.

Outside, his clothes were even more Chi-Chi; his loafers alone probably cost more than her car. His buddy wore a white suit and maroon silk shirt that flattered his olive complexion, and his black mustache and elegant hands were well-groomed. Both men had hefty gold rings on their right hands, probably for some exclusive men's club involving Cuban cigars and high-stakes poker games.

"Allie, you there?" Rianna's voice cut into her thoughts.

The men arrived, waiting as she said into the phone, "Sorry, yes. But I have to go. I'll see you at the house."

Rianna said quickly, "And you'll sign the addendum? It's a bit unusual, but with the new backup offer and housing so tight around here, I think it's a good idea."

"Yeah, sure. No problem. Anything to get my garden."

Allie hung up and the shorter man stepped forward. He had a hawkish nose and aristocratic features. "Ms. Kincade? I am Tarek Cassar. I wish to say that the episode upstairs was most regrettable."

Allie felt herself flush. "Sorry about that. Again."

"Do not concern yourself. We understand."

"You do?"

Bathroom Guy's expression hadn't changed. For some reason, she couldn't get a bead on him. In their grand total of two encounters, he'd been mad, amused, encouraging, and mad again. Yet he also seemed at home in his own skin, like no matter where he found himself, he *belonged.*

Or maybe he was just too good-looking. Like Bobby, but with more "there" there.

She glanced away. "Mr. Cassar—"

"Please, call me Tarek."

Bathroom Guy shot Cassar a surprised look, then grimaced and checked his watch. Tarek stared pointedly, and Bathroom Guy said, "Sorry. Hoping to hurry this up."

You and me both, Allie thought. To Tarek she said, "Is there something I can do for you? I have an appointment."

He bowed. "I will be brief. I am most sorry for any distress Mr. Peerless caused you, but I believe I may be able to help."

"What? You help me?"

Bathroom Guy frowned some more, and Allie gave up. Tarek was easier. He beamed now, pleased with himself, or with her, she wasn't sure which.

"Yes. It is clear that you are in need of employment."

"I can't argue with that. But, er, what do *you* need?"

"A princess. The job is yours, if you will take it."

~:~:~

Matt choked on a laugh as Allie's expression went blank with astonishment. Tarek, with his usual disdain for "needless details," said nothing further. Matt would have to elaborate before she booked it—or pulled her gun on them. Stepping forward, he held out his hand.

"I think it's time we met. Matt Wilcox."

"Allie Kincade." She shook his hand firmly, though her expression remained wary. A sprinkling of freckles on her make-up-free face added to her pixie-like appearance. Her dark eyelashes drew him in to clear, green eyes with emerald flecks that weren't visible in the bathroom fluorescents, and he lost himself for a minute.

Allie withdrew her hand, and Matt gave himself a mental shake. "Tarek and I work for GrimmLand Theme Park in Southern California. Ever hear of it?"

"I think so. Opened a year ago by the king of some tiny

country, to give his baby girl her own personal Disn—"

Matt raised a hand. "Don't say that name. Hearing about the competition pisses Tarek off."

"I see. Sorry. Didn't mean to offend."

Tarek said graciously, "You did not know."

In the three years since Matt met him in Luradel, Tarek had never shown such interest in a woman, most of whom he treated like chattel. So why now?

Matt pushed the question aside. "Back on topic. Like other character-based theme parks, GrimmLand employs actors who can't get a better gig. Because of our location, we're even farther down the pecking order."

Tarek pursed his lips, but Matt focused on Allie. He might be rusty, but he'd say she was warming to them. Or at least not inclined to shoot them. Yet.

"What's wrong with your location? Where is the park?"

"Mecca."

She waited for the punch line, then said, "You're joking. There's a place called Mecca, California?"

"Yes."

"And a king built a theme park there because his baby girl has a thing for mouse ears?"

"More or less."

"But now something bad happened, which makes you think you need a private investigator?"

This was the tricky part. "Maybe," Matt began, but Tarek cut him off.

"Ms. Kincade, three of our female cast members have *vanished.* You must go undercover and determine what has happened to them, before another princess disappears."

The *you're-a-whack-job* look came back, but this time she directed it at Tarek. "GrimmLand is losing princesses? And you want *me* to find them?"

"Yes. Most definitely I want you, starting right away."

"I can't believe I'm asking this, but who has disappeared so far?"

"Rapunzel, Cinderella, and a Little Red Cap."

The corners of Allie's mouth twitched up and she turned to Matt. "He's kidding, right?"

"Unfortunately, no. All three women were—" He searched for a PC term, finally settling on, "—difficult. The first and third, especially, thought GrimmLand was beneath them, and it's likely they found better jobs and just…left."

One of her eyebrows shot up. "Without giving notice?"

Matt shrugged. "It happens."

Tarek said, "I am sorry Ms. Kincade, but time is of the essence. My associate believes we should handle this internally. But I believe an outsider will be more objective and a better use of park resources. Speaking of which…"

He sized up Allie, then her car, which was too old to determine the make, much less the model. He removed the company checkbook from his suit coat and opened it.

"GrimmLand will be most grateful for your services, Ms. Kincade. Because your life will be disrupted by leaving today, adequate compensation is a must. I believe fifty thousand dollars plus expenses is reasonable."

Allie's jaw dropped, and Matt's followed suit. What the hell? They would've paid Peerless at most half that.

Allie cleared her throat. "Did you say—"

"Fifty thousand," Tarek repeated, uncapping a pen and beginning to write. "Twenty-five now, with the rest once the missing women are located. And the perpetrator of this heinous crime, of course." He tore off the check, then raised a determined gaze to her uncertain one. "I believe we could offer a further twenty-five—a bonus, if you will—should you resolve this in, shall we say, a timely manner?"

Allie stared at him, then asked Matt, "Is he for real?"

When Tarek made up his mind, arguing was pointless. "King Roland's coffers run deep. If the women have been kidnapped—or worse—it'd be a huge political fiasco."

Tarek held the check out, and Allie read the numbers on it and swallowed. Her hand rose, then dropped again. When she spoke, it sounded like she needed to convince herself more than anything. "What do the police say about all this?"

Tarek said scornfully, "They think I am a crazy foreigner. They found nothing 'suspicious' and will do nothing further."

At Allie's inquisitive glance, Matt admitted, "There isn't much to go on. No signs of forced entry into the women's apartments, no ransom notes, and to date, none of their families have reported them missing. Just us."

Tarek checked his watch. "Please. The details will come later. You have proven yourself energetic and resourceful. *You* are exactly what we need."

"Sorry. You guys *look* respectable, but how do I know any of this is real?"

"Ms. Kincade, would I invent such a tale? If Mr. Wilcox and I wished to harm you, would it not be simpler to hit you on the head and carry you to our limousine?"

Allie glanced at the long, black limo they'd rented for the drive from the airport. "Okay. But…today? I can't, even if I wanted to. I'm late for a meeting with my realtor."

"Ah, yes. Your house. With no job, the bank will decline your mortgage, yes? But with a nice cushion…"

He held the check out further, and Allie swallowed again. She obviously still thought they were nuts, but she needed the cash. "I really can't cancel my appointment…"

Tarek waited, the glint of victory in his eye.

"It *would* have to be Southern California in July." When

Tarek still didn't speak, she eyed him cautiously. "I'll have to get the post office to hold my mail."

Tarek smiled triumphantly. "You will come tonight then. Matt will ride down with you."

Matt rounded on him. *"What?"*

"It is a simple solution. Ms. Kincade and I have appointments we cannot cancel. You have no such commitment. And someone must explain the details to her."

"But—" *My beer. My deck. My* dinner.

Tarek said to Allie, "You will complete your business. Then Mr. Wilcox will drive down with you and go over all that is necessary for you to start on the case. Agreed?"

Allie nodded, taking the check and appearing more dazed than before.

"Very good." Tarek turned to Matt. "I will arrange a room for Ms. Kincade at the resort. You will inform me when she has arrived, regardless of the hour." To Allie, he gave a polite bow. "It has been a pleasure. I will see you first thing in the morning, after you have breakfasted."

Tarek left, crossing to the limo where the waiting chauffer sealed him inside before returning to the cab and driving them away. Headed, no doubt, for the airport and the private jet that would take Tarek down to Roland's personal airstrip in Mecca. Matt turned back to Allie and her beat up two-door hatchback and her crazy all-over-the-map energy, and thought, *Vortex: one, Matt: zero.*

Allie tore her gaze from the check and blinked when she realized Tarek had gone. "Is he always like that?"

"Pretty much. Does this thing even run?" Matt moved to the car, reaching for the passenger door.

"Don't touch that!"

Matt jumped, his fingers jerking reflexively on the handle, and the whole door yanked free, clattering to the pavement and narrowly missing his foot. Matt swore as the parking attendant hoofed it out of his booth, yelling and waving his arms, bent on saving Allie from Matt's unintentional attack. Allie herself simply glared at him. Just because he'd maimed a car that already had so many dents, a sledgehammer couldn't make it worse. At this rate, it'd be midnight before he got to the resort, not to mention the hour's drive home from there. And it was *his* foot the door almost crushed.

"Perfect." He stooped to retrieve the rusty hunk of metal. "This will be *so* much nicer than flying."

Chapter Three

Allie merged onto 101 South, then nursed the car into fifth gear. Satisfied nothing else was about to fall off—like the engine—she peeked at Matt. During the thirty minutes he and the parking attendant had worked to duct-tape the door back on, he'd barely glanced at her. Now, he scowled out the window, arms crossed, legs scrunched almost to his chest thanks to the passenger seat's broken sliders.

"Some place you'd rather be?"

"Anywhere but here, princess." He kept his eyes on the road, absently twisting his gold signet ring. It was so large it would dwarf her thumb, and was engraved with an ornate "R" surrounded by three tiny birds.

"Funny. I'd rather be here than anywhere else. Well, not *here* in this car. *Here* in San Francisco." He just fiddled with the ring some more, so she said, "Want to know where we're going?"

"Not really."

Nothing to say to that, but it was weird driving in total silence with a large, angry stranger. She'd removed her gun from her waistband, but it was under the seat within easy reach. Not that Matt seemed dangerous, but just in case.

She tried again. "I'm buying a house. I have—" He grunted, inching farther away, and she blew out a breath. "Not the chit-chat type?"

"Pretty much, princess," he said, missing her glare because he still wouldn't look at her.

"Don't call me that."

Finally he turned a gimlet eye on her. "What should I call you?"

"How about just Allie?"

"Okay, Just Allie."

This time he caught the glare, but they were having an actual dialogue, so she let it pass. "And…? What do I call you? Mr. Wilcox?"

"I'm Matt, you're Allie. I don't want to be here, I'd much rather be in San Diego, but Tarek's the boss, so I'll play nice. All right?"

"Fine."

Just to tweak him, Allie changed lanes fast, squeaking onto the exit-ramp in front of a trucker who honked loudly. Matt reached for the oh-shit handle, and she hid a smile.

"So. Where *are* we going?" he asked as she moved onto city streets.

"My house. The one I'm buying."

Matt looked dubiously at the endless warehouses passing by. "Maybe I should ask where we are."

"South San Francisco. It gets better farther in." He raised an eyebrow, and she tamped down her irritation. "It's not the prettiest place on the planet, but it's affordable. Kind of. Around here, that's the main deciding factor."

"Where I come from, form and function matter more than pinching pennies."

"That's obvious," she said under her breath. Somehow, while wrestling with her car door, his expensive suede blazer had repelled every ounce of grease, unlike her cheap jeans and shirt, which seemed to *attract* dirt and debris.

He scowled again. "What?"

"Nothing. Never mind."

She turned down her street—*her street*—would the thrill ever go away? Then she caught Matt's eye and realized he expected her to elaborate. She pulled up behind Rianna's black sedan and killed the engine.

"Look, you seem like an okay guy. But all the men who come up from LA or San Diego have the same attitude."

"Which is?"

"If something's pretty, price doesn't matter. But if not, why waste your time?"

"Is that right? I guess you think you're safe, then."

"What's that supposed to mean?"

His gaze dropped to her beat-up sneakers then trailed up her jeans to her t-shirt, lingering on her curves, before moving to the column of her throat, and finally, to her bare face. Something flared in the molten gold of his eyes, and Allie felt heat flooding *everywhere*.

When he spoke, the deep timbre of his voice resonated through her like the hum of a tuning fork. "Sometimes, no matter how hard you try, you just can't hide what's inside."

Time stopped, and for a heartbeat, she wondered what might have happened if she'd taken more care with her appearance. Then his expression went bland again.

"Let's get this over with so I can go home."

Allie's heart resumed beating with a shuddering lurch, and she scrambled out of the car. "Geez. You're a real grump, you know that?"

"Better an ogre than a princess."

She bit back a retort and slammed the door, then took a calming breath. He'd obviously meant to piss her off. Why let him ruin her mood? She was here, at her house, which she could suddenly afford again. Could life be any better?

Then she saw Matt glowering across the seats at her through the dirty car window and thought, *Okay, I could have a car with working doors and sliders, and an engine that doesn't bleed parts.*

First things first: get the house, then fix the car.

She opened her door. "Sorry. If you hadn't yanked it…"

He looked even more ogre-like, so she shut up and waited while he struggled to heave all six-foot-plus of himself across the gear shift and driver's seat. It was not a pretty sight. By the time he was out, Rianna had gotten out of her car and waited nearby.

As usual, her blonde hair was in a loose chignon with just the right amount of tendrils swirling near her pale throat. Her sleeveless silk shell and cream wool skirt were as carefully chosen as Matt's ensemble, and for the first time in a while, Allie wished she hadn't thrown on whatever was on the floor by her bed when she woke up this morning.

Matt eyed the house, a boxy two-story pink stucco with a red tile roof, and shook his head. Too plebeian, no doubt. Still, she hadn't shared it with anyone besides Rianna, and his reaction hurt more than she wanted to admit. Then he turned his gaze on Rianna, and it warmed visibly. *Men.* Luckily, most things could be accomplished without them.

Rianna had different opinions on this, and she gave Matt a slow smile. "Allie, you didn't tell me you were bringing a…friend."

"Business associate." Matt smiled also. "And she didn't mention her realtor was so…" His glance swept over Rianna much as he'd checked Allie out minutes ago, but this time he did it with obvious approval. "…professional."

Rianna laughed and touched his arm, and Allie tried not to feel like a third wheel at her own home inspection. Difficult, since Matt also hit it off with the inspector, who arrived moments later. Just because Matt had degrees in architecture *and* engineering, and was remodeling his own house, did that mean he got to monopolize *her* inspector?

And would it kill Rianna to ask if Allie was interested

in Matt—not that she was—before extending her claws?

By the time Matt and the inspector climbed onto the roof for a once-over, Rianna finally noticed Allie's mood. Maybe because Allie stomped out of the dining room after Rianna slipped Matt a card with her home number on it.

"Hey." Rianna followed her into the kitchen. "I didn't mean to muzzle in on you and Matt. Say the word, and I'll drop out of the picture."

Allie gave up and acknowledged the inevitable. "Thanks. But really, it *is* just business."

"If you're sure." Rianna's perfect brows wrinkled. "Everything else okay?"

Allie hesitated. Should she 'fess up about her job? The mortgage was in process, and the bank would find out eventually. But was there some obscure law, requiring Rianna to disclose that Allie's offer might vanish in a puff of unemployed smoke? If so, it wouldn't matter if she informed the bank or not, as the owner would reject her immediately and go with the backup offer.

"I'm fine," she said at last. "Just not a big fan of LA."

"Me, either. But you'll be in a swanky resort, with all your meals catered. Plus, if you get bored, there's always The Rock."

"The who?" Matt asked, coming in from the backyard.

Allie's face flamed. Apparently, a pitcher of margaritas and a real estate contract did not a friendship make. But it did loosen the tongue and let down the inhibitions.

Rianna turned invitingly to Matt. "Just another of Allie's…friends."

Matt's brows furrowed. "The pro wrestler?"

Rianna smiled archly. "I believe there's wrestling involved, yes." She looked like she might continue, but she was on the make and drew Matt's attention back off Allie.

"Never mind. Just girl talk. How's the roof?"

The inspector came in then, and the three of them launched into a discussion over whether Allie should ask for a roofing allowance or not. At first, Allie tried to participate, but who could compete with three people so passionate about tile versus slate versus shake? All she wanted was the house. Who cared what topped it off?

At last, everything was in order. Rianna promised to call after the owner reviewed the inspector's report and to get her a copy of the revised contract. Then Rianna reminded Matt *he'd* promised to call her the next time he was up north. Matt said he would, then followed Allie out.

As they walked away, Rianna called to Allie, "And don't forget to take The Rock! I hear purple's very *in* now."

"Why didn't I keep my mouth shut?" Allie muttered, moving ahead so Matt couldn't see her face. On the other hand, packing The Rock probably *would* be a good idea. The way things were going, she might need a distraction.

At the car, she could tell Matt wanted to drive so he wouldn't have to climb over the seats again, but she wasn't feeling charitable. To his credit, he got in without complaint. Though her mood had worsened, his had improved. Flirting with perky blonde realtors probably did that to a guy.

Then his cell rang and he answered it, murmuring to someone named Gillian that he "didn't have plans," and he'd call her tomorrow. Probably his girlfriend, though he'd been pretty abrupt with her. Had he made a full disclosure to Rianna? Not that she'd care; flings were her thing, and she wasn't particular about monogamy.

Allie decided to mind for her, and made a fast U-turn that flung Matt hard against the window with a satisfying *thunk*. He righted himself, then shot her a quizzical look, which she ignored, and they finished the drive in silence. When they reached her apartment twenty minutes later, he crawled gamely back out of the car, then contemplated the small, dirty, two-story white fourplex, not hiding his distaste. Well, who needed his good opinion, anyway?

She turned toward the stairs and came face to face with her landlord stepping out of his ground floor apartment. His round head was so red with anger, the color showed through his bottle-black comb-over, and his scraggly gray eyebrows drew down above his watery blue eyes. He wore the too-small t-shirt that was all the rage for pot-bellied older men living alone, and his wrinkled green madras shorts complemented his ancient Birkenstocks.

"Allie," he began, waving a white envelope at her, but she cut him off.

"Henry, this is my—" She stopped just in time. *New employer* was a dead giveaway that the old one hadn't worked out, a fact he could do without. She put on her best fiscally-responsible expression. "—new client, Matt Wilcox."

Matt lifted a hand to shake, but Henry ignored him. "Allie, we had a deal. I let you slide on the rent so you could make your down payment on your house."

"I know, and I appreciate it. You know I'm good for it."

"Actually, I don't. Maybe I let you slide before, and you paid up. But this is too much. *Three months*. You said you'd pay me after one. Even before that, you were late most of the time." He shook the envelope at her. "This morning, the SFPUC called. If I don't shut off the water to your apartment, they'll cut off the whole building. And PG&E says you didn't pay your electric, either."

Allie's face burned. "I can pay it! I just got an advance." She pulled Tarek's check from her pocket. "See? I can pay you, the utilities, all of it."

"Too late," Henry snarled, and Allie's heart sank.

She had to leave the apartment eventually. But it'd been home for two years, longer than she'd lived anywhere else, and she'd hoped to leave on a good note.

Matt shifted, but she couldn't tell if he was irritated on her behalf or because his getaway was delayed. Seeing her get fired wasn't enough—he had to witness this, too?

Henry pushed the envelope into her hand, his stubby fingers forcing hers to close around it. "You've been here two years. Now I'm giving you two weeks. Your house won't close by then, but you'll figure something out."

He stomped back into his apartment.

"Great," she muttered. "Just perfect."

Matt opened his mouth and she shook her head. Sympathy would only make it worse, and if he *wasn't* sympathetic… Well, better to cut him off, either way. "It's fine. I'll stay in a hotel. I needed to move out anyway."

He frowned. "Can he do that?"

Allie stepped onto the antiquated metal stairs leading to the second story. "Fastest way to raise the rent is to kick the current tenant out."

Matt put a hand on her arm, forcing her to face him. With the added height of the steps, they were eye to eye, nose to nose, mouth to—

"Does he have just cause?" His fingers were warm on her skin, making it hard to focus on his words.

"We had a verbal agreement that I'd pay by the end of the month. But legally? Yes. He can evict me for this."

Matt seemed unaffected by the electricity she felt arcing between them. "A good lawyer—"

"Would cost more than a hotel."

Nothing like a money fight to kill the mood. She

extricated her arm and climbed the stairs, and after a moment, he followed her up to the landing, waiting as she unlocked her door. Inside, the apartment was dark and cool, and she pushed away the sudden melancholy. It was just another place. She'd had lots of those, but after this, hopefully only one more.

Matt wandered around, inspecting her meager possessions, while she went to the bedroom to throw necessities into a duffel. His opinion shouldn't matter, but somehow it did. Through the doorway she saw him stoop to scrutinize the only photo she had of her dad, then move to one of her plants. From the hard set of his shoulders to the neatness of his clothes, it was obvious *he'd* never be in a mess like this.

Never mind. In seven weeks, the house will be yours, and you'll have enough left from the GrimmLand paycheck to start your own firm.

No more cheating spouses or serving summons for unpaid traffic violations, and no more Bobby, lying through his teeth and making false promises. That cheerful thought did the trick, and Allie hummed to herself as she packed. Whatever happened—wherever Fate tossed her—she always managed to take her life with her.

Well, most of it, anyway.

She glanced at the brick-and-board shelves lining the bedroom walls, all the way up to the ceiling. Her dad's books filled them, some raggedly ancient, some newer, all of them related to his passion: economics. If only she could bring them with her to Mecca. But there were too many. They'd just have to survive until she returned, triumphant, having found the princesses and collected her remaining fee plus Tarek's bonus.

It's only two weeks. If I haven't found the princesses by

then, I'll come get you. I promise.

The books weren't impressed, sitting in dusty rows as they always did, their drab browns and grays dragging her mood down again. She turned her back on them and focused on packing.

She'd almost finished and was reaching into her bedside table drawer when Matt said from the doorway, "Did you know your kitchen window's been forced open?"

"What?" Allie said, jerking around. Unfortunately, she forgot what she was doing, and his eyebrows shot up when he saw the sleek fuchsia vibrator in her hand.

"Let me guess," he said. "This must be The Rock."

Chapter Four

Allie's face turned the same color as the sex toy she held, and Matt tried not to ogle the thing or think about where it had been. Or how recently.

Belatedly, he realized he was staring at her chest instead and pointed his eyes north again. He was having a hard time keeping his gaze off her body. Not that her face wasn't worth looking at. On her, embarrassment was cute. She'd tried so hard to project confidence in the midst of the chaos. Even after getting evicted, which had to hurt, coming from a jerk like Henry right after that bastard Peerless sacked her.

Matt gave himself a mental shake. Shit happened to everyone. And her shit was, thankfully, not his problem.

Well, some of it might be.

"Anyway. Your window's busted."

"So you said."

She shoved the vibrator into the sport bag she held and bumped the drawer shut with her hip. Damn, she had nice hips. Plus, her shirt rode up again, and he caught a glimpse of that smooth, tan abdomen he'd spied earlier. Matt's jeans suddenly felt too tight and he turned fast, going back through the apartment. *Beer. Deck. Princesses.*

Better. But maybe tomorrow he'd see if Gillian wanted to hook up after all. Nights with her were fun and uncomplicated—nothing like the Allie Vortex. And he'd been rude when Gillian asked about the new addition plans for the umpteenth time. Dinner would be a way to make it up to her and get his mind off the princesses. Maybe Tarek was right, and he should leave GrimmLand as planned. If not for his debt to Roland, he could have launched the remodel business three years ago when he left the service.

Roland's ring glinted on his right hand, and his thigh ached from Allie's cramped car, but Matt sighed and gave in to his own nature. He couldn't bail now, not with everything going haywire at once. Three women missing, Laurette possibly in danger, and the man who'd tried to kill Roland still on the loose? Someday, Matt would be his own man again. But not today. Today, he'd have to play in the sandbox with Allie—vortex, tight shirts, sex toys, and all.

She tossed her bag on the couch, glancing around. Matt had already noted that nothing major appeared to be missing, not even her TV. Shelves and cupboards seemed undisturbed, as did her jungle of houseplants. He'd never seen so many plants in such a small space. Or books. She had enough hardbacks alone to open a store.

"Just hell," she said when he showed her the kitchen window. It was an older, wooden one that swung outward over her lanai and was secured with a simple metal latch.

"If I hadn't tried to close it," Matt explained, "I might not have noticed the broken catch."

Allie swore under her breath, then went through the dining nook and out the sliding doors onto the balcony. She examined the obvious splinters of wood from the frame, where the offender had likely used a crowbar for leverage. Then she peered over the metal rail to the parking lot below.

"Already checked it." He indicated fresh scrapes on the painted railing. "Looks like they tossed a grapple over the rail, climbed up, and jimmied the window. Probably just jumped back down since it's only one story."

Allie lifted a brow. "And how do you reckon all this?"

"See the spacing of these marks here?"

She stepped closer and he caught a whiff of her scent, like apricots, clean and tangy, and his groin tightened again. What the hell was wrong with him? He shook his head. Rianna was more his type. In fact, she and Gillian could've been sisters. Cool, blonde, and put-together, from their gentle feminine curves to their carefully sexy outfits.

Plus, both were petite, their heads just reaching his chin. Allie was strong—nothing "gentle" about her toned arms and firm ass—and tall. If he wanted to kiss her— hypothetically speaking—he'd barely need to bend his head to capture those full, slightly parted lips.

She moved again, her shirt stretching across the soft roundness of her breasts, their peaks stiffening in the cool of the fog rolling in off the Bay.

Matt tried to force his brain back on track, pretending deep interest in the railing. "These are new," he said inanely. "See? No scrape marks over here."

"Well, duh," she said. "I could've told you that."

Shit. Lost in his own fog of lust, he'd forgotten she was a PI who'd be as savvy about these things as he was. "Sorry. I meant to say, see the V from the joint of the grappling hook? A simple four-pronged one, maybe carbon steel. Available online or at Ninja Supply Stores everywhere."

"And you know this because…?"

"I've used one." This seemed to make her think he was a whack-job again, so he added, "In the service."

"You're military?"

"Was."

"Figures." She went back inside to the living room, where she began stuffing her laptop into its case.

"What are you doing? Don't you want to call the cops?"

"No." She sounded unconcerned, opening drawers in her desk and retrieving cables and computer accessories, which she also shoved into the case.

"Aren't you going to report the break-in?"

"What would be the point? Nothing's missing."

"How can you be sure?"

She stopped long enough to stare pointedly around the mostly bare room. "Do I look like a pack rat? If anything was taken, I'd notice. Nothing was. End of story."

"Don't you want to know who did this? And why?"

She set the laptop on the couch with the duffel, her green eyes flaring, reminding him she had a temper, and he wondered where her gun was.

"I appreciate your concern," she said, "but it happens. Probably a cheating husband I ticked off, trying to make me squirm. Why give him the satisfaction?"

"All right," Matt said, taking out his phone. "I'll do it."

"Do what?"

"Call the police."

"No—please don't!"

She dived for the phone, and he shied away. Dammit—she was too tall, or he could've just held it over her head. Feinting left, she snaked an arm around his right side and snagged the phone, ending the call before it connected.

"This is *my* apartment, so I get to choose: cops or not."

"Yeah? Well, that's *my* phone, so give it back."

"Only if you promise not to call."

He forced himself not to shake some sense into her. Something was off, and he took a mental step back, assessing the facts. Allie really didn't want the police notified. Her face had gone pink again, and her eyes were dark and troubled. Try as he might, he couldn't come up with a logical explanation for her reaction.

He stepped forward and she backed up, bumping the couch. "What is it, Allie? What are you afraid of?"

She licked her lips and held out the phone. "Nothing. Here—just please don't call them. Okay?"

She was close, and usual type or not, damn attractive. He lifted his hand to take the phone, knowing their fingers would touch. Anticipation shot through him, the thrill of the chase heating his blood, when the thing rang on her palm.

Allie blew out a breath and tossed it to him. He fumbled for it as she hurried to the kitchen. Gillian again. Jeez, couldn't she wait until Monday? Allie barricaded herself behind the breakfast bar, taking a hammer and nails out of a drawer, and he gave up and answered the call.

"Gillian. This is a surprise."

"Matt," she said coolly. Still pissed, then, or else she was with a coworker. As the park's Literary Advisor, Gillian reported directly to Tarek, just as Matt did. But they'd agreed not to advertise their relationship at work.

However, his sisters had taught him that, with women, it was always best to own up when he'd been an ass, and usually when he hadn't. He said, "I'm sorry. I shouldn't have snapped at you about the Enchanted Flounder plans."

There was a small silence, and then her tone warmed considerably. "I forgive you."

Inexplicably, that made him feel worse, and he had to stop himself from snapping at her all over again. "I'll be home too late tonight, but maybe—" He hesitated, reluctant to give up his weekend. But he did owe her something. "—tomorrow? Dinner anywhere you want?"

In the kitchen, the hammer hit something with a loud thud and Allie swore. He looked over to find her sucking her thumb and flashing him a dirty look. She turned away, but not before the image of her full lips wrapped around firm, pink flesh was burned on his brain.

"I'd love to," Gillian said and Matt tried to focus. She

was distracted, too. Instead of making Matt the center of her attention as she usually did, she said, "But I really do need those plans, so I can verify that the layouts match the houses the Fisherman's Wife demanded from the Flounder."

"Understood. But can't it wait until Monday?"

"Not really. Can you get them to me tomorrow?"

"Since when do you work Saturdays?"

"What are you suggesting?"

"Nothing. It's been a long day. I just need to get home."

"I miss you, too," she said in her most seductive tone. "Bring me the plans, and I'll show you how grateful I am."

"Gillian, you aren't listening. I won't be at the park until after midnight. I'll get you the plans next week."

Silence. "I'll let you know about dinner."

She hung up, and Matt shoved the phone in his pocket.

Allie came from the kitchen, still looking mad, and he barked, "What's wrong with you?"

"Nothing."

She began taking plants off tables and shelves, placing them on the counter. Before he could tell her she was full of crap, his phone rang. Gillian calling back. He sent the call to voicemail and turned to Allie—and it rang *again*.

"Popular guy," Allie muttered, retreating to the kitchen to drag cardboard boxes out from under the sink.

He answered the call, not hiding his irritation. "What now? I said I'd get to it next week."

"Hi, doll," said a low, husky voice, and Matt pinched the bridge of his nose.

"Sorry, Didi. Thought you were someone else."

"That's *Princess Didi* to you. How's it up north?"

He blew out a breath. "Tarek took the plane and I'm looking at a six-hour drive in a car that'll last ten minutes."

"So rent one."

Matt paused. "Well, that would make sense." He checked the time. "Damn it. We'll never get on the road if we have to pick up a car. Thanks, but I'll chance it."

"It's your funeral."

He sat down, then realized he was next to the duffel and its suggestive contents, and stood again. "So, what's up?"

Didi purred, "What? No time to flirt?"

"No."

"Fine, doll. Be that way. It's Phil." As soon as she dropped the manhunt act, her voice lowered an octave.

"Philippa? What happened to her?" The apartment suddenly felt too small, and he moved out to the balcony, ignoring Allie's obvious curiosity as he strode by.

Didi said, "Probably nothing. But she's been gone all day. With the kidnappings, we're all a little on edge."

Matt bit back a growl. "A little on edge" barely covered it when three of your coworkers had disappeared, and now your preteen daughter was MIA. Usually, Phil was more reliable than this—more reliable than Didi, in fact.

Matt forced his tone to remain calm. "I'm sure she's fine. Probably roaming the park and lost track of time. I'll call you when I get back. If she's not home by then, I'll find her. She'll be okay. I won't let anything happen to her."

"Thanks," Didi said, but he heard the fear in her voice. The same fear that roiled in his own gut when he thought of Phil alone in a vast, empty amusement park at night.

To distract her, he said, "What's she studying now? *War and Peace*?"

"She finished that. And she's halfway through that calculus book you bought her."

"Really? And she's in what grade now?"

"Seventh, maybe? With the home schooling, she really took off. I don't know how much more I can teach her."

"We'll work something out. Don't worry about it now."

"I know. Sorry to dump on you. I'm probably hormonal. Or something. The year's almost up."

She sounded hesitant, shy. Another surprise, though Matt had known it was coming eventually. "Really?"

"I saw Dr. Bauer this morning. He said everything's good for next month."

Matt cleared his throat. "Uh…congratulations?"

"Thanks, doll." She sounded wistful. "I just wish Phil could be happy for me, too."

"She'll come around. Give her some space."

"I'm trying. But I need her in at night."

"I know. Call me if she comes home."

"I will."

Matt disconnected and stared blindly at the dirty South San Francisco neighborhood behind Allie's place. Phil had *better* be all right. Of all the dumb stunts…

"Problem?" Allie asked from the doorway behind him.

"No—maybe—I hope not."

"I couldn't help overhearing. Another princess is missing?"

Matt shook his head. "The daughter of a princess, and she probably isn't missing. She's a good kid, but she's giving her father gray hairs."

Allie's brows rose. "Her father?"

"Yes. Can we just hit the road? I'm tired, and if she isn't home when I get back, I'll have to hunt her down. Even if she is, I'll have to yell at her. I'll be lucky to get any sleep tonight at all."

"Sure," Allie said, waiting for him to come in before double-locking the sliding doors. "I nailed the window shut, and I'll do the hold order for my mail tomorrow from the resort. Also, I called Bobby."

"What the hell did you do that for?"

"You wanted me to report the break-in, so I asked Bobby to check up on it. Satisfied?"

"You called the prick who screwed you out of a promotion and fired you, to ask for help?"

"He's a good PI. And odds are it's someone I ticked off while working for him, so who better to investigate?"

Matt shouldn't give a damn who she called. But Peerless was such an asshole. Didn't she have someone better to lean on? Then something else occurred to him.

"He has your key?"

"Well, yes."

"Now that's just plain dumb, princess."

She reddened. "What business is it of yours?"

He opened his mouth, then shut it. "It's not. Let's go."

Without a word, she went to the front door. He followed her to the landing, where she'd piled her laptop and duffel—and her plants, carefully arranged in four large cardboard boxes. A fifth contained a watering can, squirt bottle, garden tools, and a dozen fertilizers.

Matt said, "You pack one bag of clothes for a job that could take weeks, but you're bringing your own *vegetation?* Who the hell brings plants on a business trip?"

"Why shouldn't I?" She sounded irritated, which was rich, considering *he* was the one behaving rationally. "They won't make noise and bother the other guests, if that's what's worrying you. I can't just leave them here."

"Can't you get someone to water them?"

She shut the door, her jaw set in a stubborn line. "I don't need to. I'm taking them with me."

She keyed the knob lock and deadbolt, then shouldered the duffel and laptop as Matt assessed the boxes.

"They don't bite," she said, then gasped as he lifted the

duffel off her arm. "Hey!"

It was heavier than he'd expected, but he tightened his grip. "Don't worry, princess, I won't drop it. But I'm terrible with plants. Trust me, you're better off letting me handle The Rock." While she was flustered, he pinched the keys from her hand. "And by the way, I'm driving."

He headed downstairs, leaving her to heft a box of plants and follow. At the car, he paused. "Anything I should know about the hatch? Like, will it fly off if I touch it?"

She rolled her eyes, then did some weird bump thing with her hip, twice, before the hatch creaked open. He set the duffel and laptop next to a box of her work stuff—also containing plants—and she added the box she'd carried. She went back for the rest, and he relented and followed.

Once the car was loaded, she slammed the hatch and went to the front, wiggling over the driver's seat and gear shift and giving him a very nice view of her very fine ass.

Then she pulled her Glock out of her waistband and tucked it under the seat, and he remembered why he didn't want anything to do with her ass, fine or otherwise.

He got in and started the engine, waiting for it to splutter crankily to life. The car was so old, it didn't have a tachometer, but it was a stick and had a decent stereo, including four mid-range speakers and two tweeters.

"How about some music to pass the time?" he said and powered the CD player on.

"No!" Allie cried.

There was a split second of hushed silence, abruptly blown wide by an electric violin screeching from every speaker. A thunderous bass riff came next, joined by a driving drum beat. A woman's voice belted a feminist anthem from the early nineties, and Matt punched the power again to no avail, then turned the volume knob to the left. When that, too, failed, he tried to eject the CD.

"You can't!" Allie shouted over the cacophony. "It's stuck!" She yanked the glove box open and pulled out a package of ear plugs. Obviously not her first rodeo. She put a pair in her ears, then tossed the pack to him.

Matt twisted the key in the ignition, but she shook her head vigorously. "Won't help! Stays on when you restart!"

He shut the car off anyway, enjoying the moment of silence, then ignored her smugness when the noise resumed once the engine fired back on.

"How long does it do this?" he yelled.

Allie shouted, "It varies. Sometimes a few songs."

"And the other times?"

"It just keeps going and going and going…"

"Nice." He stuffed a pair of plugs in his ears, then pulled onto the street. Not only was he trapped in a vortex of chaos, he was about to go deaf at thirty-five. The image of a nice, new rental car popped into his head, but he dismissed it. How bad could it be? Leaving now, he might be home by tomorrow, but renting a car would add an hour, after which they'd have to drive Allie's car back here.

Besides, for whatever reason, Allie liked this junker. She'd already packed her plants; he could just imagine her reaction if he suggested she leave the car behind.

Then the heater blasted on by itself. Allie didn't seem surprised, and Matt didn't bother to ask if this, too, was normal. When she rolled down her window—only halfway, thanks to the dents in her door—he followed suit, then headed for the freeway.

With luck, the cops wouldn't be out, because the only way he'd make it home with his sanity intact was to speed.

A lot.

Chapter Five

Though sunset was an hour off, the mountains west of Mecca cast GrimmLand into early dusk. Philippa Reinhardt shifted on the tree branch, feeling for a better spot as she surveyed her domain. This was her favorite time of day, when the guests were leaving, and the park became hers again.

A warm breeze toyed with her hair, bringing with it the noxious scent of decaying vegetation and sulfur from the constant algal blooms of the Salton Sea, two miles to the south. The county commissioner said you couldn't smell it this far away, but what did he know? He only said it because so much revenue was tied up in the park, and he wouldn't admit to anything that'd drive even more business away.

It didn't bother her though, in the way that auto fumes wouldn't bother a New Yorker. To her, it meant home, and it always would, even if her dad did drag them both away to San Diego one of these days. *He can't make me,* she thought and peered through the binoculars she'd brought.

From her perch atop Marlinchen's Juniper Tree, GrimmLand sprawled in all directions. Briefly, she wondered what her dad would say to her climbing several stories above the official Treehouse, which was only twenty feet off the ground. Obviously, he'd disapprove, so she switched back to the matter at hand, panning the binoculars.

GrimmLand was much less pretty from afar, and it wasn't all that attractive up close. To the left lay *Daumesdick,* aka Tom Thumb Town, one of the park's larger sectors. It was disorderly and disorganized, thanks to the haphazard placement of trees, food stands, and gift shops, interspersed with roller coasters and other rides. To the right lay the remainder of *Hänsel und Grethel Land*, in which her tree stood and where the young kids played. They were always the first to call it a day, and the mini-rides and play structures lay still and dead in the encroaching dark.

Three more regions spread out behind Tom Thumb and Hansel and Gretel, but she ignored them, focusing instead directly in front of her: Faerie Land, home to the most popular fairy-tale castles, where royalty roamed, and where Phil's favorite store resided, dead center on a small hill.

For guests not wanting Trains of Terror or elevators that dropped thirty stories in seconds, The Princess Shoppe was GrimmLand's chief draw, a place where you entered as yourself, but came out a princess, from your authentic period undergarments to the filigreed tiara on your head. Old, young, big or small, it was a place of dreams, and some day, Phil would have the money to shop there herself.

Her dad would die laughing to know that *she* of all people—tomboy Phil—dreamed such a girly dream. Never mind what *he* went through every day, for *his* job.

Suddenly, a man in a backwards baseball cap passed in front of the binoculars. Phil stifled a gasp—not that he'd hear her from here—and zoomed in. He wore jeans, black work boots, and a white t-shirt with a cigarette pack rolled into the sleeve, and she recognized him immediately.

The man with the funny tattoo.

He'd been here before on several occasions, which was weird enough. People didn't come back to GrimmLand; they barely came once. Locals so bored with golf in Palm Springs, they took a chance down here, or tourists who didn't know the *real* cartoon characters were in LA.

Whatever. GrimmLand's guests got out as quick as they could and didn't return.

Except him. She'd first noticed the tattoo on the top of his shaved head from this very vantage point. It resembled a round castle, viewed from above, and surrounded by a moat. Since that day, he'd worn hats, but the fierce crags of his face were burned on her brain and she knew it was him, even in the dark.

Abruptly, he turned and squinted at her, and she froze. He couldn't possibly see her; they were a quarter mile apart at least. Still, she held her breath until he shook his head and resumed walking. Then she waited a few more seconds before climbing to the ground. He'd been heading toward Faerie Land. If she hurried, she might not lose him.

Where would he go this time? He never rode the rides, or ate at the food stands, or visited the shops. He just roamed aimlessly. There had to be a pattern to his route; she just hadn't discovered it yet. At least she hadn't seen him near any of the women who'd disappeared. It didn't prove he hadn't done *something,* but still.

In her pocket, her cell phone hummed, and she shut it off without taking it out. Probably her dad. He'd kill her for being out after dark. Big deal. He went off doing his own stupid thing, expecting her to follow his rules? No way.

This was *her* park, and bad things were happening, and this man kept coming back. Tarek and Matt had both left, gone off who knew where, right in the middle of the crisis.

And wasn't that just typical? If no one else would pay attention, she'd take care of the problem herself.

~:~:~

Snow White froze, caught by her reflection. *Mirror, mirror, on the wall. Who's the fairest of them all?*

Laurette Hassenpflug shook her head.

Not me, that's for sure.

But despite not being pretty, she *did* look the part. Maybe Tarek was right after all. Most of the Grimm's princesses either had fair hair or else modern audiences assumed they should be blonde.

Not Snow White. Hair as black as ebony, right there in print. *Check.* Skin as white as snow. *Also check.* And lips as red as blood. *Thanks to Revlon, a check as well.*

Laurette smoothed the heavy braids knotted at the base of her neck and examined her too-thin frame in the new dress. With its scooped-neck maroon bodice and the bright reds and golds in the panels of the skirt, she looked—and felt—like she belonged in a fairy tale. She didn't even need makeup to lighten her skin, and her eyes were big and dark.

Haunted. That's what *he* said: *Your eyes are haunted, sweet, like the deer who tries to escape her fate.*

Could any of them escape their fate? Did she even want to?

The white face staring from the mirror held no answers.

Yvonne Baptiste, wearing the poufy pink Brier Rose dress that had been Laurette's until tonight, stuck her head into the room. "Break's over. You coming?" Her glance took in Laurette's ensemble. "Nice. Snow White suits you."

Laurette inspected herself again in the mirror, suddenly self-conscious. "Do you think so?"

"Absolutely. But if you want to switch, I won't tell."

Yvonne's grin was infectious, and Laurette smiled back. Most of the other princesses ignored Laurette. But Yvonne was always friendly, and Laurette appreciated her frank good nature and common sense.

"No. I'm too sallow in pink, but with your light hair and tan, you're perfect in it. Tarek was right to switch us."

Yvonne twirled once, then sank into a low curtsy.

"Come, my queen. Our chariot awaits."

Laurette froze, sharp fear piercing her, hands clenched on the fabric of her skirt.

"What is it? What's the matter?"

Yvonne rose, the picture of concern, and Laurette forced a swallow past the thick desert of her throat. Of course Yvonne didn't know.

"I'm fine. This dress is just a little tight."

"Aren't they all? It'll loosen as you walk."

Laurette followed her to the corridor. At least this shift was short, with a dinner break at nine-thirty and only two more hours after that. Usually, she liked working evenings, but tonight she felt antsy. Maybe because of Tarek's worry about her and the other princesses. It was touching, like his concern that she play a part more suited to her. He could be so thoughtful. When he wanted to be.

She squelched the uncharitable thought as Yvonne said, "Mind if I stop for a smoke on the way out?"

"I thought you quit."

"Working on it. Never a good idea to go cold turkey."

"I'll go ahead. You can meet me later."

"You sure? Tarek told us to stay in pairs at night."

"I'll be fine," Laurette said and headed into the darkened park.

Chapter Six

Ninety minutes east of SF, the CD had played through twice, Allie's shirt was two shades darker with sweat, and she needed to pee. Matt pulled over for gas at a mega-station near the turnoff for I-5 in Tracy, and when he got out, she crawled after him, feeling like her jeans were fused to her skin. The heat outside blasted hotter than in the car, though the sun had just vanished below the mountains. She ignored Matt's funny expression as she pulled the shirt from her skin in a vain attempt at air circulation, then went to the back of the car and rummaged through the duffel.

"Need a little private time with your purple friend?"

His tone was suggestive, but she wouldn't let him bait her. She should've left the thing at home, but once he saw it, she couldn't back down. Plus, next to Bobby, it was the closest thing to a permanent relationship she'd had.

Avoiding that part of the bag, she pulled out fresh clothes, then headed for the air-conditioned restrooms.

When she came out, blissfully cooler and munching a Giant Chewy SweeTart, Matt waited impatiently by the car.

"What took so long?" he demanded. Then his gaze swept over her tank top and khaki shorts, and he appeared to lose his train of thought.

Allie waved her hand in front of his face. "Hello! Anyone home? Give me the keys."

"What?" he said blankly.

"I'll drive. Your turn to crawl over the seat."

He eyed her shorts again and his mouth curved in a slow

smile. "No dice. I wouldn't miss that view for the world."

His eyes met hers, and the spark was back—the one she'd noticed when he gave her the once over earlier. She shivered. Getting all hot and bothered by a pretty boy from the California Deep South was not what she needed. What she *did* need was to finish this job, get her money, and have her house.

"Okay," she said just to get away from him, and went to shove her sweaty clothes into the duffel.

On a sudden inspiration, she hauled herself into the back feet first, climbing over her plants and the backseat to land safely in the front without sticking her butt up in the air once. Matt closed the hatch, got in, and slammed his door hard, his disappointed expression priceless.

"Watch it!" she said. "I only have one door left."

"Cheater."

He twisted the key in the ignition, eyeing the stereo balefully. It stayed off, and Allie sighed with relief. The heat stayed off, too, and now that the sun had set, cool wind came through the open windows. Matt merged onto the freeway, leaving Tracy behind and exchanging city lights for farmland to the east and black, formless hills to the west. With no music and no scenery, it would be one dull trip.

"So," she said, after eating the last piece of candy. "Tell me about the case so far."

"Okay. The first woman who left was a Rapunzel, real name Jessica Jaimeson. She split early for the weekend, claiming she didn't feel well. Next was a Cinderella—"

"Wait—slow down. How do the princesses work? Do they rotate characters, or always play the same one? How many does the park have for each part?"

"Usually the same. In winter, we're open ten to eight, so we staff two actors per role, each working three tens plus one split. Six weeks ago, on Memorial Day, we started summer hours, which are eight to midnight. So now we need two actors per day per role. Plus, most cast members don't want full-time, so we end up with about four actors per part."

"And was Jessica a newbie or a regular?"

"They're all newbies. Except one."

"Meaning?"

"Costume character's not exactly a dream job. Even at bigger parks, the hours suck, the kids are obnoxious, and you have to be out in the heat all day." He paused. "GrimmLand's had a rough start. When Roland built it, he got out a map, saw Mecca, and thought it was a sign. He also thought it was close enough to LA and San Diego to attract business from both."

"Except…?"

"It's not. It's an hour and a half from San Diego if you speed, more from LA. With all the attractions both already have, who wants to drive way the hell into the desert, to a place no one's ever heard of, with nothing else to recommend it? Least of all an aspiring actor."

"How close is it to Palm Springs?"

"Reasonable. But people go there to golf or sit in a spa, not for a theme park. They also have a water park or two, which in desert weather is more appealing."

"Why do you work at GrimmLand?"

"Roland is a friend. I told you I was military—noncombat—I worked special intel. For a while, the US kept tabs on one of Luradel's eastern neighbors. I met Roland during that time, and when he needed a security engineer for the park, he offered me the job."

"You were a spy?" There had to be more to the story, but he exuded *not-gonna-talk-about-it*, so she dropped it.

"Did you tell Roland the location was bad?"

"Tarek did, but Roland wouldn't listen. He'd do anything for his daughter, and this is what she wanted."

"Speaking of Tarek, how does he fit into all this?"

"Park manager. Also Roland's cousin. Their fathers were brothers. Twins, but Roland's father, Bertrand, was the older."

"Luradel's in Central Europe, right? Sorry if I'm making assumptions, but Tarek doesn't seem like someone stereotypically Germanic or Austrian."

"He gets that from his mother's side. When Bertrand inherited the throne, his brother, Bernard—Tarek's father—married a woman in Zulfiqar. Tarek was born and raised there. It's where he gets his accent and…attitudes."

"That explains a lot." Allie took a swig from her water bottle and re-capped it. "Enough family history for now. Back to the princesses. Tell me more about Rapunzel."

"Jessica started a couple weeks before she left, which was June fifteenth. Got 'sick' in the middle of her shift. But another actress thinks she was meeting her boyfriend in Vegas. Says Jessica was pregnant and they were getting married. When she didn't come back on Monday, we figured she'd given her notice, but when we mailed her final check, it came back undeliverable."

"That's strange," Allie said, but Matt shook his head.

"Not for an actor. Women and men both, they come out west on a dime. It rarely works out, and they leave just as fast. She may have gone home or eloped after all."

"Anyone know the boyfriend's name?"

"Nope."

"She leave anything behind? At home or the park?"

Matt's lips pursed while he struggled with something. Finally he said, "Her braids."

A laugh bubbled out before Allie could stop it. "Are you telling me that Rapunzel—"

"Yes." His hands were so tight on the wheel, she was afraid he'd rip it off. "I know it's absurd, but the woman playing Rapunzel dropped her fake braids in the parking lot on the day she left. Another actor backed out over the bag."

"And her car?"

"Gone. No broken glass or signs of theft."

"Parking attendant?"

"No. At the guest lot, yes, but not for employees. Card keys required at the gate coming in, but not going out."

"Convenient." Allie rummaged in her purse for a pad and pen and scribbled notes on what he'd said so far. "Okay. When did number two go?"

"The twenty-ninth. Cinderella, aka Vicky Lin. She…"

He looked so inordinately put out that Allie choked on another laugh. "Don't tell me. She dropped a shoe."

"Unfortunately, yes."

His tone was repressive, and she schooled her features into a semblance of gravity. "Was it hers or part of her costume?"

"Costume, and it was more than one, it was six."

"Cinderella has three pairs of special shoes?"

"Ever read the Brothers Grimm?" She shook her head, and he said, "In the OG Cinderella, the ball lasts three days. On the first two, she wears silver slippers, and on the last, gold. Our Cinderellas wear different costumes in the morning, afternoon and evening, to signify the three days."

"Huh. Where'd she drop them?"

"In her dressing room, on a chair, but she took everything else with her."

"And did she also leave in the middle of her shift?"

"No. She got off at midnight. It takes time to get out of

all that make-up and gunk, so we don't know exactly when she left. The actress who shares her dressing space left at twelve-thirty and says Vicky was still there, but doesn't remember seeing her car in the parking lot."

"You mean her car left before she did?"

"Maybe. We just don't know."

"Think a security camera might be a good investment?"

He glared at her. "Until now, it wasn't a problem."

"Never mind. So she leaves and doesn't come back. Same deal with mailing her final check?"

"We never sent it. She'd taken an advance, supposedly to pay her father's medical bills, and still owes us money. She'd been at the park a year or Tarek would never have agreed. When she turns up, he'll probably just write off the balance. It's less than a hundred bucks at this point."

"Did you speak with her landlord?"

"Her things are at her apartment, and the rent's paid through next month."

"What about her dad? What does he say?"

"Nothing. He's in a coma. No other relatives that we know of, but feel free to search them out. That's what Tarek's paying you for."

She ignored him, making more notes. "And the last princess?"

"Not a princess. Little Red Cap."

"You think that's significant?"

Matt opened his mouth as though to argue, then snapped it shut again. "It could be coincidence, but it feels odd that the other two were princesses, but she's not."

"She's the Grimm's version of Red Riding Hood?"

"Yes. Eva Gomez. Started on Monday, didn't come in on Tuesday, and hasn't answered her phone since. It's only three days, but with the others, Tarek went ballistic. Made up his mind to hire a PI on Thursday, and here we are."

"And the cops?"

"We called them for Jessica and Vicky, but Eva hasn't been gone long enough. She's an adult, and no one else is crying foul. Also, she left her picnic hamper, but it looked…posed, for lack of a better word. On the floor outside her dressing room. Impossible to miss."

"You mean the braids and shoes might have been accidentally dropped, but the basket was planted?"

"Maybe. Plus, she gave notice at her apartment in Palm Springs, and *did* leave a forwarding address for a place in LA, but she hasn't moved in yet."

"So she could just be off having a fling?"

"Maybe," Matt said again, clearly frustrated, and she thought how hard it must be for him, as essentially Chief of Security, to have his reputation on the line.

Plus, from what she'd seen, he wasn't a rah-rah team player. She got that, having been alone most of her life. Bad enough Matt was driving her car; how would it be if Bobby had called *him* in to do *her* job?

She asked, "Why aren't you worried the women were murdered? Not to be morbid, but…"

Matt considered before responding. "The staged aspects of the disappearances. It's too much to be coincidence, and as I said, there's no hard evidence of foul play, period."

"Like your instincts say that, on the one hand, it's too obvious, but on the other, too subtle?"

"I trust the facts, princess. But yeah, my gut says they're around somewhere and will turn up eventually." He glanced at her. "Anything else you want to know right now? More about the park?"

She shook her head and put her notes away. "I need to gel what we've gone over so far."

She yawned and stretched, and Matt's glance traveled up her legs, across her exposed midriff, and lingered on her chest before snapping back to the road. She felt herself blush and grabbed her sweater from behind the seat.

"I think I'll take a nap now, if you're still okay driving."

"I'm good," he said, keeping his eyes straight ahead.

Allie rolled the window up and rested her head on the glass, using the sweater as a pillow, keenly aware of the solid male presence at her side. Apart from the zing of sexual awareness, having him near was just plain reassuring. She could almost imagine she was a girl again, driving with her dad. They'd shared many a road trip in this very car, moving from one university town to the next.

Matt changed lanes, shifting into fifth, his knuckles brushing her bare thigh, and abruptly the déjà vu passed, replaced by pure physical desire.

Great. Just great.

It didn't even help, knowing her "purple friend" was in the back. Instead, she pictured Matt's mouth on hers, his body covering her. Her body didn't care that they had no chance of a relationship. He was sexy and in the car, which appeared to be enough to set her off. She'd half decided to proposition him—why the hell not?—when his cell rang.

"Hey, Darlene. What's up?" He spoke low, but she heard every word. "Of course I know it's a date…Friday night. Wouldn't miss it."

He disconnected the call, and she turned farther into the window. Some desires even The Rock couldn't satisfy.

~:~:~

After two hours of driving, Wafi pulled into the deserted gas station, put his cap on, and went to use the decrepit pay phone. The boss was funny about orders, and there was no sense calling attention to himself.

He checked his surroundings again while fishing this week's phone number from his pocket. The bar two blocks away was, in theory, closed, but a sliver of light leaked out below the shades. Law enforcement didn't give a fuck, as long as the drunks stayed inside. Wafi felt the same way.

In the other direction, a brightly lit all-night drugstore was occupied by a lone clerk, visible through the plate glass window, absorbed in a dirty magazine. No cars passed, and Wafi shook off the sense of being watched that had clung to him all day. Dumbfucks. He was smarter than them.

He put money in the phone and dialed, then shredded the number while he waited for the boss to pick up. The line clicked open and a low voice said, "Speak."

Wafi said, "Trunk. Be there before the drugs wear off."

He started to hang up, but the boss said, "You slipped."

Fury shot through him. "No one saw me. *No one.*"

"Not this one. The other one."

"Fuck." He fought to maintain control. "Impossible. I was careful."

"Not enough. She has not told the police, but if she tries, you will take care of it. And if you *ever* alter the schedule again without permission, you are finished. Are we clear?"

"Yes." Wafi slammed the phone into its cradle.

He was *never* detected. It was why he'd advanced so far, so fast. Fuck orders. His job was snatching princesses, and if the boss didn't like how he did it, then fuck the boss.

He got back into the sedan and pulled a smoke out of the pack in his sleeve. A faint thump came from the trunk as he lit the cigarette and took a deep drag, feeling both the nicotine and the lust coursing through his veins.

The job had its perks.

And if the boss didn't come around to his way of thinking, well, Wafi had a few tricks of his own left.

Chapter Seven

Wheeled pumpkins pulled by fire-breathing bulls, driven by faceless men in black capes, hurtled down the highway next to Allie's hatchback, playing chicken. She gripped the wheel, flooring the accelerator, willing the car to go faster. Just when she was getting away, a pair of blood red braids snaked around her neck, choking, stealing her life. She tried to scream, but nothing came out, and then a man roared furiously from behind her. She jerked away— the car was crashing—she was trapped—

Then waking slammed her, the seatbelt snapping her against the vinyl seats. Her eyes popped open, heart pounding, gasping. It took a moment to realize she wasn't moving; the car was parked, and had been for a while, if the audibly-cooling engine was any indication. She drew a shaky breath, willing her pulse back from outer space.

The in-dash clock read one a.m., so they must be at the resort. She'd dozed off again after the third time of asking Matt if he was okay driving. He stood a short distance away, hands on hips, stance clearly angry, even from behind. It was his voice she'd heard, but in the dream, he'd been the Wolf from Little Red Riding Hood, intent on devouring her.

Or maybe he was the Huntsman, come to save her.

Except that wasn't right: she always saved herself.

That's my little Allie Cat, her dead father's voice echoed in her head. *Always landing on her own two feet. You can take care of yourself—you'll be all right.*

She unlatched her seatbelt, stretched, and shook her

head to clear the fog. When Matt spoke again, he sounded seriously mad, though he kept his voice low.

"Don't ever do that again. Do you understand me?"

His companion was an indistinct shape in the night, but a high feminine voice answered defiantly, "Something's wrong at the park. Don't you even care?"

"I care about you."

"Then why're you always yelling at me?"

"What did you think I'd say? 'Hi, honey, I'm home?'" His cell phone buzzed, but he ignored it. "You scared the crap out of me, in case you didn't know."

"Bull. Why don't you go back to your stupid girlfriend and forget us like you always do?"

"What's that supposed to mean?" The phone buzzed again, and he shoved a hand in his pocket, silencing it.

"That was her, wasn't it?"

"How is that any of your business?"

"Go to hell!"

"Don't speak to me that way!"

A petite form hurried around Matt and disappeared between two buildings. He moved to follow her, then kicked the gravel in the parking strip instead. A moment later he walked to the car and opened the driver's side door, and Allie blinked in the light from the dome.

He grunted. "You're awake."

Between the nightmare, the memory of her father, and Matt's surly tone, it was too much. "Apparently. Thanks to you and your *honey.*"

He looked puzzled. "My what?"

"Nothing."

His brows drew down, but then his phone buzzed again. This time he checked caller ID, then powered it off, shoving it back in his pocket.

Allie couldn't stop herself. *"Another* one? How many girlfriends do you have, anyway?"

"You tell me. You're the one keeping score."

He leaned into the car, scowling, and she skittered back against the passenger door. Unfortunately, that only allowed him to push farther in.

Annoyed with herself for letting him get to her, she ticked her fingers off, one by one. "Rianna, if you ever come up north or she comes down here. Gillian who you have *plans* with, and Didi, whoever she is. Darlene, who you have a *date* with, and now this one, which makes *five*."

He watched her silently for a minute, while she regretted her waspishness. Then he said, "You forgot Philippa," and she wanted to chop his head off with an axe.

"I thought she was your daughter."

He had a funny look on his face, like he was trying not to laugh. "What gave you that idea?"

"You said she was giving her father gray hairs, and told her mother you'd bring her home. What else would I think?"

"I can assure you, Phil is *not* my daughter."

Allie hated sounding bitter when she'd only known him half a day and didn't want to lay a claim in any case—she wasn't even sure she *liked* him—but she ground out, "Fine. Six. No wonder you were in such a hurry to get home."

Now he was downright cheerful. Not fair. Couldn't they be in pissy moods at the same time? Misery loved company, not a Pollyanna. Especially not a male one.

Matt held up six fingers also, pushing them down as he spoke. "Phil was the 'honey' who just left, bringing the total back to five, but considering she's only twelve, I wouldn't count her as a girlfriend. Besides, I plan to kill her shortly for making us all worry, so either way, we're down to four.

Then Darlene is my sister—she's getting married next week—and Didi is… Well, you'll understand when you meet her. Which leaves Rianna and Gillian."

His two extended fingers were inches from her face. *He* was in her face, and after a whole day in close proximity, it was too much. Without thinking, she reached for the door.

"Don't touch that!" Matt said as she yanked the handle and threw her weight onto it. The duct tape ripped, and with a rusty groan, the door gave way, clattering to the ground. She fell hard on top of it, the wind knocked out of her.

Matt dove forward, trying to save her from herself, and wound up hanging halfway out the car, grinning. "Nice work, princess."

"Ow." Allie rolled off the door while he pulled himself the rest of the way through.

He landed next to her, and she pretended not to notice the intense heat radiating from him. But when she sat up, he was so near, she could feel his breath like fire on her skin. His shirtsleeves were rolled up, his collar unbuttoned, and she glimpsed the strong column of his neck where it met those broad shoulders.

Her own body warmed and she fought the urge to sway into him. He reached to brush the gravel off her knees, and she jerked in response.

"You all right?" he asked, eyes dark in the shrouded parking lot.

No. Allie licked her lips, and his gaze flicked to her mouth. "I, um, think so." She stood and moved to the hatch, bumping it open. "My room over here somewhere?"

He came up behind her, resting a hand on her shoulder. "Don't you want to hear about Gillian and Rianna?"

"No." If she wasn't careful, she'd jump him anyway, girlfriends or no, which would be a Very Bad Idea. She gripped the duffel and moved a safe distance away. "I'll leave the plants 'til morning, but would you mind grabbing my laptop?"

"Sure." He shut the hatch, then glanced at the passenger door on the ground. "I'll come back for it."

Matt walked toward a building on the right, and Allie followed. He'd said the resort consisted of a luxury hotel and clusters of condos, which must be where they were now. He went to a corner unit and opened a lockbox, removing two card keys, which he used to open her door.

She stepped inside and flipped on the lights, revealing a furnished living area with cathedral ceilings, a galley kitchen, and a dining nook. A bathroom lay to the left, and the spiral stairs in the middle probably led up to the bedroom. TV, streaming device, and speakers were all provided, along with a microwave, stove, and refrigerator.

"This is all for me?" she asked as Matt shut the door and set her computer on the desk.

"We aim to please. Besides, we aren't exactly over-booked."

"What's this?" She unbolted a door sandwiched between the bathroom and a coat closet, then rattled the knob when it stayed locked from the other side.

"This is a family-friendly unit. Every unit comes with one bedroom, but between some pairs of single units are spares—sets of extra bedrooms, one up, one down. They can be unlocked and accessed from the units on either side, depending on the needs of our guests."

"Wow. This is bigger than my house."

~:~:~

Matt watched her walk away to explore the unit, and missed her jeans. The shorts were nice and all, but there was something about that blue denim hugging her sweet tush.

Then she bent over to check the freezer and what brain cells he had left said, *Thank God for shorts.* She straightened, her breasts bouncing, and his brain added, *And tank tops.*

From very far away, Allie said, "I forgot—I thought of something else about Little Red Cap."

Matt dragged his gaze up to her face. "What?" It seemed the safest response.

"She left on the wrong day."

"What?" he said again, then shook his head to clear it. "Sorry. It's late and I'm tired." *And apparently horny. Very horny.* "The wrong day? How do you figure that?"

"I had a weird dream in the car. My subconscious reviewing the case, I guess. I realized the first two women left fourteen days apart, but Red Cap only waited eleven."

"So?"

"The Rapunzel and Cinderella disappearances are very similar, but Red Cap is different in almost every way."

"And this all came to you in a dream?" Better. She wasn't using logic, a definite turnoff. Sort of. Jeez, it was late. He pictured his deck. Tomorrow. He'd sit, he'd drink, he'd be alone. Which wasn't as appealing as it had been earlier, but once he regrouped, it would be.

Allie's brows puckered. "Pay attention. I'm agreeing with you."

"Hardly. Three disappearances don't provide enough data to establish a pattern."

"Of course there's a pattern!" She glared and crossed her arms, pushing her breasts up, and he decided she should only ever wear cotton tops, or maybe a lace bra on occasion. Or a bikini. She'd look great in a bikini. On his deck.

Don't go there.

She started pacing, and he dropped his gaze to her bare legs again. Her constant motion should have reminded him of the chaos that was her life, but it also reminded him of all the reasons why women were fun to look at, and the blood in his brain drained south again.

Allie was still talking about the case. "Let's say all the women were kidnapped by the same person. He—or she, I suppose—obviously has a thing for detail. So, why break their own pattern? Whoever it is should have waited until today—er, yesterday—before taking Red Cap."

The more she moved, the harder it was to focus on her words. He dragged his mind back to the case. "One princess every other week, like clockwork?"

"Exactly," she said, then someone pounded on her door and she jumped. "Who the hell is that?"

Matt peered through the peephole, then opened the door. Tarek pushed inside, demanding, "Why did you not answer your phone? I called four times."

The argument with Allie on top of the late hour spiked Matt's temper. "I said I'd call when she was settled. We just got here. Happy?"

"No. Another princess is missing."

"Shit." Matt closed the door. "Who?"

"Sleeping Beauty. She took a break at ten and did not return, and her purse and phone are in her dressing room."

Allie broke in, "This was tonight? *Friday* evening?"

"Yes," Tarek said and sat on the couch, head in his hands. "This is it. The park is ruined. How will I face Roland, ever again?"

"Hell," Matt said. "Laurette!"

Tarek shook his head. "No. She is safe."

"You said Sleeping Beauty—"

"She has switched roles. She is Snow White now."

"Thank God," Matt said, scrubbing a hand over his face. "If anything happened to her…"

"It did not."

Allie waved her hand. "Yoo-hoo, your investigator here. Who the hell is Laurette?"

"Roland's daughter."

"I thought she was young—a little girl, into fairy tales."

Matt shook his head. "Half right. She's twenty-four. Roland built the park for her to visit, but after it opened, she wanted to stay. Roland let her, because he thought she'd be safer here than at home. But he believes she's just living at the resort, he doesn't know she's suiting up."

"She *works* here? When were you going to tell me?"

Matt shoved the irritation down. "Doesn't matter. It just didn't come up."

Allie folded her arms tight, a sure sign her temper was rising. "You don't get to decide what does or doesn't matter. This is *my* case, remember?"

Tarek's mouth pulled down, and he said to Matt, "She is right. Your job is to provide her with *all* the necessary information to do her job, and then leave her to do it."

"Fine," Matt growled. "She knows. It still wasn't Laurette."

"That is correct. Yvonne took over as Brier Rose today." Noting Allie's confusion, Tarek added, "She is the Grimm's Sleeping Beauty."

"Ah." Allie thought for a minute. "So, Roland's daughter *just* quit playing Sleeping Beauty? And the new woman in the part is now missing?"

Tarek nodded. "I know what you are thinking. Was Laurette the target? I do not know. Only Roland, Matt, and I know she is here. And the others who disappeared, she had never acted in their roles. Still…"

He was more haggard than Matt had ever seen him. Matt took his phone out and turned it back on. Six missed calls and two messages. "I have to call Didi and make sure Phil got home safe. Then you can tell us what happened."

Tarek took a handkerchief from his white suit coat and patted the sweat from his brow. "I will show you. Then Allie can see firsthand what clues have been left behind."

Damn. Allie should examine whatever evidence there was. Matt glanced at his watch: almost two a.m. With the sixty-mile drive back to his place, it hardly made sense to go home, sleep for an hour, and come back in the morning.

As though reading his thoughts, Tarek said, "Perhaps you should stay at the resort tonight."

Matt sighed. "Fine. Unlock Allie's spares."

"Here?" she squeaked.

"Yes, here. Don't argue. Someone broke into your apartment, another princess is gone, and I still don't know if Phil's safe. I'm too tired to attack you, but I might as well stay close by in case anyone *else* does. Or something else goes wrong, or—" He gave up. "Just because. I'm staying."

"But…" Allie began in the same breath that Tarek said, "Your home was invaded?"

Matt moved away and punched Didi's number into the phone while keeping an eye on Allie. Who knew? Maybe she'd erupt all over him the way she had with Peerless.

"Yes," she said, calmly enough. "But I'm sure it's unrelated. No one even knows I'm on this case."

Tarek's brows knit together. "Still…I will feel better if Matt stays with you."

"But why here? Can't he sleep in another unit?"

Matt felt a surge of impatience, but whether it was because Didi wasn't picking up, or because Allie didn't want him in her rooms, he refused to examine too closely.

Tarek said, "It is easier on the staff if we do not open another suite. It is settled. But there is another thing. I believe that was your car door in the parking lot?"

Face flaming, Allie nodded. "Sorry about that."

"It is not a problem. I will have GrimmLand's mechanics fix it tomorrow."

Didi answered then, and Matt tuned out Allie's protests about Tarek fixing her car and Matt staying with her. For one thing, when the suggestion popped unplanned from his mouth, his body had said, *Hell yes.* That couldn't be good.

His brain tried again: *Beer. Deck. Alone.*

But his body said that was a stupid plan when he could be near Allie instead.

Didi's voice said sleepily, "Doll, I said why'd you call me? Everything all right?"

"No," he said, then backtracked before her radar went up. "Yes, I'm fine. If Phil's home safe, I'll be even better."

Didi said, "I left you a voicemail. She's here," and Matt let his breath out for the first time since she'd called to tell him Phil was missing.

"At least one thing went right on this godawful day."

"You don't sound fine, doll. But you can tell me about it tomorrow."

"Tomorrow I will *be* fine," Matt said and hung up on her laughter. Then he turned back to Tarek, Allie, her broken car, the missing princesses and the reality that he wasn't getting any time off, any time soon. Tarek jerked a nod toward the door as he and Allie moved to go.

"Clusterfuck," Matt muttered and fell into step behind them. He shoved his hands in his pockets, Roland's ring weighing heavily on his finger. Four princesses in four weeks meant he *had* to be on the job. He couldn't leave.

On the other hand, maybe Allie'd bend over to examine the evidence. Working with her offered *some* perks, at least.

Chapter Eight

Allie pressed the start button on the coffee grinder she'd brought from home and waited while it went to work. Fifteen seconds later, Matt threw open the door to her "spares," as he called them, stomped out, and demanded, "What the hell are you doing? It's not even six-thirty!"

He looked tired and mad and sexier than he had last night when still put together. He'd pulled jeans on—she couldn't guess what, if anything, he wore underneath—but his chest was bare, his jaw unshaven, and his hair still off somewhere in dreamland. He also had that smooth pecs thing going on, and she swallowed a big lump of *not-my-type* while the grinder finished.

"Making coffee. Which you'd know if your girlfriends didn't do it for you."

His gaze took in the grinder, the bag of beans, the tin of European dark cocoa, and her espresso machine warming up nearby. "That's not coffee, it's a damn restaurant."

Allie's face heated. "I don't like drip." She retrieved her kitchen scale from the duffel and went to the fridge, which had been stocked with milk and other essentials.

Matt's glower deepened. "I don't care what you drink, just be quiet and let me *sleep,* for chrissake." He turned to go, then stopped when she put the porto-filter onto the scale and measured the ground coffee into it. "What in God's name are you doing now?"

"I like my mochas to taste good."

"And you do that by *weighing* your coffee?"

"And the milk and cocoa. It's important to keep the ratios constant."

"Are you *insane?*"

"You think when you buy a mocha, they dump stuff in however, and it comes out the same every time?"

"Of course not. But that's a coffee shop. At home, it's *supposed* to be random. And when you travel, you for damn sure don't bring your entire kitchen with you."

She shook her head and twisted the porto-filter onto the machine. "Of course you don't understand. Your whole family lives nearby."

"What the hell does that have to do with it?"

"Please. You moved what, fifteen miles from home? I bet you still go to the same dentist you did as a kid." His brows drew together, but he'd started to look a lot less mad and a lot more interested. In her. He glanced past the counter to her bare legs below the oversized tee she'd slept in. That and her underwear were the only things preserving a modicum of decency between them.

He raised his eyes. "What's wrong with having the same dentist?"

"Nothing. I don't, that's all."

When she didn't elaborate, he prodded, "And…?"

Mistake. She should've kept her mouth shut. Focusing on the pitcher of milk she was steaming, she said, "I moved around a lot as a kid. I had a new doctor every year."

"Okay. What's that got to do with opening your own espresso cart?" He sprawled on a barstool across from her, more awake and aware by the minute. Allie's pulse lurched and she resisted the urge to back up, concentrating on measuring cocoa instead of on the fact that he was sneaking a pretty obvious peek at her chest through the thin shirt.

Finish the job, get the money, buy the house. Do not

attempt a fling with a man who has more girlfriends than he can count on one hand, doesn't understand good coffee, and doesn't have the sense to cover his own massive chest in the presence of strangers.

She said, "We moved on short notice. I'm used to taking my stuff with me."

"Like your plants."

He sounded thoughtful, so before he psychoanalyzed her choice of traveling companions, she tilted her head at the ring on his hand. "Let me guess. Not only have you lived here forever, but you belong to the same exclusive club your great-great-grandfather founded a zillion years ago."

"Nope. Roland gave it to me. He gives them to the most trusted members of his inner circle."

She should have guessed, since Tarek had one too. "And how much ass did you kiss to get it?"

"None. I took a bullet for him during an assassination attempt three years back. He was so grateful, he nursed me back to health and brought me into the fold."

"Oh." *Well, hell.*

"Don't worry, princess. It's not all it's cracked up to be. Sure, I saved his life, but I owe him mine right back. Roland's like that. He'll take you in, but he demands total loyalty in return. Tarek's father Bernard died two years ago, and Roland gave Tarek the park job as a sort of sympathy gift. But it came with strings, and Roland's always on Tarek's case. Especially now, with the missing women."

Allie said, "Speaking of which, something's bugging me about Yvonne. Don't you think it's odd she disappeared right on cue?"

He rolled his eyes and leaned back. "Isn't that your whole point? That the kidnapper has a schedule?"

"It's too pat. You and Tarek hire a PI, and the very night

I arrive, someone else goes missing? It doesn't feel right."

"Last night you said it was weird that Red Cap left at the *wrong* time."

"I know." Allie chewed her lip, and Matt's gaze dropped to her mouth, eyes darkening. She hurried on. "Then there's the spindle at the scene. That's also over the top. You said Yvonne wasn't fully trained, that Laurette still has all her spindles accounted for. It's like someone wants to make *very* sure we know the princesses were taken in measured, calculated ways."

"You're saying it isn't *random* enough?" He raised an eyebrow, and Allie blew out a breath.

"Okay, I get it. I weigh my coffee, think the kidnapper has a master plan, and then complain when the pieces fit too neatly. Big deal. I trust my instincts."

Matt rose and pushed away from the counter. "Great. Your instincts. Would those be the same ones that gave that prick Peerless a key to your apartment?"

"That's personal, not professional."

"You use the same instincts for both."

"I told you, Bobby might be a jerk, but he's a good PI, and I've known him for years. He's loyal, in his own way."

"Whatever you say, princess."

"What business is it of yours, anyway?"

"It's not. I just wish you'd make up your damn mind about the case." He disappeared into his room for a minute, then reappeared wearing his shirt and tugging on his shoes.

Allie came around the counter. "Where are you going?"

"Since you won't let me sleep, I need to get my car back from our long-term lot, and then I have some training stuff to pick up. I'll be back in an hour."

Allie couldn't go undercover if it was known she was a PI, so Matt had said one particular princess would be the only other park employee who knew Allie's true purpose. Matt would give her a crash course on the prep side of things, and then the princess would help in the field, until she was up to speed.

"You're leaving me here? What am I supposed to do while you're gone?"

His gaze swept up from the hem of her shirt to her face, and he scowled. No doubt his girlfriends wore nothing but lace and satin. She was *so* not up to his standards.

"Call Bobby—sell mochas to the staff—what the hell do I care?" He turned and stomped to the door. "The least you could do is put on some jeans—or a pair of shorts."

~:~:~

Laurette pulled her custom Volvo into the employee lot and parked in her usual space. The sleek sedan was overkill, given she lived onsite and could walk work, but if she hadn't bought it, her father would have forced something even more opulent on her. For someone who wanted to hide her from his enemies, he had a funny way of doing it.

She picked up the deli bag she'd brought, then got out and locked the doors. Roland meant well, but even she knew you couldn't run from trouble. In two months, she'd have to go home and face the music. Just…not today.

It was barely seven a.m. and an eerie quiet hung over the park. She quickened her steps on the isolated path to the employee complex, not slowing until she was safely inside Building C, which housed the dressing rooms. The halls were dark, because Tarek insisted on using the dim emergency bulbs until eight, even though many employees arrived before then. It was one of his "economies" that bothered her, especially now. Then again, only Eva had disappeared from *inside* the complex.

Moving fast, she headed for her dressing room. She

rarely had a morning shift right after an evening one, but with so many staff changes in recent weeks, not everyone was up to speed. A thrill of pleasure washed through her. It was nice to be needed, to be *good* at something.

Her cell rang, startling her with the soft notes of Beethoven's *Moonlight Sonata*, an audible caller ID. She should change his ringtone to something less doleful. But when they were children, Wolfram had played it for her on the piano. Now, it made her sad, wistful for the carefree friendship they'd lost along the road to adulthood.

She spoke softly, so as not to disturb the building's empty peace. "Hello, Wolf."

"Happy birthday, sweet." She shivered at his deep, vibrant tone. "Did you get the necklace?"

Laurette closed her eyes, willing the tears back, then made herself move down the hall. "It's lovely. Thank you." How could she tell him the truth? That like his music, it was so beautiful, she ached. If only he'd picked it out himself, she would have treasured it forever.

"I asked Roland to forward it to you." There was no censure in his voice, yet Laurette hurt anyway. Damn her father and his machinations. "It was my grandmother's. You should have it."

"I know. Of course."

She rounded the corner to the dressing rooms—

—and a male shape knocked her back. She screamed, dropping her phone as strong arms locked around her.

"Laurette?" Wolf's voice came sharp through the cell. *"Sweet—what has happened?"*

"You had better answer him," Tarek's voice said quietly, and her heart slammed back into motion. He released her, and she stepped unsteadily away.

"Of course." Swallowing, she fumbled for the phone.

"Wolf—it's okay. I tripped."

"Are you hurt?"

She drew a deep breath. "I'm fine."

Tarek flicked an invisible speck of dust from his white suit coat, lips pressed tight, because if he spoke, Wolf might uncover her secret. How she hated the lies. But until the assassin was caught and Luradel stabilized, her father insisted no one know her location.

Did Roland truly believe her own fiancé would try to kill him? The king's death would solve a lot of problems for a lot of people, including Wolf. Everyone knew he didn't love Laurette, but he did covet Luradel's throne.

Laurette shivered. *Not Wolf. Please not Wolf...*

"I have to go," she said into the cell, watching Tarek's stony face. "I'm, uh, meeting someone for coffee."

"If you are sure you are well. I will call you again soon."

She disconnected, pushing the sadness down. Didn't his cool distance prove he cared nothing for what she did?

Tarek made no move to step away, and she suppressed a bubble of anxiety. Delaying the inevitable, she said, "Did you learn anything else about Yvonne?"

"No. We found nothing beyond the spindle." He regarded her severely.

Laurette's mouth went dry. "I'm late for my shift."

"You know I cannot allow you to continue this charade. Not now."

And there it was. The thing she'd feared since Jess vanished four weeks ago. "Please…"

"No, and that is final."

All her life, she'd been taught to modulate her tone, that hysterics were "common." Still, she couldn't keep the panic from her voice. "No other Snow White is trained. I—"

"I cannot risk it. Roland will close the park." He paused.

"What am I saying? He will close it anyway."

"No," she whispered.

Roland and Wolf didn't understand, but until now, Tarek had been willing to help her. However, with the missing princesses and Luradel's political turmoil, his life would be undeniably easier with her gone.

"Yes," he said. "Everyone will be laid off. Then you will not be the only one not allowed to play dress up."

He moved to go, but she stopped him with a hand, forcing herself to speak. "Rapunzel and Cinderella are filled, and the second Brier Rose. But we need six out at once. You *must* have a Snow White—she's a main attraction."

"Perhaps. But a new girl starts today. Matt will train her and she will suit up tomorrow."

"Tomorrow? That's impossible! At least let me do it until she's ready."

Tarek held up his right hand with Roland's ring resting heavily on his thin, elegant third finger. An elaborately scrolled R and three songbirds—her family's crest—glinted mockingly at Laurette in the poorly lit hall.

"You see this? I made a promise to your father. I cannot protect you if you continue to take foolish risks. It is settled. You are on, shall we say, administrative leave until further notice. Or perhaps you would like me to call your father— or Wolfram—to come collect you."

His demeanor was less than pleasant, and she backed up, nausea burning deep in her stomach.

Tarek nodded. "Go back to Montreal, Laurette. Better yet, go home. You are not wanted here."

Chapter Nine

Phil biked to GrimmLand early on Saturday. Her dad would be mad she'd snuck out, but who cared? Matt would be mad, too, which gave her more pause. He'd been really pissed last night. She maybe owed him an apology or something. To be safe, she stopped at the Mecca Mart and bought him his favorite chocolate bar—bittersweet with orange filling—before finishing her ride.

By the time she got to the employee lot, sweat trickled out from under her helmet and onto her neck. She locked her bike to the rack by the sidewalk, then glanced around. Huge "atmosphere walls" painted to look like snow-capped Bavarian peaks hid the complex from the view of the guests and cast long shadows over the empty lot, but didn't alleviate the morning heat.

For a minute, she wished she was back in her room in air-conditioned bliss. But she *had* to find out where the man with the tattoo went. Last night, she'd followed his weird zigzag trail across half the park, until he'd gone into the Princess Shoppe and vanished. Meggy, going over the special orders at the counter, swore no one came in before Phil, leaving her stumped.

Unless he went into the tunnels; it was the only thing that made sense. Matt'd planned the underground network for park maintenance, but cast members also used them to get from the dressing rooms to their fairy-tale abodes, so guests wouldn't see Prince Charming on his way to the john, or two Cinderellas above ground at once.

They also provided conduits for plumbing, power sources, and the like. Snaking out from the middle of the employee complex, they emptied into certain shops and attractions, as well as into the flower gardens. Could the man with the tattoo know about the exit in the Princess Shoppe? And if he did, how had he slipped by Meggy?

Even Phil wasn't supposed to know where the tunnels led, let alone go into them. This early, with the park empty, would be her best bet for slipping inside. Unfortunately, she wasn't the only one crazy enough to come in before seven.

As she got her card key out, Matt's bright red convertible Testarossa pulled into his parking space. It wasn't like he needed the car to get women. They fell all over him, regardless. Probably he was making a statement. Considering his sisters all had minivans and sedans, nothing said "screw family" like a sporty two-seater with a roll bar.

Matt got out, looking mad and like he hadn't slept. Not coming from Gillian's then, or he'd be tired and *happy.* The thought that maybe he'd finally ditched her cheered Phil up.

"Hey, Matt! How's the Testosteroni today?"

He scowled and slammed the car door. His shirt was untucked, his hair uncombed. "Why are you here so early?"

"You're in a good mood."

"You running off again last night might have something to do with that."

Which reminded her of why she'd tried to talk with him in the first place. Should she tell him now about the man with the tattoo? So far, the man hadn't done much that she knew of, except walk. Maybe chocolate first, then talking. Sugar and caffeine would probably help.

Before she could decide, Matt went on, "Plus, I have to train a new princess. Probably take all damn day. *If* she listens to me, which she never does." At Phil's blank look, he added, "I drove down with her."

"You brought the new princess *with you* from SF?"

"Crap." He scrubbed a hand over his face. "I meant to say, she sent in her résumé, and Tarek and I had business up there, so he interviewed her yesterday."

His explanation sounded wrong. "Tarek hired her *on the spot?* Mr. High-and-Mighty, three-interview-minimum park manager? She must be one wicked princess."

"You got that right."

He moved to the building entrance, and Phil followed. The tunnels would have to wait. Matt was never this distracted; he was the most focused person she knew. Maybe it was the missing princesses.

He held the door for her, and she stepped into the corridor. He moved quickly toward the wing where his office was, and she had to take two steps for every one of his to keep pace.

"So," she asked, "Why're you here?"

"I have to train the new princess in park MO, so she can suit up tomorrow."

"Tomorrow?"

"Tarek's orders."

"Why so soon? At least can't you wait until, like, nine or something?"

"Didn't get to sleep until four, so yeah, I'd rather be in bed. It's just that Allie's…" He paused. "Well, anyway. It's a huge pain in the ass." Suddenly, he rounded on Phil. "You ever help your dad make coffee?"

She blinked. "Uh, sometimes."

"How?"

"The usual. Grind the beans, add water, pour. That kind of thing."

"You don't…*weigh* it…do you?"

"The new princess weighs her coffee?"

"She did this morning. Plus, she slept in this t-shirt that must be thirty years old at least. It was…" Matt's voice trailed off and he shook himself, then started walking again. "Anyway. Tarek put me in her spares."

Phil scrambled to keep pace. "You hired her yesterday—"

"*I* didn't, *Tarek* did."

"—and slept in her suite last night?"

Matt stopped again and shut his eyes.

Phil had a good idea what went on with consenting adults behind closed doors. Thanks to her dad's obsession with openness and making sure she didn't feel the lack of not having a mother, Sex Ed was more like a dinner topic than the hush-hush stuff she was sure it was in normal families. Could Matt and the new princess…?

But Matt would never cheat on Gillian. He was too nice and had too many sisters. So maybe he *had* broken up with her. But if that was the case, why go into damage control now?

He cleared his throat and looked *reasonable*. "Tarek thought it'd be easier on the staff." Phil said nothing and he started moving again. "Besides, we had to start so early."

"Why're you training her? Why not someone else?"

Matt's gaze slid away as they rounded a corner and his office came in sight. He stopped abruptly. Gillian stood by his door, dressed like part of the boring furniture in a grey blazer, skirt, and shoes.

"Hello, darling." She walked over and kissed him. He didn't respond too much, which was another weird thing. He wasn't gross about it, but he didn't usually hold back either. Gillian leaned away. "You're here early."

"I never went home. Didn't you hear about Yvonne?"

"Of course. Poor baby. You must have been up very late. Did you find anything?"

"Nothing helpful." Matt stepped to the door, taking his keys out. "What brings you in on a Saturday?"

Gillian flushed, like she felt guilty about something. What was up with *that?* She kept her voice cool, though.

"I thought if your office was unlocked, I could find those Enchanted Flounder plans and save you the trouble."

"Jeez, Gillian. I told you I'd get them to you next week. What's the damn rush?"

Her flush deepened, but her eyes flashed. "Just trying to do my job. I don't get to drop everything and jaunt away with Tarek the way you do."

Matt closed his eyes, then turned back to her. "I'm sorry. That was uncalled for. I have no excuse, other than that I'm tired, and I have a new princess to train."

"A new princess?" Gillian looked understandably confused. "You?"

"Never mind. It's a long story."

She moved closer, saying suggestively, "If there's anything I can do to help…"

"Actually, there is." Matt stepped out of her reach, opened his door, and flipped on the lights. His office was a mess, as usual, with plans, maps and papers all over. Phil flopped into the spare chair, leaving Gillian to stand.

Some of Phil and Matt's best talks had occurred in here, while he worked and she did lessons. Especially after her mother had died. It was another of her favorite hideouts, of which she had too many. Phil repressed a snort. That a twelve-year-old needed multiple refuges from her real life should've been a red flag to someone besides the twelve-year-old. Then again, not being noticed was a big reason she needed to escape.

Matt said to Gillian, "The new princess is tall. Brunette, green eyes. What role would work?"

She considered. "How tall?"

"Maybe five ten or so."

"And her figure?"

Between Gillian and herself, Phil wasn't sure who studied Matt's face more.

"Okay, I guess. Not too thin, if that's what you mean."

He kept his composure pretty good, but turned toward his desk awfully fast. Phil almost felt sorry for Gillian. She'd never liked her much, but on the other hand, Gillian wasn't a threat to what Matt called Phil Time. He'd been dating her awhile, but made it clear it was totally casual. And now, here he was, so distracted by the new princess and her old shirt, he barely noticed Gillian *or* Phil.

"I see," Gillian said after a minute. "Rose Red is good. Less to learn, and she isn't hounded by the guests as much."

"Perfect. Thanks." Matt sounded hugely relieved.

"I aim to please." Gillian sauntered over for another kiss, obviously rattled when he barely pecked her back. "Well. Stop by my office on your way out and I'll give you a file on Rose Red. Everything the new girl needs to know."

Matt flashed her the first genuinely appreciative smile he'd given her all day. "That's a huge help. I owe you one."

"Two. Remember, you already promised me a dinner."

Matt started guiltily. "About that. With training Allie and all, I'm not sure when I'll be done."

"Darling, any time is fine. If it's late, I'll stop by Giovanni's and bring a steak over to your place."

"No, really. We should postpone." He shoved a roll of plans and a notebook into a messenger bag on his desk.

Gillian must be really desperate. Matt *never* invited women to his home. He took them out, went to their place, whatever. But his home was his sanctuary, like the park was for Phil. He never mixed his personal life with work *or* family, and though Phil had been to his house a few times, she knew how not to get in his way.

Gillian, however, didn't know when to retreat.

She said lightly, "Of course. We'll do it next week."

She gave him a lingering kiss, which he responded to more. And when she broke away, he was a little flushed. Maybe Gillian—and Phil—had less to worry about than they'd thought.

Gillian moved to the door. "See you in a bit. And if you happen across the Flounder plans…" Matt kept his head down, and Gillian's lips thinned. "Of course, I'm sure you'll be too busy, having fun with the new girl."

Matt waited 'til she'd gone, then shook his head at Phil. "Yeah, it'll be a blast, teaching the royal wave to a plant-toting, chaos-loving ninja barista who packs a purple—" He stopped abruptly, yanking the bag off his desk.

He sure was pissed. Hopefully, Allie was just really annoying. The thought that Matt usually got along with everyone popped into Phil's head, but she pushed it away. Even nice guys got mad, especially at tough chicks. Still…

She made a mental note to check Allie out as soon as possible. Matt wouldn't want her along during training. But after he went home for the day, or maybe tomorrow, she'd meet Allie and make her own mind up. She was already losing her park; she couldn't lose Matt, too.

~:~:~

The rest of the day went about as Matt expected. Allie wore shorts again, which was good, but she didn't bend over, which was bad. It was also bad how disappointed that made him. Then there were the eleven hours he spent drilling her. What most actresses got two weeks for, she got one day. When it was after six p.m. and he'd had the same hard-on since lunch, it was past time to cut and run. *Beer, deck, alone* had never sounded so good. Then she came downstairs in a black swimsuit. One piece, but man, it showed off her athletic form. She asked about using the pool, and he'd had enough brain cells to tell her where it was before making his escape.

On the long drive home, he went over what they'd pieced together about Yvonne. He just didn't buy that she'd walk off during a cigarette break. Plus, Allie was right. Her disappearance was even more contrived than the others, from the timing to the spindle, which they'd discovered came from the Princess Shoppe.

Meggy, who'd worked the shop all evening, swore inventory was accurate when she clocked in. She also said business was slow, with only two customers in five hours. Phil had stopped in, but Matt *knew* she hadn't stolen the spindle. For reasons he couldn't comprehend, she regarded the Princess Shoppe with an awe bordering on reverence. *If* she took anything, it'd be a poufy dress, not a spool of thread. But she'd never steal, period, so it was a moot point.

When he got home, he realized his cell had been off all day again. Powering it on, he discovered twelve voicemails, which he played on speakerphone while searching for food. The first eleven were from his sisters about Darlene's wedding, and he hit delete without listening to them, but the last was a surprise. Allie's voice greeted him; she must have called while he was driving home.

I'm sorry to bug you, she said, tiredness making her voice throaty and sensual. He shut his eyes, picturing her sprawled on the bed, chewing her full bottom lip the way she did when puzzling something out. She did it so often, the image was permanently burned on his brain.

I know you wanted to be alone, but Bobby called.

Matt's eyes popped open, and he was so busy trying to decide if she was happy about that or not that he missed what she said next and had to skip back.

He checked my place out. A real pro job. Nothing left behind. He's going through old files, but most are chump change, so if it's on his end, maybe they hired someone. Okay. Well, um, see you.

The speaker went silent. Ridiculous. He'd spent all day with her; he should be annoyed she'd called. Instead, he considered replaying the message, just to let her husky voice wash through him again. Christ. He'd turned down easy, certain sex with Gillian and spent the day with a woody for a woman whose life was so out of control, a circus was calm by comparison.

He grabbed a beer, then went to the deck. The stain he'd applied gave the cedar a warm glow, and he admired his handiwork. He'd built the deck himself, along the length of the house. Situated on a hill, the properties on either side angled away, so his neighbors were hidden from sight. Growing up in a small house with five older sisters had made privacy a priority. The deck faced southwest, toward San Diego and the ocean, and the view was amazing. How could Allie be excited about her boring, stucco box, crammed between equally boring neighbors on either side? She had a tiny yard, with another neighbor right behind, and no view, just the noise of traffic all around.

Thinking about her reminded him of her should-be-boring black swimsuit, and the hard-on came back. He was finally alone on his deck, and she still crowded his thoughts.

Matt took a deep breath of the evening air, sank into a cushioned cedar chair, and opened his beer.

And the doorbell rang.

He shut his eyes and channeled invisibility, sitting so still, even the birds would think he was part of the deck.

The bell rang again.

Beer. Deck. Al—

Ding! Ding!

"Damn it!"

He slammed the beer on a table, stomped into the house, and yanked the door open—tactical error number one.

Gillian stood on the porch, wearing a black coat buttoned to her throat despite the warm weather, and ultra-high shiny red heels. She looked like something out of a nineteen-forties film noir, with her platinum hair and blood red lipstick. She must have found his address in his employee file, as he'd certainly never given it to her.

"Hello, darling," she said, stepping inside to kiss him, and he was too startled to stop her.

Mistake number two. She slipped her tongue into his mouth and ran a hand over his crotch, discovering the Allie hard-on, which hadn't dissipated. She pressed closer, throwing him off balance just enough that he wrapped an arm around her to keep them from falling to the floor.

She kicked the door shut. "I knew all that 'alone' business was nonsense. I can tell how *glad* you are to see me."

"Gillian," he began, trying to get away. What was the matter with her? Had he said anything to make her think she could drop in like this? Their relationship was about sex and having fun. What had changed to make her so aggressive?

She laughed, following him across the entry. Another foot, and they'd fall into the sunken living room. She let go, allowing him to negotiate the steps while she remained above. Mistake number three. He knew better than to literally back down from an opponent.

He tried again. "I told you, tonight's not a good time."

"Of course it is. I can tell how ready you are for me."

She began unbuttoning the coat, revealing the long column of her throat, and then her bare collar bones, making it blatantly obvious she wore nothing underneath. As an offensive tactic, it was a good one. Besides, if he couldn't have Allie—not that he wanted her—was it so wrong to burn off steam with Gillian?

Yes, said his brain.

Who the hell cares? argued his body, and prepared to enjoy the show.

~:~:~

Allie shut off the lamp and thought about digging The Rock out of the duffel. But the swim was so relaxing, and she'd had so little sleep last night, further tension relief seemed superfluous. Besides, when she closed her eyes, she saw Matt. She'd just end up imagining him inside her, which would make her feel dumb and needy.

Rolling on her side, she listened to the foreign sound of the condo's AC. After two years in SF, she was out of practice at sleeping in new spaces. A wave of sadness swelled and she flopped on her back again. Rianna had called to say there were no hitches with the inspection. The owner, anxious to close, had agreed to most of Allie's demands, as proposed by Rianna, Matt, and the inspector.

One more move, and she'd never have to pack up her stuff, ever again. Her plants would get space to grow, she'd get a cat or a dog—or both—and finally have a place of her own. Assuming she could afford it, after this job ended.

Her cell rang and she shot off the bed, fumbling in the dark for it in case it was Matt. And just how junior high was *that?* Still, hope spiked when caller ID showed a restricted number. With his love of privacy, he'd never be so plebeian as to publish his contact info for all to see.

She answered the call, then swallowed her disappointment when Bobby greeted her. "Hey, babe."

"Don't call me that." She sat back on the bed, noting the clock showed well past eleven. Matt wouldn't call this late; only Bobby would be so presumptuous. Of course, with their long history, he wasn't exactly presuming, but she didn't feel like being charitable. "What do you want?"

"I forgot something when I called earlier."

"What?"

"You."

His tone was suggestive, and she didn't hide her irritation. "We broke up, remember?"

"That's never stopped us before."

The bastard had a point. "But this time, you stole from me *and* fired me. I have my limits."

He laughed, his voice deep enough, she could almost pretend he was Matt. "C'mon, Allie. You know I didn't mean it. Come back to work for me. I had to give Frank the partnership. How would it look if I promoted my girlfriend above someone else more qualified?"

"*Ex*-girlfriend. That partnership was mine. Don't think you can say sorry and I'll roll over."

In spite of everything, the offer was tempting. Maybe because of the two days with Matt, fighting both her attraction to him and the aggravation he caused. Or maybe because Bobby was *there,* the only person left from her old life. He'd even known her dad. He might not be perfect, but if she kept her expectations low, she wouldn't get hurt.

"I'll think about it," she said at last.

He gave a low growl. "Take your time, babe. Take your time."

Chapter Ten

Someone watched Allie leave the condo. She felt the hostile gaze and shivered in her bike shorts and jog-bra, despite the early morning heat. The bushes behind her rustled, and she whirled, pulse thundering. Was that a shadow hurrying between the buildings?

Nothing moved, and she unfisted her hands. Talk about paranoid. Just last night, she'd insisted she was safe and Matt should go home. Now she was jumping at the wind. Still, only once she'd jogged out to Box Canyon Road—one of Mecca's two main drags—did she breathe easier.

GrimmLand sat on a hundred acres southeast of Mecca and was comprised of the resort, theme park, employee complex, several parking lots, and a private airstrip that Roland used when visiting. The main entrance was off Highway 111, which ran from Mexicali down south up to I-10 in Indio. If she went east on Box Canyon, she'd come out on the road leading to the bottom of Joshua Tree National Park. So instead, she ran west toward Mecca and the safety of—relatively—higher numbers.

The route took her past neat rectangles of crops, mostly palm trees. According to Matt, Mecca's one draw besides GrimmLand was its winter Date Festival. Not exactly party central. Beyond the farms, empty brown hills rose on either side, the effect monotonous and depressing. Matt was right. Roland couldn't have picked a more isolated place for an amusement park if he'd done it on purpose.

The town itself wasn't much better. Not even a town:

the welcome sign proclaimed it an "unincorporated community" of Riverside County, with a population of under nine thousand. A quick pass through yielded little info, other than that most of the houses were tiny post-WWII boxes, and the people were largely Hispanic. They stared openly at her, a stranger in their midst. Likely GrimmLand's guests never came here, and just as likely, the princesses had been taken elsewhere.

Less than ten minutes later, she came out on the other side to more farmland. Just to be thorough, she turned up the highway and came back through town on a different street. This one was lined with apartment blocks that made her place seem architecturally exciting by comparison, but it didn't provide any more insight into the case. Tarek was right; she'd have to do her investigating undercover.

Today would be her first time "suiting up" as Matt called it. At eight, the infamous Didi, her new mentor, would take her for costuming. Didi was the only other cast member in the know about Allie's true profession, and with her aid, Allie wouldn't need Matt any more.

The thought of not seeing him again sent a squishy feeling to her stomach, like the one she'd got after her dad convinced her to eat raw oysters. She quashed it. Matt lived here, she lived in SF, end of story. Plus, he had that whole harem thing. For a man hell-bent on being alone, he sure had a lot of women hanging around. She had no desire to be one of them.

Keeping her pace fast, she made it back to the resort in record time. The parking lot felt less sinister now that the sun was higher, and she balanced against her car, stretching her quads.

"You don't look like a princess."

The high voice came out of nowhere, and Allie lost her

hold and stumbled before righting herself and twisting around. Her heart hammered and it took a second to process that it *was* a high voice, clearly coming from the girl on the sidewalk nearby, and not from some huge bad guy with a baritone and twelve-pack abs.

Blowing out a breath, she said, "You startled me."

The girl—under five feet tall and scrawny—shook her stick-straight brown hair, and the slashes of her brows pulled together. "You're too tall."

She made it sound like a capital offense, and Allie recognized her voice. "You're Philippa."

Phil, if that's who she was, appeared unimpressed by Allie's powers of deduction. Behind her too-large Harry Potter glasses, her bright hazel eyes remained stony. She was dressed in cutoffs that hit the middle of her skinny thighs, and a faded pink shirt that at one time might have sported a sequined four-leaf clover, but which now showed only its rough outline. Above this, white letters spelled out KISS ME I'M IRISH in curly script.

The girl put her hands on her tiny hips. "Your hair's too short. It doesn't look like princess hair."

"Yeah? Well, you don't look Irish." Allie resisted the urge to stick her tongue out and went back to stretching.

Philippa's frown deepened, but it was more puzzled now than mad. She watched Allie for a minute, seemingly unsure where to go next. Finally, she shot out, "Matt said you were bitchy and weird. He was right."

Then she whirled and ran toward the park, leaving Allie to shrug off her words. Who cared what Matt thought?

But as Allie switched legs, and the hurt didn't go away, she had her answer.

~:~:~

Thirty minutes later, she responded to the knock on her

door and finally understood why Matt was so evasive about Girlfriend Number Three, Didi.

The woman on Allie's doorstep fit his type: blonde with blue eyes. But there her "typicalness" ended. Taller than Allie, she was slim with muscular calves showing below a straight denim skirt. She wore bright red peep-toe flats which had to be size thirteen, and a sleeveless blouse that showed off her smooth arms. She had an oval face with narrowly-spaced eyes, a straight nose, full red lips—and a prominent Adam's apple in her slender throat.

Allie snapped her mouth shut, then couldn't think of a damn thing to say.

"Never mind, doll," Didi said in a low alto. "I get it all the time." Her glance took in Allie's wet hair, khaki shorts, and tank top. "Ready? Tarek wants us to get an early start."

Allie regrouped. "Ready as I'll ever be." She stuffed her cell in her shorts and grabbed her gun from a side table, tucking it into her waistband under her shirt.

Didi whistled. "Matt said you were packing, but I thought he meant you had a hot bod. Which you do."

"Er…thanks."

Allie fell into step beside Didi, trying to come up with something even remotely PC to talk about. The path reminded her of the encounter earlier, and she said, "You're Phil's…" then stopped, suddenly aware that either of the typically-gendered terms for "parent" might be inappropriate in the circumstances.

Didi smiled. "Dad is fine. Yes, she's my child. Have you met her?"

"I saw the blur. But Matt talks about her all the time."

"Then you know all there is to know. If I hadn't been there myself, I'd think she was his daughter instead." She stopped and faced Allie. "Go ahead and ask. I know you want to."

Heat burned Allie's cheeks. "Um…"

"Never mind. I'm transgendered. I was born Diedrich, tried to make a go of it with Phil's mother, and it didn't work out. I said screw that, and now I'm going to have the operation. I'm already a she, might as well make it official."

Nothing like frankness to trump political correctness. "It's not any of my business—"

"The hell with that. I know about you and why you're here. It's only fair you know about me."

"Okay."

Didi didn't seem to need a deeper response. She grinned and resumed walking. "Feel better?"

"Yes, actually, I do. Thanks."

Then the entrance to the employee buildings came in sight, and the warm fuzzies vanished, leaving Allie with sweaty palms and stomach flutters.

Didi said, "Nervous much?" Allie nodded, unable to speak, and Didi added, "Don't be."

She tapped her card key on the reader and opened the door, but Allie hung back on the walkway. "It's just that, you know, I never played dress up as a kid. I moved around a lot, and I never had friends to do it with."

"Just do what the rest of us do."

"Which is?"

"Breathe."

Didi dragged her inside, the door closing behind them, and every new school Allie'd been dropped into mid-year flashed before her: all thirteen of them. She couldn't do this—she had to leave—but Didi pulled her down the hall.

She registered vague impressions of expensive carpeting, mahogany doors, and copious turns, before they came to an open area unhappily reminiscent of a cafeteria, where several women and Phil sat at a table. The place smelled of floor cleaner and stale food, and Allie's stomach lurched. Phil scowled as they entered, and then the others turned, conversation dying out as she drew closer.

Didi beamed. "Everyone, this is Allie. Allie, everyone."

Allie's tongue was too big, too dry, she couldn't swallow. *Oh God—I'm fifteen again.*

She was the gangly, too-tall new girl who didn't know jack about dresses or make-up or shoes, who'd just been dragged *here* from Podunk *there*. She tried to smile at the popular crowd, to remember she wasn't a pimply freshman, she was a successful PI masquerading as an unsuccessful actress, but her brain was stuck twenty years ago.

It didn't help that this was clearly the GrimmLand Elite. They'd even color-coordinated: A blonde, a redhead, a brunette, and one black-haired woman who was so pale and petite, she could have passed for a porcelain doll.

This delicate vision caught Allie's eye and smiled shyly, then rose and extended a tiny hand. "I'm Laurette."

Allie tried not to break any of her bones as they shook, or to show her surprise. Laurette looked barely old enough to drive, let alone rule an entire nation. Yet she was almost twenty-five, the age when she would assume her place as heir to Luradel, assuming Roland overturned the country's sexist laws forbidding said happy event. Allie was hazy on the details, as Matt had focused less on party politics and more on what she'd need to know immediately, like where the bathrooms were and when she got her breaks.

Didi sat by Phil, who scooted unsubtly away. Didi covered her disappointment with an encouraging nod at Allie, while Laurette took over the introductions.

"This is Celia," she said, indicating the brunette. "She's—Brier Rose."

Allie noticed the hesitation. Yesterday, she'd pressed Matt further about why Laurette switched roles, but he'd brushed her off, saying it could wait. Allie wasn't so sure. What if Laurette was the intended victim two nights ago? And why was she even at work today? What little Matt had said implied she wouldn't be returning in *any* role.

"Nice to meet you," Celia said, her expression calculating. "We're practically roomies. I'm in the condo across from you. Except I hear Tarek's letting you stay at the resort for *free*."

Allie's heart hammered double-time and her blood pressure went up another notch. Crap. Many of the cast members lived at the resort, so Matt had figured it was an easy cover. But the "free" part wasn't supposed to leak out. Celia's tone made it clear just *how* she thought Allie was repaying Tarek, and Allie's face flamed.

"Ignore her, doll," Didi broke in. "She's just jealous. She tried to sleep her way into the next Spielberg pic, and wound up blacklisted in the desert instead."

Celia's eyes shot serrated knives at Didi, who lifted a shoulder, grinning. Laurette turned to the blonde next. She regarded Allie with an intensity bordering on the indecent. Like Laurette, she was pale, but in a cold, blue-veined way instead of Laurette's roses-and-cream loveliness. Her eyes were the color of Arctic ice, and her expensive grey suit contrasted with Celia's black rhinestone tee, pink shorts, and espadrilles. Unsurprisingly, she wasn't a cast member.

"This is our literary advisor, Gillian Sinclair," Laurette said, and it clicked: Girlfriend Number One. But Matt was out of the picture anyway, so it was none of Allie's concern.

Gillian said, "Matt told me you'd be starting today. I hope the packet I sent was helpful." She gave a little cough. "When I left his place this morning, he asked me to check on you, in case you needed anything…?"

This morning? Ouch. "No. I've got all I need, thanks."

"Are you sure? Matt wanted me to pick a nice, easy part, since you had to learn it so fast. He was very concerned about it yesterday, and he brought it up again last night."

Why was Gillian so hell-bent on telling Allie she'd slept at Matt's place? If she needed to worry about anyone, it was Rianna, who was *much* more Matt's type than Allie.

"Why *are* you starting so soon?" the redhead asked, and Allie suppressed a groan. Would the questions never end? That was supposed to be *her* job.

"This is Bridget," Laurette put in. "Our Rapunzel."

Bridget leaned back in her chair, assessing Allie with clear gray eyes, her long hair rippling past her waist. Probably extensions. Not that Allie had hair-related experience with anything more complex than nail scissors. Still, the effect was very Rapunzel-esque, though probably the OG was also supposed to be blonde. With so many cast members leaving, maybe Tarek had lowered his standards.

Bridget's fashion choices resembled Celia's, except she wore a miniskirt with her cropped tee. Apparently, comfort was not couture, even out here.

Allie said, "I guess there's been some turnover recently, and Tarek needs the spot filled."

Tarek and Matt had agreed that Allie should pretend not to know about the missing women. They'd called the police but wanted to keep the disappearances out of the media as long as possible. Allie didn't blame them. If the public learned four women had left the park in a month, even under their own steam, it wouldn't be good for business.

Didi arched a brow and rose. "Speaking of which, the best way to get up to speed is to start scouting the park." She took Allie's arm. "C'mon, doll. You never know what hidden talents you'll uncover if you work hard enough."

~:~:~

Laurette watched the new princess walk away. Try as she might, she couldn't hate her. Not that Laurette being forbidden to suit up was Allie's fault. But instead of another stuck-up actress, Allie seemed…lost. Laurette had never met anyone who looked the way she felt: completely out of place in a setting that should have been perfect for her. Maybe Allie would get used to GrimmLand and fit in eventually. Unlike Laurette; she'd never fit in, except in the one place she could never allow herself to be.

"You okay?" Phil asked.

Laurette forced a smile. "I'm fine. I just have to get my stuff out of my dressing room."

"Good luck with that," Celia said, pushing back from the table. "I still don't see why you get to go on vacation while the rest of us have to keep working our butts off. Everyone's leaving this damn place. Maybe I will, too."

Bridget said slowly, "I wouldn't quit just yet."

Celia frowned. "Why the hell not? Who needs this job?"

"I'm not sure, but I think Allie might be a talent scout."

Celia's eyebrows shot up and she sat again. "No shit?"

"You heard what Didi said about *scouting* and *discovering* our *talents*."

"*Un*-cover," Phil said scornfully. "Allie will find her *own* hidden talent. And anyway, why would a talent scout come way out here? There are *tons* of actresses in LA."

Bridget's own tone was scathing. "What do you know about it? Everyone in LA crawls all over each other for the next big part. A scout might come here instead, *because* it's quieter. One thing's sure, she's not an actress. Did you see how nervous she was? If she gets stage fright here, she'll never make it anywhere else."

"You might be onto something," Celia said excitedly. "It would explain a lot, like why Matt had to train her."

"She's not even from LA," Phil objected.

Bridget ignored her. "Ooh, I bet *that's* why Tarek's putting her up. I bet her agency offered him a deal on finding new princesses if he let Allie do her own scouting."

Phil's expression was incredulous. "Are you all crazy? Why would Tarek *pay* anyone to steal his staff?"

Bridget said, "How else do you explain him hiring her?"

Phil's voice rose. "Don't you get it? He's desperate."

"What about that awful haircut?" Celia asked.

"And those sneakers," Gillian added. *"So* grubby."

"I liked her," Laurette said, surprising even herself. "She seems nice."

Four faces gaped at her, and she made herself not look away. Phil chewed her bottom lip, then stood abruptly.

"Whatever. Can I help with your stuff?"

"That would be nice." Laurette rose shakily and followed Phil to the door. The other women waited until they were out of sight before erupting again into excited chatter. Laurette shook her head. "She doesn't look like any talent scout I've ever seen, but they've made up their minds without even getting to know her."

"Yeah." Phil turned pink. "Anyway. I had this idea. Since, you know, you can't dress up anymore, maybe you could work in one of the shops or something."

They were at the dressing room and Laurette stopped, touched. "You really think so?"

"Sure. You'd be good at it. You know, maybe even The Princess Shoppe. You always know what people should wear and stuff. I bet you'd be great with the customers."

Laurette hesitated. "How would I explain why I'm working, but not as a princess?"

"Oh. I didn't think about that. But it wouldn't hurt to ask Tarek, right? He could make up something. I really think you'd be great."

Laurette's heart beat an anxious tattoo. Tarek would never agree. She had no experience beyond a decade in finishing school and a bit of natural fashion flair. Plus, he wanted her gone entirely. She couldn't leave. She was happier here than she'd ever been.

Then again, what if he agreed, and she failed miserably?

Laurette stole a glance at Phil, whose normally pinched face was alight with pleasure. Laurette would *have* to ask, if only for Phil's sake. If Tarek refused, at least she would have tried. And if he said yes…

Well, she'd slay that dragon if it crossed her path. Whatever happened, she would *not* crawl home a failure.

Chapter Eleven

By six o'clock, Allie's red velvet dress was tan with dust, except where sweat stained her pits and between her breasts. The thing was beyond ridiculous in the ninety-plus sun. Its one saving grace were the short, puffed sleeves, but even these were edged with scratchy lace. Her feet were blistered in her shiny red flats, and the elaborate wig Didi'd chosen felt ten times heavier than it had eight hours ago.

It took two hours to get gussied up, but Didi swore it would be faster next time. She'd rushed into her own blue-and-white Cinderella costume, complete with long white gloves and tiara, then accompanied Allie into the park.

Since it was Allie's first day, and her training had been so condensed, Didi stayed by her side until she got used to the routine, which was pretty basic: smile and wave, have her picture taken—mostly with the children, but sometimes with randy older men—and generally pretend she was Rose Red, searching the woods for her lost bear.

The hardest part was remembering the correct versions of the Grimm's fairy tales, which differed wildly from the cartoons Allie'd grown up on. She fielded the same questions over and over from confused guests, while trying to stay in character and not hurl things. Like her breakfast.

After they parted at noon, Allie saw Didi a few times around the park, and also Bridget and Celia, who kept ambushing her like costumed snipers, probably hoping to see her screw up. Matt, however, stayed away. It was Sunday, so of course he'd rather be home than baking in the sun with a "weird, bitchy," and now decidedly itchy, princess. Still, couldn't he have called at least once to ask how she was holding up?

GrimmLand was divided into five sections fanning out from a central sixth, all with unpronounceable German names that Allie promptly forgot, choosing instead to use their English equivalents. First came Tom Thumb Town which, despite its diminutive name, had the tallest and scariest rides. Next to that was Hansel and Grethel Land—an odd placement, since it meant the kiddies were only a hop away from the screams of terror next door—followed by Frog Prince and Goose Girl, whose theme was animals.

On the other side of that was Fundevogel, which didn't have an English equivalent as it was a specific Grimm character, a boy found in a tree who later fell in love with his stepsister, then escaped a plot to be boiled to death by the family cook for reasons which, in Allie's opinion, were sketchy at best. Its theme was forests and water, though Allie couldn't discern why when she wandered through it.

Completing the park's outer circle was Riddle Valley, where Rumpelstiltskin and other tricksters resided, and where mazes and games of skill and memory could be found. In the center, connected via elaborate archways to the five other areas, lay Faerie Land, where in future, Allie would spend most of her time.

Didi had said Sundays were quiet. The weekly guests left, and the new crowd wouldn't come until Monday. With fewer distractions, Allie focused on learning the park's layout and searching for anything suspicious. Of which there wasn't much, unless she counted the busload of senior citizens who rolled in mid-afternoon. Apparently, Tarek gave them a deal, to make the park feel more crowded. Seat-fillers, Didi called them. They didn't ask questions or want their pictures taken, though, so Allie was free to snoop. When she finally dragged herself in after her shift, there were no new calls on her phone, and she sat down, yanked the wig off, and leaned her sweaty head on her arms.

Why did I think this was a good idea? There has to be another way to afford the house.

But there wasn't. Not in so short a time. Besides, she'd already spent her retainer on the down payment. She sat up, then squeaked when she saw Bridget and Celia reflected in her mirror, hovering behind her in the doorway. Both wore street clothes, looking like they hadn't sweated a drop all day, and Allie smoothed her soggy hair and faced them.

"I didn't hear you come in."

"Sorry," Bridget said, actually sounding like she meant it. "Didn't mean to scare you. Just stopping by to say hi."

Celia smiled brightly. "How'd it go? Did you, um, find what you were *scouting* for?"

Bridget elbowed her in the side, and Allie kept her expression neutral. "I guess so." Could they know she was a PI? Unlikely, but it might explain their stalking her.

"Great!" Celia smiled brighter. "We're headed to The Pink Flower. Want to come?"

"It's a bar at the main hotel," Bridget explained. "The drinks and food are decent, and no cover charge for us on Sundays, 'cuz there's fewer guests to recognize us."

"Um. I'm kind of tired…"

Bridget sounded genuinely sympathetic. "Yeah, these shifts are a real bitch. If we worked *somewhere else*, we'd only go out two hours at a time."

"Really?"

Celia nodded. "Tarek's a real slave driver. This eight-hours-with-lunch thing would never fly if we were union. Plus, he's always riding my ass about the blonde wig—"

Bridget interrupted with, "It's Laurette's birthday—well, really it was yesterday, but close enough—so she'll be there. You should come. It'll be fun!"

Allie tried to think of a good reason to decline, but none came to mind. "Okay. Let me shower and change, and I'll meet you there."

Bridget said, "Why don't you knock on Celia's door when you're ready? We can all walk over together."

Celia nodded again, like a puppet on autopilot. "I'm right across the breezeway from you."

"Sounds great," Allie said as brightly as she could.

"Perfect!" Bridget backed out, dragging Celia with her. "It's casual, so wear whatever."

They disappeared from the doorway. *What the hell?* The in-crowd never invited Allie anywhere. She studied herself in the mirror. Sticky hair pointing in all directions, red marks on her arms from the tight sleeves, and a sunburn on her nose. At least maybe she'd learn something, while not having to spend another night alone.

~:~:~

When Matt rolled into the GrimmLand parking lot and killed the engine late on Sunday, he told himself he was only there in case Allie needed more help with her part. The fact that she could—and should—go to Didi or Gillian now was beside the point.

Gillian. A pang went through Matt's gut. Damn it. She'd come on to him, for chrissake. What was he supposed to do? She could hardly blame him for what had happened.

Matt grabbed the bag of takeout off the passenger seat and headed for Allie's condo. She was probably exhausted after the long day, and from what he'd seen of her eating habits—candy and mochas—they were sub-par at best. He should have called, but Darlene had occupied him all day with wedding crap. For some reason, she'd thought it funny to make him the maid of honor, with the rest of their sisters as bridesmaids. And he'd been dumb enough to agree, not realizing he'd have to plan the shower *and* the rehearsal dinner, both of which were this week.

At Allie's condo, the lights were out. Damn. It was barely eight; she couldn't be asleep already. He knocked, lightly at first, then louder when she didn't answer. Where the hell was she? He could use his master key and let himself in, but that would be intrusive. Besides, if she was home, she might mistake him for a burglar and shoot him. Or throw a plant—or an espresso drink—at him.

He dug out his cell and punched in her number. No answer, and he didn't hear her phone ringing inside. Her car was with the GrimmLand mechanics, so she couldn't have gone far. Unless… Maybe she was at the pool.

He set the food down and headed for the hotel. But the woman in the black one-piece swimming laps turned out to be at least ninety. A fact which he discovered *after* tapping her arm, scaring her half to death, and making her splash water all over him as she screamed, "Rapist!"

Apologizing profusely, he hurried back to the lobby.

Allie'd said she wanted to explore Mecca, but surely she wouldn't walk into town alone this late. The sound of raucous laughter coming from The Pink Flower gave him an idea. Maybe the other princesses could tell him where Allie'd run off to.

The maître d' waved Matt in, with a curious glance at his wet shirt. The restaurant was empty as expected, but the bar was packed. Nearly every princess from the park was there, even the ones who hadn't been on duty, and a good number of the princes and other characters as well. They clustered around the bar itself, but what the attraction was, he couldn't tell.

"Thank God you're here," said a low voice, and Matt discovered Didi standing next to him. She wore a short skirt and tight blouse, and her hair was pulled up in a loose knot.

"Why? What's going on?"

"What the hell happened to you?"

Matt tried to wring more water from his shirt. "Nothing. Close encounter of the *Cocoon* kind. What's up?"

Didi shook her head and pushed him toward the bar. "Go get her before they make her drink any more mojitos."

"Shit," Matt said, and shoved into the crowd, expecting to find Allie trapped and trying to escape. But when he reached her, he stopped and let out a low whistle. *"Shit…"*

There she stood, surrounded, but far from unhappy. Her face was alight, eyes sparkling as she laughed at something the man next to her said. Bridget and Celia stood close by, like her new best friends, and several empty glasses on the bar attested to how much they'd all drunk.

But what stopped Matt cold was her outfit. She'd cut the bottom off one of her old t-shirts, cropping it just below her breasts. It was a tight V-neck, giving him and everyone else a nice view of her cleavage, along with an expanse of stomach below. His gaze dropped to her sandaled feet, then traveled up those long, bare legs to her shorts.

Not just shorts: *jeans* shorts. She turned to the bar, the denim hugging her ass, its ragged edges caressing the very tops of her thighs. The effect was indecent, and several of the other men checked her out as well.

One of them leaned in, hand at her back, fingers brushing the skin below her shirt, and Matt finished pushing through the crowd and tapped his shoulder. The guy took one look at him and sidled off. Matt cast a glare at the other men for good measure, and they also took the hint.

"I said I'll dance with you in a minute," Allie said flirtatiously over her shoulder, then her eyes widened. "Matt! What're you doing here?" She noticed the empty space vacated by her admirers. "Where'd everyone go?"

"Jeez, Allie." He turned his head aside. "How much have you had to drink?"

"Not much. Spilled." She indicated a damp spot on her shirt, then swayed toward him. Automatically, he lifted his arms and she fell into them. She was soft in all the right places, and suddenly, he was hard. Carefully, he set her away, while Bridget and Celia shot him dirty looks.

"What?" he barked.

Allie leaned in close again, searing him with her heat. *"Shh*—they're mad at you," she stage-whispered.

"Why?" He stole a peek down her shirt at her pink lace bra. It seemed she had at least one ounce of feminine fashion sense. Thinking about her bra made him wonder if she wore a matching thong, and his heart stopped working, followed shortly by his brain.

"They think you're cheating on Gillian."

His gaze snapped up, meeting hers, but her eyes were wide and guileless. *Fuck*. Not that he cared what Bridget and Celia thought. But Allie needed to understand.

"Excuse us." He grabbed her hand, dragging her through the crowd and out of the hotel.

"Wait!" Allie said. "Celia and I were going to walk home together. For safety."

"I'm walking you home. Celia can fend for herself."

The parking lot was cool, dark, and quiet, and Matt pulled her toward the condos. The evening wasn't turning out the way he'd expected, but if nothing else, at least he'd gotten her back on neutral ground. And by now he had a pretty good idea what he wanted to do with her.

"I don't mind," Allie said, seeming only half-aware that he was dragging her along the path at warp speed. "About Gillian. She's nice. You should have a nice girlfriend."

Her hand was warm, and he couldn't resist sliding his thumb across her palm. She made a sound like she'd sucked in a breath, but that could have been due to their breakneck pace. He slowed down as they neared her condo.

"She isn't my girlfriend. Key?"

Allie glanced at her door as he steered her to it, seeming puzzled to find it there. "Yes, she is. You're *sleeping* with her, and you have *plans* this week."

She swayed toward him, and he steadied her with an arm around her shoulder. She felt good against his side, and he slid his palm over her smooth upper arm. She shivered, and he dropped his arm to her waist, pulling her closer and resting his hand on the curve of her hip. Her height meant the creamy white of her throat was inches from his mouth, and he fought the urge to taste her clean-smelling skin, settling instead for inhaling the apricot scent of her hair.

She peered at him hazily. "Matt…"

This was nuts. She'd had way too much to drink. He had to get her inside, and then he could decide where they were going from here. If anywhere.

He released her and stepped away, telling himself, *It's just those damn jeans shorts,* and knew it wasn't the shorts. Although they weren't exactly hurting things. He stole another peek at the smooth curve of ass peeping out just below them, and said again, *"Key."*

Obediently, she rummaged in her pockets, resuming her monologue. "She spent the night with you. She told me so herself. Besides, when Bobby called—ooh—here it is!" She held the card key up triumphantly, her breasts jiggling in her excitement, and Matt turned her toward the door, helping her tap the reader. The lock clicked open, but Allie was having trouble with the doorknob.

She bent forward, her rear brushing his lap, and he swallowed. "She isn't my girlfriend."

Allie muttered something as she fumbled with the knob. She bent over more, pushing that Daisy-Dukes-wearing butt farther into him, and Matt clenched his fists and stepped back. *Get the damn door open. C'mon, Allie, you can do it.* "Gillian didn't sleep at my place last night. She came over, but nothing happened. I broke up with her."

Allie jerked, her hand twisting the handle hard, and the door finally popped open. She straightened, then slowly faced him. Her eyes were huge pools in the dim porch light, her erratic breathing making her chest rise and fall beneath that indecent t-shirt.

She also suddenly looked a lot more sober, and Matt narrowed his eyes. "Exactly how much did you drink tonight?"

"Just enough," she whispered, and stepped toward him.

Chapter Twelve

"What did you say?" Matt demanded.

He was even sexier startled, and the last vestiges of Allie's tipsiness vanished in a puff of blazing hot desire. In truth, she'd only had a couple drinks, but it was fun to play the lush and hear what people said when they thought she was drunk. However, like the rest of the info she'd garnered today, none of it was useful. Mainly guys' phone numbers and a few of the women's. No one said, *By the way, I saw the four missing princesses pigging out at Dairy Queen.*

Then when Matt swooped in, it was even more fun to let him rescue her, his blatant masculinity intoxicating in a new way. There was something to be said for relaxing her inhibitions: she could touch him, flirt, be near him, then blame it all on the booze if he objected. Which he hadn't.

Besides, if he hadn't dragged her off, she'd be dancing with some pompous prince right now, instead of staring at his mouth, imagining what it would be like to kiss him.

Screw imagining.

She stepped forward and pressed her lips to his. They were warm and soft, the rest of him hard, and suddenly she was warm and wet. He hesitated, then pushed his hands into her hair, pulling her close, bodies melding, heads tilting as he took control of the kiss, maneuvering her back into the condo and fumbling the door shut behind them. Allie fisted her hands in his oddly damp shirt, tasting the rich deep thrust of him as he filled her mouth.

The room was dark except for a blade of light coming

through the crack between the curtains, but Matt seemed to know where to go. Expertly, like he'd done it a thousand times, he walked her to the sofa, pressed her down, landed on top, his body hot and hard and *everywhere.* His clean-male musk filled her nostrils as his fingers slid from her hair, removing her hands from where she'd been exploring his shoulders, pulling them up and over her head, pinning them on the arm of the couch.

And her body said *take me now,* but that was wrong, she didn't want him to take her, she wanted to do the taking. She twisted, scrunching, using the couch as leverage to push up with her legs until Matt overbalanced, caught off-guard, and they toppled to the floor.

"Oof," he said, taking the brunt of her weight on him.

Allie straightened, heart thudding, breath slowing. Better. Not only had he released his hold on her, but from up here, she didn't feel so lost in him.

His eyes were dark, lips parted, and his hands slid under her shirt and up her spine. "Come back. I'm not finished."

"I can tell." Allie lowered her mouth to his.

He dropped his hands to her hips, stilling them, but accepted her kiss. She squirmed and his grip tightened, refusing to budge. He was hard and ready and he wouldn't let her move against him, just continued his slow exploration of her mouth with his tongue. Vaguely she recalled initiating the kiss, but somehow, her tongue was no longer in his mouth, it was the other way around again, and she went right back to thinking how she wanted him inside her, all of him, everywhere.

Take me…now…

She moaned, pushing into his chest, but he didn't take the hint, so she found his waistband and pulled his shirt free. She slid her fingers over his pecs, his nipples tightening at her touch, and she moved lower, reaching for his fly.

He pushed her hands aside. "Not yet."

His mouth still explored her, going from her lips down her cheek, then up to the place just below her ear. Allie was liquid heat, ready to burst with needing him. She touched his fly again, but again he grabbed her hands and repeated, a little more gruffly, "Not yet."

Allie suppressed her irritation, then brightened. While he was manacling her, he couldn't control her hips. She slid the length of him, pressing herself along his hard ridge and felt him shudder in pleasure. However, he still broke the kiss and dropped his head to the floor, closing his eyes in irritation. When he opened them again, his expression had closed off and he didn't look nearly as turned on as he had five minutes ago. Or even five seconds ago.

"Jesus, Allie. Not *yet.*"

He released her so abruptly she fell off and rolled to the floor, staring at the ceiling, shoving back the sudden urge to cry. Like the rest of this rotten day, sex with Matt was turning out to be a bunch of damn work for a whole lot of nothing. At least he was breathing loudly beside her. Good. If he was as frustrated as she was, maybe she'd salvage her pride at least.

After a minute, he pushed up onto an elbow, studying her in the dark condo. "What happened there?" He didn't sound mad anymore, which was almost worse. At least if he was angry, she could blame it all on him.

She refused to meet his gaze. "I don't know. You tell me. I thought we were, you know…" She waved a hand vaguely, searching for words that wouldn't sound as needy as she felt.

"We were." In the low light of the curtained room she couldn't read his expression. He trailed his fingers across her cheek and down her throat, then pulled back, hovering, his hand not quite touching the swell of her breasts. "At least, we were starting to. Why the rush?"

"No rush. But why wait?" Her voice sounded breathless to her own ears, and her heart hammered beneath his maddening non-touch.

"I've been wanting this for days," he murmured. "Now that we're here, I'd like to take my time—" His hand dropped lower, now cupping the air below her chest, the motion so sensual that even without physical contact, she shivered. "—learn what makes you tick—" His thumb moved as though to brush her nipple, and it tightened even as he once again withdrew at the last second. "—before enjoying the ride."

If he was half as turned on as she was, then he had the patience of a rock. And therein lay the problem. After two days in his company, she still couldn't read him. Maybe he wasn't turned on. So many women fell all over him, he might think this was ho-hum for all she knew.

Okay. She might be neurotic, but she wasn't dumb. Matt was turned on, all right.

"Why now?" she asked, and Matt's hand froze, then dropped to his side.

His eyes met hers, and though she could see little more in them than a flash of reflected light from the window, his confusion was clear. "What?"

"You said you've been wanting this for days. Why make your move now?"

"I'm an opportunist. Drunk women in bars are my jam."

Allie flinched. "That's it? You hit on me because I had too much to drink? What about Gillian? Or did she have other plans tonight?"

"It was a joke." His tone was puzzled. "Besides, I told

you—we broke up."

"You broke up with your girlfriend because of me?"

He leaned back, exasperated. "She wasn't my girlfriend. We dated casually, that's it. No strings. I called it off for a number of reasons, not just because of you. Now can we get on with this?"

"I thought you wanted to *take your time* and *enjoy the ride*. Why the rush?"

As soon as she spoke, Allie regretted the words. Thinking about Gillian had sent a bigger stab of jealousy through her than expected, which was dumb, because she didn't want anything more than sex from Matt in the first place. But it was too late and she couldn't take it back.

Matt stood, a dark angry shape against the shadows of the room. "I wanted to enjoy the journey, not psychoanalyze it to death."

"Wait." Allie scrambled up as he moved to the door.

"Forget it." He sounded really pissed. "It's like your damn coffee. You have to measure and weigh, judge everything against some impossible standard you've set for yourself and everyone else."

He yanked the door open, and Allie blinked in the comparatively bright glare from the porch light. "That's not true. I just wondered, you know, why me?"

He faced her, eyes glittering. "Look, you're smart and beautiful and have the best damn ass in California. But you're used to a mechanical toy that does whatever you want, *exactly* when and how you want it. I can't compete with that."

Stung, Allie shot out, "That's not fair! I've had relationships—"

"What? Peerless? He's no better than a sex toy from what I've seen. When you're ready for actual human contact, give me a call, *princess.*"

He slammed out the door, and Allie yelled after him, *"Don't call me that!"*

Then she ran up to the bedroom and flung herself on the bed, not even pretending she wasn't going to have a really good cry.

~:~:~

Wafi tossed his half-finished smoke on the ground and pressed speed dial one on the disposable flip phone, then waited for the line to click open.

"Same package, new timeline. Rush delivery," said a voice and the line went dead.

Wafi erased the call and the speed dial entry, then wiped the phone clean, broke it in half, and tossed it in a dumpster. He moved silently through the dark parking lot.

Rush delivery.

Adrenaline pumped through him, his muscles taut and ready. Up ahead, he spied her, illuminated by one of the lights spaced evenly along the path from the resort. She was with a group of bimbos from the park. Too many. He'd have to wait. But not too long.

Rush...

Besides, the stalking was half the fun. They never saw it coming.

He fell into the shadows, keeping her in his sight, listening to her unsuspecting laughter, excitement thick in his veins. Her dark hair was loose, tempting him.

She'd never know what hit her.

~:~:~

Matt's phone woke him out of a sound sleep way too damn early on Monday. It'd only been an hour since he drifted off. The long drive home gave him plenty of time to stew over Allie and her attempts to manipulate him—just like Gillian—but it'd done nothing for the raging erection he got whenever he thought about her soft breast in his hand, her mouth open for his exploration, her fingers trailing fire across his skin. By the time he pulled into the driveway, his brain and body were both thoroughly aroused in opposite ways, making sleep impossible.

The phone blared again, and he grabbed it, barking, "What?"

"He's gone!" a female voice sobbed. "He—he left me!"

"Oh, jeez. Darlene?" Matt sat up. She was so hysterical, he could barely make out her words. "What the hell are you talking about?"

"Isaac. We had a—" *sob!* "—fight. About—*hic*—about the wedding. He—" *sob!* "—walked out and—*hic*—didn't come back and—" More sobbing before she pushed the rest out in a wail. *"—andIdon'tknowifI'lleverseehimagain!"*

Matt pinched the bridge of his nose. "Darlene, calm down. Isaac didn't leave you."

"Yes, he did! I *know* he did."

"No. He didn't. He loves you. Now, tell me what happened so I know why I have to kill him."

Between gulps, she managed to explain that there had been yet another family meeting after Matt left for the resort on Sunday night. Something about wedding food: Isaac wanted falafel, but Darlene said it would clash with the seafood menu they'd agreed on. Isaac had responded that she'd agreed to the seafood, not him, and then stomped off to parts unknown.

By the time she'd finished the sordid tale, Darlene was much calmer. "I'm sorry I called you so early," she said wetly. "It was just a stupid fight. I know he wouldn't really leave me over this."

"No problem. What are brothers for?"

"*Baby* brothers. I'm supposed to give you advice."

"Do you want me to beat him up? I think I can take him, unless those pens in his pocket are secretly knives."

Darlene gave a weak laugh. "No. But thanks for the offer." She hesitated. "What if he really did leave me, though? Not over this. But what if he wants to back out of the wedding, and this is just an excuse?"

"It's not an excuse. It's falafel. He just wants to be involved—it's his wedding, too."

"I thought guys, you know, didn't care about stuff like that."

"If you mean do we care if the bridesmaids wear pink or peach, we couldn't give a rat's ass. But look at it this way: Do you *not* want falafel so much that you won't let him have input on one single part of the process?"

Darlene was quiet for a minute. "I guess I hadn't thought of it that way. Most of the time, Isaac takes the lead. At his job, dealing with his parents—you know, he's an only child—"

"Lucky bastard."

"—so they rely on him for help. Even with us—he usually drives or picks the restaurant or whatever. But does he need to have a say in *everything?* Can't just this one thing be totally mine?"

"Give him a break, Dar. When you're used to being in charge, it's hard letting someone else drive for a change. Let him have his falafel."

"You really think so?"

"Sure. It's only one thing. It'll make him feel better."

She thought for a moment, then said tentatively, "And if I give in on this, maybe he'll relax about the other stuff, and see that the world won't end just because he's not in control…?"

"Exactly," Matt said, and leaned back, then jerked up again. "Fuck. Allie!"

"What?"

"Nothing. I'm an idiot, and I should listen to my own advice."

"I'd agree with you, but you're being too nice to me." There was a short pause. "Who's Allie?"

Matt grinned, even though she couldn't see it. "Never mind. Someone at work."

"I thought Gillian was your someone at work."

"Sisters. Call Isaac, tell him he can have his falafel. I'll talk to you later."

"Matt! Wait—who's Allie? What about the shower? It's this week, and you're the maid of—"

He hung up before Darlene launched into his wedding to-do's.

Yeah, he'd been a real dumb jerk. But if Allie was still speaking to him, he'd make it up to her.

Chapter Thirteen

Allie opened the condo door on Monday, and a little old lady fell inside.

Maybe fell was an overstatement—she sort of stumbled, then righted herself—but she was clearly old and definitely little. At least a foot shorter than Allie, with neatly waved wispy white hair and large dark eyes peeping out of a heart-shaped face, she wore home-sewn turquoise polyester shorts and a striped sleeveless blouse.

Allie wondered fleetingly if Lilliputians were a Grimm's fairy tale. Next to Phil, Laurette, and this woman, Allie was a giantess. Only Matt made her feel petite: protected, instead of the protector. At least, when he wasn't yelling at her for trying to have sex with him. But she wasn't thinking about Matt and hadn't been all morning.

The old lady's eyes were screwed tight, her nose wrinkled in distaste.

"Can I help you?" Allie asked.

The woman held out a filmy plastic bag filled with takeout containers. It was covered, like anything left outside for a minute around here, by a thick layer of brown dirt. When Allie didn't take the bag, the woman thrust it farther out and Allie caught a whiff. Chinese, and not fresh.

"This yours?" Her voice was as scratchy as sandpaper, and the bag was so full, she was about to topple over again.

"I don't think so," Allie said cautiously. It was seven-thirty, and she was about to be late for her second day undercover. But the woman pushed past her into the condo, and Allie stifled a sigh.

"It was outside your door. Mebbe you forgot you ordered it?"

Allie started to tell her no, then paused. "Oh—wait. A uh, friend stopped by last night. It might be his."

The woman's black look deepened. "That rapist who attacked me at the pool? Big blond fella with a wet shirt?"

Allie choked on a laugh. "That's him. But he's not a predator."

"Hmph. Saw him leave your place last night. These men—snoopin' around at all hours, leavin' their mess behind. You watch out—he'll get you in trouble, he will."

Allie sighed. "Not anymore he won't. That ship sailed."

The woman's expression turned canny. "Like that, is it? I'm Birdie Olsen." She set the bag on the coffee table and roamed around, examining Allie's plants. She stopped near one and broke off a leaf. "You need to get some Super Thrive and re-pot this. Cut the root ball and pinch the leaves back. It's too gangly, goin' off every which way at once."

"It's a Wandering Willie; it needs to wander."

"Not like this it don't. You want it to grow, don't you?"

"Of course, but—"

"Ain't got no direction, pushing shoots out all pell-mell. Pinch it. It'll get more comfy and bush out in no time."

"Okay. Well, thanks. I'm late for work, so…"

Birdie nodded. "I can take a hint. You work here?" She joined Allie at the door, giving another distasteful sniff as she passed the food. "Tell me your name and what you do."

Allie followed her out, grabbing the smelly bag on the way. "Allie. I'm a princess in the park."

Birdie assessed her critically. "If you say so." She waited while Allie shut and locked the door. "I'll come find you in costume, give you some pointers."

"That's not necessary." Allie glanced at Celia's door, tempted to use her as an excuse to ditch Birdie, but the blinds were down. Allie hadn't heard her come in last night, so maybe she'd hooked up with one of the princes. Allie moved to the sidewalk and Birdie trailed her. She had to be in her eighties and likely came with the senior seat fillers.

"Gardenin' ain't my only *for-tay*. I cook, clean, and sew a neater stitch than anyone in Riverside County. Plus, I know jest how a lady should walk and talk."

Bypassing the obvious jibe about Birdie's elocution, Allie tried, "You probably won't recognize me—"

"Nonsense. Nothin' wrong with my eyesight. Men. Sneakin' around, thinkin' Birdie won't notice. I notice, all right. Here, now, I'll walk to the edge of the lot with you, and you can tell me about your blond fella. He was a cutie, I will say. Them's the ones you gotta watch out for, not them ugly ones. Like that other fella."

"What other fella?"

"The one I been *tellin'* you about."

"I thought you meant Matt."

"He the blond?" At Allie's nod, she pursed her lips. "Told you, I saw *men* sneakin' around, not *a man*. Other one's balder'n my Ralph, may he rest in peace, but younger. Wore a baseball cap, but all wrong, with the bill pointin' back. He's military, though. I can tell. Like Ralph was and your blond fella, too."

Allie, who'd opened her mouth to argue against Birdie's knowing anyone was military simply by their appearance, shut it again. Birdie nodded decisively.

"They got a look about 'em. A bearin'. I always know. Question is, what's he doin', snoopin' around out here?"

Allie shrugged. There were a million reasons someone would be out at night in a vacation resort, most of them legit. "Maybe a marine on leave from Twentynine Palms? Or another employee? We were all at a bar last night."

Birdie snorted. "Bars. Hmph. But you keep an eye out. That man with the cap, he's up to somethin'."

"Okay. If I see a bald man with a cap on backwards"—*of which there are hundreds, maybe thousands, even out here*—"I'll make sure he doesn't get away with anything."

Birdie nodded, satisfied. "You do that. And you tell me what you find. I can help."

They'd arrived at the path to the employee complex, marked by a sign which read *Employees Only: No Trespassing,* and Allie stopped. "Well, here's where I get off. It was nice meeting you."

She turned to leave, and Birdie gave a final sniff. "These men. Never up to any good. 'Cept my Ralph. You find one like my Ralph, you grab onto him and never let go. 'Less of course you find out he's a rapist. Then you can let 'im go all you want."

~:~:~

"Have you seen my pearl earrings?"

Laurette jerked guiltily, then reminded herself it was technically still her dressing room.

Bridget stood at the door, in full Rapunzel. The green satin of her dress complemented her light coloring, and costuming had matched her four-foot-long braids to the auburn of her hair. She chewed her thumbnail. "I left them on the makeup table, but now they're gone."

Laurette shook her head and moved in front of her own table. "Sorry. I haven't seen them."

Bridget glanced enviously around the room. "Must be nice, not having to share like the rest of us. At least you can lock the door and not worry something will be stolen."

Laurette's face heated. "I guess I won't be needing it

anymore. Maybe you can have it.”

Bridget sighed. “Never mind. I’ll ask Celia about the earrings. *If* she ever clocks in.”

Laurette’s fingers tightened on the table behind her. “Late night at the Flower?”

“Yeah. You should’ve stayed. We were having a blast until Matt dragged Allie off. Come to think of it, maybe Allie knows something. She got here bright and early. Plus, I think she and Celia are sharing a dressing room now.”

Bridget walked off, and Laurette turned back to the table. One advantage to everyone stalking Allie was that they left Laurette in comparative peace.

In the rush to get her stuff yesterday, she’d forgotten one drawer. The contents—a photo of Wolf and the necklace he’d sent—lay before her, but she couldn’t decide what to do with them. She should have couriered the necklace straight to Luradel. But that would mean dealing with it. Much easier to shove it in a drawer and forget it.

“Have you seen the new princess anywhere?”

Laurette jumped again, and whirled to find Matt filling the doorway. “Why is everyone sneaking up on me?” she snapped, then regretted her tone. He looked tired and preoccupied, and he didn’t deserve her anger in any case. “Sorry. I think she’s suiting up.”

“What about Celia?”

“Bridget said she hasn’t come in yet. Why?”

“Oh.” Matt checked his watch. “Mind if I wait here?”

“Actually, I’m not supposed to be here. I’m on *administrative leave,* remember?” She snatched the necklace and the photo off the table, dropping them into her shoulder bag, but not before Matt noticed.

“What was that?”

“Nothing.” She stepped into the hall as he moved aside.

"Laurette. I saw the photo, and I'm guessing the necklace didn't come from your father."

She glanced quickly up and down the hall, but no one was around, and she turned for the exit. "No. Wolf sent it."

"Why don't you go home and face him? Now that you aren't suiting up, what difference does it make?"

"Matt!" Laurette stopped, heart thudding. The halls were oddly deserted, but she lowered her voice anyway. "I can't. Not yet. People here are already getting suspicious."

"Exactly my point. Stop sneaking around; it'll all work out. Trust me." He paused, and Laurette felt a pang of conscience. Matt was the most honest person she knew, but he'd been keeping her—or rather, Roland's—secret for over a year. From his own good friend, no less.

He continued, "I disagree with Roland for hiding you from Wolf, but he's your father. A little paranoia is allowed. And I know Wolf will understand why you came here."

"Of course he would. My safety—"

"Not that. He'll understand *your* reasons. He…" Matt hesitated. "Never mind. Forget I said anything. Jeez. What is it with women and their men today?"

He started to move away, and she put a hand on his arm. "Please. Just a little longer. I—I'll go home in September, like we planned. Just let me have this summer."

Matt scrubbed a hand over his face. "Fine. I won't tell anyone yet." He took a step away, then stopped again. "Damn it—Allie."

"The new princess? What about her?"

"Yes, what about her?" Tarek's voice said from the corner behind them and Laurette jumped a third time and tried to remember she was a well-bred lady who never showed surprise, even when everyone kept popping out at her like demented jack-in-the-boxes.

Tarek watched Matt, who stared back, the undercurrents so super-charged, the men should have given off sparks.

Laurette said slowly, "Allie's not an actress or a talent scout, is she?"

Tarek's eyes glinted. "Now look what you have done."

Matt shrugged. "Cat's out of the bag." He said to her, "Allie's a private investigator. Didi knows."

Tarek's whole body contorted with rage. Then abruptly he deflated. "Perhaps it is best that Laurette knows the severity of the situation." He faced her. *"Now* will you return home and give up this charade? How many women must disappear before you admit you are in danger?"

"My father built this park for me—"

"So you could come to play, protected by guards, not work here, exposed." His tone was scornful. "Roland would be disgusted to learn you are working like a commoner."

Laurette started to point out that Tarek had a job, then thought better of it. Tarek's mother was a commoner, but he still considered himself nobility. When Bernard had died, leaving no inheritance, Roland had pretended it would be a personal favor if Tarek managed the park and kept an eye on Laurette, to get him to accept the paycheck.

No wonder Tarek was angry with her for working at GrimmLand, putting him in an awkward position if Roland learned the truth. Matt was right. She should never have started this. But it was only six more weeks.

She firmed her voice. "I already told Matt, I'll go home in September. Not before. And if I can't suit up, I want to work at The Princess Shoppe."

Matt's brows rose, but Tarek's expression was inscrutable. She waited, heart thundering until she thought she'd pass out. The edges of her vision were just starting to silver when Tarek finally nodded.

"Very well." To Matt he said, "Yet another reason to resolve this quickly. I must find Celia now. Many guests have complained about her dark hair. She *must* wear the blonde wig today." He started to leave, then paused. "There is one more thing. If anything happens to Laurette, you will tell Roland, not I. She is your responsibility now."

With that, he left, and Matt scowled after him. "Great. Just what I need—another woman on my hands." Then he, too, stomped away, leaving Laurette alone in the hall.

So what if she'd made Matt angry? She'd stood up for herself, for once in her life, and no one could take that away.

Well, almost no one.

She walked to the exit, the weight of the necklace in her bag taking some of the bounce from her step. If only the one person she wanted to share her accomplishment with wasn't also the one who could never, ever find out about it.

~:~:~

By the time Matt returned to the wing housing Allie's dressing room, Tarek was storming back up the hall, furious. *"Where is Celia?"*

Matt shrugged. "Maybe she's already in the park."

"No one has seen her. If she is late one more time…" Tarek's face was almost purple. "She believes I cannot fire her because we are short on staff. Arrogant! And if that blonde wig is not on her head—"

Before he elaborated on the dire fate awaiting a brunette Brier Rose, Celia hoofed it around the corner, wearing workout clothes and crocs. She looked too sweaty to pull off "fairy-tale princess" in minutes, but another thing Matt knew from his sisters was that make-up made miracles.

She pulled up short, then tried to sidle past them.

"Where have you been?" Tarek's tone was harsh, his anger disproportionate to Celia's "crime," although with the stress he was under, who could blame him? "Did you not think to call? We have been worried sick!"

Celia opened her mouth, but Matt pulled her down the hall by her elbow. Who knew what Tarek would do if Celia gave him a piece of her mind? As they neared her dressing room, Gillian appeared from a doorway further down. Probably a supply closet, since props also fell under her jurisdiction. She flushed, but before things got awkward, Tarek stomped up and shook a manicured finger at Celia.

"Another thing! You will wear the blonde wig today, or I will dock your pay, I swear I will!"

Celia yanked her arm from Matt's grasp. "Oh yeah? How come Laurette didn't have to wear the wig?"

Tarek turned the evil eye on Gillian. "Tell her. Brier Rose is blonde."

Gillian nodded authoritatively. "The literature—"

"Fuck you," Celia snapped. "Something's going on around here. People keep quitting, stuff's missing, Allie's queen of the park after one *day,* and Laurette gets to wear her own hair *and* take a vacation? I don't *think* so! When do *I* get to be teacher's pet?"

She jerked her dressing room door open, revealing Allie standing inside, looking sheepish. And hot. Very hot, in an eighteenth-century-German-fairy tale kind of way.

Celia's mouth formed an O of surprise, and Gillian's eyes flashed bright, then went cold again. Even Tarek's brows rose and he dropped his hand.

Matt swallowed. Her legs were disappointingly covered by her wide red skirt, but the fitted bodice emphasized the swell of her hips and the fullness of her breasts, the tops of which were bare above the low neckline. Her kissable throat was long and elegant, and the rich brown of the complicated hairpiece Didi'd picked for her suited her coloring. Still, he yearned to yank the thing off and run his hands through her own soft, natural hair, tilt her head back, and do all sorts of carnal things to those slightly parted lips.

She took in the strange tableau outside her door. "I heard yelling. I was waiting to come out."

Tarek steered Celia into the dressing room. "Get into your costume. We will discuss your concerns later. You"—he pointed at Allie—"Come. I need to speak with you."

Gillian frowned as Allie squeezed through the doorway in her wide skirts. "Rose Red shouldn't wear such a low-cut gown. She's searching the woods in the *winter,* not summer. I specifically told Didi—"

"It does not matter," Tarek cut her off. "Leave us."

The frown became a scowl. "If anyone wants to know how the Grimm's tales *really* go, I'll be in my office."

She stalked off, and Tarek shut Celia's door, jerking his head toward the deserted end of the hall. When they were out of earshot, he demanded, "What have you learned?"

"Not much. No one saw anything, and I haven't found anything out that you don't already know."

"That is unacceptable." There was a note of hysteria in his tone, like he'd finally reached the breaking point.

Allie chewed her lip. "I do have one lead. A guest saw a man who might be from one of the military bases."

Tarek looked at her sharply. "We have many guests, from Twentynine Palms and elsewhere."

Allie reddened. "Of course. But this woman says he was snooping around the condos. I should at least check it out, maybe visit some of the military bases or the other towns."

"Good plan," Matt interjected. "I'll drive."

"Say what now?"

Tarek glared at them both. "Do not be absurd. Any clues to be found are here in the park. What of the fairy tale references? Have you even investigated who might have the interest and the knowledge to achieve such detail?"

Matt said, "Too many to count. So far, nothing's been obscure enough to separate the kidnapper from anyone with a streaming subscription."

Tarek's mouth tightened. Finally he said, "Very well. You will take her tomorrow."

Allie's discomfort was comical. "I'm sure Matt has his own work to do. I can take my own car."

"It is not repaired yet."

Thank God, Matt thought and hid a grin.

"But both of us gone will look suspicious—"

"It is settled." Tarek walked away, leaving Allie and her pushed-up Georgian Era breasts alone with Matt at last.

She cleared her throat. "I'd better go now."

Matt stuck an arm out, blocking her. "We need to talk."

"Nothing to talk about. I was tipsy, you just broke up with your girlfriend—"

"She wasn't my girlfriend."

"—and it didn't work out. Movin' on. Or trying to."

She shoved his arm, but he held firm. "I wasn't referring to last night. I meant we need a plan for tomorrow."

"Oh. Well. Should we start at Twentynine Palms?"

"It's huge. We'd never find anything. More likely the women were taken south. There's some smaller bases down there, and also Viejas and Sycuan Indian casinos. Maybe the women are all off gambling. Besides, I need to stop by my sister's in El Cajon. We can make a loop."

She visibly struggled, then blew out a breath. "Fine. Pick me up early. Now can I get by? My public needs me."

He dropped his arm and let her squeeze past. Tomorrow, he'd have her all to himself. He wouldn't quit that easily.

Chapter Fourteen

When Matt pulled into the condo parking lot on Tuesday morning, Allie took one look at the Testarossa and muttered, "Figures."

He considered telling her the car was twenty-years-old, a gift from Roland, and secondhand to boot, but why ruin a perfectly good chance to rib her later? Instead, he gave her a long, slow smile, the one his sisters swore made women swoon, and popped the locks. "Your chariot awaits."

"Yeah, right."

She sounded unimpressed, but she slid in and Matt noted the heat had forced her to wear shorts again, so he forgave her. He could forgive a lot if she just kept wearing shorts. Those long legs leading up, up, curving deliciously under that khaki hem. He snuck a look at her white tank top while she twisted around to grab the shoulder belt. It clung to her chest almost as nicely as the yellow tee she'd worn when they met, and he forgave the "figures" as well.

When she was clicked in, he put the car in reverse and backed out of the space. He'd never been more appreciative of the two-seater, although when he first started driving it, his insistence that one person would barely fit in the buttery-soft leather passenger seat had had more to do with Family Carpool Prevention than promoting closeness.

Now, as Allie's naked thigh rested mere inches from his hand on the gear shift, his brain and body—for once in sync—both said, *Thank God for small cars.*

He said, "Where to, princess?"

Allie caught his eye, and he took the opportunity to hold her gaze just long enough to make her aware he was doing it. A blush pinkened her clear skin and she turned away, rummaging in the canvas bag she'd brought. Good. Not completely "movin' on" quite yet.

She came up with a printout of an online map on which she'd circled their destinations and plotted their route. "I thought we'd hit the Salton Sea Airport, then try the military base next to it. After that, we can drop down to Calexico and Mexicali and work our way west on I-8. It's probably a waste of time, but we should at least try."

"Sounds good. I pulled the women's publicity pics, so we can show them around and go from there."

"Okay." She put the map on top of her bag and leaned back, clearly unsure what to say next.

"It's a good plan." She seemed startled by his support, but only shrugged and looked away, so he added, "Not the chit-chat type?"

"I was once, but a big bad ogre showed me the error of my ways, and now I just keep my mouth shut."

"That'll be the day."

Ignoring him, Allie punched the stereo on, correctly assuming it wouldn't break their eardrums, then shot him a look of disbelief when the deep opening notes of the *Presto - Recitativo* from Beethoven's Ninth resonated through the eight-speaker system. "You're kidding."

"Nope," he said, and began singing along as they headed out of town. Allie looked at him like he'd sprouted horns, but he focused on the music as it filled him to the bottom of his soul, then rose and came belting back out.

The road was straight and flat, the car sleek and powerful, and the woman beside him smart and sexy. If only he didn't have four missing women to find, and he hadn't slipped and agreed to stop at his sister's. Not only was the pre-wedding Darlene more of an emotional loose cannon than Allie herself, but she would surely get the wrong idea when they showed up together. Matt never brought women to family functions, and Darlene would ignore anything he said about them being "just coworkers."

He gave himself a mental shake. There was nothing wrong with pursuing a little fun with Allie while they worked together. What did it matter what Darlene or any of his sisters thought?

He shoved Allie and Darlene both from his mind and focused on singing the *Ode to Joy*. Gradually, Allie relaxed, even humming with him, tentatively at first, then with more confidence as they reached the *Poco allegro*. The music swelled to its vibrant crescendo, until the final notes crashed through the car in a swirl of strings, the clash of cymbals, the boom of bass drums, and the blending of Matt's and Allie's voices with the chorus.

As the sounds faded, he glanced over. She studied the passing scenery but he didn't think she registered it. Her face wore an expression of intense longing, as though something in the music triggered painful memories, and he looked away before she noticed his intrusion.

The playlist switched to Mozart, *Eine kleine nachtmusik* filling the car with lighter, airier fare, and Matt said, "So, what's Allie short for anyway?"

She looked at him, emotions hidden again. "Why on earth would you want to know that?"

"I'm a curious guy."

"Why'd your folks name you Matt?"

"I asked you first. And besides, what's that got to do with anything?"

"Trust me. It relates."

"It's after Matthew in the Bible."

"Your folks pretty devout?"

"No, but after five daughters, my dad had a religious experience when I was born." He gave her another patented grin, which only made her more dubious. "Okay, fine. It was my mother's idea, but not because Matthew was an Apostle. It's because he was an accountant."

Allie barked a laugh, then caught his gimlet eye and turned it into a cough. "Actually, it fits."

"What the hell does that mean? I'm a big bad security engineer, not a bean counter."

"Oh, come on. The way you observe and analyze. You're the most detail-oriented person I've ever met. Whether it's numbers or safety and risk, your parents sure pegged you right."

There was no point in arguing with her. "Back on topic. I showed you mine, you show me yours."

She chewed her lip. "Fine. Allie's short for Ailil."

"Which comes from…?"

"It's Irish." She sent him a sideways glance. "For 'little elf.'"

Now it was Matt's turn for dubiousness. "Small baby?"

"Eleven pounds. My dad liked a good joke."

"Doesn't seem funny to me. He should've picked something that suited you, not something you'd have to fight against your whole life. What else did he call you?"

"Allie Cat." She sounded wistful, and Matt felt a scowl coming on.

"Why? Did he make you beg for scraps?"

"It's just a nickname. It doesn't mean anything." She faced the window again, and Matt let the subject drop.

~:~:~

Fate, God, or *whatever,* was against Phil. She just knew

it, even though she hadn't made up her mind yet what she believed in, if anything.

For two days she'd been trying to figure out how the tattooed man got away, but every time she got near an entrance to the Mousetraps, as employees called the maze of underground tunnels, either a cast member came out, or another went in, or Tarek showed up, breathing down her neck. He disliked her having free rein of the park, but he'd made the deal with her dad before he figured out it was a bad idea. For him. For her, it worked pretty well.

Then there was mission number two: Stalk Allie. Not for the dumb reason everyone else did. Allie was no talent scout, for sure. But she *had* fooled Matt about whoever she really was. Hadn't he been Special Ops for, like, years? Phil didn't know much about the military, except that you didn't get to be a big mucky-muck secret agent by being stupid.

But tailing Allie had gone about as well as the tunnels. With everyone hovering, from guests to princesses, Phil could barely *see* Allie, let alone what she was up to. Today, Phil had even left home early to catch her as she walked to work, but as soon as Allie came out the door, Matt whisked her away in the Testosteroni, and the whole thing made Phil so mad, she decided to break into the condo.

Which was when the old lady with the big beady eyes tapped her on the shoulder and said, "What do you think you're doing, missy?"

Phil jumped, dropping the lockpick she'd stolen from her dad's memento box, then tilted an innocent face up.

"Don't even try it. I been around, and I know what's what. You tell me what you're up to or I'm callin' the cops."

"Fine." Phil thought fast. Matt had taught her better; she might be mad, but she still wanted to do him proud. "I, uh, dropped something when I was visiting my friend. She'll be gone all day, and I really need it back. It's for school."

"You in summer school? What school you go to? I know this area, so don't you try an' pull a fast one on me."

Of all the bad luck. Phil's dad had been homeschooling her year-round for so long, she'd forgotten it was summer. "It's a new, uh, experimental school. We don't exactly have a location yet. It's mostly online for now."

"Hmph. What's it called?"

Don't hesitate. "Kilimanjaro School." Phil kept her eyes steady, chin up.

"Like the mountain?" Phil nodded, and the woman said, "All right. I don't believe you but I can't prove you wrong. Guess I'll have to let it pass." She bent stiffly, reaching for the lockpick, and Phil snatched it away and pocketed it.

The woman grimaced, then shrugged. "Well, you can keep it. It's yours, I s'pose, and I ain't no thief. But you ain't got no call to break into Allie's place. If she's your friend, you'll get your stuff back when she gets home."

"You know her?"

"We're acquainted, yes. My name's Birdie."

She waited, and Phil reluctantly admitted, "I'm Phil. My dad works at the park. He's, uh, one of the actors."

"He the big blond fella?"

Phil swallowed, then remembered if Birdie'd seen her dad's costume, she probably wouldn't have said "fella." Then Birdie added, "Allie's friend. Name's Matt," and Phil's jaw clenched.

"No, Matt's not my dad."

The door across from them opened and Celia came out. "Oh. I just wondered if Allie wanted to walk in with me."

Phil glared at her. "She's *not* a talent scout."

"Course she ain't," Birdie said. "She's an actress. Told me so herself."

Celia rolled her eyes at Phil. "I can ask Allie to walk to work if I want, whether she's a talent scout or not."

"No you can't. She's not here. She has the day off."

Celia's mouth fell open, and then her expression soured, like Phil had given her a pickle popsicle.

"You have got to be kidding me. *Unreal.* She's only worked here *two days,* and she already gets a day off? This would never happen if we were union. I'm gonna kill Tarek. And then I'm quitting—I swear to God I am!"

She flung off toward the park, leaving Birdie and Phil staring after her.

"That girl needs a boyfriend," Birdie said. "Or at least some nookie."

Phil sidled past her. "Well, I've got to go now."

Birdie fell into step beside her. "You goin' to the park? I'll walk in with you."

They were about the same height, so when Phil quickened her pace, Birdie did, too. There wasn't any polite way out of it, so Phil pretended to listen while Birdie nattered on.

It was probably just as well she hadn't broken into Allie's. Matt would be mad if he found out. Not to mention her dad. She had to return the lockpick before he missed it. Not that he still used it; supposedly, he'd put it there as a reminder of what he'd been, not where he was going. Phil thought it was harder than that for a leopard to change his spots, even with upcoming "gender affirming surgery."

They neared the main gate, and Birdie paused her monologue long enough for Phil to interject, "I have an employee pass, but I'm sure you need to buy a ticket—"

"Nope, already got one."

Phil's jaw clenched tighter. "Okay." She moved through the turnstile, flashing her badge at the guard, who knew her and was already waving her through. Behind her, Birdie still rummaged in her big shoulder bag, and Phil took her shot, dodging down a path to the left.

Birdie called out, "Hey! Ain'tcha gonna wait for me?"

Phil pretended not to hear. Once out of sight of the gate, she turned down the path that led to the new addition. Signs everywhere warned guests not to come this way, but Phil ignored them. A Mousetrap entrance was close by, and she prayed it was early enough that no one would be around.

She'd just rounded a bend and had the tunnel in sight, when the door opened and her dad walked out in full costume. He was looking down, and she veered off the path, ducking behind a mound of earth covered in bonsai and other miniature plants, à la the forests featured in most of the Grimm's tales. As long as she kept still and didn't step on the gravel path, she'd be safe.

Her dad's footsteps approached, then faded, and Phil was about to resume her quest when a cool female voice said from the hill's other side, "The tunnels are over there."

Phil jerked back again. Why was Gillian here? She'd been working overtime to ensure the new addition's design fit its fairy tale. But with construction stalled, she should've been at her desk, not roaming the park.

Then a man spoke. "You said it would be arranged by now." He had a heavy accent, but Phil couldn't place it. Something European. Maybe German?

Gillian's tone was sharp. "Matt's gone again today."

Matt? What did he have to do with it? Whatever it *was.*

She strained closer on tiptoes, leaning into the mound. Suddenly, the dirt beneath her hands gave way—she lost her grip—and fell onto the gravel with a loud *crunch!*

Dead silence. Then Gillian said, "What was that?"

Someone took a step toward the hill and Phil thought

fast. Picking up a stone, she tossed it to the left, where it landed with another, smaller crunch.

Another pause before the man said, "Probably an animal. It does not matter. I will return tomorrow, and I expect better news…"

Their voices faded as they moved away, and Phil waited until they were gone, then came around the mound. The desire to follow them warred with the knowledge that she was at the Mousetraps, *totally alone*. She could slip in and work her way back to The Princess Shoppe, and *finally* figure out how the tattooed man gave her the slip.

Or maybe *he* was the man with Gillian, and they were in cahoots.

That settled it. The chance was too good to pass up. She turned right, hurrying after them, hoping they hadn't vanished into the crowds already. The tunnels would have to wait another day.

Chapter Fifteen

After seven hours driving all over the desert, checking out the casinos and every tiny town in-between, then dipping into Mexico before finally making their way west to suburban San Diego, Allie never wanted to be stuck in a car with Matt, ever again.

She also didn't give a flying fig about Tarek or the missing princesses, except Tarek was *paying* her to give a fig, and she wasn't that coldhearted. And she really wanted her house. It was just that everything was a dead end.

So far, her two days in the park had told her zilch, except that the Grimms were sick puppies whose "fairy tales" would be rated R if anyone besides the Mouse House produced them: monsters eating children for misbehaving, animals killing each other randomly, and assorted royalty literally stabbing each other in the back made for an interesting array of "park experiences." And the food was even worse; mostly boiled sausages, parsnips, and mush.

The one good thing about this trip was that she'd persuaded Matt to go through a drive-thru, where she got a bleu cheese bacon burger, fries, and a strawberry shake. Mr. Healthy got a salad. Which only added to her irritation. That *look* he gave her—that *smile*. As if she didn't know his game plan. He could try all he wanted, but she wouldn't succumb, no matter how his muscles bulged, even driving.

Speaking of which, his car was so ridiculously small, she had to peel herself out when they finally rolled into a spot at his sister's condo. Naturally, *he* unfolded from it gracefully, muscles flexing even more.

And then there was his singing. His baritone rivaled the bass of the symphony he sang to—in *German*. Who sang in German? Besides people who lived in Germany. Or Switzerland. Or, she supposed, Luradel. Tarek kept throwing her off, with his Middle East accent and attitudes. That "common" stock his father married into had probably benefitted the inbred European gene pool he came from.

However, if she was honest with herself, the real reason Matt's singing upset her was that it reminded her of her dad. Still, no point in dwelling on the past, and therefore no need for introspection in the present. And anyway, finding the princesses, getting her house, and keeping Matt at bay were higher priority than self-pity.

Allie blew out a breath and took in her surroundings. The Paseo Del Sol Condos were more Chi-Chi even than those at the resort. Just what she'd expect from the sister of a man who drove a car that cost more than Allie's house.

Muted earth tones softened the stucco walls, while bright white walkways were edged alternately with lush green grass and rows of red stones. Natural fiber sunbrellas shaded patio tables, and each unit had its own propane grill, provided by the homeowner's association, unless it was a coincidence that they all exactly matched.

Matt stood on the sidewalk, suddenly looking put out. "You can wait out here if you want. I'll be right back."

As though after a day of catching her eye and constantly touching her, wreaking havoc with her emotional and physical responses, he now didn't want to be seen with her.

She pushed down the hurt. "What—and miss a chance to meet another of your women?"

He scowled, jangling his keys. "I don't 'have' women."

"Sure you do. Laurette, Phil, Gillian, your sisters—

probably a few more I don't even know about. Maybe they aren't your girlfriends, but they're yours all the same."

"No, they're not. Besides, what business is it of yours?"

"It's not. No need to get testy."

He gave it one more try. "You sure you wouldn't rather wait here?"

"Positive."

Reluctantly, he led the way into the complex. Darlene's unit was in a quiet area away from the hustle of the pool and fitness center. The closer they got, the more Matt's mood headed south. He knocked on the door, and Allie did a surreptitious inventory of her appearance: standard shorts, tank top, and sandals. She'd even blow-dried her hair and put earrings in, and her deodorant seemed to be working.

Buoyed by the knowledge that she didn't stink, she turned as the door opened, revealing not Matt's sister, but a pale, dark-haired man, early forties, wearing glasses, a short-sleeve pinstriped shirt, and navy slacks.

"Isaac," Matt said. "You're back."

Isaac reddened, but his tone was cool. "Matt. Good to see you." He called over his shoulder, "Darlene! It's Matt."

"Everything okay here?" Matt asked, his tone also several degrees below what Allie would expect between future brothers-in-law. He had one of his "worried about his women" frowns on, and she hid a grin. He might not realize it, but his body language—straight back, broadened stance, tense muscles—shouted, *You better treat my sister right.*

Isaac cleared his throat. "Why do you ask?"

Matt lifted a shoulder in a "no reason at all" gesture, which didn't seem to reassure Isaac. He developed a sudden need to adjust his glasses, though he kept his posture straight, too; no cringing for him. "It's fine. We're fine. Darlene, tell Matt everything's fine."

Darlene came up beside Isaac, and Allie took advantage of the all-absorbing tension of the other three to openly gape. She was gorgeous. Not just a pretty face over a super-model body. Flat-out, all over gorgeous, in a way that made Allie think functional deodorant wasn't much to brag about.

Darlene was also blonde, but where Matt's hair was the dark of a lion's mane, hers was honey streaked with sunshine, with no hint of dark roots. And while his eyes were molten gold, hers were maple syrup, bright and clear as she met her brother's raised eyebrow with one of her own. She wore a cream miniskirt and sandals, showing off toned legs and a great pedicure, and there wasn't an ounce of flab on the arms peeping from her sleeveless yellow top.

She was Matt's older sister, so had to be near forty, but her complexion was pure, too. Lightly tanned in a healthy way, not the dried leather of so many urban desert dwellers.

Allie regrouped, contrasting Darlene with her patently un-tanned fiancé. Not that Isaac was a slouch. He stood shorter than Matt but taller than Darlene, who, in heels, barely crested Allie's eyes. He had the slim-hipped frame of a cyclist, and the glasses made him appear bookish, but his firm biceps proved he was no stranger to the gym. He draped a proprietary arm around Darlene and clenched his right hand into a fist, and Allie wondered if she should've brought her gun.

"We're *great,*" Darlene said to her brother, and some unspoken Wilcox signal passed between them.

Matt shifted his cool stare back to Isaac, waiting a beat. Then he deadpanned, "Falafel?"

Isaac froze, then guffawed. Darlene wrapped her arms around him, grinning, and the tension left Matt's shoulders. Allie gave a slight cough, and Darlene's gaze snapped to her, avid curiosity replacing the worry on her features.

She stepped forward, grasping Allie's hand in a firm shake. "Hi! Don't mind us—we're getting married this week, so every day around here is World War Three."

"No problem. I'm sure you've got lots on your mind."

"I'm Darlene soon-to-be-Mendel, and this is Isaac." Her intended lifted a hand in a wave and smiled. She continued, "You must be Allie. Matt's told us so much about you."

"He has?"

Matt said, "No, he hasn't. She's lulling you into a false sense of security so you'll spill your guts."

Darlene punched him in the shoulder. "Not fair! I was being polite." She turned to Allie. "Seriously. Any friend of Matt's. We should do lunch sometime."

Allie tried to figure out a response—why was everyone suddenly inviting her for drinks and lunch and stuff?—when Matt said, "Dar, I'm here about the tux. *Nothing else.* Can you please go get it so we can leave?"

Darlene shot him an appraising look, then said to Allie, "Would you excuse us? Matt needs to try on his tux. It will only take a sec."

Matt's back went rigid again, hands fisted at his sides, but Isaac interjected, "Allie, why don't you come in and have something to drink while Matt goes with Darlene."

Matt waited another beat, then put his head in his hands. "Fine. But make it fast. We still have to get to my place."

Darlene stopped short, open-mouthed, but his head was down and he missed it. She caught Allie's eye inquisitively, but since Allie had no idea what was going on, she only raised her shoulders in a *What's the big deal?* gesture.

Darlene's expression grew thoughtful, but all she said to Matt was, "The tux is in the guest room."

They disappeared down a hall, leaving Allie adrift in the red-tiled and white-painted entry. Through an archway, a carpeted living room was visible, strewn with moving boxes, wrapping paper, and what appeared to be piles of wedding gifts. The décor emphasized a clean, Mediterranean style, and everything matched, even the tile coasters on the end tables. Obviously, Darlene cared as much for her environment as she did about her appearance.

Allie thought of her own cheap shelves and boring apartment. *Never mind. When I get my house, I'll do the magazine-décor thing. Right?*

Okay, maybe not. But it was fun to dream.

Isaac gestured through a door. "The kitchen's this way. Best to leave them alone. A Wilcox woman in wedding mode is like the Terminator meets Martha Stewart."

"Scary."

"You don't know the half of it."

~:~:~

By late afternoon, Phil was tired and hungry and none the wiser than she'd been in the morning. Trailing Gillian and her new boyfriend was a waste of time. Not only was he not the tattooed man—he had a full head of black hair— but after leaving the Mousetraps, they went straight to the employee complex, where Gillian went inside, and then Phil shadowed the boyfriend for another hour.

He was of average height with a slim build, and even from afar, his features were distinctive: Black brows, straight nose, strong chin. His long-sleeved white shirt and dark slacks looked expensive, as did his shiny black shoes. He glanced from side to side, as though searching for something. Or someone. A princess to kidnap? But apart from that, like the tattooed man, he just walked.

When the hour was up, he left the park and got into a silver Porsche parked near the rear of the guest lot. Phil chewed her fingernail, hanging back out of sight while he peeled out onto the 111. Until she could drive—legally, anyway—that was it for her career as a spy.

She turned in disgust and ran smack into her dad.

"Phil, honey, I've been looking for you all day. Where have you been?"

The worry in his eyes was tempered by his black mascara and frosted blue eyeshadow, which matched his day-three Cinderella gown, and Phil shrugged. "Around."

He looked like he wanted to press her, then thought better of it. "Let's go. I have an appointment with Dr. Bauer, but I can drop you off at home first."

"I'm not going home now."

She pushed by, but he grabbed her arm. "You're still twelve, and I'm still your father. You owe me some respect, no matter what you think."

"Respect?" Anger boiled up faster than Phil could contain it, and she yanked free. "If you respected me, you wouldn't be so selfish all the time!"

"Selfish? Honey, I know you're angry with me, but I thought maybe you were starting to understand. This is who I am. I can't help it if I was born into the wrong body."

He sounded so *calm,* which only made her madder. "Stop being reasonable! *This*—" She waved at his dress, his made-up face, the bouffant blond wig. "—isn't reasonable. *I'm* a girl—*I'm* the one who should get to play dress up, *not you!"*

"I know you're a girl—"

"Then why don't you ever treat me like one? Why are you always buying me baseball bats and footballs and things? Why don't you ever buy *me* a dress?"

His mouth opened and closed. "I—I didn't realize you wanted one. We always talk about how stereotypes are—"

"Shut up! I'm sick of being politically correct. You

never listen to me! Matt listens. Why can't you be more like Matt? I bet Mom wouldn't't've killed herself if you were."

The words tumbled out unchecked, landing in a shocked silence. Blood thundered in her ears and her fists clenched. Her breath came in gasps, and the hurt in her dad's eyes stabbed her all the way to her bones.

A tear trickled unnoticed down one of his rouged cheeks. "I'm sorry you feel that way. Be home by dinner."

He walked quietly away, and Phil watched him go, then swiped at her own eyes. This was stupid. He was stupid. She had better things to do than worry about him and his dumb operation. Like figuring out what Allie was up to so she could warn Matt. She marched across the visitor lot, then cut across the landscaping to the condos.

If Allie was home, Phil would demand to know what she was up to. If not, well, Phil still had the lockpick.

It was after four, a hundred-plus degrees out, and a hot wind rustled the palm trees. Soon, families with children would leave the park in search of air-conditioned quiet, or head to one of the outdoor pools so the kids could splash around while mom and dad enjoyed an iced cocktail or three. For now, the condos were deserted, locked tight after the cleaning crews had swarmed through.

The shades were down on Allie's windows, but that didn't prove anything. Still, her place *felt* empty, and Phil trusted her feelings. Or at least, she believed in doing what she wanted and hoping it all worked out.

She whipped the lockpick from her pocket and rapped on Allie's door for form's sake, when a bumping sound from behind caught her attention. Expecting to find Celia coming out of her digs, Phil turned quickly, hiding the pick behind her back. "I was just…"

No one was there. But Celia's door was open, swinging

slowly in the breeze, never quite closing as it caught on something and bumped open again.

"Hello…?" Phil stepped closer. "Celia? You in there?"

Silence. Phil peered cautiously into the suite. Tarek insisted the live-in rooms be cleaned daily, same as the guests', so probably the crew just didn't fully shut the door. Phil pushed it open and moved onto the linoleum entry square. Her eyes adjusted to the dim light, and she gasped.

Celia's place looked like it hadn't been cleaned today, or even this *week.* The bookcase was overturned, and from the two open suitcases on the floor, with most of her clothes strewn nearby, it seemed she'd made good on her threat to quit. An unfinished bowl of granola sat on the breakfast bar, and one of the stools had been smashed against a wall.

And on the entryway floor, not six inches from Phil's right foot, lay a pool of fresh blood.

Nausea churned in her stomach, her limbs suddenly numb. Her mind screamed *get out!*, and she willed her legs to obey. She reached for the door, then snatched her hand back when she saw the blood smeared on it.

She had to call the police. She had to—

"You again."

Phil shrieked and jerked back. Birdie stood outside on the welcome mat, eyeing her suspiciously.

"Thought your stuff was at Allie's. Why're you breaking in over here?"

"I'm not—I didn't—"

"Told ya not ta lie ta me." She tilted her head disapprovingly at the pick in Phil's hand, long forgotten in the shock of the moment.

"Please," Phil begged, trying to squeeze past her. "Let me out of here. We have to help her!"

"I'm callin' the police, that's what." Birdie pushed Phil

back inside. "Fool me once, shame on you, an' all that."

Phil avoided the blood while Birdie tried to shove the door the rest of the way open, then reached a bony finger under the weather-stripping to see what it was stuck on. She worked something loose, then straightened, flipping on the light and holding up a big gold ring with an R and three songbirds on it.

"You know anything 'bout this?" she demanded, then got her first look at the mess behind Phil. "Holy cow! You didn't do all this by yourself, did you? And—goodness—that isn't—it's not—*blood,* is it…? I don't feel so good…"

And with that, she keeled over in a dead faint.

Phil kicked the door aside, grabbed Birdie under her shoulders and dragged her out to the breezeway, then sat with her back against Allie's door and dialed 9-1-1.

So much for keeping the kidnappings quiet.

Chapter Sixteen

Shit for brains. That's what Matt had. Not only had he convinced himself Darlene meeting Allie wouldn't be so bad, but he'd also told her he was taking Allie to his place. His sister was already the mother of all matchmakers, but being a bride made her ten times worse. Yet somehow, Matt had let his tongue wag.

He wasn't even sure why, but he needed to get Allie away from GrimmLand, someplace where they could start fresh. Because if he didn't get her naked soon, his mental capacity would be zilch. He'd never find the missing princesses, never be done with his obligations to Roland, never get the damn business launched. He had to think clearly, and as long as Allie was wandering around loose in shorts and tank tops, he couldn't focus on anything else.

"So," Darlene began, once he'd re-dressed and zipped the perfectly fitted tux back into its bag, "you and Allie—"

"How about those Padres?"

She glared at him. "Matt."

"I'm not discussing this with you."

"Fine. I'll invite her to the shower myself."

"No."

"Why not?"

"Because—" Matt stopped. This was going nowhere. And it was his own fault Darlene was getting *ideas*.

Noting his hesitation, Darlene pounced. "If you'd rather, I can invite Gillian."

"No!"

"Ah, ha!"

"*No*. Not ah-ha. There is no ah-ha about Gillian, or Allie, or anyone else. I don't want you or anyone in the family mixed up in my personal or work business. And that's all this is: I'm working with Allie, that's it."

"You were *just working* with Gillian, too, at first."

"This is different. Allie is—different."

"Absolutely," she answered sweetly. Throttling her was sounding like a really good plan, but suddenly she changed course. "That reminds me—did you put 'high tea' on the shower invitations?"

"Yes." The segue was lost on him, but at least they were back on neutral ground.

"You're sure? It sets the tone. If everyone thinks it's just *tea,* they might underdress."

"It says high tea."

Darlene chewed her lip. "Because, as a guy, you might have thought just 'tea' was enough, and it's on Thursday."

"I promise you, the invitations say 'high tea.'"

"Maybe I should call everyone, just in case."

"Jeez, Darlene. *You* asked me to be maid of honor."

Her face fell, and she threw her arms around him. "I know. I'm sorry! I'm a mess right now."

He hugged her back. "No problem. I can imagine. Besides, Didi says high tea is just a fancy way of saying 'supper.' I'm sure everyone will dress appropriately."

Darlene brightened. "Didi's helping? That's fantastic. She'll know what to do. Sure you can't stay for dinner?"

"No. And just because Didi's having an operation doesn't make her a better party planner."

Darlene nodded and smiled, and Matt made himself drop the argument. If he gave her another opening, she was bound to come back to his sex life. Speaking of which…

He grabbed the tux bag and went to rescue Allie. Except she didn't need rescuing. She and Isaac leaned against the kitchen counters, drinking lemonade and laughing. When Matt came in, they started guiltily. He opened his mouth to ask what they were talking about, then thought better of it.

"Time to go, princess. I still need to drop the tux at my place, and then it's a long drive back to GrimmLand." Total crap, because if all went according to plan, they wouldn't go back to the resort tonight. At least, not right away.

Allie shrugged apologetically at Isaac, pushed off the counter, and followed Matt to the door. Isaac trailed after them, ostensibly to see them out, but Matt knew better.

He pushed Allie through the door, saying to Isaac, "You have to stay here."

"But—"

"Aw, c'mon," Allie said. "Can't we keep him? Please?"

"No. It'll be over soon."

Isaac grimaced. "Not soon enough."

"Amen to that."

As the door shut, Matt heard him mutter, *I'll get you for this, and your little dog, too.* But then Allie's nicely rounded tush swayed in front of him as she walked to the car, and he forgot everything else.

The drive to his place didn't take long, and was mostly silent. He suspected Allie was thinking about the missing women, and wondered if she was as frustrated as he about the lack of leads. Which was a stupid thing to wonder. Of course she was frustrated. Probably much more than he was, given she had an entire house riding on this job.

He stole a glance at her profile. Serious. Full lips pulled down, brows puckered. She needed to laugh more. Like she had with Isaac—or the men at the bar. That thought sent his own mood south, and he shook his head to clear it.

Focus, Wilcox. Nothing ventured, nothing gained.

He stole another glance, this one at the smooth curve of her thigh where it disappeared into her shorts. He shifted in his seat, stretching his leg to ease the tightening of his groin, then winced. Even after all this time, the scar on his thigh still ached. Allie turned her head at the movement, her gaze landing in the vicinity of his lap. Or maybe his leg. Either way, she caught his eye, then blushed and looked away.

Eyes on the prize, son, eyes on the prize.

And Allie was a damn fine prize to have eyes on.

From what Allie could tell, Matt's place suited him. Situated on a curve of road winding through the foothills of the Cuyamacas east of San Diego, it was secluded from his neighbors on every side. Only the driveway and entrance of the large A-frame were visible from the road, and the scent of the surrounding evergreens mixed with wild roses and bigger, more exotic blooms, until she almost tasted their lush cocktail on her tongue.

It was cooler up here, with a light breeze giving relief after the heat and dust of the day. Connecting the drive with the house was a short bridge, and around back, at least an acre of un-landscaped property marched down into the canyon. What her plants could do with that much space.

She swallowed, waiting as Matt unlocked the front door. No use salivating over something that simply could not be found in the Bay Area, even with money.

The first thing she noticed inside, besides the sunken living room, was the giant wall of windows facing west. The view was amazing, out over the canyon and beyond. A deck hugged the length of the house, freshly stained and glowing deep red-brown in the lowering sun. She moved toward it, past the kitchen to the left, which opened on the other side to a dining area, complete with a huge, apparently hand-carved table and chairs.

Above these two rooms was a large loft, its formerly open front now segmented by two-by-fours. A hall led from the entry behind her to the remainder of the main floor, and next to that, stairs disappeared down to the lower level. Or levels. Who knew how big the house was?

The view out the windows almost overwhelmed her. Between the canyon stretching out below, and the sun setting over the hills, Allie's heart constricted. No wonder Matt disparaged her cramped stucco box, surrounded by rows and rows of more stucco boxes. Until you got to the dirty warehouses beyond, anyway.

My place is just fine. *Who needs a view, anyway?*

Matt went to hang the tux up, and she wandered into the dining room. Rolls of paper were piled on the table, which was clearly ancient. Polished to a rich sheen, it was marked with dents and scrapes that only added character. She ran a hand over it, noting the utter lack of dust, and wondered where Matt had found it. Knowing him, he'd probably carved it himself when he was three.

Upon closer snooping—telling herself she was just keeping up her PI skills—she discovered the rolls were building plans. She smoothed them out. From the A-frame shape and the room labels, they looked to be of this house. None of the lines or squiggles made sense, though, so she couldn't tell what Matt was doing.

"Putting up walls," he said from behind her and she hastily stepped back.

He stood near the living room, his large hands thrust in his jeans pockets. For some reason, he never wore shorts, even in the worst heat. But even so, the muscles of his legs bulged against the denim.

She jerked her gaze upward. "Sorry. Hazard of the job."

"No problem." He didn't sound too upset. In fact, he seemed relaxed. Determined. *Purposeful.*

He moved toward her, and Allie shivered. What had Isaac said? Something about Wilcoxes not rushing into things, but once they made up their minds, they never gave up. Her skin prickled and she discovered she was salivating again, only this time, it wasn't over Matt's property.

She swallowed. "Why are you putting up walls?"

He nodded toward the loft. "Privacy. That's my bedroom up there."

He'd reached the other side of the table, and thinking about him and his bed—him *in* his bed—made her glad the heavy antique stood between them. Which was ridiculous. He was just a man. A man she'd almost, kinda-sorta made out with, and had been drooling over ever since. But only a man, nevertheless.

She said, "I thought you liked space."

"Sometimes. It's a pain when family stops by, especially if I want to have a…guest…over. Worrying over who's going to walk in can make it hard to get naked."

"Oh," she managed around a suddenly too *dry* tongue. "They—uh, your family—they have keys to your place?"

He shrugged. "Hazard of the job. I've tried changing the locks, but one of them always manages to copy the new key. If I have to live with them, the least I can do is keep them out of my most…intimate…space."

He came around the table, and she gripped a chair to keep from backing away again. "It's nice you have the choice. To have space or not, I mean."

He closed the distance between them, but slowly, completely unhurried. She wasn't fooled. Bobby got that look in his eye whenever he wanted to un-break-up long enough to "get naked" with her.

"You have a choice, too," Matt said softly, deliberately holding her gaze.

She abandoned the chair and took a step back, then another, stopping only when she realized her escape route had brought her closer to his loft and the bed he'd announced was waiting there.

"Look," she said, "we tried this once before and it didn't work. Remember?"

He stopped mere inches in front of her, and she smelled the tangy spice of his cologne. His arms were taut and smooth, his stance open in a clear *come-and-get-me* pose.

"What I remember," he said, leaning in, his breath warm on her lips, "is that kissing you made me so hard, I haven't been able to relax since."

"Oh," she said faintly. His hands remained in his pockets, doing nothing to force the issue, yet automatically Allie felt her chin lift, her head tilt, exposing the column of her neck, her body humming with tension and expectation.

He blew another gentle breath, tickling the vulnerable base of her throat with soft heat, then raised his eyes to hers again. "In fact, just thinking about kissing you makes me hard. I'd like to do it again. And a few other things."

He waited, desire heating the molten gold of his eyes, his intent so clear, there was no possible way to deny it. When Allie held her ground—mainly because she was rooted to the spot and couldn't have moved if she'd tried— he brought his mouth to the place where her pulse beat wildly in her throat and bit gently, then flicked the same spot with his tongue.

Allie gasped and staggered. Not away. Forward. Some primal, undeniable urge propelled her toward a gene pool— smart, popular, *built*—with which her own DNA desperately wanted to commingle. Of their own accord, her hands thrust into his hair, while he pulled her hips close so that his erection pressed into the hollow of her belly.

His mouth trailed fire along her neck and jaw, teeth grazing, tongue soothing, then *finally* captured her mouth in a searing kiss. His hands were under her shirt, dipping into her bra, teasing her. It was hot and wet and so much faster than before. Allie couldn't catch her breath, couldn't wrap her brain around the fact that *Matt*—a calculating, conscientious, never-rush-Wilcox—was urgently biting, licking, and stroking her into a frenzy.

He dropped one hand to her shorts, the other holding her steady. He unzipped and pulled the shorts down, all in a single one-handed motion, and his fingers slipped roughly over the pink silk of her underwear. She gasped and bucked against him. His mouth never leaving hers, he lifted her onto the dining table, shoving his plans aside and laying her back, hips at the edge, legs straddling him.

His mouth did move then, trailing kisses over her jaw and throat until he reached her chest. Somehow, she'd lost her shirt, too, and he made as quick work of her bra as he had the shorts. Then his mouth was on her breast, and she was lost to pure sensation. Tongue and teeth and fingers created points of white-hot fire that became her entire world. She heard his ragged breathing and knew that though he focused on her pleasure, his own increased with her every moan, every response her body made to his touch.

Then his fingers were inside her, stroking, sliding, demanding. His teeth nipped her swollen nipple, his erection pressed into her thigh. And she came, in a fiery, slippery explosion of pure bliss, the tremors wracking her body until gradually they receded, leaving her warm and languid and centered. Utterly at peace.

Oh, yeah.

~:~:~

Allie swam back up from wherever he'd sent her, and Matt tried not to look smug. Or at least, not *too* smug. Male satisfaction hummed in his veins—*me make woman scream with pleasure*—while other parts of him hummed for a different reason.

She focused briefly on his face, then on her own body. "I'm naked."

"Mostly," he agreed and shifted, still teasing her sweet spot with his thumb. Watching her had driven him wild; he figured he could manage a few more times before he literally exploded with need.

"Ooh," she said breathlessly. "You're…not…naked…"

"I will be. Trust me, princess, it's high on my list."

Her head lolled back again, and he groaned. Okay, maybe once more. But that was it. So much for taking his time and enjoying the ride. Allie arched her back, and Matt's body responded to the visual, telling him to get his pants off and himself inside her, *fast*, or it would be too late.

And then his cell phone rang.

Startled, Allie opened her eyes, suddenly seeming to realize where they were and what they were doing. She blushed and a self-consciousness crept into her eyes. He felt her retreat as a palpable thing, and shoved his free hand in his pocket, silencing the phone and tossing it on a chair.

"Shouldn't you—"

"They'll leave a message. Now, where were we?" He reached for his fly, and the landline rang. "Coincidence."

She looked alarmed, but he waited for the ancient machine to pick up after the third ring. A dial tone reached them, and he grinned down at her.

"See? Nothing to worry about. Only telemarketers call

that line." He leaned in to distract her with a kiss, when *her* phone rang. *"Shit!"*

She twisted off the table, forcing him to release her, and fumbled her phone out of her shorts pocket. "It's Tarek."

He'd known from the first ring it was GrimmLand, and probably bad news. She answered the call, listened, then raised stricken eyes. "Celia's gone. Her place is trashed and there's blood everywhere."

Matt felt her words like a physical blow, stunning him, blocking any reaction, until she added, "Phil discovered the scene. She isn't hurt, just really shook up. She wants you."

And then adrenaline shot through him, the need to shield a twelve-year-old girl from the horror she'd witnessed galvanizing him into action. He headed for the door, shoving everything else out of his head until he could determine for himself that Phil was okay. Behind him, he heard Allie tell Tarek they were on their way, but Matt didn't look back. Allie would be half-dressed by now—she'd want to get to the park as fast as he did.

For once, his own impatience might outstrip hers.

Chapter Seventeen

When Matt finally showed up, Phil wasn't surprised to see Allie tagging along. But she was so glad he'd arrived, she didn't even care he'd spent the day with The Enemy.

Still, she needed him alone, but tons of cops scurried around, investigating the scene. Birdie sat on a curb by the parking lot, a cool cloth on her head, talking to paramedics and piecing together what had happened. Hopefully, that would take at least until after Phil cornered Matt.

She patted her shorts pocket. The ring was still there, but who knew when Birdie'd remember it? Phil wasn't even sure why she'd snatched it, except that Matt and Tarek both had one, so finding it at Celia's must be super important.

Speaking of Tarek, he was also nearby, going on loudly about how if the cops had listened to him, Celia might still be here. Which was probably true. Phil couldn't decide if she was relieved or disappointed that he still wore his own ring. It would be nice to pin this on someone she didn't like.

The remaining crowd consisted of resort staff and guests, so many that the condos were busier than the park. Phil sat on the grass by Allie's windows with a female cop, who'd been assigned babysitting duty until whenever Didi finally showed up. At which point Phil would have to go give her statement to Riverside County PD, since Mecca didn't have its own station.

It was all so frustrating that when the crowds parted and Matt pushed through, Phil launched herself at him.

"Whoa there, kiddo." He staggered back—they'd never

been huggy, so he had to be wondering what was up.

Before the officer could stand, she whispered urgently in his ear, *"I've got something to show you!"*

Matt drew back and searched her face. "Are you okay? What happened? How did you find out Celia was gone?"

Phil bit back a wail. She had to get Matt's attention before Birdie remembered the ring or the officer butted in. Phil stole a peek at Matt's right hand. Thank God—there was his ring, big and clunky as ever. But the one Birdie'd found could belong to someone he knew. Hadn't he said Roland's guards were even tighter than a Navy SEAL unit?

"I'm fine," she said quickly. "I was looking for Allie when I saw Celia's door was open."

Matt's eyes narrowed. He released her, crossing his arms over his chest. *Damn.* She tried to stare him down, but he didn't budge, only lifted an eyebrow and waited.

"Okay, I was snooping. But I didn't *do* anything, I—"

"At Allie's? Or Celia's?"

"I *told* you, Celia's door was open. I was, uh, knocking on Allie's door when—"

"Hand it over."

"What?"

Allie glanced at Matt. "Did I miss something?"

Matt made a spin-around motion with his finger, and Phil gave up. "Fine. Take it." She wrenched the lockpick out of her back pocket and handed it to him. "Happy?"

"Yes," he said and slipped it into his own pocket, while Allie looked like she was trying not to smile.

It was too much—now The Enemy was *laughing* at her? Phil stamped her foot. "Can't you just go away? Stop forcing yourself on Matt. You don't belong here, and *you never will!"*

Matt's expression was furious. "Phil!"

"No," Allie said, the flash of hurt in her eyes quickly gone. "Don't be mad at her. She's right. You two should be alone for a minute. She doesn't know me, and this was all really upsetting. I'll be over here."

She moved away, and Phil ignored the stab of guilt. So what if Allie'd been kind of sensible, and, well, *nice?* Phil was alone with Matt—this might be her only chance.

Unfortunately, he had other ideas about the direction of their conversation. "What the hell is your problem with Allie? What did she ever do to you?"

"Stop yelling at me! I need to talk to you!"

Matt scrubbed a hand over his face. "I'm sorry. I know this has been a huge ordeal."

"No! Not that! It's—"

"Ohmigod! We just heard what happened!"

Bridget slipped under the yellow crime scene tape and past the two officers trying to stop the crowd from breaking through. Laurette followed her just as determinedly, dropping to her knees and pulling Phil into a fierce hug. Bridget's eyes were huge in her white face, and Laurette had clearly been crying.

"Are you okay?" She brushed Phil's hair off her brow.

"I'm fine!" Which probably sounded like she didn't care they were worried about her. So she added, "Thanks."

"How *horrible!"* Bridget's voice shook, and she twisted her purse strap around her hand. "I can't believe Celia's gone. What happened? What was her place like?"

Matt said quellingly, "Phil's been through enough without reliving it all again." He glanced at the officer still seated nearby. "Did they already get your statement?"

"No. They want my dad with me."

"Where is Didi, anyway?"

Phil shrugged, going for nonchalant. "They called him,

but he's in a doctor's appointment so his phone is off. I guess he'll be here whenever he's done." Matt's look was too probing, too *understanding.* And this was not what she wanted to talk about. She *had* to get him alone.

The officer's walkie-talkie blared and she listened, then rose and approached them. "The paramedics are taking Mrs. Olsen to the hospital as a precaution. She asked about Phil. Do you want to see her before she goes?"

Matt frowned. "Who?"

Which gave Phil her best idea of the day. She stuck her hand in her pocket, clasping the ring in her sweaty palm. "Birdie. She was with me at Celia's. You'd like her. She didn't approve of my extra-curricular activities, either."

"Activi-*ties?*"

"Um, yeah. She kind of bumped into me both times I was looking for Allie."

"*Both?* Jeez, Phil. When I taught you to—" He stopped and slid a glance at the officer, who didn't seem to have picked up on anything in their conversation.

"Anyway," Phil said quickly. "I should go say good-bye. And you should come with me."

She couldn't make it any more obvious. Laurette and Bridget still hovered, but they'd taken Matt's warning to heart and whispered to each other. Them bonding was kind of weird, but maybe good for Laurette in the long run. Over by the condos, Tarek had spotted Allie and made a beeline for her, while the officer's radio blared again and she stepped away to talk. Phil shot Matt a telling look.

"Okay," he said at last. "Sure. I'd love to meet her."

Phil tossed a "Be right back!" over her shoulder at her babysitter, then led Matt toward the paramedics as they wheeled Birdie's gurney off the curb. Phil and Matt would reach her not far from where Tarek was clearly chewing

Allie out. The ring was heavy in Phil's sweaty palm. She had to time this *just* right, slipping it to Matt and telling him where it was found before anyone saw it.

They were halfway to the stretcher, Bridget and Laurette still behind them with the officer, the rest of the cops gathering evidence or attending to other official business. The shaken guests and employees chatted in groups, while Tarek and Allie were too engrossed in their argument to notice anything else. Now was her chance—

Matt's head flew up as Tarek suddenly exploded, "What am I paying you for? You have not found one single clue!"

Allie's face was red. "There's a hundred different directions the women could have gone! And about a million reasons they could have gone on their own!"

"They did *not* leave on their own!" Tarek looked like he was having an apoplexy—whatever that was. But whenever anyone in a work of old literature got super upset, they always had one, so this must be what it looked like.

"See the blood!" Tarek shrieked. *"Celia's* blood! What will it take before anyone believes me that something *terrible* is happening to these women?"

Matt veered toward them, taking Phil with him.

"No! Wait!" Phil clutched the ring convulsively.

Allie snapped at Tarek, "Obviously, Celia didn't leave on her own, but where's the pattern? Even in the Grimm's Sleeping Beauty, she didn't vanish in a blood bath!"

Matt glanced at Phil and completely misinterpreted her expression. "Allie, tone it down," he warned, making both The Enemy and Tarek aware of their presence.

"And you!" Tarek shouted at Matt. "You were to train Allie and then leave her to do her job. Why are you still here? Have you not waited long enough to retire? Stop interfering—it is because of you she is not making progress! If you were not Roland's pet, I would fire you!"

Allie's jaw dropped, and Matt looked as stunned as Phil felt. Tarek never lost control. Not like this. Phil cringed as Laurette and Bridget hurried up. Not that it mattered. *Everyone*—cops, guests, employees—they all turned to gawk. Even the EMTs pushing the gurney stopped, and Birdie herself sat up to watch the show.

Suddenly, the silence was blasted by the un-muffled roar of an ancient Buick with glasspacks. The beat-up brown sedan screeched into the parking lot and jumped the curb. The door opened and her dad leapt out, running toward her, long hair streaming loose, wearing a t-shirt, jeans, and four-inch strappy sandals on his huge feet.

At that moment, Phil would have given anything to be the one who'd disappeared. She wrenched free from Matt's grasp and tried to back away, but her dad dragged her close.

"Phil! Thank God! I came as soon as I got the message!"

He'd pinned her arms at her sides, trapping her hands in her pockets, but she squirmed with her whole body. "Let me go! If you really cared, you would've come sooner!"

"Phil," Matt began, but her dad cut him off.

"No, she's right. I should have been here. Phil, I'm so sorry, honey. I should have made you come home with me earlier, and then you wouldn't have had to go through this."

For some reason, this made Tarek even madder. "It is a good thing you did not, or else *no one* would have noticed Celia is gone!"

Phil's dad went white and his body stiffened. He let her go and stood, clearly planning to give Tarek a piece of his parental mind. His sudden release made Phil nearly fall, so she flung her arms out for balance—and the ring flew from her grasp, glinting in the sun, sailing through the air to land with a metallic *clunk!* on the pavement right at Tarek's feet.

"Shit!" She clapped a hand over her mouth as everyone looked at her.

Everyone except Tarek. He stooped and retrieved the ring, then cast an evil eye on her. "Where did you get this?"

His voice was oddly calm, the contrast between that and his earlier yelling making him seem more angry, not less.

Her babysitter sidled up next to Laurette and Bridget, who craned their necks, trying to catch a glimpse of Tarek's hands. Allie watched with interest, and Matt had on his cool, *what-the-hell-are-you-up-to* face.

"What is it?" Birdie asked loudly, leaning forward, the paramedics trying unsuccessfully to wrestle her back onto the gurney. "Is it the ring? Did you give it to the cops? I knew it'd got to be around here somewheres."

Tarek held his palm up, displaying the ring, and everyone surged forward. Even Phil, who'd taken it from Birdie so fast, she hadn't really studied it. Definitely one of Roland's, but she saw now it was older and more scarred than Matt's. Tarek's ring was old, too, but as with everything he owned, he kept it meticulously polished. By contrast, this ring had clearly been through a lot: along with its many small nicks, there was a distinctive deep gouge on one side.

Phil heard a gasp from behind and turned. Laurette, white as a sheet, pointed at the ring. "That—that's—"

Her eyes were huge and pleading, and Matt nodded reluctantly. "It sure looks like it."

"What?" Allie broke in. "What's going on?"

"I think," Tarek said calmly, "that Laurette has recognized this as the ring of Wolfram, Crown Prince of Ruedi—her fiancé."

"Fiancé?" Allie and Bridget said together.

"But—*how?*" Laurette was so pale, she couldn't have

much blood left in her head. Phil thought maybe Matt should hold her up or something, but he was distracted, reaching for his cell.

"I don't know, but I'm going to call him and find out."

"No need," a deep, accented voice said. "I am come."

Everyone turned at the sound, except Laurette, who stood frozen in place like your basic deer in the headlights.

The man stepping onto the grass was of medium height and slim, athletic build, pale, dark-haired, and brooding, in an angry, tragic, Heathcliff-from-*Wuthering-Heights* kind of way. He wore black slacks and a white dress shirt, its rolled-up sleeves revealing a badly scarred right forearm and hand, which—along with his left one—he kept loose at his sides. His movements were controlled, his posture erect, and his gaze never left the back of Laurette's head.

He was also the man who'd been talking with Gillian, who Phil had trailed through the park earlier today. Her head spun with questions, but she couldn't find her voice.

"Sweet?" the man said, the word more a command than a question. "Will you not turn and welcome me?"

Laurette's small frame shook and Phil took a step toward her, ready to catch her if she fell. Laurette pivoted slowly, the blue veins in her face and neck standing out in stark contrast to the white of her skin.

"How did you find me?" she whispered.

"I called him," Tarek announced, and no one could miss the triumph in his voice.

No one, that is, except Laurette, who probably didn't register it while she crumpled softly to the ground, eyes rolling up into her head.

"Shit!" Phil said again, only for once—*finally!*—on this crappy, stupid day, no one noticed.

Chapter Eighteen

Laurette awoke, disoriented. Her suite of rooms below the penthouse of the GrimmLand Hotel was dark, though it must be morning by now. After Matt and Allie had brought her home yesterday, she'd slept through the afternoon and night. Mercifully, the police had detained Wolf for questioning, so she'd been given a reprieve. But she'd known it was only temporary, and she sighed.

"Wolfram."

A shadowed form rose from a chair in the corner and approached. "You are awake. How are you feeling, sweet?"

"Can you please open the drapes?"

It wasn't an answer, but after a pause, he complied. Bright sun flooded the room, and she felt a little better. She sat up, noting she still wore yesterday's silk tank and black pants. They were wrinkled, and someone had removed her bra—she *hoped* it was Allie—but it was better than one of the teddies she usually slept in.

Wolf returned to the bed, his measured pace reminding her of his namesake animal. Or part of it. He might be all leashed power and fierce pride and natural leadership, but with his black hair and winged brows, he also had the cunning look of a raven. *Wulf* and *hramn*: Wolf Raven, the perfect fairy-tale villain. Yet, with all his cunning, he had no clue about her feelings—and wouldn't care if he did.

He sat on the bed, his hip intimately close to her thigh, and took her hand, caressing it with his thumbs. His own hands, especially the right one, were scarred from the injuries he'd sustained during the attack on her father, reminding her that, when something of "his" was threatened, he fought for it at all costs.

Even when it went against his own self-interest.

The heat rose up her arm, tingling through her breasts to her throat and face. She looked away before he saw too deeply, but she was powerless to escape his grasp.

"How are you feeling?" he repeated, and she strove for control, or if not that, a little dignity.

"Better, thank you. It was just a…shock…seeing you."

"Yes."

He was silent, and she glanced up, then regretted it. His expression was unreadable, but she feared her own was not. Why was this so complicated? In their world, few married for love. Their union was advantageous for their countries. Why couldn't she be happy, marrying her best friend, perhaps bearing his children? What inside her demanded more, loving him so much, she'd rather lose him entirely than share his bed, knowing he did not love her back?

"Why are you here?" she asked, hating that she must pick at the wound, anticipating already his politic answer.

Wolf's hands stilled, her wrist limp in his grasp for a moment before she finally pulled away. He sighed—was it regret? No. More likely impatience.

"It was late when I finished with the police. Instead of going to my own residence, I decided to see for myself if you are recovered. Tarek let me in."

What had she expected? Passion? Declarations of love? That he couldn't live without her for a single second more?

She forced a light tone. "As you can see, I'm fine. You can go home now. There's no cause for concern."

"Trying to rid yourself of me?"

His teasing was almost worse, as it reminded her of the

friendship they'd shared before she learned of their engagement. How everything changed that day—how *she* had changed, losing her innocent hopes to political reality.

Wolf was so close, she saw the stubble on his jaw, smelled the musk of yesterday's cologne, felt the heat of his body calling, unconsciously, to hers. Like her, he'd slept in his clothes, and his rumpled, just-awake look tantalized her with how it would be to wake up with him every morning.

"Of course not," she said too fast and swung her legs off the other side of the bed. "Coffee?"

Without waiting for an answer, she busied herself in the kitchen, which took all of three seconds, as the machine had a built-in grinder and its own water line. It didn't buy her nearly enough time to put on the friendly mask she usually wore for his benefit.

"Laurette." His tone demanded she look at him. Eyes dark, he regarded her from the narrow space between the counter and the fridge, trapping her in. "Sweet. Do you not wish to ask me about the ring? The police had many questions. Surely you have a few."

"Such as…?"

"What is my purpose in coming here? How did my ring appear at Celia's dwelling? When did I arrive?"

"The police can't suspect *you* of harming Celia?"

"Why not? Only a handful of men received Roland's rings. That one is clearly mine—you recognized it. Tarek and Matt did as well. Many people know it was damaged during the attempt on your father's life. As I was damaged." Wolf held up his hand, displaying the thick scar snaking across it, ending at his ring finger. "If not for the ring, I might have lost the finger, or perhaps my whole hand."

She felt herself pale. "But what would be your motive?"

"That is irrelevant. It is enough for now that five women

are missing, and the only clue to be found is *my* ring."

"But the disappearances began weeks ago, and you only arrived last night." He was silent, and Laurette gripped the counter, willing down the panic. "Didn't you?"

He moved into the kitchen. "Laurette. Sweet. I have known for some time where you were hiding."

She shook her head, denying his words—denying him. "Tarek called you…"

"I found you without his aid, *sweet.*"

He made the word a harsh caress. Had she wanted passion from him? He was passionate now, but she feared it came from being denied his "due," and not from any true feelings for her. A suspicion borne out by his next words.

"I have flown to California many times in recent weeks to check on you. The police will demand my flight records and align them with the disappearances, to make a case against me. As they should." His jaw hardened. "You may wish to be rid of me, but the police have suggested I stay."

Laurette gripped the counter harder. "But—*why?*"

"Why did I come? Or why did I kidnap the women?"

Despite the ache in her heart, hot anger surged. "You didn't kidnap anyone! How could anyone think that?"

For a fraction of a second, she thought relief flashed in his eyes, then it was gone. Had he truly worried she would believe such vile lies about him?

He said, "There are some who would lay this, as well as the attack on your father, at Ruedi's door—at *my* door."

His tone dared her to contradict him and she hesitated, choosing her words. "People will always say things. They want the throne for themselves, or they don't want our countries united."

"Or they do not approve of Roland's plan for female succession."

"No," she agreed. "There are many who think I would be a poor queen."

"I, however, am not one of them."

Something in his demeanor changed—how had he gotten so close?—and his gaze dropped to her mouth. Laurette's body tightened, breasts and belly and below, heat spreading everywhere, liquefying her. They had never kissed, except for one platonic peck at the public announcement of their engagement. Heart thudding so loudly, he must have heard it, she waited, unsure of what he would do next, or what she *wanted* him to do.

"As for why I pursued you here, it should be obvious. To claim what is mine. You belong to me, Laurette. You ran, and Roland let you. But that is over. You will come home now and take your rightful place as heir to Luradel's throne. We will wed, uniting our two countries. And you…" He bent his head close. "…will be…" His hot breath tickled her lips, and she shuddered. *"…mine."*

He captured her mouth then in a kiss that fired her blood like the aged whiskey they'd shared at their engagement party. His lips were soft, his body hard as he pressed her into the counter. His tongue thrust into her mouth, tasting, teasing, as his powerful thighs captured hers, ensnaring her as fully as any forest creature, caught by the master of the hunt.

She moaned, sliding her fingers through his thick hair. For just that moment, she wanted to believe that his passion stemmed from desire for *her,* not from the benefit their union would bring. And not from the thrill of the chase.

But she knew him too well. Had they not been playmates? Had she not seen him time and again want something, a toy, a goal, anything, and then once attained, it bored him? She was important to him. She recognized that. But only because she was the toy that had eluded him.

Once Wolf possessed her, his passion would cool. And even though he did not love her, she would wed him, because she was weak and would take whatever scraps he gave her. A sob choked her, and Wolf broke the kiss, brushing tendrils of hair from her brow.

"Sweet? Why do you cry?" He sounded genuinely concerned. She dashed at the tears while he cradled her, his featherlight touch heating her blood all the more. He frowned. "Is the thought of marrying me so terrible, then?"

"No!" she gasped, stung into the admission. "I just—does it have to be so soon? Can't we wait another year, or—or two? I've been so happy here."

He stiffened. "And you will *not* be happy with me."

She shook her head, unable to force the words out, to say he was wrong—*so* wrong—but he misunderstood.

His tone was flat. "We should have wed last year. But after the attempt on his life, Roland persuaded me you were safer away from Luradel for a time." He gripped her chin, forcing her gaze up. "Hear me now, Laurette. That time has ended. You will return with me, and we will marry. Even if I must drag you back against your will *and* Roland's."

His mouth landed on hers, harder, more ruthless. Where the first kiss was all passion and heat, this was a declaration, a promise that she would not escape again. Worse, she no longer wanted to. She reached for him, a conscious surrender, when the suite's doorbell rang.

Wolf froze, the entire length of his rigid body still pressing into her. He dragged his mouth from hers, dark eyes wide with shock. "I am sorry, sweet," he whispered. "I know not what I am doing."

He moved to the door, leaving her weak and bereft, mouth swollen, emotions bruised. In fairy tales, everything was simple: meet your true love, slay a dragon, live happily ever after. Maybe the physical challenges were harder, but none of these pesky emotions reared their monstrous heads.

Then again, she'd known from childhood that fairy tales didn't come true. Past time to stop pretending they did.

Feeling calmer than she had in a long while, she joined Wolf at the door.

If she couldn't have his love, at least she could have *him*.

~:~:~

Matt wasn't surprised to find Wolf at Laurette's, though he'd wanted to talk with her alone. Unfortunately, Wolf clearly had no intention of leaving her side, his stiff body language exuding fury. Meanwhile, his fiancée avoided looking at him, but also seemed determined to stay close.

Matt cleared his throat. "Sorry to come so early. I need to speak with you both."

"Of course." Wolf held the door wide as Matt entered.

"I'm making coffee," Laurette offered.

"Thanks." She went to the kitchen and Matt faced Wolf. "I'm sorry. I didn't enjoy lying to you all this time."

Wolf shrugged with supreme indifference. "I do not blame you. We are all loyal to Roland, however unreasonable he may be."

"He had her best interests at heart."

Wolf's lips twisted cynically. "Perhaps. It was clever, hiding her in plain sight. I wasted much time searching more obscure locales first. But in the end, I *did* locate her."

Unease vibrated in Matt's gut. Wolf radiated hurt pride, and if he'd pissed a circle around Laurette, his intent couldn't have been more clear. Roland might have done more damage than he knew by taking Wolf's fiancée from him. For one thing, a heavy hand only made Laurette retreat more. Which Wolf knew. But Roland's scheme had gotten Wolf's hackles up, perhaps so much that he no longer cared if her delicate feelings were destroyed in the crossfire.

Matt watched as she poured the coffee. Her hands shook, and she seemed only marginally aware of her actions. Perhaps it was Wolf he should speak with, after all.

He met Wolf's steady gaze and lowered his voice. "Roland believed that the fewer people who knew her location, the safer she would be."

"And you agreed?" Wolf asked, also quietly. "You felt she was in such danger that even *I* could not be trusted? Or perhaps you think I *am* her worst danger."

This wasn't going well. Their shared experiences— protecting Roland, then recovering from their wounds together in his castle—had bonded them. Matt had to believe Wolf would calm down once this was resolved and Laurette was home safe. Then again, did Matt really know him, beyond the public face he put on for Roland's court?

Either way, the focus now had to be on Celia and the other missing women. "Speaking of which, care to tell me your version of how your ring ended up at Celia's?"

Wolf sank into one of the suite's velvet wingback chairs in the living area, more tired than Matt had ever seen him. "I am afraid I must apologize for my behavior. This has been more difficult than I thought it would be."

"What?" Matt sat as well. "Being questioned by the police? Confronting Laurette? Taking it out on me?"

Wolf smiled ruefully. "All of it." His gaze moved to Laurette, who lifted the coffee tray and came toward them. Intense hunger mixed with pain flashed in Wolf's eyes before he shuttered them again.

First Darlene and Isaac, now this.

Matt stopped the thought in its tracks. Not his business,

no matter what Allie said about "his" women. Thinking of her sent a surge of hunger through him, too, but he quelled it. Later. He'd get her alone and finish what they'd started. Maybe more than once. He was up for it if she was.

Back on topic. "About the ring."

The tray slipped in Laurette's hands, hot liquid sloshing over the cup rims. "I'm sorry!" She set the tray on the coffee table and reached for a napkin, but Wolf stayed her hand.

"I will take care of it. You must sit and do nothing."

She went even whiter, but she sat beside him, and Matt felt again like he'd landed in an emotional minefield.

Wolf said, "I am not sure when I lost the ring. I have not worn it much since the attempt on Roland's life."

"Do you have any idea at all when you last had it?"

"Come, my friend." Wolf's tone was mocking. "This will get us nowhere. I can say anything—I wore it to a state event last month, or I have not had it for two years—it matters not. It is my word only, with no proof."

Laurette's hands fisted at her sides. "Surely there's a photo of you wearing it, to prove when you had it?"

"Sweet. Do not concern yourself."

"But it *does* concern me—"

"Touching. I am glad my reputation matters to you."

"I was thinking of *you*, not your reputation."

Wolf made a frustrated sound and shoved a hand through his hair. "Perhaps we should let Matt ask his questions, so this can be resolved and we are free to go."

"Fine," she said stiffly. "Besides, I'm late for work."

Wolf's eyes flashed. "I understood you were no longer playing a part in the park."

"You know about *that* too…?"

"Of course. Since you were a child, I have known of your fairy-tale fantasies. But you are done with that, yes?"

Laurette stared at her hands, twisting them in her lap. Then she drew a shuddering breath. "No. Well, yes. Tarek won't let me suit up. But I'm not done working at the park. I'm starting at The Princess Shoppe today."

Her announcement seemed to strike Wolf momentarily speechless. Then his lips thinned. "Sweet, we discussed this. It is time to come home."

"No. I'll leave at the end of the summer, not before."

Until she'd asked—no, *demanded*—that Tarek let her work in the Shoppe, Matt had never seen her do anything but comply. With Roland, Wolf, Tarek, even himself. Unfortunately, she'd picked a bad time to grow a backbone.

Wolf went dangerously still. Between being interrogated by the police and having to cross two continents and an ocean, chasing down his fiancée, he was clearly not in the mood to be crossed.

"Sweet. There is no need for you to remain here. Tarek will find someone else to work in this shop. However, there is great need for you at home. In a matter of weeks, Roland will announce the legislation making it legal for you to succeed him. You *must* be at his side for it to pass. Your people must see you for the leader you are."

Her cheeks bloomed red with anger. "Why bother? When we're married, everyone will know both thrones are ruled by you, Ruedi's *and* Luradel's."

Wolf's eyes widened. "What has given you the idea that I wish to rule in your stead?"

They were off course, and maybe a redirect would help them cool off. Matt broke in, "How well do either of you know Roland's other guards? Any recent turnover?"

Wolf shot him a sardonic look. "I have not been much in Roland's court of late. Too occupied with other things."

He meant, *Hunting my woman,* but Matt let it slide.

Laurette said, "No one has left that I know of. Why?"

"Just thinking who'd have access to Wolf's ring and understand its significance."

"Doesn't everyone know why Roland gives them out?"

Wolf shook his head. "The people know nothing of them. It seems obvious to you, because the dozen or so men he bestowed the rings on are also the only men your father entrusts with your care, and you know us all."

"How archaic," Laurette muttered. "Snow White and her Dozen Armed Guards."

"Precisely my point," Matt said before her backbone jabbed any farther into Wolf's ego. He took an envelope from his pocket. "Would you go over these photos, see if anyone leaps out as having a grudge against Wolf? He checked them last night, but maybe you'll find something."

"Of course." Laurette took the envelope and stood. "Now, if you'll excuse me, I have to get ready."

Wolf rose also, and Matt followed suit, waiting politely for her to leave the room before making his own escape.

At least Wolf's Old-World courtesy prevented him from clubbing Laurette on the head and dragging her off to his cave in front of Matt. Hopefully, he wouldn't do it when they were alone, either. But maybe Matt would check on her later, just to be safe. Much as he liked Wolf, he didn't like where this was heading. And the bulk of the blame for that could be laid right at Roland's door.

Families.

Thank God Matt knew how to keep his own at bay.

Chapter Nineteen

"Allie?"

Allie's hand slipped, dragging a swath of mascara across her cheek. Which perfectly summed up the past two days. Ever since Celia had disappeared, and Prince Wolfram the Umpteenth showed up, everyone was on edge, and the case had one black mark on it after another. On Wednesday, she'd barely seen Matt or any other friendly faces, while being forced to spend another fruitless day walking the park. And here it was Thursday already, just as stifling hot as ever, and starting out just as unproductively.

In the mirror, a contrite Darlene stood behind her in the dressing room doorway. "I'm so sorry! I should have waited until you were done."

"It's fine." Allie grabbed a tissue and dipped it in makeup remover, then wiped at the smear, taking off her meticulously applied foundation and blush as well. As if she actually knew how to use all this gunk. "Urgh!"

"It's my fault. Let me help." Darlene crossed the room, dropping her purse on the table, then took the tissue from Allie. Expertly, she dabbed the mascara away, all the while blending the foundation back into place. She picked up the tin of blush and a brush, gently dusting Allie's cheek, then stepped back to admire her work. "Perfect!"

Allie looked in the mirror and had to agree. The right side of her face now glowed, the foundation hiding her freckles and leaving her complexion clear, the blush so delicately applied, no one would know it wasn't natural.

The left side was a different story. Not terrible, exactly, but compared to Darlene's pro job, definitely minor league. She couldn't suppress a sigh of despair. "Did you go to makeup school for that?"

Darlene smiled. "No, but I've got four older sisters. If you didn't learn Lipstick 101 by the fifth grade, you were excommunicated."

"Tough crowd."

"Yes." She hesitated, then said on a rush, "I don't want to overstep, but would you like some help with your makeup today?" Allie started to shout a heartfelt, *Yes!*, but Darlene hurried on. "I really don't mind, and I was going to ask you for a favor, anyway, so this would be a way I could sort of pre-pay you."

Allie paused. She already had her hands full, and Tarek was right: she *should* have found a clue or two by now. And though Matt remained supportive, he was antsy, too, wanting to be done with Roland and get on with his life.

The whole park had a figurative cloud over it. The media were having a field day, cast members and staff were on edge, and no one knew if the net effect would be bad for business, or, morbidly, bring an increase in visitors.

She said to Darlene, "Sure. Um, what can I do for you?"

"My bridal shower is today. It's a formal tea—really a dinner—at the Sofia Hotel in San Diego. It's silly to care, but we had a last-minute cancellation. My great-aunt Lula. She's over a hundred, but she was going to come, just to piss off her baby sister. *She's* only ninety-nine, and they haven't spoken in twenty years, despite living in the same nursing home. But now she—Lula—says she can't miss Bunco night, and we have an empty place. It's all paid for, no refunds, and I thought, you know, maybe if you came, Matt wouldn't go bonkers being the only guy there."

Allie stared, unsure which piece of insanity to address first. "Matt's attending your all-girl bridal shower?"

"Of course. He's the maid of honor."

A choking, gurgling noise came from Allie's throat, and she fought to swallow it before the mirth boiled over.

Darlene said cheerfully, "Oh, I know. Terrible, aren't I? But I couldn't choose one of my sisters as maid of honor, and have the rest be bridesmaids. So I picked Matt. It was sort of a joke at first, but I think he's warmed to the idea."

If by "warmed," Darlene meant Matt had stopped wanting to kill her at some point, Allie thought she might be right. Plus, this might be Allie's one chance to view him in his native habitat: not just surrounded by his women, but in charge of an all-female event. It was too good to pass up.

"Sure. I'll come."

"Great!" Darlene sounded genuinely pleased. "And don't bring a gift or anything. You saw our place—we have way more stuff than we'll ever be able to fit in the new house. Assuming Matt can ever find the time to finish it."

"Oh, wait—I don't have anything to wear."

"No problem. I already talked to Laurette, and she has just the dress for you."

Allie pictured Laurette's tiny, fine-boned elegance. "I don't think I'm her size."

Darlene laughed. "No one is. But this dress is at The Princess Shoppe. It's a short cocktail number. She's gifting it to you, as thanks for taking care of her on Tuesday night."

Allie started to object, but Darlene said, "If there's one area where Laurette won't budge, it's buying presents for people she likes."

"Okay. But there is one more thing. My car's still out of commission. I'm sure Matt's too busy as, er, hostess with the mostess, to spend hours chauffeuring me around."

"Also Laurette. Come to her room at five, and she'll help you get dressed, then whisk you away to the ball."

"My very own fairy godmother?"

"Exactly. Except her car's way better than a pumpkin on wheels. And speaking of magical transformations…"

She chose a sponge and began dabbing foundation on Allie's face, talking all the while, which could have been annoying. But Darlene offered a rare glimpse into Matt's world, and Allie couldn't resist a peek.

For instance, she learned Darlene and Isaac were Matt's first remodel clients, their home a showcase to draw in more. In fact, he already had others ready to bite, but his work at the park had caused so many delays, his reputation could be ruined before he got the business off the ground.

No wonder he was frustrated. But she had also begun to understand why he couldn't let go. She'd seen him with Laurette, heard his rushed words to Wolf before the police took him away, and knew the thought of Phil in danger scared him silly. His responsibilities weighed on him, because he cared deeply about each and every one of them.

An image of Matt, eyes heavy with desire, watching her naked body as she writhed in ecstasy at his touch sent fiery heat tingling all through her, and she bit back a groan.

She didn't want to want him. Except it was more than simple lust; she didn't want to *like* him. Yet she was desperately afraid she'd already boarded that ride, and now she couldn't get off. She also didn't want to like Darlene, or Isaac, or hear about Great-Aunt Lula and her nearly-a-century-old "baby" sister. What had she gotten herself into?

I'll find the missing women, get my check, and go back to San Francisco. End of story.

So why did that happy ending suddenly leave her hollow and unsatisfied? Giving herself a mental shake, she focused on her potted plants, her soon-to-be garden, the picket fence she'd put up to keep the dog in. When she got a dog. Which would be shortly after getting a cat, which would be right after moving in. To her house. *Her house.*

Case. Check. House.

Better.

Darlene stepped back. "I think you're ready."

"As I'll ever be," Allie said and rose, turning her back on the damning mirror. Time to face reality.

And Southern California was definitely not reality.

Laurette sat behind the counter at The Princess Shoppe during a lull in the midday crush and was amazed to discover that, after only two days, she was in her element. She was actually *good* at taking ordinary people and reinventing them in the period fairy tales of their choice. A few had even tried to tip her in appreciation, though of course she'd declined.

True, she'd been utterly terrified before her first shift yesterday, but some of that was due to her encounters with Wolf. First, there were his kisses, a far better reality than any fairy-tale fantasy she'd ever had. Then came the argument about her working, and finally, her insistence that she'd stay two more months. Even she was surprised by the determination that welled up.

On top of all that was worry about the ring and what would happen if the police began to seriously consider Wolf a suspect. Which he was *not*. Except… He'd never been this angry before. Not just with her, but in general. He'd been tightly strung all yesterday morning, and that second kiss…

Self-consciously, she touched her lips, remembering the pleasure of his mouth on hers, the pain of wanting the emotions to be real. Afterwards, he'd seemed shocked by his own behavior. He was strong. Proud. Fierce.

But, like Tarek, always controlled. What had made him snap? Was it the thought that she might not come home to him at all? He had to know she would, eventually.

And yet… What if marriage hurt their friendship? Could she spend her life with him, without at least that tiny lifeline to cling to?

She hadn't seen him since yesterday morning. Presumably he'd gone home to…somewhere near Mecca, she supposed. But was he avoiding her out of anger, or trying to give her space?

She blew out a breath, and took the photos Matt had given her from the shelf where she'd stashed them. She'd been poring over them for two days, whenever she had a moment. If nothing else, they got her mind off her emotions and back on something practical. She had yet to find anything unusual, but one more round couldn't hurt.

Many were HR headshots, but there were candid photos as well, taken of the guards at palace events or relaxing at the end of the day. She set aside the portraits, then shuffled the candids before laying them out randomly on the counter, a trick she'd learned when first put in charge of seating for a palace dinner. By mixing and remixing the seat cards, she got a fresh perspective on how the tables would flow, and how the guests would relate to each other.

She was on her third pass when something finally leapt out at her. *That's odd. What he's doing there?*

She reached for her cell and dialed, but the call went to voicemail, and she hung up without leaving a message. She replaced the photos in their envelope, then grabbed the bag with Allie's dress in it and clocked out. She waved good-bye to Meggy, then took the tunnels to the employee complex. If Matt was around she'd tell him. Or maybe Allie would know what to do. There was really no rush. The photo was three years old; surely it wasn't important.

~:~:~

"You are getting careless."

The boss was displeased, and when that happened, things went south. Not that they'd been going well anyway.

"The delay in taking Celia—the mess you left behind— all these make me wonder what I am paying you for."

"I can do better! Let me take *her*."

The boss paused, considering. "Perhaps it is time. I am tired of waiting on her fantasies. But if you fail…"

"I won't fail."

Another pause. "Very well."

The line went dead, and adrenaline and lust pulsed through Wafi.

It was time. What began with her would end with her. *Yes.*

~:~:~

"Come on," Phil's dad said, poking his head in at her door. "We're going to be late."

The room suddenly felt too small, cluttered with ancient furniture and even older carpeting. Their whole apartment was too small—a downstairs unit on the back side of your basic two-story rectangle. It was super close to the park, which was its only advantage. But that meant it was also on the local business strip, so no matter where Phil went, she had to bike past liquor stores, tattoo parlors, even a "lingerie modeling" business or two.

All that paled, however, in comparison to the ten-foot trip she was about to make now. There was no hope for it. Unless she wanted to miss Darlene's shower, she'd have to stand up, walk to her dad, and ride with him in the smelly old Buick for at least an hour and a half both ways.

Except for the occasional school lesson, she couldn't remember the last time they'd spent such "quality" time together. Mainly because she'd avoided it like the plague.

But first, the runway walk from hell.

Slowly she rose and moved toward him, keeping her head down so she wouldn't have to see his reaction. She heard his quick inhale, though, and could practically feel the emotions rolling off of him in waves.

"Phil—baby—you're so beautiful."

His voice was thick, like he fought back tears, and despite herself, she looked up. Sure enough, his eyes were shiny and wet, and his lip trembled. Today he wore a simple strapless lemon organza dress and matching low-heeled silk pumps, which she had to admit, with his light hair and skin, was pretty flattering.

Phil clenched her jaw and tried to squeeze past him.

"Honey, let me look at you."

He gripped her shoulders, but Phil shrugged out of his grasp. "What's the big deal? You bought me the dress."

She tried to pretend it didn't matter, but it did. Ever since they'd gone to the police station after what happened at Celia's, her dad had been walking on eggshells around her. She didn't need his guilt; that didn't make up for everything else. Plus, it wasn't even about making her feel better, it was about *him* feeling better.

And the *way* he'd done it—that was the worst. He'd *finally* listened when she said she wanted a dress from The Princess Shoppe. But instead of letting her pick it out, he'd chosen it for her. The dress wasn't even ugly, exactly. It just wasn't *her*. He so totally missed the point: she wanted to recreate *herself*. She didn't want *him* doing. Bad enough he'd done it the first time.

He reluctantly let her go, standing back to admire her

buttery yellow dress—also organza—how *cute*—they *matched*—covered with a layer of pale lemon tulle dotted with gold silk flowers. It was sleeveless with a super poufy skirt, and he'd bought her white patent-leather shoes that looked like they belonged on a first grader.

At least he could've picked a better color. Yellow made her skin sallow, and with her big dark-framed glasses, she probably resembled some freak-show giant moth.

"Can we just go now? Didn't you say we're late?"

Didi sighed and stepped aside, then followed her out of the apartment. Phil waited by the Buick while he unlocked her door. If only the stupid car didn't smell so bad. She should have brought perfume or something. Her dad probably had some in his purse, but never in a million years would she ask to borrow his perfume. Ick.

She aimed a kick at one of the whitewall tires, taking mild satisfaction in the dirty smear it left on her shoe. "You could let me drive."

Didi raised a startled gaze to hers. "Honey, you know I can't. Here in the parking lot—even down the block to the store—that's different. But you're twelve. I shouldn't even have started teaching you."

"In Alaska, you can get a permit when you're fourteen. Maybe even thirteen and a half."

"We're not in Alaska. And you're still twelve."

"Whatever."

She wrenched her door open, half hoping it would fall off the way Allie's had, thereby forcing them to get a rental—a nice, shiny *new* one. The door stayed firmly attached, however—the car was a *tank*—and she slid onto the ratty vinyl front seat. It was a bench, the Buick coming from an era of big families, big houses, and even bigger cars. She would've ridden in the back except the only shoulder belts were in the front, and they'd be on the freeway for most of the drive.

At least the seat was so huge, she wasn't near her dad. He started the engine, louder than ever, while she cranked her window down. Even so, the smell of motor oil was so strong, she gagged.

"I hate this car," she said suddenly, kind of surprised herself that she'd spoken. Didi glanced her way, and she scrunched toward the window.

"I'm sorry, honey. I wish we could afford a better one. Maybe after the operation…" His voice trailed off as he realized he'd said the wrong thing.

Phil couldn't stop herself. That was happening a lot lately, but right now, she didn't care. "You and your stupid operation! That's why we have to live in that stupid apartment, why we have this horrible car. Everything is horrible, just so you can save money for your *operation!*"

"Phil—"

"I hate it here! Why can't we live some place normal, like San Diego?"

Big surprise. She'd shocked him into silence. But it was only temporary.

"I thought you loved it out here. You know I'd like to take you to San Diego with me eventually. But I thought you wanted to be here. That's why I've stayed so long."

Tears choked her and she turned as far away as she could. She *did* love it here. She *didn't* want to leave. But everything was changing. Not just her dad, who couldn't change more if he grew a second head. Also the park, which overnight had gone from safe haven to dark and dangerous. And Laurette, who had a *fiancé* she hadn't told Phil about.

And Matt—she was losing Matt. She knew it, and there wasn't a damn thing she could do to stop it. She'd tried many times over the last few days to get him alone, so she could tell him about Gillian and Wolf at the park on Tuesday. She wasn't even sure why she hadn't told the police about it, except that Gillian was Matt's ex, and Wolf was his friend, and she thought he should know before the cops did. But Matt was always busy, with the case, or the wedding, or with *Allie*. He never had time for Phil anymore.

Maybe it was time to leave Mecca. It would be easier on her dad in a bigger city, with more diversity, where he'd be known only as Didi, not the woman who used to be Diedrich. Even Phil might like it better some place with more culture than a failing theme park, a nasty-smelling lake, and a bunch of date farms.

But this was her *home*. How could she leave the only place she'd ever known? The place where her parents had raised her together? The place where, later, her mother had died? She couldn't leave GrimmLand and Matt, who'd helped her through everything. He'd *say* they'd stay in touch, but when he didn't see her every day, he'd forget all about her.

Phil bit her lip, hard, the tears rolling out, fierce and silent, praying her dad would just drive and not talk any more. She really couldn't bear it if he was sensitive.

Chapter Twenty

"Darlene," Matt said dangerously. "What did you do?"

The bride-to-be turned from greeting various aunts and great-aunts to frown at him. "What?"

"That." He gestured to the flowered arch that formed the entrance to the tea room, and Darlene glanced over at it.

"Oh. That. I thought she'd have fun."

Her cheeks were pink, and she avoided his gaze. When this was over, he was going to strangle her once and for all. Poor Isaac, to be a widower so soon after getting married. But it couldn't be helped. Darlene had to die.

The shower had started off surprisingly well. The Sofia staff had outdone themselves with the decorations, using the cream and dusty rose tones Matt requested based on Darlene's color scheme. They'd also followed his instructions on the flowers: tea roses in delicate sprays, and larger arrangements of calla lilies, jasmine, ribbons, and lace. He'd known Darlene would love the old-fashioned feel. Of all his sisters, she was the most traditional.

Now, thirty minutes in, the women were chatting in groups, sipping cocktails and eating appetizers, waiting for the stragglers to arrive before being seated for dinner. Since the invitations did indeed specify high tea, everyone wore afternoon formal wear, relieving Darlene of her worst nightmare. Or at least, today's worst nightmare. She had many more stored up that she shared with Matt whenever he was in earshot. Which he tried not to be.

In short, the event was a roaring success, and Matt

hadn't even called on Didi for reinforcements. She'd arrived with a sulky Phil in tow, but Matt had barely gotten a glimpse of the poufy dress Phil wore before she ran off into the crowd. Despite her obsession with the Shoppe, the dress was too young and girly for her, and Matt wondered if Didi'd chosen it. She watched Phil disappear, then shrugged at Matt like it didn't matter. He knew how much it did, and spent his time when not reassuring Darlene, in trying to reunite Phil with her father, if only for tonight.

But even with that minor glitch, things were going really well, until Darlene's no good, underhanded deed became public, and Matt's sister's bridal shower suddenly became *his* worst nightmare.

Well, maybe that was an exaggeration.

He had to admit, he wasn't entirely disappointed Allie was here, even if Darlene had gone against his express wishes by inviting her. But he'd barely seen her in the last two days, so now that she stood under the archway in a sexy, form-fitting little green dress and five-inch heels, his libido kicked into overdrive, and all the reasons why he didn't want to mix his work, family, and personal life went right out the window.

Silky and clinging to her curves, the dress was so short, it skimmed her thighs well above the knee. Her calves sloped down to those ultra-high, black-strapped sandals, and her toned arms were bare, thanks to the dress's thin spaghetti straps. Matt nearly groaned at the hint of cleavage displayed for his viewing pleasure, thankful his slacks were loose enough to accommodate his body's reaction.

Darlene said innocently, "I'm swamped here. Can you go greet her?"

Greeting Allie was only the first of many things he intended doing to her, but his sneaky sister didn't need to know that.

"This isn't over," he said darkly, and stalked toward the archway where Allie stood, looking uncertainly around.

Her gaze met his undoubtedly heated one, and a blush stained her cheeks and flushed the tops of her breasts. He had to stop thinking about her chest, and shifted his focus farther north. She'd done something with her hair—softened it somehow, so it curled delicately around her ears and jaw, a few pieces falling below her brows. He wanted to thrust his fingers through it, tilt her head back, kiss her lush mouth, taste her jaw and neck with his tongue. Which brought him right back down to her breasts.

Disgusted with his own one-track mind, he gave in to the inevitable.

"Hi," Allie began, then squeaked when he grabbed her elbow and dragged her back through the Sofia's lobby, out the front doors, and around the side of the building to a vacant gazebo.

She tried again. "Darlene invited me—"

"I know," he muttered, moving her out of sight of any passersby. He laced his fingers with hers, pushing her against a latticed wall, enjoying the softness of her against his chest, the hardness of his body on hers.

Her emerald eyes, the same shade as the dress she wore, darkened. "Oh. I thought—"

"I know," he interrupted again. "Stop talking. We only have a minute. Which is about all I need." He kissed her, taking her bottom lip between his teeth and teasing it until she moaned.

Her fingers tightened around his, hanging on for support as her knees gave way between them. He pressed into her, tasting her mouth with his tongue, then released her hands to slide his down her bare shoulders and over the tops of her breasts. Her skin was warm and smooth, her own tongue entwining sensuously with his, and he dropped one hand to her hem, pushing it roughly up to explore her thigh and the curve of her rear.

"Matt!" she gasped. But since her hands were sliding down his chest when she said it, heading for his waistband and points below, he figured it was less a protest than an encouragement.

He had one hand inside her strapless bra, the other sliding under the thin silk of her thong, while her hands were busy pulling his shirt free and reaching into his trousers, *right* where he wanted them, when the sound of nearby laughter brought him back to his senses.

"Damn it!" He broke the kiss, then leaned his forehead on hers, waiting as their breathing slowed. He pulled her dress back down and checked that her cleavage was properly covered. "Sorry."

"Don't be." Her lids were heavy with desire, mouth plump and luscious from his kisses, and she clung to the gazebo wall as though she couldn't stand on her own.

He grinned down at her. "Not about what we did. About having to stop." He reached for his shirt, then swatted her hands when she tried to help tuck it in. "I'll do it. If you go anywhere near me right now, I'll embarrass myself, and I don't have an extra pair of pants."

She laughed and he drew her close and kissed her again anyway, then took her hand and walked her back to the tea room. "How did you get here? Tarek said the mechanics still have your car."

"Laurette drove me. Which reminds me—she noticed something in those photos you gave her. A guy in the background of one. Looks like he's talking to Wolf."

"In the background?"

"Yeah. Her second cousin, Bernard—Tarek's father, right? He's the main subject of the photo, but Wolf is behind him, near this other guy."

The uneasy feeling prickled in Matt's gut again. He'd been so busy with the shower, he hadn't given much thought to the problem of Wolf and Laurette. "She gave you a ride? Where is she?"

"She stopped in the ladies' room when we walked in. Is something wrong?"

"I'm not sure." They'd reached the archway, and he took a minute to scan the room, noting with relief that Laurette was indeed present, whole and unharmed, chatting with Darlene. He felt a stab of disloyalty for thinking Wolf would ever harm her. On the other hand, Wolf had never been so on edge before, and Matt really had no idea what he was capable of when pushed.

Allie started to enter the fray, but Matt held her back. "Hang on a minute. Did Laurette say anything about the man in the photo? Why she thought it was significant?"

Allie shook her head. "She said she tried to talk to you about it, but you were already here. She showed me the photo, but it didn't mean anything to me. Just a group of Roland's men, with Wolf and this other guy in the back. She says he's not a ring bearer, or whatever you call yourselves, but she thinks he's been in the US since then."

"When?"

Her brow wrinkled. "Maybe a year ago? She's trying to remember, but she thinks it was at the park. Why don't you just ask her?"

"I will. But Darlene's shower isn't the place for a private conversation." The irony of their own total lack of privacy wasn't lost on Allie, and she quirked a brow in that *well, duh* way she had. He added, "Besides, I wanted to get your take on it first."

She seemed surprised by that. "Oh. Well, Laurette wasn't sure it mattered, since the photo's three years old."

"And you? Do you think it's important?"

He studied her, suddenly wishing they were back in the gazebo. Her eyes were wide, her expression clearly pleased at his interest. Which made his gut twist in a new, unexpected way. Hadn't anyone ever shown faith in her abilities? Given what Matt knew of Peerless and her father, he doubted it. But frenetic, messed-up life or not, Allie was smart and quick, and unlikely to miss the important stuff.

She said seriously, "I don't know. It's a little odd that he would be at Roland's court, and then at GrimmLand. But you yourself said there are a few people at the park who worked for Roland in Luradel first. It could be nothing."

"Or it could be something. I'll stop by Laurette's first thing tomorrow." He lifted a hand, lightly brushing her jaw. "I think maybe Tarek was right to hire you."

"What do you mean?" She sounded breathless again.

"Originally, he wanted Bobby because of his reputation for handling unusual cases. But I think you're the better choice for this job."

"Bobby? His mainstay is catching cheating husbands while simultaneously consoling their wives."

He trailed his fingers around the nape of her neck, tangling them in the soft wisps of her hair. "Bastard. I'd be happy to console you, if you need it."

Her nearness was far too distracting, and he forgot their conversation, the busy room nearby, the hotel staff, his responsibilities as the shower's host. He pulled her close, ignoring her surprise, and kissed her. He couldn't seem to stop kissing her—touching her—wanting her.

"Ahem."

Allie's oh-so hot, wet mouth pulled away from his, and she stepped back, flushed and dazed. Which was how Matt felt, until he turned to find Darlene and one of his most ancient great-aunts avidly watching them. Damn it—he had to stop groping Allie in plain sight, or his family would get the wrong idea. Whatever the *right* idea was.

Leave it alone, Wilcox. Not the time to think about it.

Darlene smiled brightly. "They're ready to seat for dinner. Since Allie will be next to her, I thought I'd introduce her to Aunt Lula."

"Great Aunt Lula?" Allie's tone was suddenly suspicious.

"Oops," Darlene said. "She made it after all. Yay! But we have tons of food, and I'm so thrilled you could come!" She faced Matt. "Can you walk them in? Thanks!"

She thrust Lula's elbow into his hand, then booked it.

Allie watched her go. "I think we've been had."

"No. Really?" He stole a peek at her cleavage again and privately conceded that Darlene's machinations weren't *all* bad.

"It's time to eat," Lula said loudly, rattling her metal walker. "You're supposed to walk us in."

"I know, Aunt Lula," he said loudly back, then whispered in Allie's ear, "What are you doing for dessert?"

Her breath caught and her lips curved, and she took his other arm, running her hand along it suggestively, as though stroking a different part of his anatomy.

Matt clamped her hand to his side, then led her and Lula at a wheeled-walker's pace into the dining room. "I'll get you for that," he murmured.

"I hope so."

This was going to be one long dinner.

Chapter Twenty-One

By the time the shower was over, Allie knew more than anyone should about Aunt Lula, her sister Lola, their feud, their various medical problems dating from the middle of the last century, and how many seconds an infant Matt could pee into the air while his harried parents tried to slap a diaper on him. She'd also met Matt's mother and his remaining four sisters, all of whom greeted her warmly and pretended not to be interested in her, while plying her with alcohol and personal questions in equal measure.

When dinner had ended, the gifts were all opened, and the Sofia staff were drowning in a sea of non-recyclable foil paper and bows, Allie was more than a little tipsy. Too tipsy for anyone as nice as Matt to take advantage of, which was a real pisser.

"Take me home?" she tried again, pressing her breasts against his chest. He liked that. She knew he liked it from the way his Adam's apple bobbed while his hands slid halfway up her sides before he got them back under control.

He sighed and kissed her forehead. "Even if you were sober, I can't. There's too much to do. I'll be here past midnight."

She tried to pout, which only made him laugh. Come to think of it, it was kind of funny, and she laughed, too.

Didi wandered up, looking dead tired and like she wanted to do anything but laugh. Probably because Phil had ignored her all evening.

She said, "Darlene can't fit all the presents in her car,

so she wants me to take the rest to their place in the Buick.”

Matt said, “I’d offer my car, but…”

“It only seats one and a half, and the Buick’s a whale. I know. I don’t mind, it’s just that I have Phil.”

“Maybe she could stay with Laurette?”

Didi shook her head. “I thought of that. But with Wolf and all… I know he’s not staying with her, but she’s got too much on her mind. I never thought I’d be a single parent. Especially not one raising the next Einstein, trapped in a twelve-year-old girl’s body. But then, there’s a lot of things I never thought would happen, and look at me now.”

Her tone was so heartbreakingly wistful, it made Allie want to help, even if only in a small way. “I’ll take her.”

“You will?” Matt sounded surprised.

“Sure. Why not? Tarek moved me to a room in the hotel so I’d have more people around and wouldn’t be right across from Celia’s. I have tons of space. And I’m sure Laurette won’t mind the extra passenger. Phil can spend the night and Didi can bring her bike over in the morning.”

Allie’s brain cautioned that, since Phil hadn’t previously been enthusiastic about interacting with her, she might not appreciate a forced sleepover now. But the alcoholic benevolence flowing through Allie’s veins, enhanced by Didi’s look of utter gratitude, trumped logic. It was a great idea. It was a fabulous idea. Her brain would get that, eventually.

Didi said, “Thank you! That’s a huge load off my mind. I’ll go find her.”

She left, and Matt said, “That was a nice thing you did.”

“We’ll see. Maybe you should check on us tomorrow, in case we don’t survive the night.”

“I’ll stop by after I go to Laurette’s,” he promised, and walked her to valet parking, where Laurette’s Volvo was just being brought around.

Didi wrangled Phil into submission in record time, and while she scowled at the sight of Matt's arms wrapped around Allie, she got into the backseat without protest. Laurette climbed in behind the wheel, and Allie tried to make herself leave the warmth of Matt's body. Fortunately, he had more fortitude, or they might have stood there all night. Maybe even necked some more. Which sounded like much more fun than a slumber party with Phil.

Matt gave her one last lingering kiss, so hot, she thought she'd melt right there on the pavement. Then he held her door, told Laurette to drive safely, and waved them off.

Laurette smiled. "You're good for him."

"He's certainly good for something." Allie pulled her ridiculous heels off and rested her feet on the dash. "But me for him?"

Laurette nodded. "Yes, very. He doesn't usually get emotionally involved."

Phil said, "They aren't involved!" at the same time that Allie protested, "Oh, we're not—"

Laurette lifted a brow pointedly. "By which I mean, when he's with a woman, he'll touch her occasionally, or take her arm to lead her to her seat. I've never seen him so unable to keep his hands off anyone before."

Behind them, Phil made a noise. It sounded like disgust, but though the alcohol was wearing off a bit, Allie had enough left in her system to be charitable and ignored her.

It was true, though. Matt had spent most of the evening touching her—caressing her arm, sliding a hand over her neck as he passed her chair, copping a feel on her bottom when he thought no one was looking. And then there were the half-dozen times he'd cornered her on the way to the ladies' or out for a breath of air, maneuvering her into one nook or another for a more intense, more private exploration of her mouth and body.

But surely Laurette was mistaken about what that meant. Of course Matt was turned on. Allie was new and different, and maybe Laurette had only seen him at the end of a relationship, when the magic wore off. Besides, *she* only wanted hot sex from *him*. Didn't she?

Before Allie became too uncomfortable with the direction of the conversation, Laurette switched gears. "I think I remembered where I saw the man in the photo."

"What man?" Phil asked, leaning forward.

Allie exchanged a look with Laurette. Though Phil was a GrimmLand "insider," Didi probably wouldn't want her to get even more involved in the case. But Allie didn't want to lie outright, so she settled on, "Just some photos Matt wanted Laurette to look at."

"You mean people who got Roland's ring."

"Oh. Well, yes."

"And?"

For once, she wasn't glaring daggers, and Allie made a snap decision, hoping she wouldn't regret it. "Laurette recognized a man in a photo of Bernard at Roland's court. She thinks he was in America last year."

"I saw him at Tarek's office," Laurette said. "I remember, because he was so unusual."

"Like how?" Phil asked excitedly. "Is he bald? Does he have a castle tattoo on his head?"

Laurette's jaw dropped. "How did you know that?"

"He's been wandering around GrimmLand. I *knew* he was up to something."

"Now wait a minute," Allie cautioned. "He could just be someone from Luradel who came to work at the park."

Laurette's brow wrinkled. "That's the weird part. I

swear Tarek said he was a delivery guy."

"If that's true," Phil said, "he's been delivering a lot lately. Only he never carries any packages, *and* why would he be in the park, not the employee complex? But if he's from Luradel, wouldn't Tarek know that?"

Allie'd thought the same thing and shared the answer she'd come up with. "Maybe not. From what I've heard, Tarek hasn't spent that much time at Roland's court."

"That's true," Laurette said. "Plus, we only have one photo of him. Maybe he only visited Luradel that one time."

"And was invited to a gathering of Roland's *closest* relatives?" Phil asked dubiously.

A new thought struck Allie. "Maybe he is from Luradel. And maybe he *was* a deliveryman, but now he works security. Matt told me they have people pretending to be tourists in the park, to keep an eye on things."

"Of course!" Laurette exclaimed. "That would explain a lot. If he's in Roland's inner circle, Matt must know him, and probably gave him a promotion after a few months. When Matt comes over tomorrow, I'll show him the photo, and I'm sure he'll straighten everything out."

Phil clearly wasn't happy, but she gave up the fight. Not long after, Allie glanced back and saw she'd fallen asleep.

Laurette said softly, "Poor kid. She's had a rough time."

"What? Didi's operation?"

"That, and other things. Her mom died a few years ago, after Didi came out as a woman. If it wasn't for Matt, I doubt she'd be as well-adjusted as she is." She paused, then said softly, "Sometimes, I wish Wolf was more like Matt."

Allie thought about Phil's hero worship and decided there was a lot of that going around. "In what way?"

Laurette was silent. Finally she said, "My mother also died when I was young, and I'm an only child. We have a tradition in Luradel, dating back to the feudal system. We foster children with other noble families as part of their education. My father offered to foster Wolf. We were close in age, and though our countries fought in the past, in recent decades we've been more peaceful. I think Roland thought having a playmate would be good for me."

"And was it?"

Laurette sighed. "Better than he could have imagined. I fell in love with Wolf. I thought someday he might return my feelings."

"But…?"

"Instead, I found out our parents had planned our engagement all along. He was there for political reasons from the start. Worse, he knew it."

"Ouch. Didn't you have any say in it?"

Laurette shrugged. "I suppose I could have refused. At first I was in shock. I couldn't think clearly. And then I still believed one day, Wolf might love me, and it would all work out. Now, I just don't know. We used to be best friends. Even knowing he didn't love me, I still loved him—loved being with him. But something changed. It's why I wanted to come here, to get away and think. Now, I don't know how to get things back to the way they were."

Allie tried to think of something to say to make her feel better. But the truth was, Allie had about as much experience with men as Laurette did. And she didn't know Wolf at all, so couldn't offer any personal insights into his character, let alone his emotions.

"My mother died, too," she said at last. "When I was seven. My dad did his best, but he was absorbed in his teaching. I think it's hard to trust in relationships when the first thing on your mind is basic survival. Losing a parent sends you into crisis mode, no matter how young or old you are. And being a girl, without a mother, you don't have anyone who really gets your emotions. Even the best dad in the world is still a guy."

Laurette gave a weak laugh. "You're right about that."

Allie hesitated, unsure about giving advice where she really had no business and no clue. "Do you trust Wolf?"

Without hesitation, Laurette said, "Yes."

"Then you should talk with him, tell him how you feel, give him a chance to respond. Maybe he feels the same way, but he's just as worried as you that if he makes a wrong move, he might lose you. Just because his parents want him to marry you doesn't mean he's not in love with you. Unless his country's laws are prehistoric, wouldn't he break it off rather than spend his life in a loveless marriage?"

Laurette stared at the road a long while, then whispered, "I'm such a fool." Her eyes shone with unshed tears in the freeway lights whipping past the car. "Thank you. I owe you more than a dress now."

~:~:~

In the backseat, Phil shifted her head against the window, swallowing back her own tears. *Again.* Allie and her dumb advice to Laurette. It'd made Phil think, for half a second, that she should talk with Didi. But Phil's dad was nothing like Laurette's fiancé. Her dad was a jerk, and he didn't care about her or her feelings. What did Allie know about it, anyway? Just because neither she nor Laurette *nor* Phil had a mother didn't make them alike.

But at least Allie'd included her when they were talking about the tattooed man. Maybe spending the night at her place wouldn't be so bad. Maybe Phil would even tell Allie about Wolf being at the park on Tuesday, since she still hadn't told Matt.

Phil's eyes drifted closed. She'd been pretending to be

asleep before, but now she was actually tired. It might be nice to relax and have a nap. She stretched, getting more comfy, and let the sounds of Allie's and Laurette's low voices lull her further.

Her last thought before drifting off was that the Volvo was a *much* smoother ride than the Buick. And not a whiff of motor oil.

~:~:~

Laurette helped carry a sleeping Phil into Allie's room at the GrimmLand Hotel, then rode the elevator up from Allie's floor to her suite. She let herself in, tossed her purse on a table, and went to the bedroom. She turned toward her closet—and froze, stifling a gasp.

He was there, on the balcony. She *knew* it was him—she'd finally recognized him. She could just make out his form through the sheer curtains, but she didn't think he knew she'd spied him. The door was too far away—if she moved toward it, he'd guess her intent and grab her before she escaped. Same with the hotel phone, sitting innocently on the table by the French doors, not two feet from him.

Had it come to this? Was this how it ended? How *she* ended—trapped, both by her love, and her inability to escape, to act, to guide her own destiny? Too late, she'd realized her own foolishness. Perhaps Roland had angered Wolf by hiding her away, but this—*this* was her fault, for being so lost in her own concerns, she'd missed what was right under her nose. Some leader she'd make.

No. It would not end this way. Not without a fight.

She reached for the tube of lipstick on the nearby vanity. If Hansel and Gretel could leave a trail, so could she. Then again, they were dealing with a witch, not a psychopath. And if Laurette had learned anything from fairy tales, it was that real-life terrors were much worse than mythical ones.

Heart pounding, she took a blank card from the table by the bed and opened the lipstick. She'd only managed one letter when a whisper of sound warned her that time had run out. Hastily, she dropped the card, praying he wouldn't notice it.

She lifted the lipstick, applying it, pretending she didn't know he was *there,* right behind her, until his rough arms snaked around her neck and he covered her mouth with a white cloth soaked in something vile.

Then Laurette did fight, tried to scream, to break his pinky or jab his eye, but he was too strong, the drugs too fast. In seconds, everything went horribly, hideously, nauseously black.

Chapter Twenty-Two

Allie woke to the sound of the TV in the front room. She rolled onto her side, noting the empty bed next to hers, its rumpled sheets the only sign Phil had slept there. She sat up, then clapped a hand to her woozy head. Too many cocktails. Too many Wilcox women.

She needed coffee. She smelled coffee.

She slid out of bed and made it to the kitchenette. Sure enough, Phil had fired up the coffeemaker. The final drops of water just now filtered through the grinds, popping and sputtering, topping off a pot full of fresh dark-brown goodness. Half-and-half and sweetener were laid out on the counter, between two of the hotel's over-sized mugs.

Allie contemplated Phil, sprawled on the couch. "I think I love you."

Phil stayed glued to the TV. "Matt said you like mochas. I would've made you one, but I was afraid it would get cold before you got up."

"This is perfect," Allie assured her, pouring a steaming mug. "Want one?"

"Sure. Black, please."

Allie doctored her own cup with plenty of white stuff, liquid and powdered, then carried the mugs to the couch and sat next to Phil, who, surprisingly, wasn't watching cartoons or even a morning "news-tainment" show. Instead, C-SPAN flickered on the screen, displaying a riveting example of government process at work. A notepad rested on Phil's knee, her pen poised to jot notes, and she seemed utterly enthralled by the image of a room full of people in somber suits, shuffling papers and occasionally commenting on some nifty piece of legislation.

Allie felt even more sympathy for Didi. It had to be hard, raising a preteen girl with post-menopausal interests.

The session wrapped and Phil made a few more notes, then clicked the TV off. "Sorry. Homework."

"Your dad homeschools you, right?"

She nodded, twisting her hands in the oversize t-shirt Allie had given her by way of pajamas.

"The schools around here are pretty basic. He wanted me to learn more than they could offer. Plus, you know, he's had a lot of life experience and stuff."

Something had changed. Phil wasn't as angry this morning, and Allie didn't want to ruin their détente. But she was also curious. "If you don't mind my asking, what did your dad do before working at the park?"

Phil shot her a dark look. "You mean, before he decided he was a woman?"

"Sorry. I shouldn't have asked."

Phil toyed with her pen. "No, it's okay. Well, it's totally weird. But it's okay to talk about it. If you want."

She looked so young, wearing her adult t-shirt, her congressional notes on her lap, a huge mug of coffee nearby. Allie fought the ache that tightened her chest, remembering her own too grown-up childhood.

After a minute, Phil said, "He was a jewel thief."

"Say what?"

"My dad. He was a world-class thief. He conned people, stole their stuff, and sold it on the black market. But unfortunately, he's reformed now."

Phil sounded so put out, Allie couldn't help it—she laughed. Luckily, Phil's mouth also quirked up.

Allie asked, "Why here, though? I mean, Mecca doesn't seem like fertile ground for rich folks with too many baubles on their hands."

"It's not. He was in Palm Springs, fleecing the retirement crowd, when he got drunk, hooked up with my mom, and wound up stuck here with me."

Ouch. "Didi loves you. She'd never regret having you."

"Yeah, sure. Every transgender wants to be stuck in the boonies, raising a kid alone." Phil stood and headed for the bathroom. "I better go brush my teeth. He'll be here soon."

Somehow, Allie'd said the wrong thing after all. She considered going after Phil, but that's what Didi did, and it usually backfired. But if she didn't try, Phil might think she didn't care. While she was debating, her phone rang.

"Allie? It's Kelly."

For a moment, the name didn't compute. Then she remembered. "Matt's sister?"

"Right! Sorry to call so early. You made it home okay?"

"Um, yes." What in the world could Matt's sister want?

"Great. I hope we weren't too overwhelming last night. We're a big clan, and maybe it was too much for you."

"No. It was fun. Really." Surprisingly, Allie found she meant it. She certainly wasn't used to the whole giant family gathering thing. But she'd enjoyed herself, and not just because of the free booze or Matt's wandering hands.

"Wonderful! Glad to hear it. Care to do it again?"

"Um…" Allie's insides went raw-oyster squishy again. Kelly sounded just like Darlene had before she'd launched into the Lula story.

"It's just that the rehearsal dinner is tonight. Everyone is paired off, all the bridesmaids with the groomsmen. Which is easy, because the bridesmaids are *married* to the groomsmen. But Matt's maid of honor, and the best man's married, so no pairing there."

Allie felt the hysteria bubbling, but Kelly was unstoppable. "Anyhoo, I thought if you were free, you could keep him company."

Allie took the phone away from her ear and squinted at it for a full ten seconds before trying to answer. "I appreciate the thought. But shouldn't Matt invite me himself? If he wants to, that is?"

"It won't occur to him until it's too late. But he won't mind. Why would he mind? It's settled, then. You'll come."

"No," Allie said firmly. "I'm sorry. I really appreciate the offer. But I don't want to intrude."

There was a beat of silent disappointment before Kelly said, "If you're sure. But if you change your mind, we'll be at Mission Basilica at four, then head to the restaurant."

They hung up, and Phil wandered out of the bathroom as someone knocked on the door. Allie eyed the peephole, then let Didi in. This morning, she wore jeans and sandals, her hair in a basic ponytail. She carried a paper bag which she set on a table as she greeted Phil. "I brought you some clothes, honey. And your bike. It's locked up downstairs with your helmet."

Phil didn't answer, so Allie said, "Thanks. There's coffee, if you'd like."

"Thank *you* for helping us out." Didi hesitated, watching Phil, then turned a sad gaze back to Allie. "I think I'll pass on the coffee. Have to get to the park." She walked to her daughter and hugged her. Phil didn't resist, but she didn't respond, either, and Allie's heart ached all the more.

"Okay, honey." Didi awkwardly let Phil go. "I'll be home later. Don't get in Allie's way."

"She's fine," Allie said. "We're fine. We'll have breakfast, then figure out the rest of the day."

Phil looked up, surprised, like she'd thought Allie would kick her out as soon as Didi showed up. "I can stay?"

"Sure," Allie said. "I don't have to be at the park until noon. We can veg for a bit, and then if you want, you can help me get dressed."

"Cool."

Phil sounded excited by the prospect, and Allie felt pretty good about the whole thing until she caught Didi's eye. Didi didn't say anything. She didn't have to. The fact that she would love to share her costuming experience with her daughter, but Phil had never wanted to, was written all over her face.

I'm sorry, Allie mouthed, but Didi only shrugged and let herself out. Fragile bond or not, Allie thought Phil could use a good, direct chat about Didi, parental love, and curbing the adolescent angst.

She opened her mouth, and her cell rang again.

Perhaps sensing an impending lecture, Phil grabbed it. "Hello…? No, it's Phil… Oh—hi, Nicole. What's up?" Phil froze, clutching the phone so tight her knuckles were white. "Yeah, she's right here. Hang on." She passed the phone to Allie, scowling. "It's Matt's sister."

Another Wilcox emissary? This couldn't be good.

"Hi, Allie, it's Nicole. We met last night at—"

"Of course. How could I forget?"

"Right." She sounded sheepish. "I'm sure you're busy, so I'll make this quick. It's about the rehearsal dinner—"

"No."

Nicole paused. "Excuse me?"

"Really. I'm flattered. But if Matt wants me there, he'll invite me himself."

Another pause. Then Nicole laughed, a nice, friendly sound. Allie really had liked Matt's sisters, but she couldn't invade his personal life. Not when he valued his privacy so much, and not when she'd be gone soon, anyway.

Nicole said, "I'm sorry. You must think we're terrible."

"No, I think it's wonderful you're looking out for Matt. And it's nice of you to ask, but I really can't come."

"Okay," Nicole said. "But maybe you and I could have lunch next week, just the two of us."

"Oh—sure. Maybe. I might be going home. I don't know what my plans are yet."

"I'll call you on Monday."

Allie hung up and turned to Phil, who made a face. Allie thought about ignoring it, then dove in. "What's with you?"

"Nothing."

"At least be honest. What's bugging you?"

Phil fidgeted, looking anywhere but at Allie before bursting out, "Why are Matt's sisters calling you?"

Allie started to shrug, then stopped herself. The easy answer was, to invite her to the rehearsal dinner. But Phil knew that, and the real answer wasn't easy. Then there was the question of whether this was any of Phil's business. Considering how much longer Phil had known Matt, Allie decided she had a right to know at least some of it.

"Because they love him and want him to be happy."

"They *like* you."

This was clearly an accusation, and Allie said cautiously, "I like them, too."

"Matt doesn't *want* his girlfriends and his family getting together. Especially not behind his back!"

"I'm not his—"

"Oh, yeah? Then why don't you just *leave him alone!*"

Phil grabbed the bag of clothes and slammed herself back into the bathroom. Which would really have been Allie's biggest hitch of the morning if the phone hadn't rung again a minute later, with Matt's sister Olivia on the line, and then again five minutes after that, with his sister Helen. By the time his mother called, Allie felt about as disgusted as Phil looked.

"I'm sorry, Mrs. Wilcox," she said, as Phil flopped on the couch, crossed her arms, and scowled some more. "It's very kind of you. But I really can't come tonight."

"What on earth are you talking about, dear?" Matt's mother said. "And please, call me Eliza."

"Oh. Sorry. I thought you were inviting me to Darlene's rehearsal dinner."

"Why, whatever made you think that?" Before Allie could completely die of embarrassment, Eliza continued blithely, "No, dear, I'm calling about the wedding."

"Urk."

"Pardon?"

Allie drew in a deep breath, held it, then blew it out. "Thank you so much, but I really couldn't intrude."

"It's at noon tomorrow. Mission Basilica San Diego de Alcala."

"I really don't think—"

"And don't feel you need to bring a gift. Matt told us you're having financial troubles."

That stopped her. "He did, did he?"

"Oh, don't worry. He told us all about how you're a little, well, *unstable* right now. A bit out of control. I'm sure it's nothing, and you'll be fine once you've settled down."

"Hmm." Allie compressed her lips. *Unstable, am I? Out of control?* "On second thought, Eliza, I'd love to come to your daughter's wedding. Thanks so much for inviting me."

Eliza practically beamed across the line. "Wonderful! Now, about that rehearsal dinner…"

The call from Matt's mother *really-really* would have

been Allie's biggest problem of the morning, except that right after they hung up, Matt himself called.

"I'm at Laurette's. Get up here now. And don't bring Phil."

~:~:~

"I am telling you—it is he!" Tarek said for the fourth time, and Matt resisted the urge to tell him to can it.

"Why would Wolf kidnap Laurette, let alone the other women?"

Tarek's voice was filled with scorn. "Did you not see the troubles between them? Perhaps she has finally refused him, and he has taken her to hold for ransom, or to force their marriage so that he can wrest the throne from Roland."

The theory wasn't as far-fetched as Matt would like. Laurette *had* run away, albeit partly at Roland's behest. And Wolf had been super-charged ever since arriving in America, a walking grenade with the pin pulled out. But despite the anger and his undeniable goal of uniting Luradel and Ruedi, Matt couldn't see him harming Laurette.

Besides, there was another gaping hole in Tarek's logic. "That still doesn't explain why he would take the others."

Tarek sniffed. "Perhaps he will sell them into slavery."

The thought was so absurd, Matt almost laughed. "No."

Tarek shrugged. "Perhaps not. Perhaps he is, how do you say, a copycat, and took only Laurette? For it *must* have been he who took her. You *cannot* deny the evidence, left by her own hand."

Matt blew out a frustrated breath. Allie, sitting nearby on the sofa, shook her head helplessly. "He has a point."

They were in Laurette's suite, waiting while the police finished up their initial examination of the evidence. Which consisted primarily of a white note card found on the floor by the bed, the name "WOLFRAM" scrawled on it in

Laurette's favorite red lipstick.

Wolf himself was MIA, but then, he'd kept a low profile since bursting on the scene three days ago. Matt had assumed he was cooling off, giving Laurette space. But he wasn't answering his phone, and though he was the Crown Prince of Ruedi, his bodyguards seemed to have misplaced him. Which might be circumstantial, but it looked bad. Really bad.

And on top of everything else, Darlene's rehearsal was this afternoon, and Matt had to be there. Unless he was dead. Which, under the circumstances, was tempting. If he faked his own death, just for the next two days… But if Darlene thought he was dead, she'd cancel the wedding, and he'd have to go through all the rigamarole again after resurrecting himself.

With a sigh he sped the *live on a desert island* fantasy on its way. Tomorrow, the wedding would be over and one set of responsibilities finished. Finding the missing women was still important. Finding Laurette was personal. Roland had entrusted her to Matt's care, even after Matt failed to catch his attempted assassin. It might even be the same guy, attacking the king now through his daughter, and making Matt's failure all the worse.

He touched his thigh where the scar tightened in tune with his rage and frustration. He wouldn't fail again.

Allie said sympathetically, "I don't know Wolf, but I agree, him kidnapping Laurette doesn't feel right."

"Why do you say that?"

Allie sat forward, biting her lower lip in a way that almost managed to distract him from the current situation. Now, if she would join him on that desert island… He dragged his gaze off her mouth and focused on her words.

"Laurette told me she's genuinely in love with him."

Allie turned pink. "I may have given her romantic advice."

Tarek flattened his lips. *"What* did you say to her?"

"I suggested she talk with Wolf, tell him how she feels. That kind of thing."

It was essentially what Matt had been saying for years, but Tarek looked aghast. "You drove her to him. How could you, when you can see how volatile he is?"

"First off, I *didn't* see him act violently. Second, for all she's been hiding out for the last few years, Laurette's a smart woman. She'd know if her best friend was a wacko."

Tarek remained unmoved. "What is the first thing said of a serial killer? That he was so kind and gentle. You see? It is Wolf. He took her."

Allie wasn't having it. "Actually, you just disproved your own point. You said Wolf *wasn't* kind and gentle. Ergo, he's not the kidnapper. Or at least, not a serial killer."

Tarek clenched his fists, then deliberately straightened his elegant fingers. "He is calculating. He knows what mask to wear for your benefit. As well, he knows the fairy tales and has followed Laurette's interests. Perhaps he is teaching her a lesson by arranging the kidnappings to mimic the stories over which she obsesses."

Unfortunately, he had another point. Matt said, "First, we need to find him. He might not even know she's gone."

It was almost noon, and Allie had to suit up soon. So far, no one had noticed she spent more time with Matt, Tarek, and the cops than the other cast members. But they couldn't keep chancing it.

"Is Roland coming?" she asked.

"No," Matt said. "He absolutely can't leave Luradel now. Their parliament is about to reconvene, and if he's not there, he can't pass the law allowing Laurette to inherit."

Tarek's jaw tightened. "Passing laws is the last thing

that should be on her father's mind while she is in danger."

Matt shrugged. "Maybe. But if he dropped everything to chase after her, we'd never keep it out of the news. No one wants this turning into an international incident."

A crime scene tech approached them. "We're done here. Nothing much to find. No fingerprints, no sign of forced entry. Either she let him in or he had a key."

She and the rest of the investigation team packed up their gear and left, and Matt, Tarek and Allie followed.

As they waited for the elevator, Allie asked suddenly, "Don't the elevators all have cameras?"

Tarek shook his head. "Only up to floor eighteen. The top two floors—private suites, such as Laurette's, and the penthouse above—have separate elevators, operated with special keys. We felt it unnecessary to install cameras, which some guests might regard as an invasion of privacy."

Allie thought about that. "Are there service elevators that go straight to the top?"

Tarek's eyes narrowed. "Of course. Card key access by employees only, which automatically logs each use."

"Why doesn't Laurette live in the penthouse?"

Tarek sniffed haughtily. "Roland wished it, but she insisted she did not need an entire floor, and we should save it for our high-paying guests." His tone suggested the park wasn't attracting many of those, so it was a moot point.

The elevator pinged open, and there stood Wolf, looking like the God of Fury, every muscle in his body tenser than a bomb expert faced with an explosive.

"Where is she?"

"I guess you heard," Matt said, then failed to duck before Wolf cold-cocked him.

Chapter Twenty-Three

"Does it hurt?" Darlene asked, examining the puffy, virulent, black-green-blue mark covering Matt's left eye.

Matt shook his head, then winced. "Okay, a little."

All things considered, she'd taken her maid of honor's "blemish" in stride. They were at the parish in one of the gathering rooms, ready to start the rehearsal. Except the mother of the bride, notoriously late, had yet to arrive.

Darlene frowned. "I still don't get why Wolf hit you. He doesn't think you took Laurette, does he?"

"He wasn't thinking at all. He was feeling. Pissed."

"I get that. But why at you?"

"I was supposed to protect her. That's why I've stayed at the park, remember? He has every right to blame me."

"Hmm." Which was all of his sisters' polite way of calling him an idiot. "At least you know he didn't take her."

"Because?"

"If he had, wouldn't he play it cool? Instead of decking you?" She peered critically at the bruise. "Maybe it will fade by tomorrow. Or, with a little makeup—"

"No makeup."

"But—"

"*No makeup.* Jeez, Darlene. Next thing you'll be telling me I have to wear a dress after all."

"Fine. Stand up in front of the congregation *and* be in all the photos, with a big purple cabbage on your eye."

Matt's dad wandered up. If he was stressed by the fact that his youngest daughter was getting married in a day, he didn't show it. But he'd always been unflappable. With six women in the house, he'd developed a thick skin. Now that he was retired, with all his children moved out, he spent his days at the golf course and his nights watching sports.

Lucky bastard.

As though reading Matt's thoughts, his dad clapped him on the shoulder and smiled sympathetically. "Your mother called. She said something about traffic and having to pick something up. She'll be here soon."

He wandered off again—no last-minute wedding details gnawing at him, no errands to run, or missing princesses to find—nothing whatever to do, except show up in a suit, walk Darlene down the aisle, and head back to the green.

When this is over, that will be me. And if it never ends…

He shoved the thought away as his cell rang with a San Francisco area code. He answered it, and the caller said, "Matt, it's Bobby Peerless. Allie's ex—boss."

The deliberate hesitation wasn't lost on Matt. On the other hand, the asshole was slimier than slug guts, and not worth the trouble. "What do you want?"

He checked his watch. Even Father Don, now chatting with Matt's dad, appeared to be losing his priestly patience.

Peerless said, "Allie's landlord is trying to reach her. He left a message on her cell, but he's covering all bases, and I'm listed as her employer. I left a message at the resort, but I still had your card, so I thought I'd give it a shot."

"Got it. I'll make sure she knows. Anything else?"

"How's it going down there? Allie doing good work?"

Peerless's tone was…intentional, and Matt's guard went up. "What do you care? As noted, you're her *ex*-boss."

"Just asking. You know, she can be a little scattered."

Prick. Still, know thine enemy, learn their weaknesses, find out what they want, *before* they try to get it from you.

"In what way?"

"She's just a little…schizo…sometimes."

Matt waited, knowing Peerless wouldn't be able to stand the silence, and sure enough, a few seconds later the jerk said, "She ever tell you about the police department?"

"What about it?"

"Not sure I should say anything…"

"Cut the crap, Peerless. Spit it out."

"If you insist. When we met, she was in community college for criminal justice. Wanted to get on at SFPD. The test came up, and she failed, but only by a little. She figured she knew why, and when the next test came, she answered along different lines, on purpose."

"And…?"

"She failed again. Only this time, her score came out *way* down. Practically branded her a psycho."

He seemed to think this was funny. Matt thought it was a good thing they were hundreds of miles apart, or Peerless's face might have been on the receiving end of Matt's fist. Come to think of it, taking a leaf from Wolf's book and pummeling his frustrations out on a piece of pond scum like Peerless sounded like a really good idea.

Instead he said, "Was there a point to all this?"

"Just thought you should know who you're working with. Don't get me wrong. She's great at tailing the unfaithful. But a big case like this? If you change your mind, I'd be happy to help you out."

"I'll keep that in mind." There was a flurry of activity at the door: his mother had finally arrived. "Got to go." He hung up on Peerless's good-bye, muttering, "Asshole."

Darlene, standing next to him, said, "Don't shoot the messenger, but there's more bad news."

"What?"

"Mom brought Allie to the rehearsal."

And in they walked, the best of pals—the woman with whom he wanted to commit every carnal act in or out of the book, arm-in-arm with the woman who'd given him birth.

Helen, Kelly, Nicole and Olivia all rushed to Allie, clearly thrilled. And Allie was just as happy back, smiling and nodding and vibing "we're pals" all over the place.

Matt's dad wandered back up, saw Matt's mother and sisters fawning over Allie, and did a rapid about-face. *"Hide.* If you don't, they'll eat you alive!"

He vanished into the crowd, but before Matt could follow, his mother and sisters swarmed toward him like a colony of bees, pushing Allie ahead of them.

"Time to start the rehearsal!" Matt said to Darlene, then took the chicken-shit way out and went to get Father Don. What were priests for, if not as sanctuary in time of need?

~:~:~

Despite the black looks Matt gave his mother and sisters on her arrival, Allie enjoyed the rehearsal. She must have aunts, uncles and cousins somewhere back east, since both her parents had siblings. But after her mother died, her father had lost touch first with her family, and then with his own. Allie didn't even know if her grandparents were still alive. Bobby had offered to help track them down once, but they'd be strangers, so what was the point?

Now, it was fascinating to sit with Matt's multitudinous relatives—women and men both, this time—observing the hubbub. A few folks introduced themselves, but most left her alone. Even Matt's sisters, after their initial welcome, seemed to realize she might need space to process. Which was more touching than if they'd hovered. It meant they understood her enough to want her to be comfortable.

After the rehearsal ended, Allie waited nervously

outside the church for Matt to finish up with his family. So far, he'd avoided her. She didn't think he was mad, exactly, but he wasn't happy Eliza had brought her.

On the other hand, he'd made that "unstable" comment and deserved a little payback. Still, she'd be riding with him to the restaurant, and she had to fight the butterflies when he finally appeared at the church door, filling it with his presence, his hot gaze seeking her out and melting her in every private place she had until she could barely stand.

"Hi," he said, walking over to her.

"Hi yourself." She cleared her throat. "I forgot to tell you this morning. Your sisters—and then your mother—"

"It's not your fault. You didn't stand a chance."

He led her to the car, helped her in, then slid into the driver's seat. He sat, staring out the front, then turned, grabbed her blouse, hauled her close, and took her mouth with his. When she was tingling all over and had completely forgotten they were in a tiny car on a busy street in broad daylight, he pulled back, started the car, and peeled out.

"Um," Allie managed, and he grinned.

"Try not to look like that at the restaurant."

"Like what?"

"Like we almost had sex in my car outside my parish."

"Okay. Then don't *try* to have sex with me in front of your church. It'll be easier that way."

"No can do. When we're alone—and you're sober— I've got pretty much one goal. Get used to it, princess."

What with the heat in his eyes, and the fact that he really should focus on driving, Allie thought a change of subject was in order. "What happened with Wolf after I left?"

Matt sighed, but shifted gears, literally and figuratively. "He apologized. Sort of. Until we find her, he won't be good for much."

"Does he have an alibi?"

"Nope. That would be too easy."

"Of course it would." Allie hesitated. Matt had been more receptive to her intuition earlier in the day, but he was still Matt. Logic, facts, careful consideration; these were the things he appreciated when faced with a problem. She had very little to go on, except a strong gut feeling. Screw it—he already thought she was illogical and *unstable*.

"I don't think Wolf took Laurette or the other women. But I *do* think someone wants us to believe he did."

Matt lifted a brow. "Why?"

"Partly it's my gut. But also it's the note card."

"The one Laurette left?"

"Yes. It's been bugging me. Why would she take the time to write out Wolfram? If he was about to kidnap her, wouldn't she just write Wolf? It's faster, and it's how she always refers to him."

"True. I hadn't noticed." He assessed her. "What else?"

"The ring. Wolf knew his was gone. If he was guilty, why not find a replacement, even gouge it up to look like the original? It just feels…heavy-handed."

"You might be right," Matt said slowly. "I was thinking earlier how bad it looked for Wolf, but it's all pretty obvious. He's a smart guy. He'd cover his tracks better."

"Exactly. You know what else bugs me? The fairy tale references in the first four disappearances, which are gone in the last two. Like the kidnapper's rushed or frustrated or something. Maybe it took us too long to suspect Wolf, and now he has to really drive his point home."

"Well, Tarek's getting the message. He's tried and convicted Wolf already." Abruptly Matt smacked the wheel. "Message! Damn. I forgot to tell you Bobby called. Check your phone—Henry's trying to reach you."

Allie's gut went from pleasure at Matt's support, to the pit of despair. If Henry had gone to this much trouble to reach her, it couldn't be good. Rianna had called earlier to say the sale was proceeding, and they'd close on time, but not for another month. Meanwhile, she'd been so busy with the case, and Matt, and not tripping over her costume, that she hadn't looked for a place to live.

Fighting the dread, she found her phone and brought up her voicemail. Sure enough, there was a new message from Henry, received earlier that day, short and to the point.

The phone slid through Allie's cold, numb fingers, and she said to Matt, "Henry just evicted me. I have until Monday to get my stuff out, or he's hauling it to Goodwill."

~:~:~

"He can't do that to you!"

Matt squealed into a space at the restaurant and killed the engine. The car was too small to contain his outrage, but for her sake, he tried to rein in his temper.

"After he gave you the eviction notice, I checked it out. There's a court process: he serves you, you have five days to respond, and then there's a hearing—"

"Matt." Allie's voice was calm, and for once, she was utterly still. By contrast, Matt wanted to put his fist through a window—or Henry. Even Peerless. There must be some way to blame the prick for Allie's current situation.

Instead, he said, "Hire a lawyer. Olivia's firm doesn't do tenant law, but she could recommend someone."

"*Matt.*"

He blew out a breath. "What?"

"It's too late. Even if I had five business days, that was a week ago. I told you, it's not worth contesting. I just need a place to store my stuff until I can move into my house."

She sounded tired, worn down, and he reached for her

hand. "Allie, I know you bounced around so much as a kid that you probably expect these things. But you don't have to take it. You have legal recourse."

Her sigh sounded aggravated. Good. If she was pissed, it meant she was feeling something again.

"I don't want a lawyer. I can't afford a lawyer. I just want my house and for all of this to be over."

How could she say that? He wanted to tell her to fight, to make Henry pay for being an asshole and circumventing the court process. Then something that had bugged him after the break-in at her apartment suddenly clicked with the story Peerless had told about her flunking the police test.

She hadn't wanted the cops involved, had seemed embarrassed by the thought. Could it be she *was* embarrassed? Because she'd flunked the test so badly that SFPD branded her as too unhinged for the academy, reinforcing her belief that she didn't deserve stability? Getting evicted probably only proved the point more.

She was wrong, of course, but even he knew he couldn't just tell her that. He squeezed her hand. "If you change your mind, Olivia would help. She likes you. *All* my sisters do."

She laughed weakly, then frowned when he took out his cell. "What are you doing now?"

"Looking up storage facilities, princess."

~:~:~

Bitch.

Wafi tore the wrapper off the antibiotic spray with his teeth and aimed the nozzle at his hand. It'd been more than a day and the cut was worse, not better: red-edged but yellow in the middle. And it throbbed. Pulsed with his bloodlust. *Goddamn bitch.*

She didn't know how lucky she was that the boss wanted her unharmed. Wafi taped the bandage around his hand, flexing his fingers. He could still hit her. Stomach, legs, places it wouldn't show. At the thought, he grunted. She deserved it—breaking her plastic knife to make a sharper point. Now he just made them eat with their fingers.

The others hadn't resisted. Too scared. They'd cried, pleading for their lives. But never fought back. Just *her*.

He peered in the grimy mirror. Scratches on his cheek, too. Fuck the boss. Wafi was stuck in this shitty apartment while the bitches lived like queens. *She* got to whale on him, and he had to just take it like a pussy?

The boss's plan was whacked, anyway. Why was Wafi supposed to kidnap them and just keep them caged? At least he should get to have some fun with them. Or he could make the fake plan real and sell them off. There were men who'd pay good money for nice, clean, American women. Plus, the buyers wouldn't care if Wafi used them first.

But the boss insisted that the prisoners *must* be released unharmed. And since Wafi wanted what the boss could provide, he'd follow the rules, for now.

Except…maybe not with her.

The boss's plan to "rescue" the bitches from Wafi would still work, if *most* were saved. Wafi needed revenge. The fuckin' media would still call the boss a hero for stopping a sexual slavery ring at the park, and Roland would be exposed as a weak, useless king. Plus, the boss wouldn't need to worry that *she'd* learn the truth.

The more Wafi thought about it, the better it sounded. If the boss let her go, she'd be there in the castle with him for the rest of her life. Every day, he'd wonder if she knew how he took her throne right out from under her. But Wafi could solve that problem, and the boss wouldn't have to get his hands dirty. He bared his teeth in the mirror.

Yeah, he'd make her pay. *Goddamn fuckin' bitch.*

Chapter Twenty-Four

"Rianna? It's Allie. Sorry to call you on a Saturday."

"No problem. What's up?"

Allie shifted the phone on her shoulder. God, this was humiliating. It was her last resort, though, so she had to try.

Just do it—whatever it takes. Get the house, and you'll never have to go through this again. But if the sale fails…

Henry'd never give her a good recommendation on future rental apps. If she lost this house, she'd be homeless, with no deposit or earnest money for anything else.

She charged on. "I have to be out of my apartment by Monday. I tried every storage place around, but they're all full. A lawyer friend said the owner might rent my new garage to me before we close, so I can store my stuff there."

This *had* to work. Her only alternative was to haul the small things down to GrimmLand and abandon her furniture to charity. Not that it would be much of a loss. But it was *her* beat up, secondhand bedframe, couch, and table, part of her past, and she wasn't ready to let them go just yet.

Last night, she'd tried not to bring it up at the restaurant. This was Darlene's happy time, not Poor Allie Central. But after striking out on the storage facilities, Matt mentioned it to his family. First, they were outraged on her behalf. And then they'd put their heads together.

It was…nice…having them at her back. Different, but nice. Darlene even offered Allie the use of her condo, which would be empty as of Saturday night, when she and Issac left for their honeymoon. But besides feeling intrusive, it would be expensive to move everything down from San Francisco, and then back up after the house closed. Which was when Olivia came up with her brilliant idea.

"I'm sure the owner will be fine with it," Rianna said now, and Allie started to breathe again.

"Really?"

"Yes. He's been very accommodating, and the house is just sitting there, vacant. Plus, you'd be paying him. He should be happy to rent it to you. Let me see what I can do."

They hung up and Allie glanced at the clock. She was late. She had to go down to The Princess Shoppe, find a dress, then get to one of the hotel boutiques and pick out a wedding gift, all in less than three hours.

Not that anyone expected her to buy a present, but it was the least she could do after Darlene's generous offer. Plus, she just plain liked Darlene. And Isaac. He was a great source of Wilcox intel and had regaled her at dinner with tips for dealing with the huge clan he'd voluntarily joined.

Not that Allie would be "joining" Matt's family. In a few days, when she solved the case and went home, this would all seem like a bizarre dream.

If she solved the case. Her only leads pointed to Wolf, who her gut said was innocent. Plus, only Celia and Laurette showed signs of leaving under duress; it was still possible the other women left voluntarily, especially as no one else had reported them missing.

However, the staged aspects of the first four disappearances negated that theory, so back to someone taking them. At the same time, though, Allie's gut said they hadn't been killed. Everything was *too* obvious, so if the point was murder, shouldn't that be obvious also? Besides, according to the police, the blood at Celia's wasn't enough to indicate serious injury, let alone death.

Should Allie trust her instincts? For once, Matt thought so. But what if his friendship with Wolf—or his lust for Allie—blinded him? Maybe Bobby was right: She should go back to the agency and cheating spouses, instead of striking out on her own.

No. She could do this. She *would* do this. After she braved the dress shop, the gift boutique, and an even bigger contingent of Wilcoxes than she'd faced so far.

She picked up her purse and opened the door, finding Tarek on the other side. He was dressed as immaculately as ever, but worry lines around his eyes showed his stress.

He frowned at her. "You are here. Why are you not in the park, searching for clues?"

"I switched with Bridget for the weekend. I—well, I'm going to Matt's sister's wedding, and then tomorrow I have personal business to attend to."

"Personal business? Your *business* is finding clues, locating the missing women. You have come up with nothing so far. *Nothing!* If you do not get results soon, I will fire you and Matt, both!"

Tarek might be paying her, but after Bobby and Henry, she'd had enough of men shoving her around. "Matt has nothing to do with this. You didn't even want him helping me, remember? I looked for clues, the police looked for clues. We're all looking for clues, there just aren't any!"

Tarek's face purpled. "There are always clues! You just do not see them! What about those that point to Wolf?"

Allie forced a breath. "I know you're frustrated. So am I. I'm worried about Laurette and Celia, and the women I don't know. But with the cops swarming around, the kidnapper will lay low, unless he *wants* to get caught."

"So that is it? You will leave it to the police now—the very same who did not believe me when I told them a kidnapper was in the park?"

Allie fisted her hands at her sides. "No, of course I won't just roll over. But I can't poke around while the police are still here, unless you *want* my cover blown."

Tarek exhaled sharply. "No. I still believe this is how to stop these heinous crimes and uncover the perpetrator."

"Great. We agree, then. There's nothing I can do today. I'm going to Darlene's wedding, and then I'll be in San Francisco tonight, but I'll be back on Monday, first thing."

Tarek scowled. "You are driving to San Francisco?"

Allie hesitated, but he did have some right to know why she'd be missing her shift. "I'm sorry. My landlord asked me to vacate immediately, so I have to move my stuff into the new house early."

Tarek's lips pressed in a line. "Very well. But on Monday you are back in the park or you are fired."

~:~:~

An hour later, Allie'd made the fastest dress purchase in the history of shopping. Thank God for employee discounts. Who knew dresses could cost as much as cars? On the other hand, she drove an ancient junker that would probably *never* be fixed because its parts hadn't been manufactured in decades. So maybe the price of fabric and thread wasn't all that outrageous.

Besides, it was nice fabric and thread, really flattering, and she had visions of Matt's expression when he saw her in it. From that standpoint, the expense was justified. Now, if she could just find the perfect wedding gift, she might have time to shower and change before catching her ride with Didi. Unfortunately, she wanted the gift to be meaningful, and apparently, the GrimmLand boutiques didn't carry better schlock than any other hotel.

Allie tamped down her aggravation and examined the

glass cases again. There had to be something good here. The woman working the counter had been with another customer for ten minutes. Allie did *not* have time for this. If she couldn't speed things up, she'd lose her ride.

She thought of the trip two days ago with Laurette, and pushed down a frisson of fear. Laurette *had* to be okay.

But…what if Tarek's theory about Wolf running a white slavery ring was right after all? A theme park would be fertile ground for such an operation. Anyone making a "purchase" could browse the merchandise first, and once a selection was made, the ring leader could take that actress out of the park and ship her off.

But why bother staging the disappearances to resemble fairy tales? Or was that merely coincidence after all?

Some instincts *she* had. So far, they weren't telling her much, except that Wolf was innocent. Still, it would be good to double-check if he was connected to the park in any way. Yet another thing for her list, right after *buy fabulous wedding gift, transform into beautiful wedding-goer,* and *survive ninety-minute car ride with feuding daughter and her transgender parent.*

Oh, and then there was *move all worldly possessions into a house you don't own yet, in less than one day, then drive back here before you get fired.*

"Why are *you* here?" Phil stood at her elbow, seeming inexplicably put out. "You're supposed to be in the park!"

What was with everyone? Couldn't she take a morning off? "I'm buying a wedding gift."

Phil gaped. "Matt invited you to Darlene's *wedding?"*

"Technically, it was his mother." Phil's jaw dropped further, and Allie shifted the heavy dress bag on her arm. "What's the big deal? I went to the shower and the rehearsal. Why not the wedding?"

Phil snapped her jaw shut. "No big deal at all."

Allie didn't buy that for a minute. Based on Phil's stunned disbelief, Gillian hadn't enjoyed the same courtesies. Had Matt's family not liked her? Had they even met her? Phil likely had valuable intel on the subject but obviously wouldn't share it in her present mood.

On the other hand, Phil had good reason to be upset about any number of things. "Laurette will be fine," Allie said as reassuringly as she could. "They'll all be. The police are on the job, and Matt and I are doing everything we can."

Phil turned hastily away, examining a display of vases, but not before Allie saw the fear in her eyes. After a minute, Phil's expression cleared, as if she made a conscious effort to improve her mood. She pointed to an ornate porcelain vase, about sixteen inches tall, with intricate pastoral scenes painted on it, framed in gold leaf.

"That one."

Allie inspected it. "Are you sure? I thought Darlene had more of a clean, Mediterranean theme."

"In the condo," Phil said quickly. "But *at the house*, they're changing their whole theme. I think Darlene's even going to sell off their old stuff when they move. In case you hadn't noticed, she's really big on style."

She had a point. Darlene did like classy stuff, and it *did* all match. Plus, Phil knew Darlene better, and Allie already felt bad for breaking their détente yesterday. Add to that their impending ninety-minute carpool—each way—and taking Phil's advice was probably politic.

"Okay, I'll buy it," she said as the saleswoman finally finished with her other customer and walked up. Allie handed over her one credit card that wasn't maxed out yet and made arrangements to have the vase wrapped and waiting for her after she went upstairs to change.

She turned back to Phil. "Thanks for the help. Darlene and Isaac have been so nice to me. I really wanted to get them something meaningful, and thanks to you, I am." Phil suddenly looked like she'd swallowed sour milk, and Allie plowed ahead. "Speaking of the wedding, I don't know if your dad told you. We're riding in together."

Fury flashed across Phil's small, pinched face, lighting it with a blaze of emotion that was gone so fast, Allie almost missed it.

"Great," Phil said brightly. "I better get ready, then."

She left the boutique quickly, reminding Allie of the blur she'd been the day they met. Her moods were so mercurial, they made Allie's own ups and downs pale by comparison.

Allie shook her head. No matter what Matt had told his family, she was *not* unstable, and her life was *not* out of control. She would get her house and settle down.

But later. Now, she had less than thirty minutes for a magical transformation from grungy PI into wedding guest extraordinaire. And nary a fairy godmother in sight.

~:~:~

Matt adjusted his bow-tie, and wondered how Allie was. He checked his wedding to-do list, and wondered how Allie was. He knocked at Darlene's dressing room, ascertained that, yes, she'd be ready for the ceremony in twenty minutes—and wondered how Allie was.

By the time he'd checked with the priest, all the while thinking about Allie, he gave up and headed from the parish offices over to the church. A quick scan of the rapidly filling pews didn't reveal her, and he checked his watch.

Someone tugged his sleeve, and he turned to find Phil peering up at him anxiously. She wore another frilly, poufy dress, this one a dull lavender that made her skin look gray.

He made a mental note to drop a hint in Didi's ear. For someone who prided herself on her fashion sense, she didn't have a clue what her daughter should wear, or what she'd like. Matt was sure Phil hated being dressed like one of the Madame Alexander dolls his sisters had when they were her age, but somehow, Didi'd missed the memo.

"Hey, kiddo. You made it. Where's your dad?"

"Parking the car."

She shifted from foot to foot, glancing around the narthex, which was empty except for the two of them.

Matt waited, and when she didn't say anything, asked, "Did Allie ride in with you?"

Phil's expression clouded. "Yeah. She's in the bathroom. Look, can I ask you about something?"

"Sure, what's up?"

"I was at the park on Tuesday, at the Mousetraps."

Matt frowned. "You aren't supposed to go in those."

"I know. I didn't. I was just looking around, because there was this man—"

"You weren't following him, were you?"

Phil turned pink. "I guess I never told you about him, either. He was the first one—"

"You've been following *multiple* men around the park? Jeez, Phil. Twelve-year-old girls should *never, ever* follow strange men around. You know better than that."

She stamped a white patent-leather shoe. "Listen to me! I would've told you before, but—*damn it!*"

Allie entered the narthex, and Matt rotated like a compass to magnetic north. She wore an apricot sleeveless dress with a plunging neckline, a tight waist, and a gauzy skirt that swirled around her hips and made him want to twirl her so it would fly up, revealing her long, sexy legs.

"Hi," he managed.

What the hell was the matter with him? They hadn't even had sex yet, and he couldn't stop thinking about her. Or maybe that was *why* he couldn't stop thinking about her. He hadn't had to work this hard at getting laid since college.

He offered her his arm. "Can I show you to your seat?" Allie glanced meaningfully at Phil, glaring daggers nearby. "Oh, sorry, kiddo."

Her scowl got blacker, but he didn't blame her. When Allie showed up, everything else went right out of his head.

He offered Phil his other arm. "I shouldn't lecture you."

She hesitated, then said, "It's okay. You have a lot on your mind with the wedding and all."

"Thanks for understanding."

She was still upset but let him lead her down the aisle. He waited until Phil was seated in the middle of the pew behind his family, then leaned into Allie, inhaling her scent, like warm, rich peaches, wishing he could taste her mouth. Instead, he contented himself with a kiss on her cheek, which seemed to surprise her.

He grinned. "What?"

"I don't know. I just didn't peg you for the PDA type."

"Trust me, princess, if we were anywhere else, I'd do a helluva lot more to you." This was nuts. At least Phil was too far away to hear him making an ass of himself. "So, you'll be okay? You can get into your garage early?"

"I'm *fine.*" She sounded aggravated. "Nothing I can't handle myself. The owner is leaving me a key, and I'll rent a truck tonight, drive up, and haul everything over."

"About that—need some help with the heavy stuff?"

She avoided his gaze. "I left a message for Bobby, and I'll call him again after I get up there."

"Don't. Kelly's husband owns a microbrewery. He has a delivery truck we can borrow."

"We?"

"Yeah, for insurance purposes, he only wants me to drive it. So, I'll help you move, and we can come back Sunday night. He needs the truck Monday morning."

She clearly didn't want his help but knew it was too good an offer to pass up. *God bless insurance loopholes.*

She chewed her lip, and he groaned. "Don't do that. When I said not to rush, I didn't mean we should stop completely. So far, you've had all the fun. Let me do this, and afterward, I'm not above asking for a favor in return."

Her mouth formed an O, and he almost had to kiss her anyway, despite the crowded pews around them. When had he stopped caring who had front row seats for each new installment of *Matt's Personal Life: Allie, Allie and more Allie?* For that matter, when had her being near his family started to feel *right?* He'd kept his past flings away from his family, and except for Gillian, away from his work, too.

But Allie was now a part of all three, and it didn't bug him. Far from it. He was glad she was at GrimmLand, happy she'd be with him for the unending series of events surrounding Darlene's damn wedding, and desperate to get her alone—*finally*—for some very "personal" time.

He pulled her close. "Or you could suddenly need help with your dress in the bathroom. I'd be happy to oblige."

"Am I interrupting?" Didi said from behind them, and Allie jerked free from Matt's grasp, turning bright red.

Didi wore another dress that matched Phil's, except on her, the color was exquisitely flattering. At her arrival, Phil glared at them all from the pew. Then Father Don, standing at the altar, caught Matt's eye and tapped his watch.

"Showtime," Matt said, and went to take his place at the end of the line of bridesmaids waiting in the narthex.

One responsibility down, only a thousand more to go...

Chapter Twenty-Five

Phil *had* to talk to Matt. Everything was all messed up, and for once, she admitted she was scared and confused. She was losing the park—she was losing Matt—and she couldn't stop pushing her dad away. Soon she'd lose him, too, and it would be all her own fault.

Maybe it was her fault her mom died.

No. She'd had therapy. She knew the drill.

But her dad… Why couldn't she make herself stop? She *knew* she just wanted him to notice her—the *real* her, not the little girl she used to be, or the too-fragile-to-be-honest-with girl he thought she'd become. But even though she'd had this great emotional revelation—adolescent girl needs her father—*big* surprise—no one paid any attention.

Except Allie. And Phil didn't *want* Allie's help.

Matt *had* to hear about Wolf roaming the park on Tuesday afternoon, which gave him *plenty* of time to go to Celia's, kidnap her, and lose his ring in the process. Not that Phil thought that's what he'd done. But why had he met with Gillian? And then searched the park?

Now Laurette was gone, and maybe she wouldn't be if Phil had told Matt sooner. Something else to be all mixed up about, and even more reason to corner Matt now, before anything else bad happened.

Phil scanned the reception hall once more, with no luck. The wedding had gone off without a hitch, so to speak. Even sitting in church between her dad and Allie hadn't been as bad as she'd thought. And Matt, as the maid of honor, was awesome in his black tux, standing up with all his sisters. Even with the purple-green bruise like a giant bulls-eye on his perfect face.

If only she'd managed to talk with him before the wedding mass—before he pushed her into the pew so he could have his little tête-à-tête with Allie. Phil couldn't hear what they'd said, but he'd been anxious, like there was something going on with Allie that worried him.

Phil bit down hard on her lower lip. If Matt knew how much she needed to talk to him, he would've made more of an effort, right? What was the big deal with Allie, anyway? Although Phil had pretty much decided Allie was working *with* Matt instead of against him, because when Phil asked her about Laurette earlier, she was obviously in the know.

Thinking about Laurette made Phil want to throw up.

So don't think about it. She's fine. Matt will find her and all the other women and bring them home. Don't think about your mom, either, or your dad. Think about Allie, and how mad you are. There, that's better.

Allie could be in security or something. Phil wasn't sure what type a security expert would be, but either way, Allie's life was just too weird for someone as structured as Matt. Obviously, he had the hots for her, so maybe that's why he put up with her wackiness.

But if he was *worried* about her, it went deeper than plain old lust.

Phil's heart constricted. She'd started to like Allie. Well, until she got all buttinsky about Phil's dad. What did *she* know about it, anyway? Another reason Phil needed Matt. He *did* know about it and was always there for her.

Until now.

Phil gripped her skirt so tight, the sheer fabric started to rip. She *wouldn't* lose him, not to Allie or anyone else.

From the corner of her eye, she caught a flash of pale violet. *Shit.* Her dad. She ducked into the crowd. She *had* to find Matt, or whatever happened, it wouldn't be good. She just didn't know *what* she'd do.

And that scared her worst of all.

~:~:~

This time the bitch had gone too far. Wafi hauled her into the master bedroom, away from the other hostages, who cringed as he passed by. He'd teach *her* to fear him, too. Adrenaline lessened the pain, but his left arm was going to hurt like hell. He examined the angry red flesh— he might even need a doctor. She'd aimed for his face, and it was pure luck he'd turned just as she tossed the scalding contents of her tea mug at him.

He threw her on the bed, landing on top of her and pinning her arms above her head. "Is this how you do it with that prince of yours, *Your Highness?"*

He ground against her, then laughed when she flinched. Her fear was fleeting, though, and she spat at him. He slapped her, then ripped the front of her dress down. He shoved a hand into her bra, when abruptly his cell rang.

"Fuck." He pushed off the bed and flipped it open.

The boss's voice said, "I have a special errand for you. A field trip, shall we say. You will leave immediately."

Wafi listened to the instructions, then hung up. Finally, a job he could sink his teeth into. And not one fucking subtle thing about it.

He leaned over the bitch, still lying on the bed where he'd left her. "You just got lucky, *Highness.* But I'll be back, and I won't forget. I'm gonna finish what we started."

He twisted her cheek in a vicious pinch, then grinned at the mark his fingers left on her flawless skin. He'd finish, all right. It would be his pleasure.

Chapter Twenty-Six

"All set," Matt said and pulled the door down on the back of the wedding present-crammed delivery truck.

Kelly's husband Mike was nearby on the curb. "Thanks again. I really didn't want to unload all those gifts myself."

"Thank you for the loan. It's a big help to Allie."

"Hey," Mike said, "if it means I get home before Kelly completely passes out, it's all yours."

His wife swatted him as he dragged her to their car. "Night, Matt!" she called over her shoulder.

It was almost midnight, and Matt and Allie were the only ones still at the church. The newlyweds had left for their honeymoon trip to Greece, and the reception had ended an hour ago. It had taken Matt and his sisters and brothers-in-law that long just to load the gifts into the truck.

Allie had helped, too, but now she stood by the church door, waiting for him. She'd draped a shawl over her shoulders against the late-night chill, and she looked so soft and alluring, he couldn't resist drawing her close and rubbing his hands over her cool skin.

"Mmm," she said, low and throaty.

"Mmm, is right. Can I ask for one of those favors before we drive up?"

She pulled away and looked at him seriously. "Matt…"

"Uh-oh. The wheels are turning. What's up?"

"It's just, we keep trying to hook up, and something keeps getting in the way. Is it really worth the effort?"

He watched her for a minute, then made a decision.

Instead of telling her that it—she—was absolutely worth the effort, which she wouldn't believe, he kissed her. Long, slow, exploring her mouth all over again. He'd never tire of her mouth. Sliding his hands down her curves, he pulled her against his erection, relishing the feel of her.

He broke the kiss, keeping her close. "We have to stop doing this in public. Especially in front of the church. You pick: Darlene's or your apartment. Where's it going to be?" She laughed and he added, "The back of the truck works for me. There will be plenty of room after we unload it."

"Speaking of which, shouldn't we get going?"

He sighed and let her go. "One of these days, I'm going to get through to you—I don't give up. I want you. You want me. You can run, princess, but you can't hide."

Her gaze slid away. "Who said I want to run or hide? Can we at least get my stuff moved first?"

She moved away, but he grabbed her hand and pulled her back. "It's going to be okay. You know that, right?"

Allie regarded him silently for a minute. He thought she wanted to believe him, but something wouldn't let her. Knowing what he did of her unstable home life and lack of a support system of any kind, that didn't surprise him.

But all she said was, "Thanks."

The drive to Darlene's new house didn't take long. Matt found himself wondering what Allie would think of it. Outside of the family and the contractors, she was the first person he'd shown it to. Would she like it? Or did she really not care what she lived in, so long as it was affordable?

They pulled into the semi-circular drive, and Allie's jaw dropped. "Wow. You really went all out."

"This is my showcase house."

"Then you should have no trouble getting clients."

He'd designed the house in the style of Frank Lloyd

Wright, considering the property's natural landscape and incorporating regional materials and motifs. Matt had taken Darlene's preferred Mediterranean feel a step further, combining it with the Southwestern Pueblo Revival style. The house was even built around a central garden, as California's early Spanish settlers' homes had been.

Allie stepped out of the truck onto the flagstone driveway, taking it all in, the palm trees, curved adobe walls, flat tile roof. He felt a stab of pride at her obvious admiration, but then her eyes narrowed.

"Is it like this on the inside, too?"

"Of course." He got out also, and went to roll up the truck's cargo door. "Inside and out, very natural, very Santa Fe mixed with Spanish-Mediterranean."

"So…I'm guessing Darlene and Isaac really aren't into the whole French Louis XIV thing?"

"Not even remotely." He almost laughed at the thought, but Allie looked so stricken. "Something wrong?"

She eyed the house balefully. "Not a damn thing. But if you happen to come across a white box about so big—" She held her hands eighteen inches apart. "—with a gold bow, could you set it aside?"

"Princess, you just described half these gifts."

She surveyed the giant mound in the truck. "I know. Never mind. Let's get started."

~:~:~

"Wake up, princess. We're here."

Allie stretched groggily, her hand smacking into something warm and solid. Opening her eyes, she discovered it was Matt's chest as he leaned over her in the cab. He brought her fingers to his lips and kissed them. Allie shivered, but not from the morning San Francisco fog.

A slow smile curved his mouth. "I thought you were

cute asleep. But you're sexy as hell when you wake up."

She shook her head to clear the fuzzies. "Did I snore?"

Either way, it was embarrassing that she'd sacked out in front of him, again. Especially since, also again, he'd had to drive the entire four hundred and fifty miles by himself. He must have broken the sound barrier, because as near as she could tell, it was barely seven a.m.

"Hungry?" He waved a drive thru bag under her nose.

"What is it?"

"Nothing healthy. Bacon, egg, and cheese biscuit, hash browns, and coffee. No mocha. Sorry."

"This is great." She snatched the bag and dug the biscuit out. It was heavenly, and she moaned. "Did you eat?"

"Yogurt and an oat muffin."

She rolled her eyes and pushed the door open, unfolding onto the curb and stretching the kinks out. She'd changed into sweats at Darlene's, and Matt wore jeans and a t-shirt. When she'd wolfed down the rest of her breakfast, they headed upstairs to her apartment. Obviously, she had to leave eventually, but this made it so real.

After today, she'd never live here, ever again.

After today, she'd be homeless.

Giving herself a mental shake, she opened the door and flipped the lights on, and Matt followed her in.

"Well, this shouldn't take long."

He was right. Futon, brick-and-board "entertainment center" with a cheap TV and speaker in the main room. Formica table and two ancient vinyl-cushioned chairs in the dining nook. A box's worth of dishes in the kitchen—the appliances weren't hers—and then in the bedroom, just her bed and more shelves, housing more of her dad's books.

She'd even brought all her clothes to Mecca already, along with her plants. If not for the books, she might have abandoned the rest. Thirty-plus years of her life, and it would all fit in a truck half the size of the one downstairs. Darlene and Isaac had gotten more wedding gifts than the sum total of Allie's possessions.

Matt understood her mood, and worked beside her silently. It took less than an hour. He carried her toolbox down, while she finished packing the books left on the bedroom floor after they'd disassembled the shelves. In their dusty stacks, they weren't as imposing. Even less to show for her dad's life than for her own.

She sat on the floor and lifted the top one off a pile, tracing the embossed title with her fingertips. *Economic Growth and Innovation in the Latter Half of the Fourth Century: Rome, Great Britain and Beyond*, by Patrick Kincade. She turned to the dedication:

For my wife, Sara Jane. And for my little Allie Cat,
who always came to the library with me.

It was the only book he'd published, and he'd autographed it for her, signing his name with a flourish on the title page. The other tomes he'd used for research, or were written by his colleagues.

This is it. A pile of books and his car. That's all I have left of him.

The tears welled up. For her dad, her crazy life, and this apartment that was nothing special, but which had been her home. Matt was right. She was unstable, still adrift, tossed by the tide even when she thought she'd gained control.

She couldn't control anything. Not her feelings, not this case she was supposedly investigating, even though the police had taken it over, and certainly not buying her house. The seller was fully in charge on that one, adding so many clauses to the contract, she'd lost count. And she'd signed them all, desperate to close.

She would close. She'd solve the case and get the house, and she'd never, ever move again.

"Hey, babe. Why the sad face?"

Allie jerked her head up. "Bobby? What on earth are you doing here?"

He stepped into the room, as movie star handsome as ever in a button-down shirt with the sleeves rolled up and khaki slacks. "You called and asked me to help you move. Remember?" His glance took in the almost empty room. "I didn't know you had other help."

"Oh. Right. I said I'd call when I got here. I didn't expect you to just come over."

Bobby squatted beside her. "I'm always here for you." He brushed a tear off her cheek with his thumb. "What's wrong? I saw loverboy downstairs. Did he do this to you?"

Allie swiped at her nose. "He's not—we're not—oh, never mind. No, I was just thinking about my dad."

"Ah." Bobby sat, reaching for her, and somehow, she ended up in his arms, head resting on his shoulder. She should have pushed him away, but it felt so good to be comforted by someone who *knew*.

"You remember him, right?" she asked after a minute.

"Your dad? Of course."

His sympathy hurt even more, and a fresh lump rose in her throat. "He died so long ago. And I—I don't have anyone else to remember him with. Sometimes, I start to forget…"

She choked on a sob, and Bobby tilted her chin up. "Hey, it's okay. I remember him." He paused. "I remember this, too."

She didn't pull back fast enough, and his lips touched

hers. She held still and a few seconds later, he broke the contact, searching her face. After a long moment, one side of his mouth quirked up sadly. "So that's it?"

She drew a ragged breath. "I'm sorry. But yes, that's it."

"Is it Wilcox?"

She took too long to answer, and he said, "Ah," again.

"No. We're not—it's not serious or anything."

But that only made it worse, because somewhere inside, she'd finally acknowledged that she wanted it to be serious with Matt. They never would be; they were too far apart, separated not just by the miles between San Diego and SF, but also by their personalities, their backgrounds, their futures.

Yet unconsciously, she'd tried to fit into his world; not just at his work, but also with his family, his friends. And look how that had turned out: she'd put her faith in a twelve-year-old with a grudge. Darlene was going to hate that vase, and though she might not hate Allie for buying it, the whole thing just proved again that Allie would never learn the secret handshake, never be one of the Beautiful People.

But even with that realization, she couldn't go back to Bobby. Not after knowing what it was like with Matt.

Bobby let go, leaving her bereft, and she said quickly, "I'd still like to be friends…"

"Ouch." He softened the word with a smile, then sobered. "I blew it. I'm sorry. I could've been a better friend, a better lover, and a better boss. If you change your mind, the partnership is yours." He took an envelope from his pocket. "I even put it in writing this time."

He held it out, but Allie was too stunned to take it from him. So instead, he opened her dad's book and slipped the envelope inside.

"Take your time. There's no expiration date."

He stood, then leaned down and kissed her forehead. "Good-bye, Allie."

She watched him go, hugging her knees, a fresh wave of tears sliding down her cheeks. What the hell was she supposed to do with that?

~:~:~

Matt leaned against the loaded truck as Peerless came back down the stairs. It'd nearly killed him, not following the smarm up in the first place. Still, he'd checked his watch, giving them ten minutes before he went in after Allie. Whatever passed between them, it hadn't taken that long. Peerless's expression was shuttered, and Matt flexed his fist. If the bastard had hurt her in any way…

Peerless raised his hands. "She's fine. Well, she isn't fine, but not from anything I did." He gave Matt a considering look. "You should go up there. She needs you."

Surprised, Matt pushed away from the truck. "Okay."

Maybe he'd misjudged Peerless. Maybe he wasn't so bad, after all.

Then the slug said, "But first, there's something I need to tell you that Allie doesn't know. Not sure why I didn't come clean. I should've told her right away."

Matt narrowed his eyes. "Told her what?"

"Your friend Tarek asked me for intel on her."

Matt frowned. "You mean he asked for a reference?"

Peerless shook his head. "No. He hired me, for a background check. Wanted all her deets—past history, present situation, the works. I should've sent him packing, but it was easy money. I knew most of it without searching, and I was still pissed about her leaving. I'm not proud of it. But I'm telling you now. Any idea why he'd do that?"

Matt considered. Why would Tarek hire a PI he didn't like, to investigate a PI he'd chosen to hire? "Buyer's remorse? Maybe he wanted to see what he'd got for his money. He must have liked whatever you gave him, because he hasn't said anything to me about it."

Peerless studied him, and for once, Matt felt like *he* was the clueless idiot. Then he remembered the last time they'd spoken on the phone. "What are you up to?"

"What's that supposed to mean?"

"That little story you told on Allie, about the SFPD. Pretty obvious you were trying to undermine her. So why are you so concerned about her welfare now?"

Peerless had the decency to look chagrined. "I was an asshole. You may not believe it, but I actually thought if you fired her, she'd come back to me."

The muscle in Matt's jaw worked some more. Finally he ground out, "Allie's never coming back to you."

"I know." Peerless's piercing gaze held Matt's for a long beat. "Take good care of her."

"That's the plan."

Matt waited while Peerless got in his car and left. Then he took a deep breath and did something he should have done sooner: He examined his feelings.

Shit.

Allie appeared at her door, setting down a box of books, then went back in and reappeared a moment later with another. She locked the door and headed for the stairs. Her expression was neutral, but tear tracks ran through the dust on her cheeks.

Shit, shit, *shit*.

He jogged up the stairs and took the heavy box out of her hands. "Give me that."

She went back for the final box and they added both to the truck. He lowered the cargo door and moved to the cab.

"Let's go, princess. We still have a long day ahead."

Wafi checked the timer on the detonator, then his watch. She should be here soon. The boss had said to give her time to unload first, so the activation key was set to go off in two hours. Wafi slipped from the side yard around to the front of the house. Perfect. The neighbor had a chain-link fence. Wafi took the Ruedian crest he'd torn off a military jacket and snagged it on the fence near the end of the drive.

Then he crossed the street to the nondescript sedan he'd stolen. He'd wait until she arrived, in case he needed to reset the timer. The boss wanted her to know she'd been warned, but not to be inside when it happened. She was due back at the park on Monday, so she'd have to leave right after unloading. Wafi would wait until she arrived and then split before she noticed him.

He hunkered down behind the wheel, and was rewarded fifteen minutes later when a delivery truck drove up and backed into her driveway. She got out on the passenger side, and her big blond boyfriend got out on the other.

The boss hadn't said he would be here. But he also hadn't said he wouldn't be. Wafi reviewed his options. Either way, the boss was pissed. She wasn't taking him seriously and needed to know he meant business. That could be accomplished with or without Wilcox's presence.

Decision made, Wafi assessed the size of the truck. An hour and a half should give them plenty of time to unload, even if the thing was full. Besides, if they left before the explosion, she'd find out about it on the drive home.

Wafi reinserted the screwdriver into the car's ignition, jiggling it until the engine turned over. He put the car in drive and made a U-turn out into the street. He checked the house one last time in the rearview mirror as he sped away.

Hasta la vista, baby.

Chapter Twenty-Seven

Matt had been quiet on the drive over from her apartment. Not that Allie felt like talking. She suspected Bobby had said something to him on the way out, but if he had, Matt wasn't sharing. She still didn't know what to think of the whole encounter. Bobby had always been her safety-net; not as bad as everyone thought he was, and a solid, warm body when she needed one. Problem was, a warm body by itself suddenly wasn't enough.

But he had put the partnership in writing…

Allie watched Matt's stern profile as he unloaded the truck. The bruise had faded, but it still gave his face an angry edge, reminding her of the ogre he'd been on the day they met. Helping her move no doubt reminded him of all the reasons his perfectly ordered life was superior to hers.

Best to get this over with and return to GrimmLand before Tarek blew a gasket. She could deal with Bobby's offer later, once the missing women were found and San Diego, Matt, and everything else was behind her.

Quickly, she found the key under the rock Rianna had described and inserted it into the padlock on the old-fashioned garage door, then flipped the panel up and open.

The garage was small, but big enough for her meager belongings. Because there were no stairs here, it took even less time to unload the truck than it had to load it. Plus, she didn't have to unpack. Within thirty minutes, they were down to the dregs, and Matt's frowns were getting on Allie's nerves. Enough was enough, already.

She grabbed the last box from the truck and followed him into the garage. "Hey—strong, silent type. Something on your mind?"

"Yes." He set down the chairs he was carrying, then took the box from her and set it next to them. Then he placed an arm on either side of her, pushing her against a wall, expression serious. "You."

Despite the warm-jello feeling spreading through her limbs to her belly and below, Allie rolled her eyes. "Is sex really the only thing you think about?"

"Princess." His voice was low, vibrating over her sensitive skin. He dropped his molten-gold gaze to her mouth, leaning in close, his breath warm on her lips "This stopped being only about sex a long time ago."

He kissed her then, and there was something different about it, an awareness that hadn't been there before. He laced his fingers through hers, then closed the space between them. But when he pressed against her, it felt somehow less…urgent. More…gentle. Like they had all the time in the world to explore each other and whatever this was between them.

And somehow that made it all even hotter.

Matt touched her lips with his tongue, and when she opened, he slid inside, tasting her, letting her taste the warm spice that was him. Against his solid chest, her breasts tightened, and her palms pressed flat into his. He nibbled her lower lip, then trailed kisses across her jaw to her ear, where he nipped and licked until Allie could barely stand for all the heat pooling between her legs.

A car drove by outside, and she whispered, "Matt…"

He placed a soft kiss on her mouth before releasing her to go pull the garage door down, giving them privacy. At least the wall at her back allowed her to defy gravity and stay vertical, and thanks to the small window in the backyard door, there was enough light to see by. He caught her hand again and led her to the futon, which they'd set up in the far corner. He sat and guided her down next to him.

And Allie let him, unable to think clearly about any of this. Matt was acting so…tender…and she didn't know what to do with that, except that she liked it.

No, she loved it.

She loved him.

And before she could process that terribly-timed revelation, his hands slid over her bare arms and under her shirt, caressing her collar bones with his thumbs until her breasts were on fire from the proximity. He pulled her shirt off, then bent his head, suckling first one side, then the other, through the silk of her bra, until she ached for more.

And with that, the passivity that had overtaken her vanished. She whimpered—God help her, she never whimpered—then she pulled his shirt free of his jeans and began her own exploration of his chest, the hairs tickling her fingers, the tiny buds of his nipples hardening at her touch. A low growl came from deep in his throat before his mouth closed over hers again, the intensity of his kiss increasing from a simmer to a boil.

He pressed her into the futon, the length of his hard body covering hers, cradling her close. Her bra was gone— how did he *do* that?—and he traced slow, sensuous circles around each of her breasts.

Allie finished removing his shirt. She would have torn it off, but the unhurried pace he'd set was contagious. He teased her—she wanted to tease him back. He drove her wild by brushing his fingers over her most sensitive places—she traced the hard ridge of his erection lightly with her palm, relishing in his sharp in-drawn breath. He pushed her sweats down; she unbuttoned his jeans.

And though they weren't hurrying, before she knew it, they were naked, and Matt was every bit as magnificent as she'd imagined. His body was hard and muscled and lived in. He stretched out next to her, and she reached over to touch a vicious scar that snaked from the middle of his left thigh up to his groin.

He flinched and she snatched her fingers away. "I'm sorry. Does it hurt?"

He shook his head, then wordlessly captured her hand and brought it back, placing it on the thick, roped tissue. Gently she followed the jagged line, realizing instantly how lucky he was. A few inches higher, closer to his spine, and he could have been paralyzed. Or he could have bled out, if his femoral artery was involved.

"The attempt on Roland?" she asked, and he nodded. "It looks serious."

"It was. I almost lost the leg. It took a lot of physical therapy before I could walk or run again. It's still painful."

"How…?"

"The shooter was up close and personal. I tried to wrestle the gun from him and it went off. I let go, and he got away."

His expression was unreadable, and she thought he might be reliving the scene, probably kicking himself for "letting" the assassin escape.

"Matt, you're lucky to be alive. I'm sure Roland is grateful you saved his life and survived."

"I suppose." He watched her. "You're the first person I've told this to. In fact, no one but Roland, his doctors, and now you know how bad it was. And, of course, the shooter."

"Not even Wolf? I thought you recovered together."

"He was also hurt in the attack, yes. Arm and hand

sliced by the guy's knife. But we didn't compare war stories. We both felt we should have tried harder to catch the guy, so any suffering we went through, we deserved it."

Which was ridiculous. But he was a man, and an über-responsible one at that, so she thought of a way to make him feel better. She bent and softly kissed his scar, starting near the bottom and working her way up. No wonder he never wore shorts: the thing crawled over his whole thigh.

At the first touch of her lips, he sucked in a breath. By the time she reached the top of the scar, right at the groin muscle, his body was rigid. And then she moved her mouth over and kissed him *there*.

"Allie…" He said it like a prayer, and before she knew it, he'd caught her, pulled her up, was kissing her, hard. He paused long enough to roll a condom on—probably conjured it from the same dimension he'd sent her bra to—then leaned over her, tracing his fingers over her cheek and brushing her lips with his thumb.

"Princess," he murmured, then pushed inside, opening her, sliding, thrusting, hands steadying her hips, all the while holding her gaze. She couldn't look away, though everything she felt must be laid bare before him. His own expression was as tender as his lovemaking, as he moved slowly out, only to plunge in again, and again, and again.

Finally, when she couldn't stand it another second, he groaned. "Allie—"

"Hurry," she gasped.

His mouth landed on hers, the urgent pressure of his kiss mirroring the pressure he built deep inside her. She pushed her hips up to meet him—and then everything was heat and white light and muscles contracting and endless, endless release.

Matt collapsed on top of her, breathing heavily, the

sweat from his body cooling her skin, and Allie wrapped her arms around his broad shoulders and held him close, still cradled deep inside her.

I love you, she thought. And if she was honest with herself, his eyes had hinted he might love her back. Problem was, she didn't have a damn clue what to do about it.

~:~:~

Phil stared at the TV without processing the images flitting across it. The apartment, which had seemed so small a few days ago, now felt big and empty. A little scary, though it was broad daylight out, and a lot lonely.

Phil, honey, are you sure *you'll be all right while I'm gone? It's only overnight, and Amy next door will check on you. After I got dizzy last time, Dr. Bauer doesn't want me driving, and wants me to stay in Indio for observation...*

Phil swiped at her nose. No, she wouldn't be all right. She was horribly, awfully, terribly afraid she'd never be all right, ever again. Only she hadn't said that, because physically, she was fine. She was twelve, and totally okay staying home by herself. But emotionally?

I'm fine. Just go! The hospital shuttle's waiting...

A long time ago, she'd tried telling her dad how she felt—how scared she was by what he was doing, but that she wanted him to be happy. How she wondered if he was scared, too, and wished he'd say that no matter what, he loved her and she'd be okay. She wanted to ask him about being a jewel thief, and why he'd done it. Why he'd stopped, and if he ever missed it.

And she wanted to ask about her mom.

That was the worst, because they both hurt so much, and they needed to talk, but they couldn't. She'd tried. She'd really tried. But she was so young then, and either she didn't say it right, or he didn't hear it right, and the hurt only got worse, until eventually she gave up.

Now, when she wanted to try again, she didn't know how.

Except for schoolwork, they barely talked anymore. He tiptoed around like she was an unexploded mine he might step on. And she—she couldn't stop herself. When she wanted to say *I love you,* it came out *You're a freak!* When she desperately tried to say *I need you,* her mouth shouted *Leave me alone!*

And she did need him, because whatever was going on inside her, maybe it was what went on inside her mom before she died. But at the same time, she couldn't say that to her dad, because what if she was right? And what if he tried to pretend she wasn't, just to make her feel better?

She hadn't even told Matt that part, though he'd helped her through some—most—of her worst moments. He always told her to talk to her dad, but he understood that if she couldn't, it was better she talk to him than no one at all.

But now he was gone, and Laurette was missing, and even if Matt didn't care about Phil anymore, and the police had taken over the case, shouldn't he still be here, looking for the missing women?

She remoted the TV off, then picked up the phone and dialed his cell again. After four rings, it went to voicemail. At his home, she got his machine, and she didn't have any of his sisters' numbers. If she'd had Allie's, she would've tried it, even if it killed her.

Damn it! Where are you, Matt? Why aren't you here?

He was probably at Allie's. Phil had tried the hotel, asking to be connected to Allie's room, then hung up after one ring. What would she say if Allie answered? What if *Matt* answered?

She couldn't stand the thought of losing him, but

especially not to Allie. And the reason for that was even stupider: she liked Allie, had started to trust her. She even knew it wasn't Allie's fault if Matt liked her. But if he did, and Allie liked him back, then Phil would lose them both.

Isn't that what grown-ups did—focus on the object in front of them and nothing else? For sure, her dad did it with his stupid, all-consuming operation that kept them in this crappy apartment, with that horrible car, unable to move or do anything because every dime went for hormone treatments, or doctor's bills, or into savings for the Big Day.

Phil gave the coffee table a savage kick, but it was so beat up already, she didn't make a mark. She picked up the remote and lobbed it at the wall. The back popped off and the batteries jettisoned out, but it was otherwise undamaged. She got up to see if maybe she'd dented the wall, at least, when her gaze landed on the keys to the Buick, hanging on a nail by the door.

Before she could think too clearly about what she did, she grabbed them and ran outside, not looking back and not stopping until she was at the car. She yanked the door open and climbed in behind the wheel. She could barely see over the dash, but her dad had let her drive a few times in the parking lot and once to the convenience store a block away. She'd never driven in reverse, but how hard could it be?

Shoving the key in the ignition, she turned it until the engine roared to life, then buckled her seatbelt, took a deep breath, and shifted. Carefully, she lifted her foot off the brake and the car inched back at a snail's pace.

Relief washed through her. She could do this. It was only a mile to GrimmLand, a straight shot down Box Canyon Road. Plus, it was Sunday, and as usual for late July, so hot that everyone was locked up tight indoors. The county sheriff's patrol rarely bothered with Mecca, and if she did get stopped, so what? She had to try.

She had to find Matt. Even if he was in Allie's hotel room, she had to talk with him.

She had to talk with someone. She just *had* to.

A short while after the most meaningful sex of Matt's life, he reluctantly left the warmth of Allie's body and found their clothes. He would much rather have made love to her for another day or two, until, just maybe, he was satiated. But it was past eleven; they'd been here almost two hours. Leaving now would put them in San Diego by seven, where they still had to exchange the truck for his car and drive either to his place or Allie's hotel room, whichever she chose.

It was amazing to realize he wanted her at his place. But then, she was amazing. His feelings were too raw, too new, so he'd tried to show them to her with his body. He even thought he might have succeeded. The way she'd honored his scar—sweet Jesus, but her mouth was ecstasy and agony all at once on the damaged tissue—then watched him with perfect trust while he made love to her, burned her even more deeply onto his soul.

But now, when he tried to catch her eye, she blushed and her gaze slid away. A little space, that's all she needed. This was new for her, too. Who knew if she'd thought herself in love with Peerless, but it was the first time Matt had felt like this. The thought that he might lose her before he "had" her twisted his gut.

Give her time, Wilcox. Don't scare her off.

When they were dressed, he opened the garage, then closed up the empty truck and slid behind the wheel. Allie got in beside him as he cranked the engine over and started to roll forward down the driveway.

"Wait!" she said suddenly. "I forgot to shut the padlock."

He shifted into park, idling while she jumped out and ran back behind the truck to the garage door. Matt saw her framed in the side view mirror, kneeling by the lock. She stood again, and he looked away quickly, not wanting to be caught ogling her in the mirror.

And then everything behind him exploded in a giant ball of fire and deafening thunder, glass and cement and burning wood raining down like shrapnel.

"Allie!" He hurled himself from the truck, pounding back to where he'd last seen her, but the smoke was too thick, too black—he couldn't find her.

Dear God, let me find her…

~:~:~

Phil kicked Allie's door so hard, her foot throbbed.

She wasn't there. Matt wasn't there. Wherever they were, Phil *knew* they were together, and she couldn't reach him—she couldn't even reach Allie.

Unwanted tears blurred her glasses and she stumbled back down the hall to the elevators. Blindly she pushed the button and rode down, then fled across the lobby and through the spinning glass doors into the blazing heat of the circular drive. She ran to where she'd left the Buick, jumped inside, started it, put it in reverse, and backed out of the parking space. Miraculously, she didn't hit anything, because she hadn't even tried to be careful.

Then she sat in the middle of the parking aisle while the glasspacks went off like fireworks and the smell of motor oil engulfed her.

Where should she go? Where *could* she go?

Nowhere. This was Mecca, and her dad was in Indio, and Matt was God knew where, with Allie, doing God knew what.

It was then she saw it: Allie's car, dead ahead, in a spot way at the far end of the aisle by the hotel's west wing. Phil recognized it from the night Matt drove Allie down from San Francisco. GrimmLand's mechanics must have finally fixed the door, and Tarek probably had them park it so far away because it was the only car in the lot that was older and uglier than the Buick.

Matt. Allie. Her car.

Phil sat for a minute, staring at it. She looked around the interior of the Buick, at the ratty seats with the stuffing coming out, the stained floormats, ancient food wrappers, crumbs, dirt, sand.

Matt. Allie. Her car.

Her car.

Phil reached for her seatbelt, securing it tightly across her chest and lap. She took a deep breath of motor-oil-infused air. She put the Buick in drive.

And then she floored it.

Chapter Twenty-Eight

"NO!" Allie screamed, running up the drive. "Not my house—goddammit, not my house!"

Matt tackled her from behind, lifting her bodily from the ground and half-carrying, half-dragging her toward the street, away from the blazing inferno destroying everything she owned. She fought him—she had to get inside—dear God—her dad's books—*his* book—it was in there. She was losing the only piece of him she had left.

"No!" she sobbed, but Matt's hold was like iron.

"Allie, you can't go in there!"

She tried to bring her arms up, to force him to let go, and when that failed, she kicked him. He jerked at the impact, but held tight.

"Listen to me! There's nothing you can do. Allie, sweetheart, I'm sorry. I'm so, so sorry." He turned her to him, using his strength to absorb her fury as she pummeled her fists against him.

Eventually she realized he was no longer gripping her so tight she couldn't get away. But by then, the fight had left her. He rubbed her back and rocked her like a child, murmuring soothing words into her hair.

"I'm sorry, sweetheart. I can't let you go in there. I can't lose you—I can't."

The distant sound of sirens reached her ears. "I don't have anything left," she whispered against his chest, and his arms tightened around her.

"You have me, princess. You'll always have me."

~:~:~

The rest of the day passed in a blur. When the smoke cleared, they discovered that the entire house hadn't been destroyed after all, just the garage and part of the neighbor's fence on that side. There was fire damage to the wall between the garage and the house, but the bomb was fairly self-contained. Whoever set it hadn't bothered pretending it was an accident, and the police and emergency crews recovered quite a bit of the casing, as well as the timer, from which they hoped to get fingerprints or DNA or some clue as to who the perpetrator was.

The police took statements from Allie and Matt, but when Allie showed her PI license, and Matt's military record and high-level security clearance became known, they were told they didn't have to stay in San Francisco. They could return to San Diego, as long as they promised to come back if necessary.

Allie was so numb with shock, she let Matt lead her to the truck and help her in. Somewhere in the back of her mind, she knew hours had passed since the bomb went off—almost the entire day—but she had no sense of time. He buckled her into the center seatbelt, then got behind the wheel, wrapped an arm around her, and drove one-handed.

She should've been grateful for the contact, for his support, but she couldn't feel anything, physically or emotionally. He glanced at her, then nudged her head down onto his shoulder, kissing her hair.

She digested that, like it was something happening to someone else. Yes, it felt good to be next to him. Yes, she was exhausted. Yes, she needed him. She let herself relax a tiny bit, and felt some of the tension leave his body.

"What do I do now?" she asked, not really expecting an answer.

"It's going to be okay, sweetheart."

"I don't even know what the legalities are. The house wasn't mine yet. Does the owner's insurance cover it?"

"The police will notify him. It will all get taken care of."

Allie jerked upright again. "Oh my God—I don't have renter's insurance. I signed a contract, renting the garage from him. And the garage is the only thing that blew up." She started to laugh, then choked on a sob.

Matt dragged her back to him. "Shhh. Don't worry about it now. We'll figure it out. And we'll get the bastard who did it. I swear to you, princess, we will hunt him down and get him for this."

~:~:~

It was after midnight when they got to San Diego. To Matt's eternal relief, Allie'd gradually come back to him. Exhausted beyond measure, she'd slept for a bit, and when she woke, there was color in her cheeks and a spark of anger in her eyes at whoever'd done this.

Matt had a hunch it was the same guy who broke into her apartment. And he was more and more convinced that both events were related to her work at GrimmLand. If what she'd said about Peerless's typical cases was correct, Matt couldn't imagine exposing an extramarital affair would induce someone to blow up her garage.

Besides, who even knew her not-yet address? Maybe Peerless. Her realtor. Matt. No one down here even knew she was from SF, except Matt's family and Tarek. Plus, the sale wasn't final yet. He didn't know much about real estate law, but until she'd officially closed, her name shouldn't appear on any public records related to the property.

Beside him, Allie stretched and sat up. "Where are we?"

"Almost home." Shit. "I'm sorry. I didn't mean—"

"It's all right. I'm okay. I'll be okay."

Matt exited the freeway, and they drove in silence to the church. He parked the truck, locking it after they got out. Kelly would drive Mike over in the morning to pick it up, and Matt would return the spare key later.

Allie walked slowly to the Testarossa. He couldn't take seeing her so destroyed again. Bad enough when she'd been evicted. Now she'd lost everything. Except her plants, her espresso machine, and her car.

And him.

He unlocked the passenger door. "Where to, princess? Back to the hotel? Or we can head for my place." She didn't respond, and to be sure she understood her options, he pulled her close. "Either way, I'm staying with you. I'm not letting you out of my sight for at least a month."

He felt a small laugh against his chest, then a sigh. "Matt, you don't have to do this. I can take care of myself."

He lifted her chin, meeting her uncertain gaze. "I know you can. Believe it or not, this isn't about you. I—"

His throat closed around the words. Damn it, why was it so hard to say? Or…were his instincts telling him not to scare her off? He was in love with her, and logically, it should be a no-brainer to tell her. But given the intensity of his feelings, and how quickly he'd realized them, she'd likely mistrust them. Considering her experiences with the other men in her life, Matt couldn't blame her.

From inside the car, his cell phone rang. He'd left it there during the wedding, then thanks to Allie absorbing his entire focus for the last two days, he hadn't realized he'd never retrieved it. He considered ignoring it, but any call that came in after midnight couldn't be good.

He released Allie and grabbed the phone, noting Didi's number on the screen. Shit. Allie watched with concern as he answered the call.

"It's Phil," Didi said, nearly incoherent with tears. "She was in a car accident—she's in the hospital. Oh God, Matt—she could have died!"

~:~:~

Wafi was asleep in his shitty apartment when the boss's call came.

"I gave you very simple instructions. You have failed me again."

Abruptly he was wide awake. "What the fuck? I did everything you asked."

"Your instructions were to blow up the house, not merely the garage. And you were to do it after she left, not before."

"What difference does it make? I blew it up, didn't I?"

"I did not want her hurt. What sort of hero will I be if she dies? And you were to leave her a sign to let her know we are serious. There was nothing—*nothing*—to connect this with the kidnappings."

"What are you talking about? I left the fucking patch on the fence."

"It was too close to the bomb. It was destroyed, and no one saw it."

"Yeah, well, I didn't have time for your fucking details. Like that fucking notecard. I almost got caught, wasting time on that, and it didn't even work. Maybe that bitch PI isn't as dumb as you thought."

Silence. Fuck. He hadn't meant to say that.

"Forgive me—"

"You are relieved of your responsibilities. You will leave Mecca and return home tomorrow. Your plane leaves at three."

The call ended and Wafi hurled the phone at the wall.

Fuck. Fuck, fuck, *fuck.*

Light filtered through the filthy window, but the sun wasn't far over the horizon. A cold smile curved his mouth. He still had time. He'd finish what he'd started with *her*.

The boss might own him, but nobody controlled him. Nobody.

~:~:~

Phil's eyes fluttered open. The room was dark, the curtains closed, but it didn't feel like home. Where was she? What had happened?

And then it all came back. The rage, the despair, and the utter calm as she'd floored the Buick and barreled head-on into Allie's car. The Buick was a tank; Allie's two-door compact didn't stand a chance.

Phil remembered slamming into the hatchback, lifting and carrying it as the Buick jumped the curb and plowed over the parking strip into the hotel's west wing, knocking through the bricks, the Buick's hood folding up like an accordion as it squashed into and with the smaller car.

She felt again the seatbelt slamming her back, and then the entire front bench lifting, lurching forward, her head hitting the windshield, her shoulder wedged into the ancient, wide-open steering wheel, before the car came to a screeching, grinding halt.

After that, she didn't remember much. The paramedics must have come; she thought they'd had to cut her from the Buick, but she couldn't be sure. And now she must be in the hospital, though she didn't remember whether they'd brought her in an ambulance or Life Flight or what.

"Phil, honey, are you awake?"

Her dad's voice drifted into her consciousness and she realized he'd been sitting in the dark by the bed the whole time. He leaned forward. It was hard to see his face, but she couldn't miss the tears rolling down his cheeks as he took her hand in his. And suddenly, she was crying, too, deep chest-wracking sobs.

"Baby—I—" He stood and before she knew it, he'd stretched out on the bed, enfolding her in his arms, like he'd never let her go.

"Oh, baby, I'm so sorry. I should have paid attention. I knew how hard this was on you, but instead of making it easier, I just asked you to deal with more and more. I should never have started this now. I'll stop. I'll wait until you're older. We can stay in Mecca, or move anywhere you want. Just please, baby, don't ever scare me like that again."

"Daddy!" she sobbed and clung to him. "I want you to be happy—I want you to have your operation. But I don't want you to leave me."

"I won't ever leave you. Never, ever, ever. Baby, baby, baby…"

He murmured it over and over, holding her close, until she'd cried herself out and begun to drift back to sleep. And still he held her, and she knew when she woke up, he'd be there. And maybe the stupidest thing she'd ever done in her life would bring them both the most happiness.

~:~:~

The next time Phil woke, she felt like Dorothy from the Wizard of Oz, waking up in her bed in Kansas, with her aunt and uncle and all the farmhands crowding around.

Except Phil definitely wasn't in Kansas anymore.

She was in Indio, in the hospital, and her dad wasn't in bed with her, but he was sitting in a chair so close by, she knew he'd only gotten up because she had visitors. Daylight streamed through the windows, and the clock on the wall said it was ten a.m. Her shoulder and her head ached, but she didn't have any casts on, just an IV, so she must not have been hurt too bad.

Her regular glasses had been busted in the crash, but her dad had brought her old pair, so she could see well enough. Matt was there, white and worried, with Allie by his side. Phil blushed when she saw her, but there was no accusation in Allie's expression, only concern, so maybe she didn't know yet that it was her car Phil had plowed into.

Even Bridget was there, and Phil suddenly felt bad for all the mean thoughts she'd had about her. At the time, it'd seemed natural to dislike her and Celia, a kind of protectiveness for Laurette. But really, Bridget hadn't done anything all that bad. And now Celia, her closest friend, was missing. But still she'd taken the time to drive up here.

Phil was starting to think a lot of her problems could be laid at her own door. So maybe her dad could save on the therapy bills after all.

"Hi," she said, to the room at large. And suddenly, everyone was talking at once.

"Kiddo, if you ever pull a stunt like that again, I'll kill you myself."

"Honey, do you want some water?"

"Ohmigod, Phil! I was so worried about you!"

"Phil, I'm really sorry if anything I said upset you."

That last came from Allie, and besides her dad, she was probably the one Phil owed the biggest apology to. She cleared her throat. "I'm sorry, too. I was really mean to you. About the vase, and—some other stuff."

She couldn't bring herself to confess about the car just yet. Maybe when there were less people around.

"That's okay. You've been through a lot."

Pale and exhausted, Allie had dark circles under her eyes and Matt's arm planted on her shoulders, like he was afraid she'd drift away if he didn't hold her down. But instead of it bugging Phil, she was happy for him—for both of them. Just knowing her dad had heard her made her realize how awful she'd been to the people who loved her.

"Are you okay?" she asked, startling Allie, who exchanged a glance with Matt. He gave a slight shake of his head, and Phil said, "Don't worry, I can take it. I won't go driving into anymore walls or anything."

Allie choked on a laugh. "I'm fine. Really. Something did happen, though, I won't lie to you. But it can wait until you're feeling better."

"Okay," Phil said, fiddling with her blanket. "I'd like to hear about it. I mean, if you want to tell me. But if you don't, that's okay, too."

"I'd like that," Allie said. Then she added something that surprised Phil more than anything else. "Maybe you could help me find another present for Darlene and Isaac."

Phil jerked her head up. Allie was serious. That had to be the biggest olive branch ever offered. Matt watched them both, looking confused. Allie must not have told him Phil had tried to sabotage her relationship with his sister.

"Thank you," she whispered, knowing she didn't deserve a second chance, but so, *so* happy to take it.

Bridget came forward then. "Speaking of presents, Meggy sent this over. There's no one else to mind the Shoppe, or she would've brought it herself."

Draped over her arm was the most perfect dress Phil had ever seen. It was a simple sleeveless sheath, no fancy bows or embroidered flowers, and not a pouf in sight. The light green fabric—a much better color for her than yellow or lavender—had darker swirls on it, making it feminine but not too girly. It had an empire waist, which would flatter her small frame, and when she wore it, she knew she'd look like she was actually twelve, instead of the eight most people assumed she was.

"It's beautiful," she breathed. "Thank you!"

Bridget grinned. "The dress is all Meggy. But these are from me." She opened her shoulder bag and brought out a pair of cute green sandals. They were Phil's size, but were much more sophisticated than the little girl shoes she normally had to buy to fit her tiny feet.

Phil was so overwhelmed, she couldn't speak. Fortunately, a nurse came in then and asked everyone to leave except her dad. Matt kissed her forehead on his way out, and she realized she still hadn't talked with him about the man with the tattoo, or seeing Wolf.

"Can you come right back? I really need to tell you something."

"Of course," he said seriously. "I'm sorry I didn't listen to you before."

"That's okay. I just didn't know how to get your attention."

"You've got it now, kiddo. Promise."

~:~:~

Once out in the hallway, Allie headed straight for the coffee pot in the lounge. Halfway through her first large mug, Bridget followed her in.

"Allie, can I talk to you?"

She was bone-tired, and the coffee hadn't kicked in yet. But Bridget was wan, and despite the brave face she'd put on for Phil, Allie knew she was terrified for Laurette and Celia and the others.

"Of course. What is it?"

Bridget seemed embarrassed. "You're not a casting agent, are you?"

Allie's jaw dropped. "No-o. Um…"

"It's just, Celia and I figured out you aren't an actress, and somehow—I really don't know how—I might've, sort of…said I thought you were a talent scout."

Allie snapped her jaw shut. "I'm not," she said at last, trying to hide the hurt. At least now she knew why the popular crowd had included her. She turned back to the coffee pot, and Bridget came to stand beside her.

"I know it looks like we only hung out with you because we wanted something. But—I don't know how to say this without sounding dumb. I've had a lot of fun with you. So, you know, maybe we could still hang out sometimes. If you want." Allie's shock must have been apparent, because Bridget's face fell. "If you're too mad, I understand."

"No! It's just, you're right. I'm not an actress."

She hesitated. Screw it. Tarek's obsession with keeping her undercover wasn't working, anyway. If he wanted to fire her, let him. She'd probably lost the house anyway; she might as well be jobless, too.

"I'm a private investigator," she said, then smiled at Bridget's floored expression.

"Oh. My. God! I should have known! How cool!"

"What?" Matt asked, coming into the lounge.

"I spilled the beans," Allie said. "About being a PI."

"Good for you," he said emphatically, and Allie felt a worry dissipate she hadn't realized she held. All part of craving his approval, she thought, only a little cynically. Knowing his integrity, he'd be glad the deception was over, even if it had been for a good cause.

"Hey," he continued, "Phil wants to talk to me. Under the circumstances, I'd like to stay and hear her out. But I'm your ride, and you're already late for the park."

"I can drive you back," Bridget offered.

"Sure," Allie said. "That would be great. Thanks."

~:~:~

Laying his plans took Wafi longer than he'd hoped. It

would have been simpler if he could've just taken her to his apartment, but the walls were too thin, and he was going to make her scream. Loud.

But he couldn't just drag her into the master bedroom and leave the other bitches unguarded in the front room. He doubted they'd have the guts to attack or escape, but there were five of them, plus *her,* if she was still conscious, and he wasn't stupid.

So, he had three choices: Cuff them together, which would take time and wouldn't stop them from opening the door, as there was nothing to cuff them to that they couldn't drag with them. Or he could blockade them in one of the smaller bedrooms by piling furniture against the door. Or he could replace the inside door handle with one that had an electronically coded lock.

Bingo.

By the time he'd herded the bitches into one of the bedrooms while he worked, and then herded them all back out again, it was late morning. He closed the padlock on his toolbox, then stood. He couldn't miss his flight—he had no idea how the boss would react when he found out what Wafi was about to do to *her,* but by then, Wafi would be on his way home and out of reach. Hell, when he landed, he might even just disappear. He was good at disappearing.

Yeah. He'd have some fun, take advantage of the boss's offer of a free escape pass, and then just fade away.

Wafi faced the bitches. "You." He pointed at *her*. "Get in the bedroom, now."

"No."

Her voice was flat, not scared. She stood stiffly straight, fists balled at her sides. Fine by him. He grabbed the nearest bitch and flipped his knife open, nicking her throat just enough to create a trickle of blood.

"Move it. Or she dies."

The woman whimpered, and he moved the knife to her jugular, pressing against the skin, until *she* said, "Okay! All right, just please don't hurt her."

She backed toward the master bedroom, then stopped, waiting for his next move. That was okay, too. He liked it when they tried to fight back. Emphasis on the *tried.*

He shoved the other bitch aside and strode to *her,* pushing her backwards through the door. She stumbled but didn't fall, her eyes never leaving his. Yeah, she knew what was coming. The front of her dress, which he'd ripped during their last encounter, hung loose, exposing the thin silk and lace of her bra. It did nothing to conceal her tits from his viewing pleasure, and lust pulsed through him for the violations he'd perpetrate on her perfect body.

He turned, shutting the door and locking it. Then—*fuck!*

White-hot light exploded from the back of his skull. He raised his hands to his head, fighting the pain, willing himself to turn and grab whatever weapon she'd used against him. Before he could complete the move, she hit him again, harder. Something metal made a thick, wet sound against his skull, like a hammer into a melon.

His last conscious thought was, *I'll fucking kill the bitch.*

Chapter Twenty-Nine

Back at GrimmLand, Bridget offered to come up to Allie's room and wait while she showered and changed, then walk to the park with her. Allie'd never had a girlfriend before; it was nice. Now that the air was cleared, they both relaxed. And apparently, Bridget didn't think being a PI was geeky; far from it. Instead, she plied Allie with questions during the car ride, and even more in the elevator.

By the time Allie unlocked her door, she was laughing helplessly. "Enough! Seriously—enough about me. Let's talk about you for a while."

"But I'm boring!"

"Hardly. You're an actress. You must have some great insider stories or fun roles to talk about."

"Yeah, that's why I'm stuck out here." Bridget's grin flashed again. "No, really, I only got into this because of Celia. It's fun and all, but she's the ambitious one."

Her face clouded, and Allie touched her arm. "We'll find them. The police are on board now, and Matt and I are still working on it. They'll be okay."

"But what if they aren't?"

"There's no indication they've been harmed. You have to keep believing that."

Bridget smiled wanly. "Thanks. I'll be fine. Go shower. I'll just nose around in all your drawers and stuff."

"Feel free. I have nothing to hide." Allie paused. "I have nothing, period."

A few minutes later, as she was getting dressed, Bridget

squealed from the main room, "Ohmigod! It's him!"

"Who?" Allie asked as she came out of the bathroom.

Bridget stood at the kitchenette table, the photos of Roland's ringmen spread before her. Matt had brought the copies over so Allie could show him which man Laurette had recognized. Matt didn't know him but had left the photos with Allie in case anything else jumped out at her.

Bridget held up the one of Bernard, pointing at the tattooed man. "Him!"

Holy crap. "Where did you see him? When?"

"This morning, here at the hotel. I came to find you after I heard about Phil. I went through the back lot, past the service elevators. He was there, using a card key to get up to the penthouse."

Allie'd never felt thunderstruck before, but that's how she felt now. "Are you sure? How do you know he went to the penthouse?"

"Only certain employees are allowed on the penthouse level. They get a special card key, not white like ours—red. He used a red key to activate the elevator, so he had to be going to the top."

"Oh. My. God." Allie grabbed her phone, dialing Matt's cell. "Pick up, pick up, pick up!"

"What's going on?" Bridget asked. "Who is he?"

Matt's phone went to voicemail, and Allie hung up. She was almost sure, but she had no proof, just her instincts. What if she was wrong? What if she stormed up there or called the cops, and it was just some head of state and the man was his employee? Her credibility with the police—at least in San Francisco—wasn't great. If she was wrong about this, she'd never live it down.

But…what if her instincts were right?

Phil had seen the man in the park, and Laurette saw him

a year ago—*and* he was at Roland's court before that, and now here, at the penthouse. Hadn't Tarek implied it was vacant? Could someone be holding the missing women up there without his knowledge? Maybe even…Wolf?

She didn't want to believe him guilty after all, but her gut said tattoo guy wasn't acting alone. And from how close they were in the photo, Wolf had to know him.

If the women were here at the hotel, and had been all along, then the kidnapper was either beyond arrogant or really smart. Like how Roland had hidden Laurette in plain sight, knowing no one would look for her here.

And if Allie's garage had been bombed by the same person, maybe he was tiring of the game and getting reckless. The women could be in more immediate danger now than before. She had to trust her instincts; they were all she had left. She ran to the safe, unlocked it, and retrieved her gun, loading it quickly.

Bridget gasped. "Ohmigod! They're in the penthouse?"

"I think so." Allie shoved the gun into her waistband "Call the police—tell them to meet me up there. Then keep trying Matt." She scribbled his cell number on a piece of paper. "Tell him about the tattooed guy having a red key."

"Aye, aye, captain!" Bridget pulled out her cell and began dialing, and Allie ran for the elevators.

Dear God, she'd better be right.

~:~:~

Laurette's plan had delivered mixed results so far. Celia and Yvonne were with her, but the others were so frightened, they wouldn't fight back. Not Laurette; she was going to fight until her dying breath.

At least she'd learned some things about herself from this experience. Like, that her confidence at the Princess Shoppe wasn't an aberration. That she could, in fact, lead when called to. And that no matter how nerve-wracking it was, or if he didn't reciprocate, she had to tell Wolf she loved him. She couldn't die without him knowing that.

Speaking of which, one thing she'd gleaned from the bits Wafi let slip was that whoever he worked for, it wasn't Wolf. Not that she'd ever thought it was. Despite his recent anger, Wolf was a *good* man, the best she knew, even including Matt.

It must be Monday now. She'd woken on Friday with a horrid drug-induced hangover, to discover she was locked in the penthouse at the GrimmLand Hotel with all five of the other missing women: Jessica, Vicky, Eva, Yvonne, and Celia. They were unhurt, with the exception of Celia, who'd sustained a small cut on her leg during her kidnapping, and thanks to the luxuriousness of their prison, they were well-cared for.

On the downside, the penthouse had privacy-glass windows, so no one on the outside could see in, even if they weren't so high above the ground. Plus, the other women were so terrified of their captor, it hadn't occurred to them to try overpowering him.

Not Laurette. She'd begun considering her options immediately, keeping her eyes and ears open, using small resistances to test Wafi's response.

Which led to her first piece of useful intel. "Non-violent restraint" was not in Wafi's vocabulary. But those were his boss's orders, especially where she was concerned.

So, she pushed harder. If she drove him to the violence he craved, from which he'd have to constantly check himself, maybe he'd slip up, and she could disable him.

Ironically, it was Wolf who gave her the idea. Normally, he was so composed and contained. But something she'd said or done had pushed him so far, his response had shocked him as much as her.

She didn't blame him, though. After talking with Allie, then having three days with nothing to do but think, she realized how badly his pride was hurt when she ran from him; he'd truly had no other outlet. What that said about his feelings, she didn't know. But she was going to find out.

And the Wafi part of her plan had worked, maybe too well. She'd infuriated him so much, he'd become obsessed with punishing her, to the exclusion of everything else. Now, he wanted to hurt her a *lot*, maybe even kill her.

Still, she *had* to try, to get herself and the others to safety. Yet even as late as this morning, she hadn't known how she would "disable" him when he made his move.

And then God gave her a gift: Wafi brought a toolbox into the room, and a large wrench slipped unnoticed under the settee. Somehow, she'd retrieved it and tucked it inside the back of her torn dress without him seeing, and miracle of miracles, the other women kept her secret.

Unfortunately, after she knocked Wafi out, the solidarity ended. She tried again to marshal her troops.

"Ladies! We have to work together! We can't just sit here and wait for him to wake up."

Proving her point, Wafi groaned from the floor where she'd dragged him. Celia and Yvonne had bound and gagged him with ripped bed sheets, but Laurette wasn't naïve enough to think these would hold him for long. He clearly had military training, as well as bulging muscles that could probably pop his bindings off without much effort. If he was coming to already, they had to hurry all the more.

"But we can't open the lock!" Eva wailed, panic rising in her voice. She was the third woman kidnapped, but acted like she'd been there the longest. "And he moved the hinges to the outside of the door, so we can't unscrew them!"

"Shut up!" Yvonne snapped. "At least Laurette did something. Now think—can we break the lock open? Or just remove the whole thing?"

Laurette shook her head. "He also put those screws on the outside, and I don't want to smash the box and put it into lock-out mode. Maybe we can reprogram it?"

The others looked at her hopefully.

"Okay," she admitted, "I have no idea how to do that. But there must be some way to override the combination."

If only the door wasn't a fire door. If it was wood, they could smash it to pieces and escape that way.

Suddenly, Jessica shrieked from her position on the floor, where she'd been watching Wafi. "He's awake!"

Laurette whirled and met his malevolent gaze above the gag. On his other side, Vicky shook so badly, she almost dropped his knife, which Laurette had ordered her to hold at his throat. Sensing their fear, Wafi twisted and hit Vicky with his legs, knocking her over, the knife flying out of her hands, while he simultaneously flexed his arms and snapped his bonds as easily as Laurette had feared.

"Get the knife!" she screamed at Yvonne. Then to the others, "Help me get his arms!"

She threw herself at him, but only Celia joined her. Jessica was so terrified, she backed away, shaking her head, while Eva ran to where Vicky lay crumpled on the floor.

Wafi thrashed like an enraged bull. Laurette tried to pin his arms at his sides while Celia fought to help. He landed a blow to Celia's head, and she fell back, stunned or unconscious, Laurette couldn't tell.

Wafi had stretched the bindings on his feet almost to the breaking point. He forced his arms out of her grasp, bringing them up and then back down, pinning her own arms at her sides. He gave one final kick and his legs broke free. Then he rolled, forcing her onto her back, and punched her in the stomach.

Laurette had never been punched. All the air left her, and she couldn't get it back. The pain was excruciating and she needed to vomit. Wafi was so livid, he would either beat her to death now, or rape her and then kill her. Either way, she'd die without seeing Wolf again. She fought back wildly, but Wafi was a two-hundred-and-fifty-pound weight crushing her hundred-pound frame.

He drew his fist back again, aiming at her head, his eyes alight with lust and rage. Vaguely, she heard cries and screams from the other women, but it was hopeless. He was too strong, and they were too uncoordinated.

And then chaos erupted. Someone fired a gun outside the door—she heard it bursting open—Wafi looked up, stunned, then down again, face blotched with fury—he grabbed her throat—tightening—so tight—she couldn't breathe—her vision silvered, then went black—another shot—he fell away, and Laurette gasped in air.

It didn't make much difference though. Thanks to the shock of it all, she passed out anyway. Again.

Chapter Thirty

When Matt reached Wolf's private estate in the hills west of Mecca, it was nearly noon. Apparently, Wolf had purchased the property after discovering Laurette's hiding place, to use as his home base when in town. Matt gave his name at the electronic gate, was buzzed in, and drove up the winding drive.

After parking behind Wolf's Jag, he found Wolf in an Adirondack chair on the wide, well-irrigated front lawn. He didn't smile, just waited silently as Matt crossed the grass and sat in the chair by his. There were circles under his eyes and an unhealthy pallor to his skin, and Matt felt like an ass for grilling him while Laurette was still missing. But if there was even a chance Wolf was involved, he had to know.

"Want to tell me why you've been sneaking around GrimmLand with Gillian?"

Wolf's gaze jerked up, eyes bright with anger before despair darkened them again. "It is of no consequence. Once I realized Laurette was here, I began checking on her. I worried for her safety. With good reason, as it happens."

The accusation was warranted, so Matt let it pass, and Wolf continued. "I confronted Roland with my concerns. I suppose you know already that he located the park in Mecca, specifically because it is so remote?"

Matt's brows rose. "Really? He never shared his reasons with me. But…it makes sense. Laurette was so obsessed with fairy tales, and with America, and he wanted to make her happy but keep her out of harm's way."

"Precisely. He feigned ignorance of the land and put the park where it was least likely anyone would search for her."

"What does any of this have to do with Gillian?"

"I was not convinced Laurette was safe, even out here. You are adding a new section, and many laborers come and go each day. I introduced myself to Ms. Sinclair and suggested the addition of more security cameras near the construction site, particularly at the entrances to the—how do you call them? The Mousetraps. She wished to confer with you first, but you have been rather busy."

Crap. No wonder she'd hounded Matt for the Enchanted Flounder plans. "Why didn't you come to me directly?"

"I did not wish Laurette to know I had found her. The secret—her escape—was important to her. And I feared your loyalty to her would outweigh our friendship. Much simpler to ask Ms. Sinclair." He lifted a shoulder. "Also, I hoped to conceal my interference from Roland. God willing, he will one day be my father-in-law. I do not wish to antagonize him."

Wolf had a point. Family ties were messy under the best of circumstances, but when entire nations were involved, they could really be a bitch.

"Have I satisfied your curiosity?" Wolf asked, only a touch sardonically.

"Almost." Matt took the photo of the tattooed man from his pocket and passed it over. "Recognize him?"

"No. Should I?"

"He's talking to you."

Wolf squinted at the photo, then shook his head. "No. He is not. You see—there—that is someone else's hand, a person next to me, obscured by Bernard's head."

Matt took the photo back and squinted himself. Holy shit. Wolf was right. The tattooed man was talking to a third person that Laurette and Allie, even Matt, hadn't noticed. He'd have to show the photo to the police, get them to enlarge it, in case they could get more detail from it.

"Anything else?" Wolf asked.

"No. I'm sorry. You know I had to ask."

"Of course." The anguish in Wolf's eyes was absolute. "My friend, I only want her back. I need her back." His voice broke. Then his cell phone rang, and he brought it out, answered the call, and put it to his ear.

A second later, Matt's phone vibrated in his pocket. He'd forgotten to turn the sound back on after leaving the hospital, and he pulled it out, noting several missed calls before he answered the unfamiliar number showing now.

"Ohmigod!" Bridget's voice squealed. "Allie found them! She found the missing women!"

Listening to his own call, Wolf's expression erupted in pure joy. He raced for his car, with Matt right behind.

~:~:~

By the time she'd finished lunch, Phil was tired of being stuck in bed. After she'd unburdened herself to Matt, her dad had stayed by her side. They'd talked. Shyly at first, then getting better as the day wore on. She told him some of the things she'd been keeping inside, and he told her how scared he was, but also how he knew the operation was the right thing to do. He said again that he'd wait, to give her more time to adjust. Just him saying that helped. If he was willing to delay something so absolutely, utterly huge, for her, then there was no way he was abandoning her.

Then Matt called to say the missing princesses had all been found, and Phil and Didi both had cried for joy. She knew he wanted to go to them, especially Laurette, so she'd told him she'd be okay without him for a while. And she would, because now she knew he'd be back soon.

What was even cooler was that Phil was right about the man with the tattoo. He was the kidnapper, but no one knew who he worked for, because he'd been killed when the police couldn't make him stop choking Laurette. Phil shivered. If Allie and the cops had gotten there a few minutes later, Laurette would be dead.

But she's not dead. She's safe. They're all safe.

I'm safe.

And bored. Very bored.

She moved restlessly, then sat up and unhooked her IV. She was fine. She'd drink some water or something. She got out of bed and wandered into the lounge. Maybe she could find a deck of cards and play solitaire or something.

The lounge served the whole floor, so there were kids' games on shelves, and grownup magazines on tables, and a big TV with an old DVD player. A handful of other patients sat reading or drinking coffee, and as Phil walked by, a gravelly female voice said, "I know you."

Startled, Phil looked up and met Birdie Olsen's sharp gaze. She sat in one of the upholstered chairs, watching a local talk show. Her small, bony body was almost as lost inside her too-big hospital gown as Phil's was in her own.

"Oh—Bird—Mrs. Ols—"

"Call me Birdie. Probably wondering what I'm doin' here, aintcha?" Without waiting for a response, she said, "Been here since that mess at that girl's place. I'm fine. Too cranky to die, but they won't let me go. Keep sayin' my blood pressure's too high. Pfft."

Phil wasn't sure what to say to that, but Birdie was another one she felt bad about, so she tried, "I'm sorry I ran away from you."

Birdie hunched a shoulder, her gown almost sliding off on that side. "Enh. I shouldn't've bugged you. Young girl like you, you got stuff to do. Don't need an old lady like me crampin' your style. Whatcha doin' in here, anyway?"

"Oh."

Embarrassment heated Phil's face. The whole thing had been so stupid, and even though she and her dad were talking again, they hadn't talked about what she'd done yet.

Everyone kept calling it an "accident," but Phil was scared it wasn't accidental. Didn't suicides run in families? What if she was like her mom? What if she really had been trying to kill herself? It was bad enough thinking about it inside. How could she say it out loud to her dad, when he was already so scared for her?

Birdie watched her intently. "Never mind. I already know. It's pretty good gossip around here. You really drive your dad's car into a wall?"

Something about her was so nonthreatening that Phil sat down, slumping low in the chair. "Yeah." She paused, afraid to meet Birdie's gaze. "I think I might've been trying to kill myself."

There. She'd said it. Not to her dad, but to someone who didn't have anything to do with anything, someone not emotionally invested in any of it, who didn't know her, or her mom, and who didn't pussyfoot around the hard stuff.

"Huh."

Phil looked up, but there was no censure in Birdie's eyes.

"That's a scary thing to think."

Phil nodded, throat suddenly clogged with a fresh round of tears. Would she ever stop crying? This was ridiculous.

Birdie considered the matter. "If you'd really tried to kill yourself, I bet you wouldn't just think so. You'd know."

Phil shrugged. She'd started the conversation, and now she didn't know how to continue it. Or if she wanted to.

"You don't look too dinged up." Birdie examined her cuts and bruises with a critical eye.

"What's that supposed to mean?"

"If you was tryin' to kill yourself, you did a pretty poor job of it."

Of all the stupid things to say. Shouldn't Birdie be trying to make her feel better, not worse?

Phil scowled. "I was wearing my seatbelt."

"Ah-ha! There you go. If you was tryin' to kill yourself, you'd'a left your seatbelt off." Birdie's expression was kind, and gentle, and knowing. "So I guess you wasn't."

Phil stared at her. The tears spilled over and she threw herself into Birdie's waiting arms.

"Thanks," she whispered, and Birdie held her tight.

"That's okay. When you're all done cryin', you want to play gin with me?"

"Yes."

"No hurry. I ain't goin' nowheres."

~:~:~

Matt found Allie up in the penthouse where, apparently, the missing women had been kept this whole time. Now they'd all been taken to the hospital, or else checked over by the paramedics and released, and the dead man had been carted off by the coroner. Despite all the cops still combing the room for evidence, Matt pulled Allie into his arms.

"Princess, if you ever go in anywhere with guns blazing again, I swear, I'll—" He stopped, because he really didn't know what he'd do.

She gave him the *you're-a-whack-job* look he loved so much. "First off, I'm a professional. Remember? And second, except for shooting the door handle off, none of the blazing guns were mine. It was all the cops."

That clearly irked her, and he hid a smile, his relief at

her safety overwhelming. "But it was you who figured out where they were. How'd you do that, anyway?"

Allie brought him up to speed, and he told her about Wolf's discovery in the photo.

"Wow," she said. "Can't believe we missed that."

"The guy's almost totally blocked by Bernard, but I'm hoping the crime lab can get something more out of it. What do we know about the guy here?"

"Laurette says his name is Wafi. Ring any bells?" Matt shook his head, and she continued. "He definitely worked for someone, but Laurette didn't learn who. She's sure it's not Wolf, though."

"Me, too. He loves her too much." Matt studied Allie's profile. Maybe now was the time to bring the conversation back to something more personal to them, as well. Then a thought struck him. "Where's Tarek? How did he not know someone was up here this whole time?"

"That bugs me, too. No one can find him. He left for an errand this morning and hasn't been seen since. Wafi had a red card key, but no one knows how he got it. None were reported lost or stolen, but the police will check the elevator logs to see who it was issued to. It's possible the suite's been vacant so long, the card just wasn't missed."

"So Wafi steals the card, sneaks the women in, and uses the service elevators regularly, and no one notices? This whole time?"

"Yes. Maybe *now* it's time for more cameras…?"

He grinned. "All right. You and Wolf win. Here at the hotel, in the employee parking lot, and by the Mousetraps."

"Wolf? What's he got to do with it?"

"Long story. Look, are you done here? Can I ride with you back down to your room?"

Allie glanced at him curiously. It must be obvious he

wanted to get her alone, but all she said was, "Sure."

In the elevator, Matt considered which tough subject to tackle first. Darlene was married, Phil and Didi were reconnecting, as were—hopefully—Laurette and Wolf, and the missing women were safe. None of it thanks to Matt, but at least they were taken care of. Yet somehow, he still had a few burdens weighing on him.

"Allie," he said once they were in her room, "I've got something to tell you."

"Uh-oh." She smiled, unsuspecting. "More bad news?"

"Kind of. It's about your car."

Whatever she'd thought he was going to say, it clearly wasn't that. "My car? What about it?"

This would kill her. But she had to know. "Remember how Phil crashed the Buick by pushing another vehicle into the hotel?"

She nodded, waiting for him to continue. And then she got it and sat down hard on the sofa.

He sat, too, taking her hands in his. "You okay?"

"Okay? I've lost everything I own except my plants and my coffeemaker. I've been evicted and lost my house, since the seller will probably declare a fail-sale after I blew up his garage. The clauses he put in mean my deposit and earnest money are forfeit, so I can't buy anything else. And the one thing keeping me going was that I still had my dad's car."

She started to laugh, and for a second Matt thought she was going off the deep end, the way she had the first time they'd met. Not that he blamed her. This was as good a time as any to lose control. Instead, her laughter sounded genuine and normal, and she wiped at her eyes.

"As Bridget says, *ohmigod!* I have nothing left. Nothing."

"About that. Allie—sweetheart—"

The alarm in her eyes set warning bells clanging in his head. After the bomb went off, when he'd been terrified that he'd lost her, the endearment had slipped out so naturally that she hadn't noticed.

She'd noticed now.

"Matt—"

"Hear me out. You're right: you've lost your apartment and maybe your house. Definitely your car; it's totaled with a capital T. And your old job. You don't have any reason to go back to SF now, so—move in with me."

Allie's jaw dropped. Then she snapped it shut again, a muscle twitching below her ear.

He hurried on. "I know it's sudden, and I've never wanted to share my space with anyone before. But I've been thinking a lot over the last few days. You were right. Ever since I let Roland's assassin get away, I've been trying to make up for it by taking care of everyone else. Laurette, Phil, Darlene. Except for the wedding, I'm not exactly batting a thousand, and even that was more Darlene than me. But you—I can help you. I want to help you."

Matt waited. It hadn't come out very well, but at least he'd said it. The thought of sharing his home—his *life*—with her should have scared the hell out of him. Instead, it filled him with such joy, he didn't know what to do with it all. Surely she'd see this was the best option.

"No."

"What?" He must have misheard. "Take some time—"

"I'm not moving in with you." Her jaw was clenched so tight, he was surprised she'd gotten the words out.

"Why?"

His cluelessness released the floodgates. Allie yanked her hands from his and stood, walking away only to whirl around and stomp back. "Because you said it yourself: this is what you do. You take care of people. I can take care of myself—I'm not one of your responsibilities."

"Allie, this isn't about responsibility."

"Yes, it is. You think I'm out of control—unstable. That you can swoop in and reorder my life, and I'll be grateful and drop everything and go wherever the hell you want."

Clusterfuck. He'd forgotten her father had dragged her back and forth across the country, never realizing she might have put down roots before he yanked her away again. And she'd watched him treat her mother the same way.

"Allie, it's not what you think. I love you."

"No, you don't! You feel bad because, in your view, you failed Roland, and you couldn't protect Laurette or Phil. So you think by saving me, you'll redeem yourself."

So much for his big admission. He stood, gripping her shoulders. "Listen to me. I've never felt like this before. I don't know how to say it right. Obviously. But I love you!"

"If you loved me, you wouldn't ask me to drop everything and leave my home!"

That did it. He gave her a shake. "Dammit! You don't have a home! I do."

She jerked free. "Then why don't you go there?"

He glared at her. How the hell had declaring his love and asking her to move in with him gone so far south? He had to get through to her. He forced himself to calm down.

"If you don't move in with me, what will you do?"

Some of the fight left her, also, and she shrugged. "I'll figure it out. I'll find another apartment, start saving for another house."

"How? With the money Tarek's paying you?"

"Maybe." She hesitated. "Bobby apologized and offered me the partnership again. In writing. I'm going to take it."

Matt's jaw dropped. "You can't be serious. That prick? You'd go back to him rather than move in with me?"

She had the decency to blush. "Bobby's not so bad. I keep telling you that. And he knows me—knows what I'm like. He doesn't want to change me."

"Sweetheart, I don't want you to change."

"Then why did you tell your mother I'd be okay, *after* I got my life under control?"

Shit. He hadn't meant it like that, but there was no reasoning with her now. She'd never believe him, no matter what he said. Before he could figure out how to explain, she went to the door and opened it.

"Matt, please. Just go. I don't belong down here. I've been trying to fit in—I'm not even sure why. I can't leave San Francisco. You have to understand—my dad's grave is there. I have nothing else of his left. I can't leave him."

There were tears in her eyes and Matt's gut twisted. "Allie—"

"I'll be okay. You don't need to worry. I always land on my feet."

He wasn't about to give up that easily, but it was obvious he'd lost round one. He moved to the doorway, then paused. "That's why he called you Allie Cat. Because no matter where he dropped you, you made the best of it."

She looked away from his penetrating gaze, and he sighed and stepped out. She closed the door with a soft click, and he stared at it for a long minute. After growing up with five sisters, he'd thought he had at least some inkling of how to deal with women.

Apparently not.

Chapter Thirty-One

There was a commotion outside Laurette's door. One of the two police officers stationed there said loudly, "I'm sorry, sir. No one is allowed in."

"I am her fiancé!" Wolf's furious voice came through the door. "If you do not let me in, I—"

Laurette rushed to the door and opened it, sparing him the necessity of detailing what he'd do to her hapless guards should they continue denying him access.

"Laurette—sweet—"

He charged between the officers, and once they understood he wasn't a threat, they backed off. She shut the door and turned, to find herself wrapped in his arms.

"I was so worried." His voice broke and he squeezed her harder.

"I'm okay," she said, though just having him there was making her fall apart all over again.

"Truly? You are not hurt? He did not—" Wolf hesitated. "He did not abuse you?"

Laurette shook her head. "He—he tried to. He hit me once, in the stomach. And he tried to choke me."

Wolf drew in a sharp breath. He lifted her hair, lightly touching the bruises on her neck. The sensation set fire to her skin, and her breasts tightened. She shivered, and he quickly withdrew his hand.

"I am sorry. I did not mean to hurt you."

"You didn't. I—"

"Shh." He pulled her close again. "This has been a

nightmare for you. You will need time to recover. I—I will not pressure you. About the wedding, or anything else."

Though he still held her, she felt him withdrawing. He thought he was protecting her. Somehow, she knew that now. All the times he'd been distant, it was because he feared his power and intensity would overwhelm her.

Roland was also powerful and intense, but the difference was that her father threw his weight around to get his way. Wolf's people bowed to his will because they knew he cared for them and made his decisions based on their welfare, not his own needs. She had to make him understand that, in fact, it was those very qualities she loved about him. And she had to know if he loved her back.

"Wolf, listen to me." She tilted her head so she could see his face, but didn't try to leave his arms. His expression was serious, closed off. She plowed ahead. "It was awful. I won't deny it. But it was…good, in a way, too. I didn't fall apart. I fought back—I knocked him out. We almost escaped, and we did survive, because of me."

She couldn't keep the pride from her voice, and his eyes lit warmly. "But that is wonderful. I am proud of you, sweet."

She smiled shyly. Now or never. "Why do you call me that?"

"What? Sweet?"

"Yes."

He gave a puzzled frown. "Surely it is obvious."

"It's not. Please tell me." He regarded her for another moment, and she repeated, "Please."

He sighed. "Very well. It is because I am deeply, desperately, hopelessly in love with you. I have loved you all my life. I had thought that, perhaps, once we were engaged, you would grow to love me, too."

Laurette's heart beat a wild tattoo and she tried to make her voice work, but she couldn't force out a single sound.

Wolf watched her, but her overjoyed expression must have seemed merely shocked, and he released her. "I am sorry. I will begin the process to dissolve our engagement when I return home."

No! He thought she didn't love him. They'd had too many misunderstandings, too many times when they hadn't spoken the truth to each other. And now that she wanted to, she couldn't make her voice work. He started to turn away, and she grabbed his shirt, pulling him back. His brows lifted in surprise. The way her mouth worked up and down, with no sound coming out, would have been comical if she wasn't so desperate.

There was nothing else for it. She let go of his shirt, thrust her hands into his hair, and lifted her mouth up as she brought his head down. She put everything she had into the kiss—the years of love she'd felt, but was too afraid to speak aloud—her hopes and dreams for their future—and the bone-deep desire of her body as it cleaved to his.

The first contact of her mouth froze Wolf in his tracks. She pushed the tip of her tongue against his lips, startling him into opening them. But it was when her tongue twined with his that she finally got through.

He broke the kiss, cupping her face in his hands, the hope in his eyes piercing her to her soul. "Laurette? Sweet?"

His expression was urgent, and suddenly, the barrier was broken. "Yes—I love you. I've loved you for so long. Please—just, please…"

That was all she could manage, but he understood. "Darling—are you sure? Your ordeal—"

She put her hands over his, pressing them tighter against

her cheeks. It was such a cliché, but it was how she felt, so she said it anyway. "Make me forget."

"Sweet—"

He brought his mouth down to hers again, the depth and heat of his kiss searing the blood in her veins. His hands were everywhere, stroking, gentling, assuring, igniting. He scooped her up and carried her to the bedroom, kissing her all the while, his tongue loving her mouth until she thought she might die from it.

Setting her on the bed, he stretched lightly on top of her, eyes filled with wonder, shining with unshed tears. "Is it true? Does the kindest, warmest, most beautiful woman I have ever known truly love me?"

That a man as strong and proud as Wolf would be moved to tears by her love made her own eyes well up. She turned her head, kissing his palm. "I'm the luckiest woman in the world."

He made love to her then, in every sense of the term. As he undressed her, he worshipped her body with his. He showed her first with his hands and mouth what their lovemaking could be. And he encouraged her to explore the hard planes and smooth muscles of his body, until he finally caught her hands in his.

"Sweet—I cannot take much more." He moved on top of her again, nudging her legs apart. He stretched her slowly, then began a gentle rhythm, an ancient dance, increasing the intensity little by little, minute by minute, until she was crazed with wanting.

"Wolf!" she gasped at last. "Stop being so damn gentle!"

A deep laugh burst from his throat. "I love you, sweet."

It felt good—he felt good, and so right. "I love you, too."

Incredibly, her fairy tale had a happy ending after all.

~:~:~

Allie stared, unseeing, at the photo of Wafi. She'd been studying it for thirty minutes without processing it. Instead, she thought about Matt and his absurd, impossible offer. She acknowledged he'd been sincere and might even really think he loved her. And she did love him. He was kind and generous and sexy. Intelligent, conscientious, and incredible in bed. What wasn't there to love?

But what happened when the novelty wore off? When he realized she'd never be "stable" or "in control?"

Even she knew that now. Maybe once she'd hoped she could be. But in the ten days since coming to Mecca, she'd already moved twice. Stability was not in her genes. She just kept gravitating back to what she knew: Total Chaos.

And who she knew. Her cell rang, and she answered it.

"Hi, Bobby."

"Babe. I got your message. What's up?"

"I—" How to begin?

Hey, remember how I quit just before you fired me? And then I dumped you and you still offered me my job back, but I refused? You were really nice and I kicked you in the teeth. Remember that? Good times. Well, now I've lost two homes and my car in one day, while irreparably hurting the man I love after he also tried to be nice to me. So I've decided to come back to work with you after all. How about it?

"Babe?"

"Sorry." She took a deep breath. "We found all the missing women, and I've almost solved the case down here. I'm coming home in a few days, once I get a couple things settled." *Like finding Wafi's boss, getting my second check, and buying another car. Oh, and avoiding the hell out of Matt.* "I'd like to take you up on that partnership offer."

Silence radiated through the line. She hadn't expected a party, but she'd thought he'd be a *little* happy at the news.

"Bobby? You there?"

"I'm here." He paused, then sighed heavily. "You're going to hate me. But this is for your own good. I'm taking the offer back again."

"What?"

"I told you you'd hate me. Look, when I wrote the offer, I thought it would be great for you to come back. Like old times, only better, because I've matured, blah, blah, blah."

Allie's jaw hurt. She forced it to unclench. "But…?"

"I know how you feel about loverboy, and how he feels about you." She tried to deny it, but he barreled over her. "And I know you. You think you're too different, that you can't fit in. That somehow you belong on the sidelines, instead of out in the game. Allie—babe—everybody's too different. We all feel that way. But instead of letting it rule your life, you've got to get out and play anyway. You might be the best thing that ever happened to me. Which is why I'm telling you—go. Be with Matt. Take your chance at real, honest-to-God happiness and run *with* it, not from it."

It was the longest speech he'd ever given her. It sounded a lot like a lecture. And—he might be right. She did love Matt. So why was she running from him?

"But…I can't leave my dad."

"I know, babe. I know."

She'd half-hoped he'd have an answer for that one, too. "And I'm homeless."

"Temporarily. You'll close in a few weeks, right?"

"Not exactly." She told him about the bomb, finishing with, "My dad's book is gone. Plus, my car's a pancake."

There was a pause. Then she heard a low chuckle, growing to a laugh, and then to great guffaws. He finally regained control, wheezing, "Allie. Babe. You're so messed up, you *have* to start over. The universe is telling you to stay in San Diego. I finally put the partnership in writing, and you get it *blown up?* You don't even have a ride up here…" He started to chuckle again, and she felt herself smile.

"I know. I'd at least like to find the bastard who did all this. I'm pretty sure it's the guy behind the kidnappings, but we still don't have any solid leads. How the hell did he know where my house was, anyway? And my apartment. The break-in happened like an hour after Tarek hired me."

Bobby stopped laughing. "Shit!"

"What is it?"

"Babe, you're going to hate me even more."

"Bobby, I could never really hate you. You know that."

"You might change your mind in a minute. There is someone who knew the address of both the house and your apartment. I didn't put it together at first, because we thought the break-in was from one of our old cases. Half an hour after you left that day, Tarek called and—I'm really sorry, babe—asked me to run a background check on you. I gave him the basics immediately over the phone. Including your address."

Allie's head spun. Tarek had known where she lived? How long had it taken to complete the inspection, then drive with Matt to her apartment? At least a couple hours. Plenty of time for a man accustomed to acting quickly to have her apartment searched. But why? Whether it was Tarek or not, she still didn't have a clue what the purpose was.

Then all at once an image of the photo of Bernard and Wafi flashed before her. "Ohmigod! Bobby, I've got to go. Thanks for telling me—I don't hate you. I don't know if I'm coming back or not, but I don't hate you. Okay?"

"Thanks, babe. I don't deserve it. But I'll take it."

She hung up, then retrieved the photo and brought it over to the window where the light was better. There. How had she missed that? The hand behind Bernard was smooth and manicured, free of Wolf's scars or even Wafi's callouses. Not exactly effeminate, but definitely…elegant.

Plus, the skin tone was more olive, compared to the "Snow White" Luradellians and Ruedians. Perhaps because its owner was half…Zulfiqarian?

She had to show Matt. It was a little after one-thirty, so he was probably in his office. Grabbing her purse, she shoved the photo in it, then ran for the door and opened it.

Tarek stood on the other side.

"You have ruined everything," he said. Then he used the gun in his hand to force his way in.

Chapter Thirty-Two

On his way through the hotel lobby, Matt ran into Didi. She fell into step with him, more relaxed and at peace than she'd been in a long while.

"Things better with Phil?"

"Yes. We're going to be okay. *She's* going to be okay."

Matt understood. Not many people knew about Phil's mother's suicide. When he'd learned what Phil had done, it had crossed his mind to wonder. But after talking with her, it seemed more like she just wasn't being heard and had run out of options for getting anyone's attention.

"Good," he said.

"Yes." They walked in silence toward Matt's office for a bit, then Didi said, "So. I saw Tarek waiting outside Allie's door."

"He's back, then? Maybe we can figure out how this Wafi guy got into the penthouse."

Didi slanted him a look. "I also went to see Laurette, but Wolf is with her. After all the drama, I thought you'd be getting busy with Allie." Matt grunted, and Didi laughed. "Like that, is it?"

"Yes. No. I don't know." Matt blew out a breath. "I told her I loved her and asked her to move in with me."

"And she said you were insane and broke it off."

Matt grunted again, and she laughed again.

"Damn it, Didi. What was I supposed to do? I love her, and I know damn well she loves me. When people love each other, they say it. That's what you're supposed to do."

"Must be nice, having all that certainty. Knowing your place in the universe—where you've been, where you're going, and where you belong."

"I get that she didn't have any of that growing up. But I can *give* it to her now. Why won't she let me?"

Didi said seriously, "I haven't known Allie long. Is there anything in her makeup that indicates she wants to be dependent on someone else? Even in a small way?"

"She wouldn't be dependent! We'd be living together—hell, she can pay rent if she wants."

"It would still be your house. Your town. Your family. Even your friends. What part of that would be *hers?* If, God forbid, you ever broke up…"

Matt stopped. "Shit."

"Exactly. She also might be feeling a lack of confidence on your part."

"That's ridiculous. She's smarter and more capable than anyone I know. Look at what she's had to overcome, and how well she's done." Didi just watched him. "Okay, I know at first I said her life was a mess, but all things considered she's done damn well. I have complete confidence in her." Didi didn't budge, and after all, she'd had a point with the dependence thing. *"Fine.* How so?"

"Let me ask you this: when the women went missing from the park, and Tarek told you he was hiring a PI, how did it make you feel?"

Matt opened his mouth, then shut it. He tried to figure out how it was different, except it wasn't—it was exactly the same.

Didi's mouth quirked up on one side. "By offering to take her in, you told her you don't think she can fix this herself. And she *has* to fix it, or she'll never get past it."

Matt started moving again, thinking. They were almost

at his office. "But she said she's going back to work with that prick, Peerless."

"Did you call him that to her face?"

"Of course."

"So now you don't trust her judgment."

"What the f—"

He stopped at the door to the employee complex and stared right through it. *Damn.* Allie'd said more than once that Bobby wasn't as bad as Matt thought. She was smart enough that, over a ten-year period, she wouldn't keep wasting her time on him if he was really awful. Matt was sure she wasn't in love with Peerless, and didn't think she planned on anything physical. *At least, she'd better not.*

But from her perspective, maybe a business partnership with someone she'd known a long time, in an established agency, in the closest thing to a hometown she'd ever had, wasn't as dumb an idea as Matt had suggested. To her.

He pinched the bridge of his nose. "So when I thought I said *I love you*, what I really said was, *You're weak, incompetent, and not very smart.*"

"Pretty much."

"Why do you have all the answers?"

"Doll, if the glass slipper fits…"

~:~:~

For the next hour, Matt holed up in his office. During the last week, he'd done virtually nothing for his "real" job, and now mounds of paperwork were piled everywhere. Something as mindless as filling out reports and filing was perfectly suited to his current mood.

He kept replaying the conversation with Didi. She was right: he should have considered Allie's history and feelings before making his "magnanimous" offer. The question now was, how to fix it? Every idea he came up

298

with had some kind of obstacle, and by the end of the hour, the only two things he knew for certain were that Allie was going to be part of his life if it killed him, and he had a headache a mile wide.

Beyond that, something else niggled at him. Didi'd mentioned finding the right person for the job, much as Tarek had wanted to hire Peerless because of his supposed reputation for "unusual" cases. But when Matt mentioned that to Allie, she'd said Bobby mainly handled cheating spouses.

So why would Tarek think such a thing? And once he realized his mistake, why not immediately leave and go to another agency, instead of trying to hire Peerless anyway?

The answers to either question eluded Matt, and he suddenly realized he'd filled out a purchase requisition for new security cameras on a form used for incident reports. He threw down his pen in disgust and looked up to find Wolf coming into his office.

Matt assessed him. "You look…well."

A satisfied grin split Wolf's fierce face. "Better than I have ever been in my life." He sat in the chair, his expression growing more beatific by the moment. "She loves me. We have straightened everything out and we are to be married next month. You will be my best man."

"No."

Wolf laughed, a sound of unrestrained joy. It was nice to hear after Wolf had been through so much pain. But it didn't change Matt's mind.

"I mean it. I'm done with weddings." He almost said *with other peoples' weddings,* but stopped in time. If Allie wasn't ready to move in with him, he doubted she'd find marriage a satisfying alternative. Not that he was considering marriage.

Was he considering marriage?

He was considering marriage.

Jeez. After ten days.

Wolf said, "Laurette thought you might feel that way. If you will not be my best man, perhaps you would prefer to be her maid of honor instead."

Matt put his head in his hands. "Fine. You win. I'd rather bat for your team."

"Consider it a personal favor. My friend—you realize you are done? With your obligations to Roland? You are free to get on with your life."

"Not quite. We still don't know who Wafi's boss is."

"Even so, Roland has decided to close the park at the end of the year. Laurette will come home with me now. There is no need for you to stay. Go. Take care of your own personal matters."

Once Wolf started smiling, he hadn't stopped. It was getting on Matt's nerves. He picked up his pen and a new, blank purchase form. "I'm kind of busy here."

"Have you understood me?"

"About the park? Yes. It doesn't surprise me. I'll be gone before then, anyway. But today, I have work to do."

"Ah."

"No. Not *ah*. Just work."

Wolf sat back in his chair. "What is the problem? You love her, yes?"

Matt threw the pen down again. *"Yes."*

"But…what? She does not love you?"

"Of course she does. Look, it's great you and Laurette sorted everything out. It's not that easy for the rest of us."

Wolf's expression grew thoughtful. "Is it your injury? Do you fear disappointing her in the act of love?"

"No. What in God's name gave you that idea?"

Wolf threw up his hands, palms out. "No insult intended, my friend. It is just that Tarek mentioned the extent of your wound and its location. I understood there was some concern that you might lose your leg. Naturally, I wondered if anything else had been affected."

"My equipment is fine, thank you. Perfectly functional."

"Merely…functional?"

"No! Better. Allie has been fully satisfied. *By me.*"

If Wolf hadn't been his friend and the Crown Prince of Ruedi, Matt might have—*Hell!*

He shot up, knocking the stack of papers off his desk. *"What did you say?"*

Wolf looked confused. "What? When?"

"A minute ago, at the start of this absurd conversation!"

"That Tarek told me—"

"My God—*Tarek* is the one who tried to kill Roland."

Wolf stood. "What? You are certain? But how?"

"No one knew the severity of my injury—*no one*—except Roland and his doctors—and the man who shot me. If Tarek told you that, then either he's the gunman, or he employed the man who was."

Wolf's face blazed with fury. "Where is he? May God damn him for eternity—*where is the bastard?*"

"He's with Allie." Matt couldn't believe how calm his voice sounded, when his soul was being ripped to shreds. "Didi saw him at her hotel room an hour ago."

Wolf's ashen expression did nothing to reassure Matt. "No. He is at the airstrip. Laurette wished to leave today, so I contacted the controller. Tarek's plane was to depart at three—and it is now half past two."

Something cold and hard gripped Matt's heart. "We don't know he took her…"

"He left the hotel—she was in his car. I saw them, not ten minutes ago. I will call the police." Wolf retrieved his cell phone, but Matt's face must have shown his impotent rage and agonizing fear. Wolf gripped his arm. "My friend, you *must* think clearly. Hit me—it will help."

Matt did want to hit something—preferably Tarek. But even if Wolf thought he owed Matt for having hit *him* when Laurette disappeared, Matt couldn't bring himself to do it. Instead, he turned and kicked a gaping hole in the wall behind his desk.

"Let's go," he ground out, and didn't wait to see if Wolf, still on the phone with the cops, followed him.

~:~:~

"Where are we going?"

Tarek didn't acknowledge that Allie'd spoken, and she went back to studying the passing scenery. She already knew he was taking her to Roland's airstrip; that was obvious. *Why* he was doing it was the part she hadn't figured out. And she needed to know. For one thing, puzzling it out kept her from hyperventilating.

She still wasn't sure how he'd gained control over her so easily. She'd been in tough spots before, although admittedly, none as tough as this one. For one thing, the police had taken her gun as evidence, even though she'd only shot the door handle with it, not Wafi. But it wouldn't have mattered if she'd had it, as Tarek had patted her down and made her leave her purse and phone behind.

Still, she'd always pictured herself kicking the gun out of an assailant's hand if the need arose. And she'd certainly never imagined she'd just cave and let herself be walked from her hotel room to Tarek's car without putting up a fight.

Of course, he kept the gun on her the whole time, albeit

in his coat pocket. Plus, his grip on her arm showed surprising strength. She had the advantage of an inch or two of height, but he was more muscled. And more cold. He'd shoot her without a second thought if she resisted.

He was also supremely arrogant. Maybe the chance to brag about his own brilliance would buy her enough time to figure out an escape plan.

"From what Laurette overheard with Wafi, we get that you're running a white slavery ring, planning on shipping the princesses off to your buyers back in Zulfiqar."

That did the trick. He gave her such a look of scorn that she flinched.

"Do not be absurd. The women were not in any danger."

"But Wafi said—"

"Wafi should have kept his mouth shut and performed the task to which he was assigned. It is well the police terminated him. I should have shot him myself long ago."

His indifference sent chills down Allie's spine. It was clear the only reason Tarek *hadn't* hurt the hostages was because it didn't fit his master plan. Whatever that was.

The gate to the airstrip lay ahead, and past it, a waiting plane. *Crap.*

"Are we picking someone up? Roland, maybe?"

"Imbecile."

Allie wasn't sure if he meant Roland or her. "Okay. Not picking someone up. We must be going someplace. Where? And why?"

The car rolled up to the security gate, and Tarek lowered his window while the guard verified his identity. Allie moved in her seat, and instantly Tarek's gun was pressed into her temple. The guard, likely from Luradel or even Zulfiqar, obviously wasn't paid to have an opinion about his employer's actions, and remained expressionless while returning Tarek's ID.

"Your plane is almost ready, sir. Please proceed to the airstrip."

He raised the barrier arm and Tarek drove through. As far as the guard knew, Tarek was Roland's right-hand man and had authority to do whatever he wanted, with whomever he wanted.

Shit. Shit, shit, shit.

Okay, Allie Cat. How can I land on my feet this time?

An image of Matt rose before her, and with it came a surge of panic. *Dear God, I just found him. Let me get back to him—just let me get back.* If—*when*—she got out of this, she'd find a way to make it work. *Dad, I love him. I need him. But I can't leave you. I can't leave either of you.*

Tarek moved the car onto the dirt near the runway, putting it into Park with the engine idling. The plane sitting on the tarmac was a large jet, and Allie's heart sank. Tarek wasn't planning a short jaunt; he was taking her very far away. And since he hadn't killed her outright, maybe he was implementing the white slavery thing after all.

Movable stairs butted against the plane's side, two men in military dress at their base. The entrance gate lay a few hundred yards behind the car, across wide open space where Allie would be an easy target. And like nearly everywhere else in this damn region, the far side of the airstrip was formed by steep, dead hills, leading up-up-up into steeper, deader mountains.

Tarek still aimed the gun at her head, and the men waiting by the plane weren't going to help her.

"Why are you doing this?" she asked. "If you're pissed, why not just shoot me and escape?"

A slow, cold smile spread over his face. "It is not you that I am, as you say, *pissed* at. If I were to shoot you, the end would be quick. Painless. However, you suffering—alive, but unreachable—for years on end…” His voice trailed off, and he watched while she processed.

“Matt. You’re punishing Matt. But—*why?* What did he do to you?”

Tarek gestured impatiently with the gun. “Stupid, stupid woman. *This* is why I hired you! Why could you not remain this thick-witted all along?”

Despite the gun and the dire straits, Allie’s jaw dropped. “You hired me *because* you think I’m a bad PI?”

“Of course. For me to frame that interloper Wolfram, someone else must discover his guilt. Roland would be suspicious if it came from me. You clearly are unable to think objectively during times of stress. Yet instead of following my clues, you ignored what was right beneath your nose.”

Everything was coming together. Allie thought fast. “You tried to kill Roland, but Matt stopped you. You’ve been waiting for another chance, working alongside Matt this whole time. That’s why you kept telling him to get on with his life—you were afraid he’d put it together.”

And the final piece clicked. “You’re next in line for the throne. If Roland is killed or deposed before legalizing female succession, you can stop being plain old Tarek from Zulfiqar and instead be King of Luradel.”

“As I should have been all along.”

“I don’t understand—”

“Fool! Bertrand was the elder twin, by one minute. *One minute.* My father should have been king, but when their mother’s womb was cut open, they feared for Bertrand’s life and delivered him first. He was sickly. *My* father was strong, as I am stronger than Roland. If Laurette is queen, she will have no control. Who would obey a woman? And that idiot Wolfram will be no better. Weak, all of them!"

He seemed to have forgotten they were in the still-idling car. The passenger door didn't open from the inside, and he leaned against the driver's door, blocking her access. His eyes were glassy, focused not on her but on his grievances.

Maybe she could grab the gun and gain control of the car. The men on the tarmac were armed but far enough away that she might escape before they shot the tires out. The plane would be ready soon—she had to keep him talking. If he got her onto the plane, there'd be no hope.

"Okay," she said, "you tried to kill Roland, and it didn't work, so…you decided to wrest the throne from him by framing Wolf? That doesn't make sense."

His crazed eyes zeroed in on her. *"Stupid cow.* With Laurette's lover in disgrace and her precious park exposed as a slavery ring, who would allow her to inherit the throne? Who would support legislation from the man who encouraged the union with Ruedi in the first place?"

Humor him—remind him how brilliant he is. Get him off balance—it's the only hope.

"Isn't stabilizing Luradel's borders a good thing?"

"Not with Ruedi!" The distraction worked. He gestured with the gun, intent on correcting her ignorance. "Roland depleted the royal reserves building this absurd land of fantasy! Ruedi will sap Luradel's remaining resources until she is dry. She will never recover, and her people will succumb to the interlopers. Roland is ten times a fool for giving Laurette to Wolf."

"So," Allie said slowly, "disgrace Wolf, get Roland deposed while there's no one to support Laurette, then swoop in and save the country, after taking credit for rescuing the women." She was running out of topics—she needed more time. "But what I still don't understand is why you broke into my apartment and blew up my garage.”

For a second, she thought she’d said the wrong thing. His eyes darkened and his finger tightened on the trigger as he pointed the gun at her forehead. Then he regained control, and she let out an inaudible sigh of relief, shifting imperceptibly, waiting to make her move.

“That imbecile, Wafi. He was to blow up your house as a warning. But he could not even set the bomb properly, and the clue you were to find was destroyed.”

“Clue?”

“A Ruedian crest.”

God, he was arrogant, assuming everyone would believe the absurdity of his framing Wolf. Like the notecard, on which they now knew Laurette had written a W for Wafi, before Tarek ordered Wafi to add the “OLFRAM.” But then, short though their acquaintance was, the one thing Allie knew about Tarek was that he believed himself superior in every way to those around him.

He shifted impatiently, so before he realized she was stalling, Allie said, “Was it your idea to make the crimes follow the fairy tales? To further point the finger at Wolf?”

“I see you are not a total loss as an investigator. Yes. Laurette was obsessed with fairy tales, and Wolfram made it his business to study them as well.” His gaze hardened. “However, neither you nor Matt were smart enough to pick up the obvious clues I left for you. Perhaps I should have employed your former lover, Mr. Peerless, after all.”

“You’re insane,” Allie said. She couldn’t help it, and from his unchanged expression, it didn’t matter anyway.

“Perhaps. Many great rulers were misunderstood by their peers. Choices that seem unusual to you may be viewed differently by the grateful citizens of my realm.”

A shout came from the gate and Tarek turned. Allie

didn't wait for a second chance. Lightning fast, she knocked the gun from his hand, then lunged across him and yanked his door open. Her weight and momentum pushed him backwards, his foot hitting and releasing the parking brake, and suddenly, they were moving forward.

They were half in the car, half out, rolling toward the plane and the two guards, who Allie heard running toward them, though she couldn't see around the swinging door. Tarek had a death grip on her arms. She couldn't get away—she strained her body forward and caught the door handle, then wrenched herself back, slamming the door into Tarek's head. He released her and she swiveled, grabbing the wheel and shoving her feet down to the pedals. She was sitting on him—the guards were almost to them—she yanked the wheel around and stepped on the gas.

The car spun, tires crunching, and she aimed it toward the gate. A gun went off behind her and she scrunched down. Tarek grabbed her waist and she clung to the wheel, refusing to give him purchase. There was a police car on the other side of the gate, a red sports car beside it—*Matt*—he was getting out—shouting—he spotted her—he ducked under the gate, running toward her, the cop car following, breaking through the barrier arm. She slammed the brakes, and Tarek's car fishtailed to a dust-cloud stop.

"Allie!"

Matt reached her—pulled her out—was she okay— yes—releasing her—*don't go anywhere*—jerking Tarek out by his lapels—punching him square in the face—Roland's ring *crunching* his hawkish nose before he dropped to the ground, out cold, blood staining his perfect white suit coat.

Then Matt was back, and she never wanted him to leave, and he held her tight and it was going to be okay. She would *make* it be okay.

Chapter Thirty-Three

"Matt—"

"Talk later. First, *this.* "

He pulled Allie close and covered her mouth with his. Her sweet-spicy apricot scent filled his nostrils, the taste of her tongue sliding over his and arousing his body so much, he ached.

After they'd been cleared to leave the airstrip, he'd managed to get her to GrimmLand and into his office with the door shut and the blinds down. It was the closest place he could think of that would afford some privacy but wouldn't have the bad memories of the condos or her hotel room. If there'd been time, he would have taken her to San Diego, but as it was, he'd barely kept his hands off her on the five-minute drive over here.

"Jesus," he muttered. "Don't ever scare me like that again." He slid his hands up her rib cage, feeling the soft weight of her breasts, the buds of her nipples as he ran his thumbs lightly over them. She was so responsive—so *alive*. "When I think what might have happened…"

Fear still coursed in his veins. He needed the affirmation that his worst nightmare *hadn't* happened, that she was there, in his arms, and he was never going to let her go. He moved his lips over hers, coaxing her mouth open, using his tongue to meld them together, crushing her against his chest, next to his erratically beating heart.

After a minute, she broke the kiss. "Matt—really—we need to talk."

"I know. But I'm telling you right now, we are going to live together, and nothing you say will change my mind."

"Matt—"

"I mean it, Allie. I'm done with Roland, the park, all of it." To prove his point, he yanked Roland's ring off and threw it across the room. God, it felt good, literally a weight off his hand.

Allie said, "I'm trying say that living at your place—"

He shook his head. "Not at my place. Your place. I'm leaving San Diego. Whatever you do—wherever you go— I'm coming with you."

Her shocked expression was about what he'd expected.

"You can't leave your family, your friends— everything!"

"Watch me."

"But—"

"I thought you might need persuading." He dropped to the carpet, pulling her down beside him, then quickly removed his shirt.

Allie stopped looking shocked and started to laugh. "Are you crazy? Here?"

"Okay, if we're going to make this work, we need ground rules. Number one: Never laugh when I take off my clothes. And no, not crazy, unless you mean with lust."

He pulled her shirt over her head before her half-hearted protest was fully voiced, then unhooked her bra with one hand.

"You have *got* to show me how you do that," she murmured, then gasped and arched her back as his mouth closed over one luscious peak. The way her nipple hardened as he sucked it sent heat straight to his groin, and he unbuttoned his jeans, kicking them and his briefs off in one motion. He unzipped her shorts, sliding his hands inside to caress her rear, pressing his erection into her soft heat while he tongued her other nipple to a tight peak.

Her hands tangled in his hair, holding his head to her breast, while she writhed beneath him. He shoved her shorts and panties out of the way, then reluctantly abandoned her breasts to extract a condom from his wallet and pull it on. Thank God he still had one left after their trip to SF.

Before he could turn back, Allie rolled on top of him, her mouth meeting his as he rose up to her, her sweet tongue making him wild. He reached for her—she was slippery and ready—and he held her hips and rocked up and into her.

Then he forgot his own name as she slid up and almost off, then down onto him again, over and over. *Down*-up-*down.* Matt groaned. He was so close already—she did this to him, all thoughts of going slowly lost in the urgent need to spill himself inside her. He dropped one hand to the place where they were joined, stroking and teasing her, watching her eyes close in pleasure. Now—this was the time.

"Allie, look at me."

She forced her eyes open. He saw the effort it took her, still sliding slowly up and down, still driving him to the brink, only to pull back at the last second.

"I love you," he said simply. "You're smart, you make me laugh, and you don't take crap from me or anyone else."

He increased the pressure of his thumb, ever so slightly, and she sucked in a sharp breath.

"You're so hot, I can almost come just watching you. And when I'm inside you, I never want it to end, but at the same time, I can't hold back."

Her muscles tightened on him, and he knew she was about to go over, that he was sending her there, and that when she went, she'd take him with her.

"Sweetheart, let me be with you—let *us* find out where

this is going. Please, Allie, give us a chance."

He moved his thumb once more and she cried out, clenching, pulling him deep, deep inside. He rocked up, hard, harder, and then he was flowing into her—every part of her—she was *his*—no matter how often she denied it.

~:~:~

When Allie was finally spent, and Matt had stilled, she rolled off, waiting while he removed the condom. Then she snuggled against his shoulder and kissed his neck. Their hearts gradually slowed, and she wished this moment could go on forever. Except…

She pushed far enough up on her arms to look down at him. He had that male *I-could-sleep-for-weeks* post-sex expression on his face, and she almost hated to disturb him. But they needed to talk.

"You know," she said, "it might be nice to do this on a bed sometime. The whole table-garage-office-floor thing is romantic and all, but my knees are starting to hurt."

He grinned without opening his eyes. "You don't have a bed. Or a table."

"Or a garage. I know. About that…"

Matt's eyes opened, his expression abruptly sober. "You'll figure it out. I'd like to help if you'll let me. But not because I think you can't do it yourself—"

She put a finger over his lips. "I know. Let me talk. I was trying to tell you this before but you, um, distracted me." Matt looked smug and kissed her fingers. "Stop it! You're doing it again."

"That's the plan. When you get all serious like this, it's not good news for me. How about we skip the talk and I persuade you some more instead?"

"Matt!" She couldn't help laughing. "Listen to me!"

He sighed, aggrieved. "Okay. But it won't do you any

good. My mind is made up, and in case you haven't figured this out already, I'm persistent."

"I know. I've figured a few other things out, too. Not just about you—about me. And my dad."

Matt's eyes flashed, but he didn't say what she knew was on his mind. He didn't have to, because she'd finally realized something she'd never understood before.

"You already know how my mom gave up everything for my dad. How he dragged her around the country to different universities until she died, and then he kept on dragging *me*. And you know how that affected me, how I absolutely need to settle in one spot, and not give myself up like she did."

"Allie, I get that. You need to be your own person, and not live on someone else's terms."

"I know." She smiled at him, her heart so full of love, she could barely contain it, let alone express it in any way that made sense. "I'm not worried about you controlling my decisions; my dad's the one who's been doing that."

Matt looked confused. "Your father? But…he's dead."

"I know," she said again. "It took a lot, but I finally realized he's been gone for ten years, and he's still dragging me with him. I kept thinking I couldn't leave San Francisco because I needed to be near his grave. Then I lost every last piece of him—his book—his research—his photo. Even his damn car. And suddenly, I'm free. He can't force me to pack up and leave, and he can't make me *stay,* either."

Allie took Matt's face in her hands, memorizing the feel of his strong jaw, leaning in to kiss that slightly crooked nose, then pulling back to watch as hope flared in those fiery gold eyes.

"I love you, Matt. I love you so much. I love your family, your friends, your ridiculous car. And I love your house. If you'll still have me there—"

"Yes." He pulled her back down, his mouth hard on hers, arms encircling her, hands sliding over her naked back. "But don't call it my house. Make it *your* house. If you want a room to yourself, it's yours. Any room—all the rooms. I don't care, as long as you're there."

"Thanks, but I love your—*my*—house the way it is. The open space is fabulous."

He pulled back. "If you want more space, I'll tear down the wall to the bedroom."

She grinned. "There's a metaphor in there somewhere. But all I really want is somewhere for my plants to grow. And I want you."

"Don't forget your espresso stand. You'll need a whole counter just for that." She laughed, the movement bringing their bodies into closer contact. He hardened against her, and his eyes darkened. "You know, I still don't get the whole coffee thing. If I'm going to give up that much of my kitchen—listen to that noisy grinder every day—I might need some persuading of my own."

Allie rolled onto her back, and Matt came with her, his body covering hers. She slid her hands up his chest, lightly teasing his nipples.

"Like this?"

He sucked in a breath, and she moved her hands down, circling his growing erection.

"Or this? Can I pretty please have my espresso maker in *our* kitchen now?"

Matt growled, lowering his mouth to hers. "Anything you want, princess. Anything you want."

My tale is done.
See the mouse run.
Catch it, whoever can,
and then you can make a
great big cap out of its fur.

~Hansel and Gretel

…AND THEY LIVED
HAPPILY EVER AFTER

A Quick Favor Please?

Before you go, would you please leave this book an honest review online? Reviews are so important for authors, as they help us reach more readers. Please take a minute to visit one or two retailer/review sites, such as Amazon, BookBub, or Goodreads, and leave this book a review. I promise it doesn't take long, but it would mean the world to me! This Book Riot article breaks it down into six easy steps, if you need tips: http://bit.ly/BookReviewTips.

Thank you for reading, and thank you so much for being part of this amazing journey!

~Kerry

***P.S. Turn the page for a sneak peek at* PUBLISH OR PERISH…**

Excerpt:
Publish Or Perish
©2019 by Kerry Blaisdell

Chapter One

*Nicholas, Patron Saint of: Maidens, Murderers,
Newlyweds and Thieves*

On Valentine's Day, a Friday, Emma O'Manny woke up with two kids, a minivan, a house in the Portland suburbs, and a husband with a sick sense of humor. Three days later, she woke up with a headache, a bottle of Tums, no Kleenex—and a purpose.

"God *damn* him!" she said into her cell's speakerphone as she turned left onto Terwilliger. "I *am* going back for my master's, no matter what he and his *girlfriend* say. If that son-of-a-bitch thinks I'll lie down and take this, or that he'll get the kids or the house—"

Emma hit the steering wheel, her sweaty palm sliding off, and the car swerved toward the nearby jogging path. Tall firs loomed in the gray pre-dawn, dark and menacing, and she jerked the wheel, over-compensating, before settling back into the rain-slicked lane.

"Emma!" Karen James, best friend extraordinaire, sounded worried. "Be careful! Hang up and call me from the lab!"

Emma inhaled the musty heat of the defroster. Counted to ten, blew the breath out, and took another one. "I'm fine—don't hang up—please."

"Okay. But you have to calm down—it won't help if you…get in an *accident*."

Shit—her kids were up. Karen couldn't say "if you go over the edge and die," because then they'd ask what the hell Mommy was doing—when they should be asking, what was *Daddy* doing?

As though reading her thoughts, Karen repeated, "I really didn't know. Honest—if I'd had any idea, I never would've taken the kids for the weekend. Screw him."

"I know. It's not your fault."

"I'm really sorry, Em."

Deep breath. Blow it out. Focus on the taillights of the car ahead.

Her hands on the wheel felt foreign. They didn't belong to her any more than did the white face and purple-shadowed eyes she'd seen in the mirror this morning. *She* was not-quite forty, blonde with brown eyes, a mother, a wife, about to go back to school and get her M.S. in Computer Science. The woman in the mirror was middle-aged, haggard from two days of lying in bed, nursing ginger ale and crackers, and about to be a divorcée.

A *Catholic* divorcée.

Karen's voice was hesitant. "Do you want to talk about it?"

Emma laughed—a sound that was also foreign. Brittle. But then, she was brittle.

"What's to talk about? He brought me flowers, a box of candy, and—" *Deep breath. Hold. Don't cry.* Don't *cry.* "—seduced me and then shoved the divorce papers at me and left."

Except that was a lie. He hadn't seduced her; she'd been more than willing. Which was the truly humiliating part.

"Bast—what a fu—" Karen choked. "I can't even say how pissed I am, because, well…"

"Kids are there."

"Yes."

"And you can't call him a bastard because that's a 'bad' word, and he's their father."

The father of her children—*her husband of fifteen years*. And she'd had no clue. None.

Bored with his life? Girlfriend? Taking her to *Hawaii*?

She tried to relax, to un-grip the wheel, just a tiny bit, but her hands weren't hers, and wouldn't do what she wanted.

In ten minutes, they'd have to.

Get in. Get her stuff. Get out.

"Emma—are you sure you want to go to the lab today?"

"I have to. You're taking the kids to school, but I have to pick them up. This is hard enough. I need to do it before I see them."

"I'll call in sick. If you wait a couple hours, I'll come with you."

"Thanks. But if I wait, Oscar and the other lab rats will be there, and I can't face them. It's too much—they *know*. I'm sure they've known all along."

"I understand, honey. Do you want me to come over tonight?"

The tears threatened, and she swallowed hard. "No—really. I have to tell the kids myself."

Tell them Daddy had dumped Mommy, gone to Hawaii with another woman, and was moving out when he—*they*—came back in ten days. How exactly could she explain all that? To an eleven-year-old boy and a six-year-old girl?

"If you're sure. But tomorrow, I make lemon drops and we burn his boxers."

Emma laughed in spite of herself. "Thanks, Kar. You're the best."

"Hey, you did it for me. Although even Rob looks better next to Dan. At least our dumping was mutual." Karen hesitated. "Have you…told your mom?"

Emma's fingers were so tight on the steering wheel, she'd never uncurl them. "Look," she said finally, "I'm almost to the hospital. I'd better hang up now."

Silence. Then Karen said, "You're *sure* I can't help?"

"I'm sure. I have a plan."

"That can't be good. You won't do anything dumb, will you?"

"Define dumb. Would that be marrying a low-life, cheating, scum-sucking bastard? 'Cause I already did that."

"Just be careful, okay?"

"Always. I'll call you later. Tell the kids I love them."

Emma hung up and turned left at the sign for St. Elizabeth's, taking the back way on the narrow, one lane street lined with evergreens and small post-World War II houses. Old habits died hard. Five months since she'd been up to the lab—since Dan-the-bastard O'Manny had, oh so magnanimously, said he didn't need her as an admin assistant anymore.

Take some time off, honey. It's too late to apply for grad schools this year, but Juney's in first grade, Justin's in fifth. You can prep for next year. Oh—and the real *reason is so I can put that skank I'm screwing in your place. In your bed, at your desk, in your role.*

Shit. She was going to vomit again.

She turned right, right again toward the tiny church, left up the hill, past the odd mix of patient clinics and administrative buildings, then into the lot serving the tightly clustered research buildings that comprised the upper-hill portion of the Oregon Scientific Health University campus. Another old habit. She still had her parking pass, in case Dan's car was ever out of commission. With a five-year wait on the permit list, it seemed prudent not to cancel. Plus, you never knew when you'd have to come back.

Ha.

She rolled into a spot and killed the engine, and the sudden stillness slammed into her.

Since Friday, she'd done little more than run to the bathroom every few hours to throw up. Her whole body had been in turmoil, her mind whipping from utter denial to wondering what she'd done wrong—*why didn't Dan love her anymore?*

She shoved the door open, yanked herself up and out, and slammed it shut. Then she stomped across the courtyard to the Sion Institute for Advanced Biomedical Research.

Sion. "Idealized, harmonious community," her ass.

There wasn't a single Principal Research Investigator who wouldn't stab a fellow PI in the back if it moved his grant app to the top of the pile, or his research into publication faster. Discoveries were great, but if another PI published first, it was career homicide. They were like spiders, hiding in their lab-webs, coming out long enough to sabotage each other's work before scuttling back into the dark.

Except Dan. Loyal, honest, above-the-muck Dan.

Breathe.

Get in. Get her stuff. Get out.

She made it to the heavy glass doors just as the auto-locks clicked open at six-fifteen. Two elevator doors, nine floors, and one card key swipe later, she emerged into the beaker-, vial- and paper-strewn lab that had been her second home for ten years. She flipped on the fluorescents, saw the orange light on the alarm pad, and punched in the code before it notified security of her presence. Then she faced the room.

Everything looked the same.

If nothing changed in ten years, why would five months make a difference?

Except something had changed. She'd stopped coming in—*take a break, sweetheart*—Mollie McBride had started—*she can be my admin* and *a postdoc*—and Emma's desk had been rearranged.

Bitch.

Get in. Get her stuff. Get out.

But her stuff wasn't there. Laptop, file boxes, photos of her kids—all replaced by a new desktop system, metal wall files, and pics of Mollie's friends. What had she expected? God—she could *not* vomit again—or cry. Not now. Her stuff. Where the hell was her stuff?

She checked once more on the crowded desk, shoved into a corner outside Dan's office. The space was so tight that with his door open, the desk disappeared. She'd always hated it, put there as an afterthought—just like her marriage.

The anger boiled, and she shoved it down. This was so unlike her. She had to get a grip—for her kids' sake, if nothing else.

Her gaze roamed the lab. Long rows of metal-topped counters crammed with machinery, books, papers, and research paraphernalia of all descriptions—but not her stuff. The food fridge, where lunches were kept. The bio-sample fridge, for anything *not* food, that should never, *ever*, be anywhere near food. But not her stuff.

And then her gaze landed on Dan's office. Of course. She tried the door. Locked, and her key didn't work.

Good for him. He'd changed the locks.

Bad for him. She was handy with a coat hanger.

Emma grabbed Mollie's lab coat off the nearby stand, pulled it off the metal hanger, and threw it on the floor, stepping on it for good measure. Then she untwisted the hanger, hooking an end between the door and the jamb, around the simple knob lock. All she had to do was jimmy it up and down and—

Pop! The latch was forced open and the hanger jerked free, throwing her back. The door hung open for an instant before starting to swing shut and—*she'd got it!*

Pulling herself up and into the office, she flipped on the light. Sure enough, a cardboard box under the desk held a jumble of her personal effects, topped by her precious laptop.

Asshole.

The rest of the room was as unchanged as the lab. Big corner office with picture windows.

Okay, it was scientist-big, not CEO-big, but it was still more impressive than her tiny desk behind the door. Which was now *Mollie's* desk behind the door, so maybe there was some justice after all.

She grabbed the box and one of the portable files. She'd have to make two trips. Maybe on the second, she'd find a Sharpie and scribble all over Dr. Dan's big freaking windows.

Vandalism could be your friend, if you knew how to use it.

~:~:~

Day One, Hour Two on the Job, stuck in a cruiser, staring at a gas station while they drank their coffee and waited for something—anything—to come across the scanner. And so far, Vin Bronislovas was unimpressed with the kid they'd given him as a partner.

Except it was the other way around. He might be twenty years older than Joey Zitface, and have come from a precinct in South Deering, Chicago—Area 51, for cripe's sake—to l'il ole Portland, Oregon, but *he* was the new guy. *He* was the rube.

Damn it. Bad enough the state-to-state move meant he'd had to go through the Academy a second time—the *Advanced* Academy, but still—did he have to start at the bottom when he got out? If only the detective position he'd coveted hadn't vanished in a puff of bureaucratic smoke. If he hadn't promised Azi they'd be here for Thanksgiving, and Tony hadn't kicked his renters out to give them a place to live.

If, if, if.

He'd *had* to leave Chicago. Even now, six months later, he would've taken a desk job, anything, to get away—from the Deering Darling—the Long Island Lolita of the Midwest.

Isadora Higuera.

Vin shuddered.

At least the uniform spot had materialized. And the low-key northwest lifestyle was *exactly* what he wanted. Quiet. Simple. Not complicated and messy, like Chicago.

If only his partner wasn't a twelve-year-old.

Right on cue, the kid piped up again. "So, what does Vytautas Bronislovas mean, anyway? It's Polish, right?"

Vin deliberately unclenched his jaw, reminding himself most people would've guessed Russian, which was worse. "*Lithuanian*. From *Lithuania*."

"Lithuania? Where's that?"

Vin closed his eyes, waited a beat, then said, "Next to Poland."

"Oh. So they're, like, the same?"

"Not really." *Shut up. Just shut up while you can.*

"So what does it mean?"

Vin sighed. Shrugged his shoulders, working the kinks out, his duty belt creaking. Drank from the paper cup he held. The station coffee was better here. Northwesterners knew how to do coffee—and beer. He took another sip. Joey looked at him expectantly. Ah, fuck it.

"Vytautas means 'chasing the people.' Bronislovas means 'protection and glory.'"

Joey's jaw dropped. "You're kidding, right?"

"Unfortunately, no."

"'Cause that's as bad as my Phys Ed teacher, Mr. Court. I'm not making this up. Your dad's a cop, too, right?"

Another sigh. "Was. Yes. He's dead."

"Funny sense of humor. How'd he know you'd go on the Job?"

"I have no idea." Vin should have picked another profession on purpose. But this was what he wanted to do—always had, and nothing else mattered.

"Hey—what about Tony? That's *Italian*."

The kid actually sounded suspicious and for the first time in a long while, a smile sneaked onto Vin's face. Joey was persistent, he'd give him that. In less than an hour he'd weaseled out most of Vin's vitals, including that he had four brothers, three sisters, and a dozen nieces and nephews; that Tony was the only sibling not still in Chicago; and that Vin and his Uncle Azi had moved here last fall, were crashing at Tony's rental house, and were neither of them encumbered by anyone of the female persuasion.

Thank God. The last thing Vin wanted was a woman needling her way between him and Azi. Az was a handful all on his own.

Vin scowled out the window, then realized Zitface still waited for an answer. Cripes. "Tony's short for Antanas—Lithuanian for Anthony."

"Like Vin for Vytautas?"

"Sort of."

"Does Vytautas mean Vincent?"

"No. Look—"

The radio crackled on. Joey zeroed in on it—more points for him—and when the dispatcher finished, he yanked his seatbelt on. "That's us!"

"Relax, kid. It's just a tripped alarm. Probably the owner

punched his code in wrong. Happens all the time.”

The look Joey shot him was expressive and explicit. “You’re shitting me, right?”

The look Vin shot back was equally so. “What?”

Rolled eyes. You’re-a-dumbass shake of the head. You-don’t-know-how-stupid-you-are twitch of the lips.

“Not just *any* alarm.” Joey shoved the car in gear and screeched right onto Sam Jackson Park Road. “The *only* alarm on the Hill that bypasses campus security and goes straight to us. OSHU authorized it last month. Big dealy bop PI, researching vaccines or something.”

“PI?” Vin had only learned today that the OSHU campus, or the Hill as it was called, would be his beat, and while he knew it was a teaching and research hospital, he had no clue how it worked. South Chicago hadn’t been a hotbed of biomedical science. More like of drug and gang violence.

“Principal Investigator,” Joey explained, as he veered back and forth up the twisting, two-lane road carved onto the hillside, knocking Vin hard against the door.

“Jeez. Whose bright idea was it to put a hospital up on a hill with lousy street access? Slow down, will you? I’m telling you—I’ve got a feeling about this. We’ll get up there and find the monkeys got out of the cage or something. This isn’t a career-breaker call.”

“No. But it could be a career-*making* one.”

Vin just shook his head. Kids. Who the hell let kids become cops anyway? He’d never been that young, had he?

Surreptitiously he gripped the oh-shit handle and hoped they weren’t about to careen off the edge into the canyon. Oh for the unending flat of the Midwest. At least when you floored it, you went in a straight line. None of this hairpin curve crap.

Then he grinned for real. Ah, fuck it. At least they were

moving.

Emma sat back to check her handiwork. This was so far out of character, it was like admiring someone else's artistry. It'd taken longer than expected, but was still faster than a pen. Thank heaven the minivan still had junk in it from December—a.k.a., Holiday Craft Month.

Yes. Dr. Dan and *Mollie* would get quite the shock when they returned from *Hawaii*. Maybe they'd come in to catch the sunrise while sipping their coffee. Thanks to the angle of the building, both Mt. St. Helens and Mt. Hood were visible through the windows.

Emphasis on the *were*. Now the only thing visible was yards and yards of Smith's Pink Spray Tree Flocking-in-a-Can. She'd run out or she would've done the desk, too—but white was almost as good. And gold and silver added nice touches to the filing cabinets and shelves.

But the *pièce de résistance* was Dan's monitor. He'd *needed* it to complete his research—*had* to have a bigger screen, so he could finish his vaccine paper and rush it to publication, before someone else got there first, and he lost a decade of work. Or worse—his position at the university, or even his lab. But back then, the Sion was in start-up mode, bleeding money left and right, and none of his early grants covered equipment. So he'd been *forced* to dip into the kids' college funds to pay for it.

Now, thanks to his soon-to-be-pubbed research, the National Vaccine Research Endowment had funded him to the tune of one million dollars—which was lucky for him, because his five grand, flat-panel, goddamn huge display was now solid fuzzy green, front and back, except right in the middle where she'd sprayed a huge red, furry "FUCK YOU."

Merry Christmas—and Happy Valentine's Day.

So what if her blouse was a rainbow of pink-gold-silver-red-green? Or that she'd mis-aimed one can and half her head was crusted white? It was all worth it.

Get in. Get her stuff. And vandalize the flock out of the place.

Queasy panic jolted through her, but she shoved it down. Wrecking Dan's office was juvenile, petty, and wouldn't help in the long run. But he deserved it. Jesus—he'd dumped her on *Valentine's Day*. She would *not* feel remorse for giving in to her anger, just this once.

Emma set down the last can. Drew in a deep breath. Counted to ten. Exhaled.

And felt as free as it was possible to feel, when the whole rock-solid foundation of your life had just exploded.

She rose and flipped off the lights, bending to retrieve her keys from the floor. Started backing out of the office, still stooping, through the door she'd propped open earlier. Glanced to the right of the doorframe, just above floor level—and noticed the red blinking light of the new, additional security pad a fraction of a second before her rear bumped into something very large, very muscular, and very not-messing-around.

"Shit."

"Yep," a deep male voice said. "That's about the size of it."

About the Author

Kerry Blaisdell is the bestselling and award-winning author of the acclaimed Dead Series, including DEBRIEFING THE DEAD and its sequels, which InD'tale Magazine recommends for "fans of shows like 'Constantine' or 'Supernatural.'" She also writes award-winning Romantic Suspense (PUBLISH OR PERISH, a Publishers Weekly BookLife Prize Quarterfinalist) and Historical Mystery.

She has a B.A. from U.C. Berkeley in Comparative Literature (French/Medieval English), and a Master's in Teaching English and Advanced Mathematics from University of Portland. Kerry lives in the gorgeous Pacific Northwest with her family, assorted animals, and more hot pepper plants than anyone could reasonably consume.

To connect with Kerry online, visit http://linktr.ee/kerryblaisdell to join her Facebook Reader Group, follow her on social media, or subscribe to her Very Occasional Mailing List for freebies, news and more!